STARS FROM THERE TO HERE

Mae Wellcome

Grosvenor House
Publishing Limited

This book is published by
Grosvenor House Publishing Ltd
Link House
140 The Broadway, Tolworth, Surrey, KT6 7HT.
www.grosvenorhousepublishing.co.uk

This book is a work of fiction. Any resemblance to
people or events, past or present, is purely coincidental.

A CIP record for this book
is available from the British Library

ISBN 978-1-83615-283-5

DEDICATION

For Dusty,
whose dearest wish was to visit Ireland
but was never able to.

Foreword

I am fortunate enough to be able to call Mae Wellcome a close friend, and whose wisdom I have come to rely on and trust over the years. Mae actively listens, gives gentle advice when needed and above all offers non-judgemental support. I believe it is these human characteristics and her life experience that have allowed her to draw such pleasure from writing this book and enabled her to connect with each character on a deeply personal level.

In the tapestry of human experience, family bonds create narratives rich with love and resilience. "Stars from there to here" invites readers on a heartfelt journey through interconnected families, each navigating unique challenges while drawing strength from their heritage. Mae's ability to understand and articulate the dynamics of family relationships profoundly influences this work, offering valuable insights that resonate throughout. She beautifully captures the essence of family – how experiences shape us, challenges forge deeper connections and love remains a guiding star.

As you read, you may find echoes of your own experiences, and inspiration to cherish the relationships that matter most. Let this book remind you that while the stars may seem distant, they illuminate our paths as we travel together. Welcome to a celebration of familial love and the challenges that strengthen our family ties.

Lauren Barson
April 2025

Preface

Apart from some wonderful holidays, I have no connection with Ireland other than my love for the country and a huge respect for its history, so I hope my readers will forgive any gaps in my knowledge.

The characters and some of the places in the story are fictitious and drawn entirely from my own imagination. However, readers will note that I have referred to some actual events. It was never my intention to explore these in detail; that was not the purpose of this book, and I hope that this will not be seen as trivialising their importance or their significance in Irish culture.

M. W.

Acknowledgements

A thousand thanks to my long-suffering partner Chris for his endless patience and for always having confidence in my efforts, and to my wonderful family: Joanie, Anne, Catherine, Anthony, Nicky, Paul, Will and Jack for their motivation and encouragement even though there were times when I wondered if my book would ever be finished!

As a new author I am eternally grateful to Grosvenor House Publishing Ltd for all their help in bringing my book to publication and for guiding me through the process every step of the way with such expertise and dedication – always with the personal touch.

I am greatly indebted to the team at Monster Creative for their imaginative and thoughtful cover design.

And finally, special thanks to my lovely dear friends Jude Helen, Lauren Barson, Karen Davis, Jo Carter, Janet Clarke and Roger Grigg, all of whom have given me such support and inspiration; in particular to Lauren for her constructive feedback and wise words throughout.

M. W.

Introduction

When stargazer and amateur astronomer Neville Garth and his wife Lois decide to retire to Spain for health reasons, the impact on the life of their daughter Nell and her growing family is enormous. As events unfold, can she mend the failing relationship with her mother, support her beloved father through the worst dilemma of his life and later help her own daughter through an agonising trauma, all at a distance? And when faced with her greatest predicament yet, can Nell follow her conscience and overcome her doubts without sacrificing her own ambitions?

And in Ireland, how will Kathleen react to unexpected opportunities which affect not only her own life chances but those of the family to which she has become inextricably linked?

Two families – poles apart – yet joined by the merest chance. Across several generations, the complexities of the various relationships are tested with surprising results.

Set against the background of Sussex, southwest Ireland and Spain, the story follows members of both families as they face unexpected challenges and the toughest of choices through tragedy, success, exploitation and personal triumphs, none of which could have been foretold in the stars.

Prologue

November 1996

If it hadn't been for the pedestrian stepping out in front of her vehicle, the driver of the car behind would have been unable to catch her up after a long pursuit and the story might have ended differently.

As it was, the elderly man sauntering across the road seemed oblivious and unaware that he had caused Nina to carry out an emergency stop to avoid an accident. The driver of the car in her rear-view mirror had also been forced to slam on his brakes, narrowly avoiding a collision with his quarry. As soon as it was safe to move off, she did so, but not before she had registered the fact that whoever was chasing her was driving her own car. With a sickening lurch of her stomach, she realised what had happened.

Nina Mason had borrowed her friend's car for this journey, intent on keeping it a secret and remaining anonymous, at least until her objective had been completed. But clearly, something had gone wrong, he had found out. He had probably forced Jessie to tell him; he could be very persuasive, she thought grimly. Now, she could tell, he was determined to thwart her at every turn. She had no other option; this was to have been her last chance.

As she accelerated out of Kirchington in the hope of shaking off her pursuer, she looked down at the fuel gauge. Damn, it was on the red. She had meant to stop for fuel on the way but the realisation that she was being followed had derailed her plan. Trust Jessie to forget to mention that her car was nearly out of petrol, but of course Jessie probably ran her car on fumes most of the time because she was permanently broke. That was why her friend had come to her in the first place and then the whole plan was hatched.... but that knowledge didn't help her now.

By now she was on the approach road to Rivenden, leaving the countryside behind. She might be able to lose him if she navigated round the back streets – she knew the layout of the town better than he did; there was still a chance of escape. But just then, her car started to judder and misfire, and Nina had no choice but to admit defeat and steer it into the nearest lay-by. He stopped immediately behind her, leapt out of the car and opened her driver's door.

"I hope you weren't planning to do what I particularly asked you not to do" he said, eyeing the overnight bag on the back seat.

"You know I have no choice. And anyway, it's none of your business. I've made up my mind".

"It is my business, and you do have a choice. I told you I'd take care of everything".

"You can't take care of this. It's never going to work. Let's just leave it at that and go our separate ways".

"I will not leave it at that" he said, grasping her arm, not roughly but firmly enough to let her know that he would not be deterred. "Now get out of the car and I'll drive you home. You can't stay here. Don't worry about Jessie's car, I'll arrange for that to be picked up later". Furiously, Nina picked up her bag and made her way to the car behind.

"I suppose you pestered her until she told you" said Nina bitterly. "And I don't want to go home, I want you to leave me alone. This has all been a terrible mistake".

The man ignored her and drove off at speed, leaving Nina with no option but to spend the rest of the journey wondering how she could retrieve what was left of her plan in time. It would be even more difficult than before, she acknowledged now that he suspected, or had Jessie spilt the beans? He would not take his eyes off her; she would have no chance.

For the thousandth time she wondered how she had ever allowed herself to get into this situation; a trap so easy to fall into in one careless moment but so impossibly difficult to extricate herself from. Ruling all her actions now was fear – fear of reprisals, of repercussions, and the realisation that he was now in control.

During the journey back to the house Nina tried to compose her thoughts, and decided that compliance, at least outwardly, would be the best strategy. At least it might buy her some time, and that was now in short supply, more so with every day that passed.

But during the days that followed, he watched her like a hawk. She was under house arrest in her own home; there was no other way of describing it. There was no opportunity for her to escape; he raided her handbag for her mobile phone and kept the external doors locked, always taking the house keys and house telephone handset with him, even when he went to the bathroom. But it could not be for ever, she knew; once the possibility of her taking the action he feared was past, she would be free again. Free to do what though? Free to face a permanent reminder of a time she bitterly regretted. Freedom to be tied to someone whom she now despised and who had already shown himself to be ruthless. Or freedom to be subjected to a lifetime of censure and most probably violent retribution. How had she become faced with such appalling choices?

But she had one trump card. Nina knew the reason for his urgency and had also discovered that he was motivated solely by money. Something she had, and he desperately needed. She felt sure that he had a plan as well; by being irrevocably tied to her, he would try to gain access to it. Well, perhaps she could still find a way to salvage something. What had occurred to her to do was extreme, shocking; something that was no doubt illegal and that would appal most right-minded people. But the alternative was worse, and too horrifying to contemplate.

* * *

It was late July the following year. There were three people in the darkened, stuffy room: Nina, Jessie and the man.

For a long time, nobody said anything.

"No one is to know about this, absolutely no one. Do you both understand?" Nina spoke sharply, the insistence in her voice disguising weariness and exhaustion. "If this gets out, I shall know it was one of you, and you will regret it. I will report you; I mean it. You both owe me, never forget that".

"Are you absolutely certain this is what you want? There's still time to change your mind". Jessie was clearly anxious. What she had done – was about to do – was, she knew, very very wrong. All her instincts railed against it. If only things had been different…. if only she hadn't been forced into this position.

The man remained expressionless, as if determined to show no emotion or remorse.

Nina smiled weakly, and for a moment her tone softened a little. "Don't you see, this is a way out for all of us? No one is going to suffer; we have planned this. Now clear every trace from this room and get out." She pointed to some envelopes on the table. "Take these, it's what we agreed. And…. remember, this stays between the three of us. Always. We shan't be meeting again". Her voice tailed off and she turned away, as one by one her companions did as she asked, then picked up the envelopes and left the room, closing the door silently behind them.

No one saw them leave.

* * *

PART ONE

Chapter One
October 1981

"Are you absolutely sure we are doing the right thing?"

Lois Garth tripped slightly as she ascended the top step of the narrow stairway, and her husband put a hand on her elbow to steady her.

"We've been over this so many times dear" murmured Neville, following his wife into the first of the attic bedrooms, noticing a tear slipping from the corner of her eye and down her cheek.

"I don't suppose I shall come back up here again" said Lois, looking around the room and landing, trying to take in every detail and commit it to memory. "It's just too difficult. Even if we do return, I won't be coming up these stairs, into these rooms. It will be a flying visit just to sit in the drawing room for a cup of tea. I know how difficult things have been, for both of us," she sighed and looked around again as if to make sure she had missed nothing of the familiar view across the back garden stretching to the little orchard, the field beyond, the immaculately weeded flower beds and the secluded al fresco dining area on its beautiful York stone patio. "When I think of how I used to run up and down these stairs chasing Nell from room to room, playing hide and seek" .... her voice tailed off.

"Lois". His voice was gentle and compassionate but with a firm edge. "You cannot manage these stairs – any stairs now. You would have fallen a moment ago if I hadn't been there to catch you. I'm surprised you managed to climb up

1

to the top floor. It would be so disruptive to make this house suitable for you, do we really want all that upheaval just when we should be winding down for retirement? And we certainly don't need all this space. So many rooms that we never really used". He waved his hand in the general direction of the doors leading off the landing. But he too felt a silent pang of regret, glancing round his own attic 'observatory' room where many years ago he had positioned his telescope on its tripod, facing to the southwest. Here, while Lois spent time reading, worked on her tapestry in the drawing room, listened to classical concerts on the radio or played the piano, he had enjoyed many evenings studying constellations, the courses of the planets, comets and especially the moon, after which he had renamed the house, such was his fascination with the cosmos and all the mysteries of the heavens. He struggled sometimes to understand quite how the Greeks had attributed shape and form in the stars sufficiently to name the various signs of the zodiac, but as an enthusiastic amateur and as a mathematician he had taken solace in astronomy and refuge in his many books and charts that had lined the walls. These items were presently all boxed and packed, awaiting shipping to their new home.

And then there was the garden.....from his vantage point on the second floor he looked out at the clumps of dahlias, even now in their final flourish of late October colour, the roses he had planted decades ago that he had tended with such care and increasing expertise, with the promise of a few buds still to open before the first frosts came; the mature shrubs that he had trimmed and shaped with the precision he gave to everything he did. He must leave all this behind. The lawns, carefully manicured and free of weeds were soon to be run across by small feet, trampled on and later rutted by bicycle and scooter tyres, the precious blooms broken by footballs......

But fearing it would weaken his resolve and knowing that Lois would be quick to spot any flaw in his argument, he said nothing, guiding her back down the uncarpeted staircase to the first floor.

"You're right of course". Lois looked up at Neville and smiled, although her voice was still hoarse with emotion. "I know I need a wheelchair now, at least some of the time. The house is no longer practical for me". She always used to trust his judgement, yet these days he was less sure that she did. Lois made one more attempt. "But we could install wheelchair ramps, a stairlift….? We could still have lots of holidays in Spain. I have met you halfway over this, Neville".

"No". Neville's voice was tinged with slight impatience. "We've made our plans now. And however many changes we might make to this house we could never improve the weather, the climate. You need warmth and sunshine all the year-round Lois, and a single storey home with sea air. That is what we have decided and what I have promised you. In a few weeks we will be there, and we will have no regrets". He said it as a statement of fact with a tone that brooked no argument, no contradiction.

Neville had hoped that the move to Spain would mark a new beginning for them both. His original plan was for them to retire there as a couple. The disease from which Lois suffered was slowly advancing, he knew it, despite her frequent denials. Most of the time she did not complain, remaining stoic and matter of fact about her illness, saying that with help she could manage very well. But that help had to come from one particular quarter, he had begun to realise. During her recent holidays in Spain, the Mediterranean climate had significantly improved Lois's symptoms, but nevertheless he had witnessed a decline in the last three months which had prompted him to bring forward his retirement and to move permanently to their home in Solibrio, near Nerja, on the Costa del Sol. He had been renting an apartment there for Lois to make regular visits, and the owner had recently agreed to sell it to them. Lois assumed that it would be just a holiday home that they might visit two or three times each year and had not even contemplated a permanent move. That was typical of Lois, thought Neville; always preferring to think things would be how she wanted them to be, rather than how they actually were. She cannot face too much reality, he thought. Had someone famous once said that? he asked himself. There had been many arguments and recriminations in the days that followed. Neville could see how much difference the holidays in the warmth and perfect weather of Solibrio had made to Lois, but she was adamant that she did not want to leave the home she had lived in for so long and where for a brief time they had been so content. All her best memories were here, and she felt that by moving she would never be able to recapture those times, and they would be lost for ever. Was that the real reason, he wondered? At times she seemed to live in the past more and more. But Neville knew that there was another force at work, turning her head against the plans he had made for them both and for their family home. He had been suspicious for some time but had no idea how to deal with the dilemma, pinning all his hopes for a solution on a move abroad. But even that was now fraught with difficulties; a predicament from which he could see no way out.

They had been so blissfully happy in those early years, then things started to go wrong, life did not turn out as they had planned. Lois's health – mental and later physical – had gone from bad to worse and she had retreated gradually into private grief. She was seldom hostile or cold but always distant, and eventually, without either of them venturing to speak openly about their sadness they withdrew from each other incrementally, going through the motions of affection but each settling for a quiet understanding which was never analysed, never discussed. Could a complete change of scene help to heal their sorrow and the divisions between them? Neville hoped so. If only they could be facing this new challenge together, just the two of them. He had made the biggest compromise of his life by giving in to his wife's wishes. Outwardly they were a devoted couple; only Nell knew of her parents' heartache and during her growing-up years she learned to accept their unhappiness without ever referring to it. But now Nell could see an even greater threat; the rift in her parents' marriage that had come from an unexpected direction; a subtle, insidious influence that had started to tear them apart without Neville realising what was happening until it was too late. Lois was being swept along on a tide of manipulation and lies, and she was the only one who could not see it; Neville, in an effort to avoid conflict with his wife, had allowed the status quo to continue until the problem was so deeply entrenched that he could see no way of resolving it.

Lois continued to look round her, memorising the four spacious bedrooms, comfortably furnished, no longer in the latest style of décor but with an eye for good taste and quality. Moving into the master bedroom she stroked the dark green velveteen of the bedroom chair, twitched the heavy curtains to let in a little more light and ran her fingers across the smooth surface of the antique walnut dressing table. "Neville this was our first home, it's been our only home, this is where we started our married life together, and this is where I nursed Nell through all those sleepless nights. Of course I'm sad and emotional". Once again, a sob that she had been trying to suppress broke through and sent a shudder through her slender body.

"I know, my dear". Neville's voice was tender and soothing as he went to place a comforting arm round her shoulders then noticing how she stepped away avoiding his embrace, he moved to the window. There had just been a light shower of rain, and a blackbird was pecking for worms on the lawn. He fixed his gaze on the magnolia tree outside, which in March was a cloud of pale pink waxy blossoms. Lois always complained about the mess when the petals dropped. He would miss that too, the first real sign of spring that he always looked forward to. He remembered so well the day when it was planted.

"But this house really needs to be full of people, a young family with lots of comings and goings, visitors, noise, activity. We've never been able to do it justice. In my grandparents' time it came into its own, but we have been marking time with it in a way for thirty years, we've been its custodians, but I think that it has a whole new chapter to be revealed, and the next generation may be the ones to bring it alive again". Neville made a fresh appeal to his wife, realising that persuasion would achieve far more than cajoling.

"Yes, Neville I hope so". Lois sighed again. "I really do hope you are right, because there will be no going back on this decision. I think we should tell them later, don't you? We'll ask them round this evening. And be tactful. He's a proud man, you know". She swayed slightly and clutched at the doorframe. "I'm tired, let's go back downstairs now. I need to have a rest before dinner".

As if finally convinced by her own argument, Lois glanced round the bedroom again, checked the bathroom, looked into the three remaining rooms and crossing the broad landing to the main staircase began a slow, careful descent, with Neville a step behind her.

Chapter Two

Geoffrey Garth, entrepreneur and beneficiary of a handsome legacy from his father's estate, decided that the gentler climate and cleaner air of Sussex would be more to his liking than the industrial landscape of the Midlands, so moved south and established the Garth Brick & Clay Company in 1866. Foreseeing the expansion in house building due to the growing population of Lamberham and the recent arrival of the railway, he invested heavily but wisely. Within five years he had courted and married Alice Conway, daughter of the manager of Lamberham Municipal Bank, and within another fifteen years he had made his fortune, had a thriving business with a workforce of twenty-eight men, and a desire to settle permanently in the area which had contributed to his success.

Rather than commission a new building using the very bricks which had done so much to ensure his prosperity, after several year's searching he chose instead to purchase The Gables, a rambling, early Victorian house in the nearby village of Drover's Cross; a substantial dwelling with sufficient grandeur suited to a man of his standing, but with enough character and originality to satisfy his eclectic taste.

He moved in with his wife Alice and three children (two boys and a girl) in the spring of 1888, together with five domestic staff. A third son was born two years later.

Despite his hopes that at least one of his sons would take over the business, none of Geoffrey's children did so. Leo, his eldest, being in fragile health succumbed to tuberculosis at the age of fourteen. Thomas, the second son, having persuaded his father to advance his inheritance, emigrated to Canada in 1902 to take up an opportunity in a timber plantation in New Brunswick. Geoffrey agreed, unable to deny his ambitious son the chance to succeed in business as he had done. Emily, his only daughter married young and moved to Bristol with her husband, a merchant seaman. Geoffrey disapproved of the match, and news of Emily dwindled to a few letters each year. He and Alice eventually lost contact with her; it was thought that she and her husband had settled in Antigua. Thomas married later in life, but his wife Anna was eighteen years younger and gave birth to two sons, Neville and Henry within three years of their marriage.

Frederick, the youngest son of Geoffrey and Alice, joined the regular army in 1911 as a commissioned officer and was posted to France at the beginning of the First World War. He married Phoebe Ward, his childhood sweetheart during his first brief spell of leave late in 1914.

So, with no prospect of any of his family taking over the running of the Garth company, and with war in Europe looming, Geoffrey sold his business in 1912 with the proviso that it would keep the Garth name, which it did until its demise in 1914 at the outbreak of the First World War. He continued to live at The Gables with Alice, but his health was by then poor. Both Geoffrey and Alice died in 1916 within six months of each other, and Frederick was the only one of their children to inherit the property.

So, in the time of Frederick and Phoebe Garth, the next occupants, the house was still known as The Gables, and Frederick, returning from Passchendaele in 1917 with a seriously damaged leg peppered with shrapnel and an even more severely damaged mind, saw no reason to change it, if indeed he ever thought about it at all.

It was an uninspiring name which did not do justice to its grand proportions, its quirky and unusual layout (the flight of fancy of a long forgotten Victorian architect whose indulgence of design was no doubt suitable for a nineteenth century household with large families and servants to accommodate) but when Frederick's nephew Neville inherited the property in 1951 the amount of space and number of rooms to heat, furnish and maintain could have been seen as a challenge rather than an advantage, society having changed so much since the end of the Second World War. In the early 1950s only the wealthiest continued to have live-in staff; and help at home, for those who could afford it amounted to a cleaner and a visiting gardener. But Neville loved the house with all its imperfections, even though one of the saddest times of his life had been spent there.

By the time Neville took ownership along with his new wife Lois, The Gables had for many years suffered from if not actual neglect by the previous owners, lack of care except for basic structural repairs and essential maintenance. This was not due to penny pinching or shortage of money on Frederick's part, more to indifference and general apathy, the result of many years of shell shock, pain and immobility that had gradually robbed him of any interest in his surroundings. It was only at the insistence of his wife Phoebe that roof slates were replaced after storms, damp problems attended to, and sagging floorboards repaired, but the niceties of fresh wallpaper, newer appliances and modern conveniences had bypassed The Gables, and it remained trapped in the past.

The Gables was the last dwelling in the village of Drover's Cross, being situated halfway up Hasker's Hill beyond a sharp bend, after which the road continued for half a mile, winding its way through dense woodland before dipping down steeply into the neighbouring hamlet of Wharnden. At this point the road followed the river Haske for a further mile then branched off in the direction of Lamberham.

The property was arranged over four floors including basement and attic rooms, together with two acres of land which boasted an apple orchard, field, lawns and shrubbery, none of which had been tended adequately for many years, and like the rest of the house the garden had, by Neville's time, fallen into decay except for a small kitchen garden where a few soft fruit bushes still flourished alongside some abandoned runner bean canes.

The proportions of the rooms were generous with high ceilings and wide doorways. On the ground floor the entrance porch led into a broad tiled hallway with a low oak door at the far end which opened onto stairs to the basement. Also leading off the hallway was a formal dining room, a breakfast room and a commodious west-facing drawing room with a cast iron tiled fireplace. This room was large enough to accommodate a grand piano, once owned by Phoebe although she seldom played it. A bathroom and large kitchen/scullery were reached by several stone steps down at the far end of the hall, these rooms being situated at a lower level than the rest of the house and must have been inconvenient for housemaids carrying trays and buckets of coal in former times. A panel of call-bells was still fixed to the kitchen wall, although it was many years since these had either rung or been answered. At the rear of the property was a corridor leading to a single storey extension, once housing a butler's pantry and storerooms. Adjoining the north side of the house were two further ground floor rooms with a separate entrance and flat roof, their purpose unknown but possibly to provide self-contained quarters for a resident nurse in Geoffrey's declining years. Clearly these had been added later than the original construction as the brickwork was of a different style and featured casement windows back and front instead of the double sash variety that were evident in the main part of the house, except for five dormer windows on the top floor and the narrow arched Gothic window at the turn of the staircase. This staircase led to a broad landing and the first-floor bedrooms, two at the back and two larger at the front, all with spacious wardrobes; also a bathroom with an ancient roll-topped bath, rusty and stained, which had obviously not been used for decades.

The stairs leading to the attic rooms were narrow and steep, the bare wood splintered and treacherous in places. The top floor had been unoccupied and unused in Frederick's time other than for storage, but it was possible to imagine one room being used as a nursery with a tiny boxroom leading off it where a nurserymaid might have slept in times gone by, and the remaining three comprising the accommodation for several housemaids and a cook.

The overall structure was sound, but nothing was uniform or symmetrical. Neville felt that the unconventional design added to its charm and since visiting it many times as a boy, exploring the top floor, hiding from his brother in the wardrobes and running around the grounds, he never dreamed that one day this unique and distinctive property would be his own.

Surprisingly, Frederick lived for another thirty years after his medical discharge from the army and survived the Second World War but late in 1948 he contracted influenza and never recovered. His wife Phoebe outlived him by only eighteen months. They had no children. So, it was in 1951 that The Gables came into Neville's possession.

Lois, Neville's wife was impressed by the faded elegance of the house, thinking of how it could become a family home again, and made elaborate plans for refurbishment and modernisation. Neville allowed her free rein in the design and choice of décor, trusting her artistic flair and creativity. It gave her occupation and purpose during the early years of their marriage while he was busy concentrating on his career and setting his sights on advancement.

Neville renamed the house Moongarth. He felt that the house, which held so much promise for them both, deserved a more fitting title. Garth was obvious – his family name. It was also the Old English word for 'garden'. That was appropriate too – he would in time, with the help of Lois's eye for colour and structure, transform the wilderness outside and bring it back into order, gaining new skills and knowledge. Moon was added to the name because of Neville's passion for astronomy.

Over the years the house had witnessed success, loss, fear, happiness and tragedy. Yet those early days were, for Neville and Lois, full of ambition, hope, possibilities. They were so fortunate. War was over, they had each other and a magnificent home that they would take such joy in restoring. Nothing could blight their happiness.

Chapter Three

Neville was born on the 21st of March 1920 in Saint John, New Brunswick, to Thomas and Anna Garth, and his brother Henry followed eighteen months later. Thomas was keen for his sons to benefit from an education back in England; and being satisfied that peace in Europe was assured after the end of the First World War and that his sister-in-law Phoebe would be willing to offer a home to the two boys at Drover's Cross during their holidays from boarding school, arrangements were made for Neville and Henry to make the trip back to Sussex in the summer of 1931.

Anna resisted the plan; she felt that both the boys were too young to be sent away so far from home; Henry would be homesick and still needed his mother. A perfectly adequate intermediate school could be found here in Saint John, she argued. But Thomas wanted his sons' education to be more than adequate and was insistent. Privately he was concerned that Anna was too inclined to fuss over Henry, and that he was becoming soft. Anna was overruled, reassured in part by the promise that the separation would be five or six years at the most, and by Thomas's assertion that Neville and Henry would leave Canada as boys but would return as young men, ready to take their place in his business. In particular, he wanted his sons to be educated at his former school which had a fine reputation and excellent examination results. Boarding School had done him no harm, he said firmly to his wife, although Anna retorted that he had not been three thousand miles from home.

Phoebe was nervous initially about taking on this responsibility, having no children of her own, and knowing that her husband Frederick who was suffering from the effects of wartime injuries might not welcome the presence of two noisy children in the household. But she agreed, partly because of a desire to assist her husband's family despite never having met them, and in the hope of some respite from the constant demands of a stricken, broken man and the thought that perhaps in some way their situation might be happier with some laughter and fun that the visits of her two nephews might bring.

Neville enjoyed the sea voyage, being of an outgoing disposition and at an age where everything was an adventure. He was interested in the navigation of the ship and was allowed, under supervision to have a tour of the engine room and to talk to the ship's company when they were off duty. He learned how long ago, sailors set a course by plotting the positions of the stars, and later with an early version of a sundial.

In contrast Henry, who was of a more delicate constitution, hated every moment of the sea crossing, suffering frequent bouts of seasickness and constantly missing his home and especially his mother. By the time they docked at Southampton he had lost weight and looked pale and sickly. Nevertheless, finding Aunt Phoebe to be kind and motherly, and that there were to be four weeks of holiday and settling in before school started in September, Henry's spirits recovered, and he began to enjoy his new life in England.

But they were never to see their parents again.

Fenborough Academy, a boarding school for boys aged ten to eighteen was situated in the gentle rolling hills of the South Downs about five miles from Drover's Cross. The first year was exciting for Neville but harder for Henry. Neville made friends easily and did well in the mid-term tests, having a quick brain and an appetite for learning. He also enjoyed sports; never actually making it into the First Eleven but always giving a creditable performance which rendered him a reliable and steady team mate on the playing field. But Henry struggled. He was not academic like his brother, preferring to read, watch sport rather than participate, or just walk around the grounds, often alone. He took piano lessons and showed promise; but practising was a solitary pastime; he had not yet reached a standard sufficient for the school concert, and in any case nerves and intense shyness might have ruled out any public performance. Neville did what he could to encourage Henry to take part in activities in his own year group, but was aware of how it would look to the other boys if he protected his brother too much. Besides, their father had written to Neville expressing a hope that the discipline and rigours of school would toughen Henry up a little.

Both brothers found it slightly irritating when their classmates tried to imitate their accent, and as with many Canadians, they did not appreciate being taken for Americans. These minor annoyances soon passed, however. The Academy opened up many possibilities for Neville, who readily adapted to life at Fenborough; Henry, who was only used to a small local day school back home in Saint John, found it harder.

"I don't like it here" said Henry dismally to his brother as they walked back from the school chapel together one Sunday morning. "I want to go home to Canada".

"We can't go home" said Neville gently, wondering how he could comfort Henry, knowing that being overly sympathetic might make his brother more emotional. "We have to make the best of it". He said 'we' to show some solidarity and to give Henry the impression that he was equally homesick, whereas in fact he was already embracing school life and all it had to offer. "It will get better, I promise you. Just try and join in more, you'll make friends that way". Henry shrugged, and no more was said.

But there were always holidays at The Gables to look forward to. Both boys were allowed the freedom of the house and garden, made camps and played games in the nearby woodland on Hasker's Hill. Henry became animated during those times and enjoyed life more under the care and affection of Aunt Phoebe who seemed to recognise his vulnerability. Strangely, Uncle Frederick, who was often short tempered and irritable developed an unexpected bond with Henry, who would sometimes sit and read the newspaper to him, bring him his meals or just listen while Frederick talked about the house and its history. This was a subject in which Frederick came into his own; for a short time, his pain and trauma troubled him a little less and it was possible to glimpse the strong, fearless and interesting man that he once had been. For Phoebe it was a relief from a life of thankless service to a man who now needed a nurse rather than a wife.

"I remember when there were eleven people living here", he said to Henry one day as they sat in the drawing room after breakfast. Henry had just gone to fetch the newspaper for his uncle and was about to suggest a game of chess. "There were six of us, and five servants. We had three maids, a cook and a gardener. He was a handyman as well" he added, suddenly realising with guilt that all the work of the previous domestic staff now fell on Phoebe's shoulders.

"Why don't you have servants now, Uncle Frederick?"

"Your aunt wouldn't like it", he whispered conspiratorially. "She likes to do things her way". What Frederick really meant was, he wouldn't like it. He preferred Phoebe to do everything for him, he felt uncomfortable about his disabilities in front of strangers and disliked the thought of other people in the house, talking or complaining about him. Yet somehow, he didn't mind the company of his young nephew who seemed to accept his crotchety behaviour and who didn't criticise or judge him.

"We used to play in the woodland up the road, just like you and your brother", he said. "That was, your father, Emily and me. I was the youngest. Not Leo, he died the year I was born". He looked away for a moment. "At harvest time we would have a long table out in the field and the servants would join us for a big supper. And Christmas was great fun too, there was always a party for the servants, and we gave them presents then".

The only time Frederick would ignore Henry was when the boy, with innocent curiosity, asked him about his wartime experiences and what happened to him in France and Belgium. At those times Henry was ordered summarily out of the room or Frederick himself would struggle to his feet and shuffle off wordlessly into the garden or into another room.

Henry soon learned that the subject was off limits and was careful to avoid any reference to the war in their conversations.

The boys looked forward to their first Christmas at The Gables. Phoebe was excited too, having long given up hope of sharing the festive season with anyone except Frederick, who would often drink to excess and fall asleep without even touching his Christmas dinner. This time though, it would be different. She took trouble to decorate the house from top to bottom, hauling in greenery and branches laden with berries. Candles twinkled in every window and a wreath of holly adorned the front door. She stayed up late wrapping presents, baking and making every preparation with such love and anticipation as if Neville and Henry were her own sons. The dressing of the tree she would leave until the boys were home from school; they would all enjoy doing that together on Christmas Eve.

She secretly hoped that Henry could be persuaded to play the piano for Christmas carols and arranged for the grand piano to be tuned specially in advance of the holiday.

Phoebe collected the boys from school in her Austin 12. She had learned to drive out of necessity soon after Frederick had been invalided out of the army, and although she seldom drove any distance it was a lifeline to her and there were times on Frederick's better days when he liked to be driven around the countryside or for brief business trips into Lamberham.

Henry was overjoyed to be going to The Gables for Christmas and having three weeks away from school. "I'm so looking forward to Christmas, Aunt Phoebe" he said excitedly, stowing his small suitcase into the boot of her car. Phoebe smiled at him but inwardly she was brimming over with happiness. "There's plenty of work to do, young man", she teased. "We have to trim the tree, bring in lots of firewood and deliver Christmas cards". Henry sighed blissfully; it was going to be a wonderful holiday.

Neville shook hands with her formally and asked after his Uncle Frederick. Phoebe was impressed by his good manners and noticed how he had grown up, both in stature and in maturity since the summer. The two boys were so different, but she loved them equally and offered up a silent prayer of thanks for this chance to have the nearest thing to a family of her own.

Snow fell on the twenty third of December; thick whirring flakes and clumps that blotted out the sky and soon transformed the landscape. Drover's Cross was like a scene from a Christmas card, and The Gables was cloaked in a soft blanket with the reflections of candlelight streaming across the front lawn.

This promised even more fun for Neville and Henry. They were given permission to raid the sheds and outbuildings, and armed with some of Frederick's long unused tools, they set about making sledges from cast-off broken furniture and unrecognisable wooden items. While Phoebe was busy doing last minute errands and cooking, the boys were sliding down Hasker's Hill, shouting and yelling in excitement, then taking it in turns to haul each other back to the top.

Of course they were used to snow in Canada; snow that came in October and often stayed until April. But they could only remember the piles of slushy greyness lining the streets of Saint John for weeks on end, so different from the pristine white carpet covering the countryside around Drover's Cross; so unpredictable here in Sussex and rarely sufficient even to build a snowman. But this year enough fell for plenty of snowball fights and snowy walks through the woods.

Christmas Day was magical for the boys and even more wonderful for Phoebe who had never enjoyed Christmas so much in her life. From the moment the boys opened their stockings in the morning there were shouts of laughter and exclamations of thanks, surprise and delight. Phoebe had surpassed herself; a magnificent turkey dinner was served with every possible accompaniment, followed by her home-made Christmas pudding and mince pies. While Frederick had a nap after the meal, the three of them wrapped up against the cold and trudged out to the edge of the field and watched some deer feeding by the treeline in the afternoon dusk. The evening stars were beginning to appear in a clear sky and Neville pointed out the Plough, Orion's Belt and the constellations of Perseus and Aries. Phoebe was astonished at his knowledge and made a mental note to buy him a book on astronomy for his next birthday. After the candles were lit indoors, they sat around a roaring log fire in the drawing room, the boys ate a great many sweets and Henry agreed to play the piano. They sang their favourite carols and even Frederick joined in for a time. Neville had memorised a couple of verses of the Canadian Huron Carol: 'Twas in the Moon of Wintertime' and Henry sang along with him.

Their presents from Phoebe and Frederick were brand new bicycles and Phoebe said that as soon as the snow had cleared, they could test them out and ride to the village and back. This happened within a couple of days of Christmas – the temperature suddenly went up overnight and a thaw set in. It was agreed that the bicycles would remain at The Gables to be used during holidays.

Neville and Henry did not miss their parents as much as might have been expected. Letters were exchanged throughout the year, and Christmas cards had arrived from Canada containing money for presents and treats. But such was Phoebe's kindness and determination that the boys would have a happy time and not be homesick that they did not dwell too much on their homeland three thousand miles away. They both began to look on Phoebe as a second mother and she did nothing to discourage that, feeling that as circumstances had denied her any sons of her own, she was blessed with two loving and affectionate nephews who made her life worth living once more.

The holiday drew to a close and in the first week of January the two brothers returned to school, a few pounds heavier and in glowing health. During the weeks that followed, Henry started to come out of his shell; he was visibly taller and fitter now than the frail feeble boy who arrived in England six months earlier. Phoebe's care and loving attention had not only increased his vigour and stamina but had also given him a degree of confidence and the beginnings of independence from Neville. School was no longer to be dreaded; his aptitude for learning improved and he at last made a friend, Barnaby, who was a new boy that term.

Neville studied hard. His best subject was mathematics – he grasped difficult principles and formulae with ease and was consistently near the top of his form in tests and exams. His maths master considered him to be well above average – in fact the headmaster's comment on the next end of term report sent home to Thomas was that Neville was intelligent beyond his years.

Half term came and went, then the Easter break, and with each holiday at The Gables a greater bond was formed by both boys to their Aunt Phoebe, and cautiously with Frederick, who always seemed pleased to see them and was somehow less prickly or bad tempered during their visits.

They broke up for the summer holiday in the third week of July. Seven weeks of freedom, fun and home cooking stretched ahead. Neville and Henry went for long bike rides around the Sussex countryside, enjoyed substantial picnic lunches sitting on the Downs or on the shingle beaches, swam in the sea, sat around a campfire in the summer dusk in the meadow at The Gables and lazed in the garden on hot days, listening to the bees in the lavender and the blackbirds' shrill piping. They helped Phoebe around the house sometimes, and Henry kept his Uncle Frederick company while Phoebe did errands in the village. Neville, now a strapping twelve-year-old, mowed the grass, chopped a good supply of logs ready for the winter and under Phoebe's direction, planted rows of spring cabbage and carrots.

It hardly seemed possible that they had been in England more than a year already.

But with the arrival of August, Neville reluctantly turned his mind to his studies. He had some important exams later in the autumn term and was expected to do well; the results would determine his class streaming for the following academic year. He did not want to let his parents, teachers and most of all, Phoebe and Frederick down. So, every afternoon on weekdays he spent three hours with his books, tackling mock test papers and making notes.

The exams were to take place in mid-November, and it was a relief that they would be over in time for Christmas. This left the half term holiday at The Gables for final revision. So, during that week, instead of the boys roaming together through the countryside, playing games in the woods or cycling to the seaside, Neville studied and Henry was left to his own devices. He did not mind; he had made friends with Ben; a boy whose parents ran the village stores. On the Tuesday afternoon of half term, he and Ben decided to go fishing in the Hasker's Brook, the other side of Drover's Cross. Phoebe packed him some sandwiches and reminded him not to take any risks; it had rained non-stop during the preceding week and the brook would be deep and in full spate. Henry promised to be careful, and balancing a rod and a bait tin on his handlebars, he rode off to meet his friend.

Hasker's Brook was a favourite spot with local anglers; pike had been seen there but today the boys were hoping to land some small brown trout. The brook was a tributary to the River Haske which flowed southwest, bypassing Drover's Cross through water meadows until its course ran near to the road at Wharnden. The road was damp from overnight rain and the hedgerows were a tangle of Old Man's Beard and rose hips, which glowed brightly against the drabness of the fields. The weather was overcast but ideal conditions for fishing, the boys agreed. They chose a position close to the old stone bridge, where the stream flowed more gently.

No trout were caught that afternoon; the boys found it difficult to sit still and quiet for long enough or to wait patiently for a bite. But they did manage to land two grayling, both of which were of a decent size and were quickly dispatched, ready for Ben to take home to his mother. "My turn next time" said Henry, pleased that Ben was as eager as he was for another fishing trip the following day.

Twilight was starting to fall as they left the river; there was a slight mist rising from the water and birds were beginning to roost. It was late October; darkness came earlier at this time of year but both boys had lights on their bicycles, and neither were far from home. They parted company in the village with shouts of "See you tomorrow" as Ben turned down into the Main Street towards Drover's Stores and Henry continued up Hasker's Hill.

At The Gables, Phoebe glanced at the clock.

George Harding, on his way home from Lamberham in his Morris Cowley was not driving fast. Visibility was hampered slightly by the mist, but this seemed to recede a little as he neared the top of Hasker's Hill from the direction of Wharnden. He descended the hill at normal speed and passed by The Gables on his left. He could not possibly have seen the lights on Henry's bike as he approached the sharp bend near the woodland. But swerving to avoid a deer that suddenly leapt out from the undergrowth, he took the curve on the wrong side of the road, straight into Henry's path.

The impact was instantaneous and fatal.

Two police officers from Lamberham were on the scene within half an hour and broke the news to Phoebe and Frederick.

Phoebe was inconsolable. A torrent of emotions overwhelmed her, devastation that her nephew, this young boy she had come to love as dearly as her own child had been taken from them, with no opportunity for her to save him, to be there with him at the end, or even to say goodbye. Her next thoughts were of guilt; Thomas and Anna had trusted her with their young sons, and she had failed them in the worst possible way. And lastly, that she herself had purchased the bicycles – gifts intended to give fun and independence to Neville and Henry, but which instead had brought about tragedy.

Neville, completely stunned, was unable to speak for a long time, and when he did, he was incoherent and unintelligible, his voiced racked with sobs, his body shaking.

Frederick, who had developed an unexpected closeness with Henry, also felt tears running down his cheeks. Henry, who as a small boy would sit at his knee and read to him, listen to tales of his childhood and with wisdom beyond his years had somehow understood him, was dead. To Frederick it seemed all wrong; it was he, Frederick, riddled with pain and ill temper and with no longer anything to offer the world who should have been taken, not this little boy whose life had barely begun. Not knowing what else to do, he poured three large glasses of whiskey, handed them round and then took Phoebe awkwardly in his arms, something he had not done for a very long time.

Later that evening the police arranged for Henry's body to be removed, and after measuring the road and examining what remained of the tyre marks, they took George Harding into Lamberham police station for further questioning. George was physically unhurt except for some minor bruising, but deep shock was etched into his face as he climbed into the back of the police car, with realisation dawning that a split-second action on his part had taken the life of this young innocent boy.

And in the small hours of the night that followed, Phoebe sat at the table in the breakfast room to compose a letter to her brother and sister-in-law; it was the most difficult thing she had ever had to do.

The whole village turned out for the funeral; local shops and public houses were closed for its duration and people lined the main street to watch the little procession behind the horse drawn hearse make its way to the parish church of St Luke the Evangelist. Henry was not well known except to the shop keepers and of course to Ben – he had only lived in Drover's Cross during school holidays – but many knew how he and his brother had brought untold happiness to Phoebe Garth who was a respected neighbour, and wondered how she would ever get over her loss.

Barnaby Todd, Henry's friend from school attended along with his parents, and the headmaster from Fenborough took a seat in the back pew.

The congregation sang "All things bright and beautiful" – the hymn chosen by Neville as the most fitting description of his little brother – and Frederick, limping determinedly to the pulpit, read a passage from St Matthew's gospel. The rector gave a short address and spoke about how Henry had always enjoyed his holidays here at Drover's Cross and how he spent his last days with people he loved, and his final hours fishing happily with a friend. Afterwards, Henry's body was buried in a quiet corner of the churchyard, near a cherry tree which would flower in the spring and scatter soft white petals.

No wake was held; Phoebe did not have the heart to entertain company, so great was her grief and desolation. There had been no time for Thomas and Anna to make the journey from Canada for the funeral; in any case Anna was expecting a child that month and was not able to travel. Thomas had written to Phoebe and Frederick; his letter clearly speaking of his shock and anguish at losing his son so far from home and how hard it was to come to terms with never seeing Henry again. It was a tribute to Thomas's fair-mindedness and respect for his brother and sister-in-law that despite his distress, there was no word of blame or censure in his letter; he had quickly realised that Henry's death had been a tragic accident. Anna would have been less generous and understanding but for the fact that her attentions were focused on her forthcoming confinement; instead, under the insistence of her husband, she wrote a brief personal letter to Phoebe, expressing her sorrow and thanking her for all she had done for her two sons. Thomas sent some money to Frederick for the funeral costs and asked him to arrange for a headstone to be put in place when the time was right. They would consult about the wording at later date. He promised to visit Sussex very soon, but no definite plans were made.

There was no inquest; three months later George Harding was prosecuted for involuntary manslaughter and went to prison for five years. To Phoebe and Frederick, it seemed a trivial punishment for taking a life, but over time they accepted that it had been an accident, even though the consequences had been so terrible.

* * *

Neville returned to school a fortnight after the funeral, having missed the beginning of the second half of term but still in time to sit the exams in November. Surprisingly he did well; but over the past few days since the funeral, he had resolved to spend as much time as he could with his schoolwork – it seemed the only way in which he could find any purpose in life. His father wrote to tell him that he had a new baby sister, Josephine, born the day after Henry's funeral, but this news left Neville completely numb; what possible comfort could that be compared to the loss of his brother?

He continued to study hard, so much so that his form tutor, knowing of the tragedy had started to worry that he was overworking. But the suggestion from the headmaster that Neville should take some additional time off in the weeks before Christmas was met with dismay – work was his only distraction from grief, and much as he wanted to go back to The Gables and see his aunt and uncle, the thought of Christmas without Henry was like a knife to his heart – especially when he remembered the last happy and carefree Christmas they had enjoyed so much. In the end, a compromise was reached, Neville returned to The Gables on the fifteenth of December, and with Phoebe he attempted to make the best of the holiday season, but it was half hearted; neither of them could find any pleasure in the preparations, and Frederick spent a great deal of time alone in the drawing room, or with a bottle of whiskey for company.

So followed the next three years, hardworking ones for Neville as he prepared, at the age of fifteen for his School

Certificate. Terms were punctuated by visits to The Gables as usual; he was always welcomed by his aunt and uncle and his presence provided Phoebe with much needed solace. Together they visited Henry's grave, sometimes to take flowers, sometimes just feeling the need to be there at his resting place. The light had gone out their lives, and though now they no longer talked continually about Henry, thoughts of him were always near the surface. Occasionally their loss seemed too much to bear, and the unspoken grief at those times was palpable. The fact that the place where Henry died was only two hundred yards from The Gables meant that reminders of the tragedy were seldom far away and were like a scar that was never able to heal. As he often did, Neville turned to activity to cope with his feelings and set about helping around the house and garden. He noticed with concern that parts of the building were falling into disrepair and during his holidays he did whatever he could, with limited tools and skills to put things to rights. But it was a losing battle. Frederick had for many years been incapable of work of any kind, and Phoebe, once so energetic and particular about keeping her home in good order seemed to have lost all motivation, so only the most urgent repairs were attended to.

But on the date that would have been Henry's fourteenth birthday, they planted a little magnolia tree at the edge of the front lawn in his memory. It was a mild September day, the sun warm on their backs as Frederick, Phoebe and Neville stood in silent contemplation, each lost in their own thoughts.

There was no further mention of Thomas making the trip from Canada to see them, but early in 1937 Anna wrote to Neville to tell him that his father had contracted pneumonia, and the outlook was not hopeful. Within a month, a second letter told of his death.

The distance and length of a sea voyage made it impossible for Neville to attend his father's funeral. He wrote to his mother a perfunctory letter of sympathy; any closeness he had once felt for Anna had long since faded – she was now almost a stranger to him. Nevertheless, he enquired after the health of his sister Josephine and expressed a hope that they would one day meet, although in his heart he knew this to be unlikely.

* * *

That same year Neville gained his School Certificate with Distinction. He was by then seventeen and needing to make decisions about his future, but England was unsettled politically and war in Europe seemed inevitable. He expected to return to The Gables, help Phoebe around the house for a while then find some sort of paid work – he needed to earn a living now, he could not expect his aunt and uncle to support him. The provision made for him by his late father was due to cease altogether when his education was finished, although he would come into a legacy under his father's will when he reached twenty-one. He would be leaving the Academy at the end of the summer term. However, one day in early July, Ian Hathaway, the headmaster invited Neville to take tea with him in his study. He came straight to the point.

"Garth, I've asked you here today to discuss your career intentions".

Neville nodded and waited for Mr Hathaway to continue.

"Have you made any plans?"

"Well sir, I will need to get a job quite soon. But if possible, I would like to train to be a teacher eventually. Mr Harris, my form tutor suggested it".

Mr Hathaway took a sip of his tea. "As a matter of fact, I have spoken to Mr Harris about you. I agree with him, you have the makings of a fine teacher, Garth. Your maths results are excellent, and I think you have the right qualities to be able to teach it, and science, come to that. You would have to wait until you are eighteen to go to Teachers Training College of course. But I have a proposition for you in the meantime". He leaned back in his chair.

"I'm sure I don't need to tell you that this country is likely to go to war. It may be sooner than we think. But whenever that happens, I'm certain to lose some of my teaching staff.

Some of the younger men are bound to enlist, even though teaching will be a reserved occupation".

He passed Neville a plate of biscuits.

"So, what I am offering you is a temporary post here at Fenborough, assisting the Maths master. It will be unofficial, that is, it will not be a recognised post as you are untrained, but if there's a war on, I doubt if that will be a problem. You will receive a salary and have accommodation here at the Academy. You are still very young I know, but I think you are ready for this. It will give you some teaching experience, you know the ropes here, it will help me greatly to have you join my staff and you can still go to college to train later. What do you say?"

Neville was dumbfounded for a moment. This was the last thing he had expected, and the thought of being able to continue at the Academy as an assistant teacher was the most wonderful opportunity. He didn't need to think about it. He stammered his acceptance and gratitude.

"I won't let you down, sir", he said, feeling that his words were inadequate. "I will always do my best for the school".

"I have no doubt of that, or I would not have offered you the post". Mr Hathaway was smiling. "We can work out the finer details later. Go off now and spend the summer with your aunt and uncle, then come back in September ready to take the new first form for maths".

Neville could not wait to tell Phoebe his good news when she collected him in the car a fortnight later.

Phoebe was equally excited, partly because it meant that Neville would not be far away. The prospect gave her a rare moment of happiness. There was also relief; she had realised that if war came, Neville would be of an age to join the armed forces, with all the uncertainty and anxiety that enlistment would bring, and resolutely she had pushed the unwelcome thought to the back of her mind.

"I am so proud of you", she said, hugging him close.

So, in the autumn term of 1937, Neville took up the post as junior maths master at Fenborough Academy. He had a study bedroom and a small salary; the first money he had ever earned. Teaching without any training would not be easy but he felt equal to the task, remembering how not so long ago he had been a new boy in this very school and how some of the teachers had inspired him to learn and recognised his potential. If he could do the same for just one boy he would feel he had made a good beginning.

The first year as a junior teacher was challenging for Neville; the adjustment from student to assistant maths master was difficult at times, but Mr Hathaway had wisely arranged for him to coach the new intake of ten-year-old boys; teaching those who remembered him as a fellow pupil would not have been so easy. He found that the staff accepted him as one of them with equanimity, and two new teachers who had not known him as a student gave no thought to the fact that he was only recently a sixth-former.

It was in September 1939, just as Neville started his third year as a teacher at Fenborough that war broke out.

Mr Hathaway had been right; within weeks, several of the younger members of staff joined up. At nineteen, Neville was of an age to be conscripted, but teaching was to be an exempt profession. He had at first felt duty bound to follow his colleagues and enlist, but was persuaded by the headmaster that he could equally well serve his country by remaining on the staff and filling some of the gaps in the maths and science department; education was still important even in wartime, he said. For a while, Neville wrestled with his conscience. It seemed as though he was escaping danger when so many young men were willingly putting themselves in harm's way.

He spoke to Phoebe about it during the October half term. She was careful in her reply, not wanting to show her apprehension at the thought of Neville in the army, flying a fighter plane or being torpedoed at sea. She had lost one nephew in tragic circumstances; she was terrified of losing another.

"You must do what you think best, Neville", she said at last. "Uncle Frederick and I will support you whatever you decide. I know, because you have thought about this very seriously, that you will make the right choice. But there are other ways you can help the war effort, you know. It doesn't all have to be on the front line".

This gave Neville food for thought, and within a few days he gave his answer to the headmaster; that he would stay on at Fenborough but that he would like permission for time off on some evenings to join the rota of fire watchers in nearby Lamberham.

In the end he took on other duties to help the Home Front. He assisted the Air Raid Patrol warden – there were only a few dwellings near the Academy but from time to time he was asked to help out at Lamberham. His bicycle, now parked in the cycle shed at school was essential for these journeys. He was given responsibility for the blackout at the school, realising that a hundred and twenty young lives depended on his vigilance, and that many of the boys' fathers were away fighting the enemy.

Regardless of the privations of wartime and the interruptions to lessons, Neville took to his new role teaching maths and science to the first years with enthusiasm. There was something satisfying about imparting information and seeing difficult problems overcome. Perhaps it was because the age gap between himself and his pupils was not great, but he was popular with the boys. He understood, remembering his own brother's sadness during his first weeks at Fenborough how homesick ten-year-olds could be, now even more so with all the uncertainties of war.

The school was spared any damage despite the Battle of Britain being fought overhead in the skies above Sussex and Kent. But a Hurricane and a Messerschmitt crashed during a dogfight on the downs above Drover's Cross and it was a sobering reminder of how close the war had come to their doorstep.

Early in 1941 Neville broached the subject of teachers training with the headmaster.

"Sir I am very happy here at Fenborough, but I should like to apply for college soon. I've spent longer here as an assistant teacher than I expected, and I'm so grateful for the opportunity you've given me. But it's important that I gain my Teaching Certificate".

To Neville's surprise, Mr Hathaway was sympathetic. "I won't deny that we would miss you tremendously, Garth", he said at last. "You've been an asset to the school, and we will find it difficult to fill your shoes. But yes, I agree, you do need to get through college now. Have you any thoughts about where you will apply?"

"I was considering Falcon Hill, Sir".

"It's a good choice, and not that far away from your family. You need to talk this over with your aunt and uncle. There's the matter of financial support, for one thing. Come and see me again after half term. I have an idea that may help".

Phoebe was delighted to hear of his plans. "It's so right for you, Neville", she said, once again trying to hide her relief that he was not contemplating a military career. "Please allow your uncle and I to help you. We will support you through college. It's what your father would have wanted", she added, not actually knowing if Thomas would have wanted Neville to go into teaching but feeling sure that he would have approved of them helping their nephew.

A fortnight later, Neville sat with Mr Hathaway in his study. "I am going to suggest that you apply for a one-year course, Garth", he said, looking up from some papers. "There is already a shortage of teachers, particularly in the maths and science subjects, and as the school leaving age is likely to be raised before too long there will be even more demand in peacetime, whenever that may be".

He continued. "I will give you a first-rate reference, you have a Distinction in School Cert, and I think that with the two and a half years' experience in front of a class that you have already had, there can be no doubt that you will be accepted".

"Will that mean I will be fully qualified Sir?"

"Yes, at the end of that year you will receive your Teaching Certificate. In fact, it will be a little less than a year. And it goes without saying that I would welcome you back on to the permanent staff here, but you would of course be free to take any other post, it would be your decision".

So, in October 1941 Neville began his Teacher Training at Falcon Hill Training College, funded by some of the money left to him by his father, and by a generous allowance from Phoebe and Frederick. The following July he was granted his formal qualification.

He returned to stay at The Gables to spend some time with his aunt and uncle and to consider his future. By then he was twenty-two, and under normal circumstances he would have hoped for a chance to travel or at least to experience life outside of the classroom. But this was still wartime, and the idea of foreign holidays or pleasure trips was impossible.

Ian Hathaway's words returned to him. There was a permanent post waiting for him at the Academy, he knew. But much as he appreciated that offer (and in many ways he felt he owed the headmaster a great deal), he did not want to spend any more years at the same establishment; he needed a total change, to meet different people, live independently and most importantly to test himself in a completely new working environment where he would succeed or fail on his own merits and without the safety net of the school where he had spent half his life.

Having made that decision, he wrote a personal letter to Mr Hathaway, telling him that he had qualified as a teacher. He thanked him again for all the help he had received over the years and for the valuable experience as an assistant teacher but went on to explain that he now felt the need to branch out.

The headmaster wrote back, congratulating him on his achievement but understanding perfectly why Neville might wish for a change in direction. He ended the letter wishing him every success and reminding him that there would always be a vacancy for him at the Academy should he change his mind.

Feeling that he had in some way received Ian Hathaway's blessing, he applied for the vacancy of maths teacher at Kirchington Boys' Grammar School, about ten miles from Lamberham. It was near the end of the summer term, but within a week he was invited for interview and was offered the post there and then. So, promising to visit Phoebe and Frederick as often as possible and satisfied that he had done the right thing by everyone, in September 1942 he moved to Kirchington, rented a small flat and looked forward to the next chapter of his life.

It was at Kirchington Grammar School that a few years later he met Lois Oakley.

Chapter Four

If Constance Oakley had been able to arrange for her daughter Lois to 'come out' as a debutante in order to find a suitable husband, she would have done so.

Unfortunately for Constance, if less so for Lois who was appalled at the prospect, there was neither money nor connections sufficient to make this a realistic possibility, and by the time Lois was of a suitable age, the tradition of the most well-connected young ladies being presented at Court was beginning to die out.

Constance, by then widowed for ten years, had felt it her duty, if not her right (because of a long-held belief that she had a distant, if unconfirmed link with a minor royal), to ensure her only daughter married into society. The reality was that Constance had aspirations without the financial means to act on them and eventually was forced to abandon the project entirely. In addition, Lois was painfully shy, uncomfortable in company and had little conversation, which caused her mother to despair that even if her daughter were to meet an eligible man, he would find her boring or lacking in the qualities of a society hostess. But her hopes rested on Lois's beauty; she was indeed beautiful; slender, with dark hair and deep grey eyes, fine bone structure, a clear complexion and an engaging smile.

But not ready to give up completely on her plans for Lois's future, Constance decided that if marrying into the aristocracy was out of reach, then academia was a feasible and respectable alternative. Lois herself had received only standard formal education, but her mother had ensured that her daughter was well versed in ladies' accomplishments: French, piano playing, painting and needlework. Lois had shown early promise of artistic flair and would have liked to pursue training in brush techniques and composition, but Constance was not minded to allow that talent to be nurtured any further, fearing that any such association might encourage undesirable bohemian tendencies. Her daughter's achievements seemed sufficient, as far as Constance was concerned, for a young woman who by securing a well-to-do husband would never need a career or an income of her own.

But although Constance's alternative plan for Lois was well thought out and there were the beginnings of some suitable introductions, their timing was outside of her control. Reaching the age of eighteen in 1945, Lois was required to sign up for war work and joined the Auxiliary Territorial Service towards the end of World War Two, taking a clerical role in a searchlight unit. She was assigned shared quarters with four other girls and provided with uniform. It was her first experience of living away from home. Constance, initially heartened by the fact that women in uniform were at that time considered to have a certain glamour, and were likely to meet officers or pilots, hoped that another opportunity would present itself. This however came to nothing; the uniform was dull, and working long shifts with little free time meant that Lois rarely met any young men, eligible or otherwise. However, in the post war years of the late 1940s, having undergone some basic secretarial training while in the ATS, Lois took a post at Kirchington Boys' Grammar School, typing notes, reports and examination papers for the senior masters. She rented a room in a local lodging house – a further step away from her mother's control. It was the nearest Lois came to a career of her own, and it was here that she met Neville Garth, who had joined the staff a few years previously.

Constance was not happy about this development. Her ambitions for her daughter in the sphere of education included marriage to a Vice Chancellor of a prestigious university, not an unknown teacher from an obscure provincial school. But by then, Constance's health was failing. She lacked the energy and determination to do more than voice her objections. Lois saw this as a chance to make her own decisions and within twelve months of meeting Neville, they were engaged.

Their courtship had been brief. The Second World War had injected an urgency into relationships. Long engagements overseen by protective parents to ensure couples were kept at a respectable distance were by then a thing of the past.

It may not have been a grand passion but Neville, seven years her senior saw in Lois an attractive, cultured and sensitive woman who would be a supportive and loyal wife, whose background was impeccable (whilst realising the control her domineering mother had long exerted over her), and whose creative talents would complement his own scientific and analytical mind.

Neville had not had any serious relationships with girls. His life until then had been spent in male company, with a few exceptions of local dances at Christmas and 'socials' following the school summer garden parties or parish fêtes. Even then, ladies at these functions had either been in short supply or already spoken for. But in any case, he had no desire to play the field.

Lois was not motivated by wealth or status, despite her mother's influence, more by a need for emotional security and a modicum of independence. Growing up without a father in her formative years and with no siblings, she recognised what she had missed in the way of family life, and a future with Neville promised all these things.

They married in 1951, just as Neville came into his inheritance from Uncle Frederick. Lois received a modest settlement from her mother. Together with Neville's salary, they would be comfortably off.

Constance, by now bedridden and unable to attend the wedding was comforted a little by the fact that Neville had inherited a sizeable property, although she was never well enough to visit and witness the scale and magnitude of the refurbishment task that lay ahead for the couple. She also felt a sense of relief that her reserved and socially awkward daughter had at last found someone who would give her a comfortable home and who understood her complexities and shy temperament.

She died the following year, content that Lois had married well.

Chapter Five

For Neville and Lois, the first few years of their marriage were idyllic. As a couple they were devoted to one another; social life was unimportant, they were content with working on their plans for transforming the house and seeing their ideas gradually come to fruition. The design was predominantly Lois's domain: once any structural repairs were completed, she came into her own, spending hours choosing wallpaper, the right shades of paint and the most exquisite fabrics and furnishings. Never had she expected to have the freedom or the means to exercise such choice over a home of her own, let alone a house on the scale of Moongarth, or to express her own tastes – her mother's disapproval had always put a dampener on any artistic aspirations she might have had. Gradually, her shyness became less; she ventured into Drover's Cross to the local shops instead of leaving all the errands to Betty, her daily help. As her attentions switched to the overgrown jungle outside, she realised how little she knew about plants and flowers, and plucking up courage she joined the local Women's Institute, which she guessed would provide a wealth of knowledge about gardening and whose members would be only too happy to share their expertise. She was not wrong. The ladies of the WI welcomed her and instead of Lois being known merely as the 'lady from the house on the hill' she very soon formed a small circle of friends and was invited to coffee mornings and afternoon tea. Now that Moongarth was fully restored and resplendent in new furnishings and décor, Lois lost no time in returning the invitations, knowing that every detail of her home would be the subject of local gossip for a while but feeling proud that her efforts would stand up to scrutiny from the most critical of her neighbours.

To Neville, teaching was more than a career, it was a vocation. Every boy in his form was important to him, regardless of their level of ability. He was a dedicated and gifted teacher, with an ability to inspire the most promising children and encourage the less able. Mathematics was his core subject with science as a secondary, and nothing was more rewarding to Neville than when pupils struggling endlessly with a mathematical problem could, under his guidance and patient instruction, suddenly understand. Their sense of achievement at those times was matched by his own. He did his utmost to make lessons relevant and interesting, however dull the subject matter might first appear. As a result, he was highly respected by both students and other members of staff but also had a reputation for being firm and strict in class. Keen to share his enthusiasm for astronomy with the boys, he established the Star Society as an after-school activity to promote some basic knowledge of the solar system and how to identify objects in the night sky. He expected it to be of limited interest but to his surprise over thirty boys of various ages asked to join, and the venture proved popular. Neville's zeal and energy did not go unnoticed by the headmaster, and in 1953 he was promoted to head of the junior department, with responsibility for the maths and science curriculum.

Together, he and Lois tackled the garden; Lois armed with suggestions freely given by her WI friends (who, having seen its neglected state were more than ready to share ideas knowing that a team of gardeners was to be engaged to carry out the hard landscaping). Over time, fresh turf was laid on what had originally passed for a lawn, flower beds and borders dug and weeded, fruit trees and shrubs pruned; those considered not worth saving were consigned to the compost heap or bonfires. A winding stone path was created, weaving its way from the edge of the lawn through the shrubbery and disappearing out of sight of the house at the far side of the orchard. A magnificent York stone patio was laid adjoining the lawn, and a timber summer house at the lower end of the lawn completed the picture. Beyond the orchard, hedged with hawthorn and gorse bushes was a meadow of about an acre in size; the far side marked the boundary of the property. No plans for its use had yet been decided so in the meantime it was a haven for foxes, rabbits and occasional deer, and a carpet of wildflowers in the summer months.

There were several existing outbuildings, surprisingly still in a good state of repair. Once cleared of decades of rubbish they were adopted as a tool shed, a log store and a garage for Neville's newly acquired Wolsely.

The driveway at the front of the house was freshly gravelled, the small lawn restored, the hedge trimmed and broken paving slabs on the front path replaced. A purple wisteria, long overdue for pruning and shaping had been brought back to order and now it clung to the front wall, its flowers tumbling in profusion over the mellow brickwork during the early summer months. A mature magnolia tree stood at the corner of the lawn and promised an abundance of waxy flowers in spring. The overall effect was transformative, the outdoor space now rivalling the refurbished interior for style and charm.

Neville and Lois planted the borders and flower beds together; this was an activity they had both looked forward to, deciding against engaging professional gardeners for this part of the work. Their tastes were vastly different – Neville preferring bold, bright colours with banks of tall structural plants; gladioli, delphiniums, dahlias and peonies whereas Lois favoured smaller, low growing flowers in muted colours of pink, mauve and pale blue; stocks, lobelia, forget me nots and nemesia, interspersed with white alyssum and bacopa. The combined effect was charming – the garden had never been so well tended or nurtured with such care and imagination.

There was just one cloud on their horizon; despite their hopes, there was no sign of a baby. The couple were both in good health and there seemed to be no reason why Lois did not conceive. After nine years of marriage, she and Neville had all but given up hope. Then miraculously, soon after their tenth wedding anniversary, Lois announced that she was pregnant.

This came as a wonderful surprise to them both, even more so because Lois was by then thirty-four and had been only too aware that her chances of having a child were slipping away. But seven months later, after a trouble-free pregnancy, she gave birth to a daughter, Eleanor Phoebe.

Neville was overjoyed. "She's so like you" he said fondly, looking down at them both as he cradled Eleanor in his arms for the first time.

"It's impossible to tell when she's only an hour old!" Lois laughed despite her exhaustion. She too was brimming with elation. She felt that a spell had been lifted, a spell that for ten years had plagued her, telling her subconscious that she had no right to expect such happiness when she already had so many blessings.

Lois took to motherhood with such delight and contentment, and as Eleanor grew and thrived, Lois blossomed too – in health, confidence and enjoyment of life. Neville worked long hours, such were the demands of his position at the Grammar School and could rarely join in – but Lois was determined to give Eleanor every attention and experience that she herself had lacked as a child. The simple pleasures were the best. She took Eleanor to picnics on the beach and played games with her in the back garden, took her to the zoo, to children's parties at Christmas arranged by the WI, and they walked through the snow on winter's mornings and made snowmen. During the school holidays Neville was able to accompany them on outings and sometimes took them to London to the best toyshops. When Eleanor, by then known as Nell reached the age of four, she took riding and ballet lessons, both essential accomplishments, Lois decided. For a time, they were the perfect family.

But this blissful state of affairs did not last. Later Lois felt that the spell had returned, that fate had somehow dictated that she had by then had more than her fair share of happiness, and that the balance was to be redressed.

For several years Neville and Lois had hoped for a brother or sister for Nell. But just as Nell was about to start school, Lois suffered a miscarriage.

It was a bitter disappointment. They had thought that as Lois had been able to conceive, have a problem-free pregnancy and deliver a healthy baby that another child might be possible. It was completely random, they were told by the family physician, Dr Ferris; it was not due to anything they had done or not done, and although Lois was by then 39, there was no reason why she should not, after giving her body time to recover, have a further successful pregnancy and carry a baby to term.

Nell was too young to understand but she knew that her mother was sad and unwell, and needing to rest. Having just started in her first year at the village school, she craved comfort and reassurance, but Lois was distracted. The timing couldn't have been worse. Neville took two days compassionate leave but was unable to take more. One of Lois's friends from the WI, Shirley Fox, took Nell to school along with her own little boy who was about the same age, and collected her and brought her home in the afternoon. Neither Neville nor Lois had family to call upon, but with the help of Shirley, and Betty the daily help, they managed. It was a time of great sorrow for them all, and for a while the atmosphere at Moongarth, once so full of hope and positive energy, was bleak and sombre.

Life was never completely the same after that, but gradually Lois became philosophical about what might have been and looked to the future. Family life slowly went back to normal, Nell sensing a return of closeness to her mother again, Lois picking up the reins of her household once more and Neville feeling relief that they seemed to have overcome a crisis without lasting damage. It was a setback, nothing more.

But eighteen months later, the same thing happened – another miscarriage.

Their sense of loss was profound – but as with the previous miscarriage, there was no obvious reason. Lois struggled to cope with this second blow, blaming herself despite all the well-meaning reassurance that it was no one's fault, that these things sometimes just happen.

This time Lois found it harder to recover, both physically and emotionally. She decided at that point to give up hope of having another child; she saw the miscarriage as a failure on her part and could not risk another. Together she and Neville resolved to avoid any further pregnancies.

Having come to terms with this latest disappointment, Lois and Neville did their best to put it behind them. Nell was now six and a half and doing well at school. Lois learned to drive and bought a little car. She was able to take Nell on trips again, this time further afield and one summer the two of them went for a short holiday at the seaside. Neville's career was in the ascendant and despite all the personal upheaval of recent years he applied for the position of head of senior school curriculum when this post became vacant and was successful.

But fate can sometimes play cruel tricks, and attack in the most insidious of ways.

Their decision to give up on having any more children had been taken jointly and for the most compelling of reasons: to spare themselves any future heartache, to protect Lois's health and to accept that they were fortunate in so many other ways. So, it was a total shock that soon after Christmas 1970, Lois discovered that she was pregnant again.

Neville was full of trepidation although he tried not to show it, saying instead that this time things would be different. But he had grave doubts and took steps to ensure that as the pregnancy advanced, Lois had every possible paid help in the house and the very best medical care.

Lois steeled herself for another miscarriage. She was by then forty-four and it seemed inevitable. But after the third month came and went with no sign of any problems, she allowed herself to hope that all would be well.

By the seventh month they decided it was time to tell Nell, in simple terms that she would soon have a new brother or sister. It was becoming impossible to disguise the pregnancy, and Nell was starting to ask questions. She was excited at first, but Neville explained that there were still several weeks to wait, and that her mother would need lots of rest and quiet.

Ever cautious, and taking nothing for granted, Lois continued for another month in good health and spirits. Then suddenly, inexplicably, she sensed something was wrong. She had not felt the baby move for several days. But a scan, paid for privately by Neville, did not reveal anything abnormal. "It's just a sleepy baby", the midwife said, after careful examination of the images and carrying out a thorough check up. "There seems to be a regular heartbeat. Try not to worry. We will see you next week and do some more tests if you haven't felt any movement by then".

Partly reassured, Lois went home to rest. But two days later she was in premature labour, and after an agonising thirty-six hours she gave birth to a still born son.

Lois was numb with shock for several days and barely spoke. She returned home, pale and silent, rejecting all offers of help, company and sympathy. There was no way to comfort her. Beside herself with despondency and recriminations, she became distant and withdrawn, not sleeping and seldom emerging from her bedroom. Even the sight of Nell upset her, and she refused to have anything to do with her little daughter. Neville was in despair. It was Shirley who once again came to the rescue, walking Nell to and from school and ensuring that she had clean clothes, giving her meals and trying to keep up a sense of routine. Betty, the daily help was persuaded to take on extra hours. Lois neither acknowledged their help nor thanked them for it, such was her utter devastation and sense of loss.

Neville too, blamed himself, but for different reasons. He held himself responsible for allowing the pregnancy to happen in the first place; they had made a pact that they would not try to have more children. Yet he had assumed that with Lois being in her forties she was unlikely to conceive again, and he had become careless. Their lovemaking had been so rare at that time that he was reluctant to spoil the mood by talking about not taking risks.

His sorrow was heightened by the memory of his brother Henry, and how as a boy he had grieved for him in this very house without his parents to console him. He felt the same sense of unfairness now as he had done then as a twelve-year-old boy, and something more – that feeling of guilt, albeit unjustified, that had he acted differently both tragedies could have been averted.

His colleagues at school were unsure how to deal with the situation. Although they held Neville in high esteem, they had always found him to be a very private person and felt reluctant to intrude on his grief. Some were torn between expressing their condolences or saying the wrong thing, so said nothing at all. Only Frances, the school secretary said how sorry she was to hear about his bereavement.

As Lois distanced herself from her husband and daughter over the days that followed, Neville and Nell became closer. Neville had until then left the majority of Nell's upbringing to Lois, and accustomed as he was to teaching boys, his relationship with Nell did not come naturally at first. But it fell on him to tell her why there would be no baby; that a little brother had been born but had not survived. It was difficult to explain to a nine-year-old and even harder for Nell to understand. She cried for a long time, and he cuddled her in his arms, not knowing how to console her, also realising that she longed desperately for her mother and that he had no idea how to make anything right again for his family.

They named the baby Laurence Henry.

It was a sad, small funeral procession that followed the tiny white coffin, carried by Neville. St Luke's, the little parish church in Drover's Cross was decorated with just a few white lilies. For a time, Neville had doubted whether Lois would come at all. She had received the news of the funeral arrangements with a look of horror, the reality too much to take in.

Shirley, Betty, a few close friends from the WI and two of Neville's work colleagues attended. Nell held tightly to Shirley's hand; her mother seemingly unaware of anything going on around her. Laurence was to be buried a few yards from Henry's grave. Shirley thought that the sight of the coffin being lowered into the ground would be too much for Nell and took her home straight after the service. But somehow Nell understood the finality.

A prolonged absence from school for Neville was out of the question and finding it impossible to impose any further on Shirley and Betty for help, he was on the point of engaging a resident nanny for Nell. This prospect however, seemed to shake Lois out of her melancholy; the thought of another female taking her place in the household and possibly in Neville's attentions was a step too far. So, Lois gradually returned to family life, capable of taking care of Nell in a practical sense, looking after their home and garden and giving quiet companionship to Neville. But for many months there was no warmth or tenderness, it was as if a light had been extinguished.

It was from that point that Nell, even in a nine-year-old child's way, decided that the right thing to do was to avoid her mother whenever she could, not to be noisy or a nuisance, not to ask for things and to try to be good for both her parents. She would make herself as inconspicuous as possible and not add to their troubles.

Chapter Six

As she grew older, Nell became aware of how her relationship with her mother had changed since her earliest memories. The shift was almost imperceptible, yet it was real. There was less closeness, less warmth. Nell lacked nothing in terms of correct upbringing and education; every material need was met, but she was not spoilt, nor did she seek or crave the trappings which other girls of her age took for granted. Yet there was something missing. It was as though Lois, instead of cherishing and pouring out love on her only child, was looking for somewhere to lay the blame for the loss of three others. Of course, this was unspoken and would have been emphatically denied if such a thought were ever given voice. It was just a feeling that Nell had, because it would have been impossible to raise the subject with her mother. She did sometimes try to talk to her father, who always listened to her when he had time. But he became awkward and dismissive, saying it was just how Lois was, she had been through a great deal, and that they both loved Nell very much.

So Nell carried a great deal of guilt as a child; guilt that she did not understand. If she had been able to confide in anyone about it, she would have been reassured that she was not to blame for her mother's sadness, and the circumstances would have been explained to her. It was even more poignant to Nell because she could remember a time when things were so different. The emotional bond between mother and daughter which had existed in Nell's early childhood, without her even knowing what it was, had gradually faded.

Unable to avoid the subject, her father had told Nell in the simplest way he could that her baby brother had not lived, and she knew that he was buried in the village churchyard near to her Uncle Henry who had died as a little boy in a tragic accident very near to their home. So, she understood something of her parents' sadness, and in a subconscious way resolved to give them no more worry or add to their sorrow.

School became an escape for Nell, she was bright, intelligent and a quick learner like her father. But unlike Neville she showed little aptitude for maths or science; her favourite subjects were English and History. She was a great reader from an early age; the Beatrix Potter stories were read and re-read, but sadly these were seldom read to her. When other children were enjoying outdoor games, Nell would be curled up on her bed, losing herself for hours in a book, finding that stories had the possibility of opening up new and exciting worlds for her. At the age of ten she moved on to classics such as Little Women, What Katy Did and The Railway Children, and wondered if one day she could become a great writer. Deep down, she was desperate to do something to make her parents proud of her.

When Nell moved up to Lamberham Girls High School, she was a little overawed at first; the transition from the local village school was daunting. Lois had never encouraged Nell to bring friends home for tea, so feeling unable to reciprocate, Nell could not accept invitations from girls at school, and this did little to establish any firm friendships for some time. But after a few months settling in at school she found a kindred spirit in Caroline Brooke, and this went some way to easing her loneliness. Together the friends compared marks, discussed homework and walked to catch the school bus; and as time went on, exchanged confidences.

Caroline had a boyfriend. "I don't think I shall ever have a boyfriend, let alone get married", sighed Nell one day, as they walked to the bus stop. "I never meet any boys, I don't really know any".

"You need to go out more, then you will. You're so beautiful Nell; boys will be queuing up to take you out". Caroline was keen for her friend to have more fun; Nell had told her a little about her home life and to Caroline it sounded so dull, even allowing for the fact that they both took their studies very seriously.

English literature lessons provided solace; at fourteen Nell was consistently top of her class and relished every set text and book that she was required to read, learning how to compile character studies, take a glimpse into the mind of the writer and to understand the social or historical commentary behind the words. Her solitary childhood had somehow given her a certain insight; the complex, tempestuous story of Jane Eyre and the wild romanticism of Wuthering Heights she found gripping, and the irony and witticisms of Jane Austen were not lost on her. When Nell was awarded first prize in the fourth form for a Shakespeare essay, neither of her parents attended Speech Day to see their daughter receive the honour – Neville was unable to take time from work, and Lois seldom went into company without her husband.

By the age of sixteen, Nell had blossomed in looks, with beauty rivalling her mother's. She was tall like her father, being above average height, but had inherited her mother's slender frame, dark glossy hair, and deep-set pewter grey eyes which at times seemed to have a distant look, and which people sometimes mistook for inattention.

Also like her father, she concentrated hard on schoolwork, especially the subjects she enjoyed most and did well at 'O' Level with nine passes: History and English Literature at Grade 1. Following discussion with her form tutor, Nell opted to take French, History and English Literature at 'A' level. This meant transferring to Kirchington Sixth Form College, but her father approved of this move as the college had a record of high achievement and had the advantage of being in the same city as Kirchington Boys Grammar School where Neville was head of department, so he could take her by car in the mornings.

"Mummy please can Caroline come over at the weekend? We are going to work on a project together". Nell had decided to test the water with her mother.

Lois was taken aback by this request. "I suppose it will be all right", she said at last. "But on condition that it will only be Caroline. I don't want hordes of people here".

Nell, who in any case had only one friend to whom she was close enough to spend time with out of school was encouraged by her mother's acceptance, however unwilling, and together with Caroline she made plans for the beginnings of a social life.

Caroline's boyfriend Simon invited both girls to a party in Lamberham the following Saturday. It was the first grown-up party Nell had been to – in fact even attending children's birthday parties had been a rarity. She drank two glasses of cider in quick succession, after which she felt light-headed and slightly sick. Everyone seemed to be enjoying themselves immensely and Nell felt awkward and left out. For a few moments she wondered if she had inherited her mother's inability to socialise. Perhaps it would be different if I had a boyfriend, she said to herself miserably. But feeling it was too early to leave the party and make a run for it, she hung around, pretending to look at the record sleeves, her eyes scanning the room every now and then to see if there was anyone she recognised. There wasn't. The only two people she knew seemed to have disappeared.

After another half hour had gone by, she was asked to dance. She accepted, glad to have a break from the boredom but all the time wondering if the young man had asked her because he felt sorry for her. The thought made her feel even worse. Her partner was polite and friendly enough, but Nell felt he was not her type. "But what is my type?" she asked herself later. "And how will I ever find out?" She resolved to avoid parties and forget the idea of finding a boyfriend for now; there were exams coming up, and her studies were all-important.

But things changed for Nell soon after she made that decision.

* * *

It was around this time that Lois began to notice some worrying physical symptoms. She shrugged them off at first, attributing them to her age (although she was at that time only fifty-one) but the feelings persisted.

The initial change was that of fatigue. Excessive fatigue that left her feeling exhausted before she had even started a task. Every limb ached and her body felt intensely weak; even the smallest chore was a huge effort.

After a while, the decline in her health became impossible to disguise, and Lois, who for some time had made valiant attempts to keep it hidden, could no longer deny that she felt unwell. Nell, who missed nothing about her mother, was the first to notice although she knew better that to raise the subject, but Neville, by chance witnessing Lois stumbling as she stepped down into the kitchen one morning, voiced his concerns and a heated altercation followed. Lois reluctantly admitted to experiencing pain and tiredness but made light of it. She refused to see a doctor, insisting that the condition was only temporary and that her strength would return.

But it didn't; over time the symptoms worsened, and Lois reluctantly began to ask Nell for help, at first with small things, such as fetching and carrying, then more frequent assistance was needed. One morning Lois asked Nell to help her dress. She couldn't do up the buttons on her blouse or buckle her belt.

Nell was happy in a way to oblige; she had long hoped for her mother to need her or for them to share personal moments like this. But it was so unusual for Lois to ask for help of this kind that Nell confided in her father later that evening, when Lois had gone to bed.

"Daddy, I think there's something wrong with Mummy. She is not managing everyday things very well; she is struggling and has been asking me for help. I don't mind that, I will always help her, but should we get some advice?" Nell's voice faltered uncertainly.

Neville listened to what Nell has to say, his face grave.

"Your mother is not well, of that there is no doubt" he said at last. "But I have no idea what is wrong with her. Yesterday she complained about numbness in her hands, she can't play the piano as well as she used to. She is so weak and can't carry things, sometimes walking a few steps tires her".

"What can we do, Daddy?" Nell's anxiety was plain to see.

"I am going to arrange for her to see a doctor, whether she likes it or not", said Neville after a few moments. "She can't go on like this and if she is asking you for help then that is unusual. Your mother has always been so ...well private. She would never do that unless there was a real problem. Leave it with me for now. I shall telephone Dr Ferris tomorrow and ask him to visit. In the meantime, can you do something for me? Help your mother get ready each morning, before you go to college. Can you travel on the bus for a while instead of coming with me in the car? That will give you an extra twenty minutes or so. You don't need to be as early as I do".

"Yes of course Daddy. I'll get breakfast too, and clear up a bit before Jenny comes, then I'll go and catch the bus".

Jenny was the daily help, successor to the faithful Betty who had retired two years previously.

Neville kissed his daughter and Nell felt at last that she had been given some responsibility, that she was being useful to her parents, and that helped alleviate her worries a little.

So It happened that Lois began to rely on Nell's assistance and a new arrangement was established without it ever being openly agreed or discussed. Lois was clearly distressed at being unable to manage bathing and dressing on her own, but realised she had no choice but to accept her daughter's help in the mornings, and once she was up and had taken breakfast, she would start to feel a little better. Jenny, having been briefed about Lois's situation started to arrive fifteen minutes earlier and Nell, reassured that Jenny was perfectly capable of looking after her mother, departed for college a little later each day.

The bus to Kirchington was convenient in one way because it stopped right outside college. The only problem was that it arrived ten minutes later than the start time of her first lecture on Wednesdays.

She explained to her tutor that her mother was unwell and needed her help in the mornings, but that she would ensure she caught up on any work that she missed during that time. Mr Harvey, realising that Nell was one of his brightest and most diligent students that year, was understanding and for a while this routine continued.

* * *

Kirchington Sixth Form College was at that time undergoing extensive refurbishment in order to accommodate additional students from the secondary schools at Haskebourne and Rivenden whose sixth forms were due to close the following year.

Patrick Walsh, who had arrived in Sussex from Ireland three months previously had found work initially as a labourer for Keane Construction on the college contract, but when his foreman discovered that Patrick had also done some training as a bricklayer, he was swiftly moved on to the team constructing the new Science and Engineering block. At the age of twenty-two he was earning good money; enough with overtime to rent a small bedsit, run a van, save a little, send some home to his parents in Ireland each week and have enough over for Friday nights in the pub with his workmates.

Life was good here, he thought, he had made the right decision to travel to England to work, as had so many of his friends who had made the journey across the Irish Sea. None of them had regretted the move or so they said, apart from missing their homeland now and then. He felt settled, independent, and for the first time he had prospects. He was full of optimism; things were going his way and there was every chance that life was going to get even better.

He first caught sight of Nell running through the car park one Wednesday morning. She was rushing, obviously late for a lecture, her long dark hair streaming out behind her in a tangle and her complexion glowing. Despite being in a hurry, she glanced at Patrick who was carrying a bag of tools towards the construction site and noticed him looking at her. Then she looked again at him and smiled. From that moment he was captivated.

He searched for Nell on the campus every day for the next week, whenever he could find a reason to leave the site, to fetch something from his van or when he took his sandwiches to eat on the college green at lunchtime. He had to be careful in case his frequent absences were noticed by his foreman. When at last he spotted her again, she was walking in the grounds with a friend during the lunch break. She saw him and gave a little wave. He was encouraged by this. But he didn't dare approach her, he needed an excuse. He would wait, but he wouldn't give up. An opportunity would present itself.

* * *

Dr Ferris, the family doctor visited Lois the day after Neville telephoned him. He examined Lois and asked her several questions. Her symptoms could be caused by a number of conditions, he concluded. He wondered if Lois could be suffering from depression; given the earlier trauma she had been through, it would not be surprising. "Depression could cause a huge range of physical manifestations", he commented, and he could not discount the possibility. He prescribed a course of anti-depressants, to be taken for several months before any improvement could be seen, and some pain relief medication for her aching joints. But feeling slightly out of his depth, he spoke to Neville privately at the front door.

"I would feel happier with a second opinion". Dr Ferris was nothing if not cautious. "It's not immediately obvious what is causing the pain and weakness. Your wife needs to see a neurologist. I will make a referral".

Neville, feeling that there was no time to lose decided to pay privately for Lois to see a specialist, and within a few days they attended the consulting rooms of Mr Hugh Clifford in Kirchington.

Mr Clifford was kind, congenial and thorough. He carried out an examination of her hands, finger and knee joints, and watched Lois walk a few steps up and down the room. He observed her ability to pick up and grasp various objects. An eye test was performed. He then asked numerous questions and made notes. Lois became impatient, saying she had already given Dr Ferris a great deal of information.

Mr Clifford smiled. "I realise it's very irksome, Mrs Garth" he said, looking up from his writing. "But I do like to start from the beginning with all my patients. Every detail you can give me will help find the cause of your affliction". He had a faint Scots accent and an old-fashioned way of speaking, which, if Lois had not been so anxious, she would have found reassuring.

Neville, who had sat silently up until then, cleared his throat. "Mr Clifford, I wonder if you're aware that some years ago my wife had a series of miscarriages and then a still birth? Could this be relevant?"

"It's possible, but unlikely, given the amount of time that has elapsed", Mr Clifford said at last. "I think we must look further to ascertain a reason for these symptoms. I can't give you an answer today, I'm afraid. I have a theory but until it's confirmed I cannot say any more".

A series of blood tests was ordered, a scan and lastly an X-ray. Neville took time off to attend these appointments with Lois, realising how frightened and confused she had become. He told Nell that the procedures were all routine, and that Mr Clifford just wanted to rule certain things out. He didn't want to worry her unduly until a diagnosis was given.

Ten days later Lois and Neville returned to Mr Clifford with some trepidation to hear the results of the tests. He came directly to the point.

"Mrs Garth, the tests show that you are likely to have a chronic condition called Rheumatoid Arthritis", he said, leaning forward in his chair and looking Lois straight in the eye. "It's what we call an autoimmune disease. It occurs when the immune system goes haywire for some reason and starts attacking its own tissues".

Neville and Lois looked stunned.

"It's not clear what causes RA", he continued. "It could be genetic, it could be as a result of a viral infection, or it may be completely random. I realise that's not much comfort, it's natural to want an explanation for such things, but any opinion I gave would be pure speculation on my part".

He gave time for his words to sink in, then continued.

"There is no cure for RA, but there is some good news. The condition can be managed. The tests show that you are in the very early stages and therefore any interventions we make now will help slow down its progress. Also, there are likely to be long periods of remission; I'm not saying you will feel completely back to normal during those times, but you will feel better than you do now and be able to function day to day".

It was a great deal to take in, and although Mr Clifford asked them if they had any questions, they were unable to think of any at that moment. "I'm sure you will want to know a great deal more, once you have had time to come to terms with this", he said gently. "I am going to give you a prescription which will relieve the aches and pains a little and that will in turn help with your mobility. Come back and see me again in a month's time and we will talk in a bit more depth about treatment in the longer term".

Later that evening they sat down with Nell in the drawing room and Neville explained the situation in a way that would cause her the least alarm.

"Your mother has been prescribed some medication that will make her feel better quite quickly" he said, pausing to watch Nell's reaction. "But she will need some regular help at home, more than Jenny is able to give. I am going to look into this". Lois said nothing but for a moment the look on her face reminded him of the time he had almost employed a nanny for Nell. That time she had resisted, and, in a way, it had helped bring her out of her malaise. But this was different, he told himself.

Nell, although shocked and dismayed to hear about her mother's illness was somehow heartened by the fact that her parents were talking to her as an adult, and she felt that they were trusting her and wanting her to be involved. "I can help too, Mummy", she said, not knowing what else to say, and went over and took her mother's hand. Lois did not pull it away as she once would have done. It was a tiny gesture, yet it spoke volumes that perhaps the bond between the two women still existed, however fragile and hidden.

Of one thing Neville was quite sure; he was not going to let Lois's illness interfere with Nell's education. A little help in the morning must not be allowed to become full time care. In any case, Lois may manage without too much help during the periods of remission, he thought. But the following day he contacted a home nursing agency and asked if they had a suitable trained female nurse/companion on their books.

Strangely, Lois seemed more accepting about her condition now that she had a definite diagnosis. She became almost cheerful and as the pain reduced, and she could move around more easily, her day-to-day life improved. She was still reluctant to go out, especially on her own, but she showed interest in life again, reading and listening to music. The numbness and stiffness in her hands and joints curtailed any activities requiring dexterity, so needlework or piano playing were no longer possible, but she took pleasure in tuning into concerts and afternoon plays on the radio.

After a few weeks, Neville interviewed several prospective nurses, and Lois, who naturally wanted to make the final decision herself, agreed that Mrs Evelyn Kemp was the most suitable. Evelyn would not be resident but would come every morning after Nell had left for college and would stay until mid-afternoon. Everything was arranged very quickly by the agency and Evelyn was willing to take on extra hours when required, depending on any periods of flare-up. It seemed ideal although she had negotiated a much higher salary than Neville had anticipated, but Lois seemed to have taken to Evelyn, and he wanted someone in place without delay. Soon Neville and Nell were able to relax a little, feeling that not only was Lois in good hands but that she had willingly accepted the prospect of being looked after by someone who was after all a stranger, however well qualified.

Within a couple of weeks, Evelyn had established herself at Moongarth. On the surface she seemed amiable and competent. She was a no-nonsense woman in her early fifties, with a great deal of experience as a sister in a general hospital as well as having spent the last two years in private nursing. Lois, once so reluctant to welcome strangers into her home, found Evelyn's presence reassuring and felt that she was in safe hands. Evelyn, a firm believer in routine, made sure that Lois carried out the daily gentle exercises that Mr Clifford had suggested, but was perceptive enough to notice when Lois was in pain or needing to rest, and the regime was adapted accordingly. But it was clear from the beginning that Evelyn considered herself to be in charge of the household and had sharp words to say to anyone who contradicted her or who ventured to interfere in her treatment plan.

Jenny was the first to have doubts about Evelyn, although she did not mention these for several weeks. She was at first suspicious that Evelyn would usurp her position as part time housekeeper and was relieved to find that Evelyn's role was intended to be completely separate from her own. But there were times when Jenny resented the older woman giving her orders about meals, mealtimes and the priority of various domestic tasks, and neither of the two women, whose paths inevitably crossed were prepared to give way, so raised voices could be heard frequently in the kitchen. But Neville and Nell were not there during the day to witness these disagreements and if Lois heard the altercations, she never commented on them.

One evening after the first week, Jenny voiced her concerns to her husband.

"I don't know, Phil. There's something about her I don't trust. It's not just that she tries to boss me around, you know me, I can stand up for myself when I have to. But she's sneaky. She pokes around a lot, and she's a nurse, she has no need to go into the attic rooms or into the spare bedrooms. She was definitely snooping this morning".

Phil knew his wife was perceptive and would not have mentioned anything without good cause. "If I were you, I'd just keep your eyes open for now. If you see anything more serious you will have to tell Neville".

Over time, Lois's health stabilised. As predicted, she had frequent periods of remission from the illness, and together with medication, Evelyn's attentive care and a sense that this was not a death sentence but a condition that with help she could come to terms with, her life was as comfortable as it could be. Evelyn encouraged her to take a little walk if the weather was fine and mild but did not press the point when she could see that Lois was already fatigued, and as it was early February the weather was still unreliable.

Evelyn was soon almost indispensable to Lois. Neville was hugely relieved that she was receiving excellent care from someone who had quickly become a trusted friend to his wife as well as a nurse. Although Nell still sometimes assisted her mother in the mornings, Lois gradually managed a little better without help but the relationship between mother and daughter had progressed, and Nell felt that she had crossed over to adulthood during that time.

One afternoon while Lois was resting, Jenny noticed from the kitchen that Evelyn had gone upstairs. Thinking that she had gone to wake Lois, Jenny thought no more of it for a few seconds, then heard footsteps continuing up to the top floor.

Feeling curious, Jenny followed silently and found Evelyn looking through drawers in Neville's observatory room.

"What do you think you're doing?"

Evelyn spun round in shock.

"I'm just tidying up. Poor man, he works such long hours, he doesn't have time to do it himself".

Jenny was furious. "You have no business in here. This room is private. I do the housework in this house, and I only clean in here when Neville asks me to. Now get out". Jenny spoke with authority and Evelyn had no choice but to obey. But she gave Jenny a vicious look as she left the room.

Jenny was in a quandary. She didn't know whether to report Evelyn's behaviour or not but knowing how much Neville had been through with his wife, she didn't want to add to his concerns and give him unnecessary worry. She decided to have another chat with Phil later.

Phil thought for a while, then advised caution. "Some people are just nosey" he said at last. "It's a bit weird and she was out of order being up there, but you warned her off in no uncertain terms so unless anything else happens, I should keep quiet for now".

She took her husband's advice and no more was said, but the uneasy feeling persisted, and Jenny felt even more convinced that Evelyn was up to no good.

Heat seemed to help Lois's condition; it meant that her joints were less painful which in turn improved her mobility. Evelyn suggested that Lois might benefit from a holiday in a warm climate. This was something that had never previously occurred to Neville, but he began to make plans for a trip to Spain, to the Mediterranean coast.

It was to be a turning point.

* * *

It took Patrick nearly two weeks to think of a pretext to speak to Nell, and then it was only to ask her if she knew that the normal route to the Arts building was out of bounds due to it being used by the builders to store a delivery of materials. Nell did already know this but seemed to be glad of the opportunity to stop and chat. During that brief two minutes he introduced himself and Nell did likewise. Nervously he asked her what subject she was studying, and although his knowledge of nineteenth century literature was scant to say the least, he would have willingly shown interest in advanced mathematics if it had meant he could talk to her for a few moments longer.

"You're punching above your weight there my friend".

Patrick's workmate had slipped out during a break for a quick cigarette and had watched the exchange with amusement.

"We'll see". Patrick grinned back at him.

He had met Joe Clancy on the ferry from Ireland, and finding each other in the same situation, searching for employment in England being their priority, they had sought construction work together. They had worked side by side on the college contract for several months and relaxed over many pints of beer on Friday evenings.

"All the same, don't expect too much", said Joe, grinding his cigarette butt into the ground and picking up his coffee mug. "These posh girls are all the same over here, they might have a banter with you in school time, but they'll never take you home to meet their Mam and Dad".

"She's not like that at all", said Patrick, hoping his excitement was not too obvious. "In fact, I'm seeing her again at the weekend ".

This was not strictly true; no date had been planned or even discussed. But Patrick held on to the hope that it might, just might be possible, if with luck on his side he managed to talk to her again before then.

In the end it was easy. On the Thursday of that week, he saw Nell making her way across the courtyard, leaving to catch her bus. When she saw him, she smiled and waved. Walking quickly to catch her up, he decided it was now or never and asked her if she would like to go for a cup of coffee with him after college the following day. Work on the site finished early on Fridays so they could walk into town together. He had originally thought of asking her for a drink at the Bridge Tavern which would be his normal Friday evening routine after work, but not knowing if she was legally old enough to drink alcohol and reluctant to put a foot wrong in case he blew his chances of future meetings, he opted for caution. Also, the thought of his workmates being present with their inevitable joking and comments after a few early pints was not the impression he wanted to give on a first date.

So at four thirty on that Friday afternoon Nell and Patrick walked through the town to Markham's coffee shop, and over a hot chocolate for Nell and a pot of tea for Patrick, their lives began to change forever.

They managed to find a corner table as far away as possible from the hiss and clatter of the espresso machine, but the coffee shop was noisy and crowded with late shoppers and it was difficult to talk. So as soon as they had finished their drinks, and seeing a queue for tables was forming, Patrick paid the bill, and they made their way outside. They threaded their way along the busy High Street and no passers-by gave a thought to the smart college girl in the company of a builder still in his working clothes.

Patrick was of average height, broad shouldered and muscular, his powerful build showing his physical strength. But most eye-catching was his hair, red and crinkly, worn fairly short, and a closely trimmed beard which was of a slightly deeper colour. He had a smattering of freckles across his nose. Nothing could have been of greater contrast to an onlooker than Nell's svelte, slim figure, glossy long dark hair and pale clear skin.

Crossing the bridge over the Haske at the far end of the street, Nell showed Patrick a short cut down some steep steps to the river. They sat on a bench and watched the swans glide by for a few moments. It was late February; the river was in full flood and the willows on the opposite bank were trailing their graceful branches in the fast-moving water – still bare but showing a faint hint of green.

Conversation flowed easily, with no awkwardness, no uncomfortable silences. Nell found herself telling Patrick about her life at home, her quiet and secluded upbringing, her parents' sadness, her mother's illness. She was not seeking sympathy or pity but understanding, feeling that she somehow had to explain why she was not like other girls of her age, and had not experienced much of life. She said little about the house where she lived – she felt that would have been insensitive. Patrick listened intently, holding on to every detail. It was exactly as he had said to Joe a few days before – Nell was special. He was gratified that there were no signs of snobbery or condescension about her, even though she was poles apart from him socially. He was spellbound, all the more so because she was happy to sit and talk to him as an equal.

After a while Nell turned to Patrick. "That's enough about me. Tell me about your home in Ireland and why you came to Sussex. You must find it so different here".

She listened, enthralled as Patrick told her of the farm near Ballymere where he had been brought up, the dairy herd that grazed outdoors on pasture most of the year, yielding the creamy milk that contributed to so much of Ireland's economy and their livelihood, yet only providing a modest living. He had six brothers and sisters, he was the third son; money was perpetually tight, and space and privacy were hard to come by. One of his younger sisters, Kathleen was recently married, as was his eldest brother Connor who helped their father run the farm and would eventually take over, but knowing that the farm would not support another family the second son Sean had emigrated to America the previous year to settle in Boston, and he himself had decided to try and make a living in England.

Patrick went on to tell her of the wild dramatic coast of West Cork where the huge breakers rolled in from the ocean, of people harvesting seaweed after stormy high tides, of horses ridden across the surf at sunset, the circles of standing stones guarding their ancient and mysterious secrets, and the beam of the Fastnet Lighthouse, perched on its precarious rock in the Atlantic, the 'Teardrop' which was the last glimpse of Ireland for the millions who had emigrated to America over the years.

When he described the little town ten miles from his farm, with its narrow streets, often hung with flags and bunting, brightly painted houses festooned with hanging baskets of flowers, its bustling Friday market, the sandy beach and the river that wound its way through the town, not much more than a stream at first then broadening as it flowed out into the wide sweep of the bay, she was entranced. As a student of English, fascinated by words and language, how could she not fall in love with names like Clonakilty and Inchydoney? If Patrick had told her that it was like Brigadoon and only appeared once every hundred years, she would have believed him.

Her eyes widened with horror and disbelief and a tear slipped down her cheek as Patrick went on to tell her of the Potato Famine, the Great Hunger that had so cruelly decimated the population of West Cork a hundred and thirty years previously and which only one of his great grandparents had survived. He was touched at her reaction, feeling that Nell understood on some deep level the things that were important to him about his heritage and the struggles of the country to which he was so devoted. He was careful not to refer to the tension between the Irish and the British that had grown up over centuries, mindful that her knowledge of politics and history might not be so great; instead, he attempted to lighten the mood by recounting how Ireland's fortunes had improved in recent years, although life in West Cork was slow to change.

Nell felt that in comparison the Sussex countryside in which she had been brought up, with its gentle sloping downs, shingle beaches and temperate climate was far less inspiring than the coastline Patrick had depicted. She told him that it was the only place in which she had ever lived. Her family circumstances were different too – as an only child of an only child on her mother's side and no relatives that she had ever met on her father's side, she felt very keenly the lack of siblings or cousins. She confided in him her ambitions of becoming a writer or a teacher like her father, and of her love of literature which since her teenage years had been her only means of escape and excitement.

If Patrick had no clue about the great writers such as Thomas Hardy and Jane Austen, he disguised it very well and vowed privately to learn more about the authors Nell had mentioned, just so that he could converse with her on a more equal footing.

"Would you like to meet up again?" Patrick asked her, pinning all his hopes on a second date. "We could see a film, or just go for a walk?"

"I'd love to". He noticed that Nell answered him with no hesitation, as if she was just waiting for him to ask. This was even better, he thought, she wanted to see him again. They arranged to meet the following Friday evening. His spirits soared as he made his way home; from then on he was smitten.

It was the first of many dates – kept secret at first by Nell. Patrick was her first boyfriend, and she had little experience of men except for her father and teachers. Contact with boys of her own age had been few and far between, and certainly there had been no one special to her until now. She had taken the decision a few months previously that she would concentrate on her studies until her 'A' levels – but then she had not been looking for anyone on the day she met Patrick, yet here he was, and she wondered where this might lead.

For Patrick, the fact that this warm-hearted, beautiful, cultured girl had agreed to come out with him at all was something unbelievable and at times he had to ask himself if it was really happening. The difference in their backgrounds troubled him a little if he allowed those thoughts to intrude on his happiness, but mostly he pushed them to the back of his mind, determined to do everything in his power to make Nell happy and to enjoy every moment of this new life that she had opened up for him.

They met often after that first occasion, sometimes just for a cup of coffee, to the cinema or for walks along the river or in the countryside. After a few weeks Nell told her mother that she had a boyfriend, feeling she needed to explain her more frequent absences. Lois was vaguely interested on days when she was coping better with her pain, and in some ways, she felt that Nell did ought to have more fun. It might have been a different story if Evelyn had not been there to give constant support and attention to Lois, and so no difficult or searching questions were asked as long as Nell was home by ten thirty in the evening, and Neville too thought that was quite late enough. He had asked about Patrick's occupation, and Nell told him that Patrick worked at the college. Feeling that this was not actually a lie, and that a little more planning was needed before she told her parents that Patrick was in fact a builder, she left it at that, and her parents enquired no further.

One evening Nell and Patrick went to a party given by one of his workmates; there was as expected a great deal of heavy drinking taking place, but his friends noticed that Patrick was far more restrained than usual since he had met Nell. They left early, both feeling perfectly content just to be alone with each other – Nell having grown up unused to crowds and noisy gatherings, and Patrick precisely because being used to a household of nine, it was a welcome relief to experience the calm and space of being listened to and not having to compete for attention – Nell gave that freely because she was so interested in everything about him. This he found incredible, that someone so different from every girl he had ever met could think of him that way. Nell in turn was touched by his devotion, his affectionate nature and his care of her, always mindful of her comfort and safety, never keeping her waiting or allowing her to travel home alone. On the occasions when he dropped her off in his van at Moongarth he did not make any comment about the fact that she lived in a big house although now and then this fact served to remind him that there remained a gulf between them.

Nell was impressed by Patrick's determination to better himself, both at work and intellectually. With this in mind, she cautiously suggested buying tickets for an open-air performance of 'A Midsummer Night's Dream' which was being staged by a local amateur theatre company in Lamberham Park.

Patrick was doubtful. "That kind of thing isn't for the likes of me", he said, not wanting to offend Nell but feeling a little out of his depth.

Nell chose her words carefully. "Shakespeare is for the likes of all of us, Patrick. He wrote for the masses; it was the main entertainment of his day. Just give it a try, we needn't stay if you don't like it". In the end he agreed to go, with Nell explaining in advance the theme of the play within a play, the various characters and that it was in a way a teenage love drama with fantasy and comedy thrown in.

Despite his reservations, Patrick followed the play without any trouble and found himself laughing at the plot, not even noticing that some of the actors were under-rehearsed and needed to be prompted several times.

After the play had finished, Patrick bought them each a glass of wine from the outdoor bar and they strolled along the pergola in the moonlight. A local string quartet was playing Mozart nearby. It was early May, clematis and honeysuckle were in bud and their tendrils climbed over the lattice work of the roof and cast gently moving shadows on the stone path. The atmosphere in the park was magical.

He felt that he had taken a huge leap forward in his life that evening. He, Patrick Walsh, bricklayer from Ireland with little formal education could go to see a Shakespeare play with this beautiful girl in these lovely surroundings and understand and enjoy it. Whilst not planning to tell his workmates about his evening's entertainment, the realisation gave him confidence that with Nell's encouragement he could achieve more if he put his mind to it, and he resolved to speak to his foreman about taking on more demanding work.

Chapter Seven

During this time, Neville had been giving serious thought to Evelyn's suggestion. The idea that a Mediterranean climate might improve Lois's condition or at least ease her symptoms was a compelling one, and it prompted him to make some enquiries in order to find the right accommodation. The problem for Neville was that his summer holiday from school – late July to early September – would be at the very hottest time of the year in Spain and undoubtedly too hot for Lois. June would be a more suitable month, pleasantly warm but not oppressive or exhausting. But he would be unable to take his holiday then.

The travel agent, a dark suited young woman in her mid-twenties with immaculate hair and makeup, wearing a badge which bore the legend "Laura – here to help you" had been obliging but at first could not find any accommodation that would be both acceptable for Lois's needs and available during June. Neville was ready to compromise on the location so long as it was accessible for Lois and within a short distance of the sea. There was silence for several long minutes as the agent studied various brochures and travel catalogues. Shaking her head, she selected a folder from the shelf behind her and leafed through it. Eventually she looked up.

"There is an apartment that may be suitable for your wife, I think, Mr Garth" she said at length. "It's only on our books because it was a holiday rental several years ago, but the owner has been trying to sell. I could contact him for you and see if he is willing to let it to you during June or July. I can't promise, of course, but we can ask. It may take me a while so why don't you pop out for a cup of coffee and come back in say, half an hour?"

Twenty-five minutes later, Neville returned, fortified with a double espresso in the expectation that he was still in for a long wait. But the agent looked up at him and smiled.

"Success, Mr Garth. The owner has agreed to let the property to you for the dates you want, but he wishes you to understand that it hasn't been let for over a year and so it will need a thorough clean and check over to make sure it is up to standard. He will arrange for this to be done".

"Thank you so much", said Neville, thinking that this sounded hopeful. "But please can you go through the details with me before I sign? I need this to be absolutely right for my wife". Neville went on to explain that it must be appropriate in every detail for a disabled person and her companion.

The spacious apartment in Solibrio, near Nerja on the Costa del Sol seemed to fit the bill. Laura confirmed that although the accommodation was on the ground floor, it enjoyed an elevated position, accessed by a sloping ramp and no steps, and therefore boasted a sea view as well as all the other features essential for a comfortable holiday home. She showed him a photograph of the apartment from a previous season's brochure. It did seem to be exactly what he was looking for, allowing for the fact that some travel agents, like estate agents might showcase the good points and often gloss over any drawbacks. Nevertheless, satisfied that he had found the best possible solution, Neville signed some forms, paid for three weeks holiday including flights and returned home to give Lois the good news.

Lois was excited – more animated than Neville had seen her for many months. She immediately thought about making arrangements for a passport, never having travelled abroad before. She then sat with Evelyn who compiled a list of travel necessities and holiday clothing. But her face fell when Neville explained that he would be unable to accompany her to Spain. This was a major blow for Lois and initially threatened to compromise the whole plan. Despite the distance that had developed between them over the years, Lois acknowledged that deep down, Neville was her security, her rock – they had never been separated overnight in all their years of marriage except for her time in hospital. The thought of spending three weeks apart from him was to her almost an impossibility.

However, when it was explained that Evelyn was to accompany Lois to Spain as nurse/companion, she became visibly relieved and accepted that a holiday with Evelyn, who was now a friend as well as a nurse might be a solution, even if second best and not her ideal plan. Arrangements were made and Lois began to look forward to the trip.

"I shall take the opportunity to put in some extra planning time for next year's curriculum" Neville told Nell when he outlined details of the holiday. "There are also a couple of astronomy lectures coming up at the Planetarium that I'd like to go to".

"It's a shame you can't go to Spain too. You work too hard Daddy". Nell was slightly taken aback by the sudden announcement of the holiday plans but hoped that her mother would feel some improvement with some warm sunshine and relaxation. "I'm sure Evelyn will take excellent care of Mummy, and I shall be fine here, we shall be like ships that pass in the night, won't we?". They both laughed.

* * *

The following week, Jenny heard Evelyn talking on the telephone in the hallway one morning. She couldn't hear exactly what was being said, but she seemed to be making an appointment. Despite knowing that it could have been a perfectly innocent conversation, nothing that Evelyn did was above suspicion to Jenny now.

At two-thirty Lois went upstairs for her rest and at three o'clock Jenny left the house and cycled down Hasker's Hill. An unknown car passed her on the opposite side and continued up the hill. She had only gone a few yards further when she remembered she had left her wristwatch on the draining board, so she turned back to Moongarth and as she approached the drive, she could see the same car parked on the gravel. Mystified, she tucked her bicycle into the hedge and walked quietly across the front lawn to the back door. Silently letting herself in, she listened from the kitchen and overheard voices, although only the odd word was distinguishable. Had Evelyn called a doctor to Lois? It was not Dr Ferris's car.

As she waited, hardly daring to breathe, the voices became louder, and footsteps could be heard moving along the hall and towards the drawing room. It was unmistakable. Evelyn was showing a man around the house and explaining in detail all the features of the accommodation. It sounded as though he was taking measurements as now and then dimensions were discussed.

Jenny didn't dare risk being discovered in case they came into the kitchen next, so she crept out of the back door into the garden and crouched down behind a tall shrub at the side of the house. She waited for about half an hour and was just beginning to feel stiff and cramped when the man came out of the front door and took his leave of Evelyn, thanking her and promising to send her figures by the end of the week. She waited until Evelyn had shut the front door and the man had driven off before she emerged cautiously from her hiding place.

Shaking, Jenny recovered her bicycle and started for home, overwhelmed with shock. There could be no doubt. Evelyn was pretending to be the owner of Moongarth and was having the house valued.

She thought about nothing else for the next two days and became more and more convinced that Evelyn was involved in something shady. Subconsciously she began to monitor Evelyn's every move. For a while, nothing seemed untoward. Preparations for the trip to Spain were in full swing and most of the time Evelyn was busy upstairs with Lois, doing her packing and ensuring she had enough medication for several weeks. So as was her usual routine, Jenny greeted the postman each morning and a few days before the holiday a large cream-coloured envelope arrived, addressed to Mrs L Garth.

Knowing that Lois rarely, if ever received personally addressed letters, Jenny made a momentous decision. She realised that she was risking her job and her reputation, but with a silent apology to everyone concerned if she were wrong, she slipped the envelope unopened into her handbag.

* * *

Early on the tenth of June, Lois and Evelyn departed for Spain. It was a tearful goodbye for Lois and for a while she clung to Neville, last-minute nerves and doubts crowding in.

"Darling you will have a wonderful time, and the change will do you so much good. Go and enjoy yourself, I will see you in three weeks' time complete with suntan and lots to tell me". Neville kissed her and handed their suitcases to the taxi driver.

"Please don't worry, she will be fine". Evelyn said reassuringly to Neville as she climbed into the taxi. Nell kissed her mother and waved her goodbye as the car disappeared down the hill. She felt a pang of envy, just for a moment. She could barely remember the week at the seaside she had spent with her mother when she was much younger, and there had been no family holidays since the death of baby Laurence.

She felt a little deflated as her father dropped her off at college, but her spirits soon rose at the thought of seeing Patrick later that day.

He met her after college, and they drove up onto the South Downs for a walk.

It was late afternoon but nearly midsummer and the sun was still high in the sky as they strolled hand in hand up the track to Low Barrow. The trees and bushes were in full leaf and the colours were a fresh vibrant green, the meadows a haze of buttercups and the hedges beside the lane were a riot of dog roses, pale pink with their petals wide open to the warmth. As they climbed further, they could hear a skylark high above, its melodious notes the only sound to break the silence.

After an hour or so following fairly level paths, they passed through a wooded vale where ancient yew trees offered some shade for a few welcome moments, then leaving the edge of the woodland behind they came to an open slope, steeper now, where they stopped to take in the view. They sat down amongst the dry grass, cropped short by sheep and rabbits, and Patrick produced a flask of tea and some bars of chocolate from his rucksack.

Low Barrow, in defiance of its name was the highest point for miles around. They had not quite made it to the top but from where they were sitting, they could see the yew forest they had just passed, the valley with small villages clustered together and the town of Kirchington, its church spire rising up from amongst the rooftops. Beyond that was the coastal plain and further still the azure and silver glint of the English Channel.

"It's beautiful here" said Patrick, scanning the panorama and screwing up his eyes against the glare. "I didn't realise Sussex was like this. I've only seen busy towns and the odd quaint village"

"It's so much more than that. But it's all I really know" said Nell, sipping her tea. For the first time she realised how much she loved the area in which she had been brought up, just as Patrick felt fiercely proud of his own country. But she was aware that having travelled so little, she had nothing to compare it with.

They sat there together for a further hour, relishing the warmth, the peace and the beauty of their surroundings. At times there was no need for either of them to say anything, the silences communicating more than words could have done.

"I'm going to be made up to foreman". Patrick suddenly sat up and put an arm round Nell's shoulders, thinking this was a good moment to tell her his good news. "John Preston is leaving; he's moving out of the area. So, I asked the boss, like you said, and he's given the thumbs up. I start next week".

"That's wonderful Patrick" Nell was delighted. "I knew you could do it". He had told Nell on several occasions that

71

he wanted to better himself; she had encouraged him to try for promotion as she called it, and her faith in him had given him confidence he needed. "I would never have done it without you behind me", he added, stroking her hair. "And I can stay on the college contract until the work's finished".

"Isn't it a coincidence that you are in the building trade, Patrick. Especially as you are trained as a bricklayer. My great grandfather Geoffrey founded a brick-making company here in Lamberham back in the nineteenth century. The Garth Brick and Clay company it was called. It's long gone now, but many houses you see in Lamberham and around here were built with Garth bricks".

Patrick was immediately interested. "I had no idea", he said, thinking he would look at the local Victorian brickwork with fresh interest now that he felt a kind of link with its history. "See, I'm learning new things about you and your family all the time".

"It was Geoffrey who bought Moongarth, the house where I live" added Nell. "It was called The Gables then, and it's been in my family ever since. It was Dad who changed the name". She went on to explain. "I want to learn more about your family too, and West Cork. I should love to visit Ireland, I want to see everything you have told me about", she said contentedly, lying back and watching tiny wisps of cloud barely moving across the sky, which was now becoming deeper indigo on the horizon as almost imperceptibly the light began to fade. Bees were still droning in a patch of tiny orchids and purple vetch.

"Just don't be thinking that it's all Top of the Morning and Leprechauns" Patrick said seriously. "That was for Hollywood and maybe the tourists fifty years ago. Life in West Cork is hard, very hard, especially in winter". He had a way of repeating important words, which Nell found endearing. "You have to be tough to live out there. There's nothing to do, it rains a lot, the weather comes in full force from the Atlantic. And it's dark, so dark, there are no streetlights where we are. The skies are like black velvet".

"Like Guinness?" Nell said mischievously.

He laughed. "Maybe. But it means you can really see the stars, so clearly, not like here with all the light pollution, but out there they are so clear, so bright...when it's not raining of course". He laughed again.

Nell thought how much her father would love to study the stars in those dark Cork skies and resolved to tell him about it when the time was right.

"Not everyone who moves to Ireland stays there, people find it too difficult. It's hard to explain. It may be the weather, or because it's hard to make a living or it could just be that it takes a long time to be really accepted. Yet the Irish are the most welcoming and hospitable people you could wish for. There are those who want to settle there and can't, and many who were born there who leave. People have always emigrated from Ireland, mainly to search for a better life in America. Some may have found it; I don't know about the others". Patrick's voice tailed off as he thought about his brother Sean who had left for Boston a year ago and whose letters home said little, maybe hiding disappointment.

Nell said nothing. She suddenly remembered being taught about the 'huddled masses' – the inscription on the Statue of Liberty in New York Harbour. Patrick's words made the picture come alive for her more than any history lesson.

They walked slowly back along the track at dusk. The heat of the day had diminished, and the first stars were beginning to appear in a clear sky. A pair of tawny owls hooted to each other from a distant copse of trees. The air was still, the atmosphere timeless. Patrick pulled Nell to him and kissed her, not roughly but leaving her in no doubt of his longing. She kissed him back, realising somehow that she had fallen headlong for this shy, modest, loving man who worshipped her and made her feel so special. She knew, as much as any inexperienced seventeen-year-old girl could know that she was in love, and that despite all the sadness of her childhood, no one could be happier than she was at that moment.

Chapter Eight

The house was even quieter than usual without Lois and Evelyn, and with Neville busy elsewhere during the evenings. He had agreed with Nell that Jenny should have some time off too, so she would work just one day a week instead of four during the remainder of June.

On the day that Jenny was working, she stayed later than usual so that she could speak to Nell when she returned from college.

"Nell I'm sorry to bother you with this but I do need to talk to you about Evelyn".

"It's ok Jenny. Go on, what did you want to tell me?"

Jenny took a deep breath. "It's like this. She may be a qualified nurse, but Evelyn isn't all she seems, in fact I think she's up to mischief. Well mischief might be putting it mildly, I believe she is doing something illegal or at least attempting to".

Nell was horrified as Jenny went on to describe the events of the previous week when she had witnessed a man being shown around Moongarth while Lois was asleep.

"She waited for me to leave at three, but she didn't realise I came back for something I forgot. I hid in the kitchen and then behind a bush near the front lawn. I heard him say that he would send her some figures, then he left".

Despite still feeling certain that Evelyn's behaviour was highly suspect, Jenny could not bring herself to confess to intercepting the letter that had arrived soon after that visit.

"What could that possibly be about?" Nell was equally mystified. "I suppose she might have invited someone over to discuss her own personal business, but then why would she show them round our home? And you think they were taking measurements? It doesn't make any sense".

"I thought so too. I couldn't get it out of my mind, I've been so worried. But just this morning I put two and two together". Jenny went on to tell her about the time she had caught Evelyn rifling through Neville's desk. "Now I think about it, I reckon she was looking for something that day. The deeds to this house. That man was an estate agent".

Nell was lost in thought for an hour after Jenny left. Could she possibly be right, was Evelyn impersonating her mother and having Moongarth valued? It seemed so preposterous that she could scarcely believe it to be true. Anyway, surely there were safeguards to stop anything fraudulent taking place? Nell knew so little about matters of this kind that she felt completely overwhelmed.

Well Evelyn is in Spain now, nothing can happen for a while, she thought. She was reluctant to tell her father of Jenny's suspicions; well in fact they were more than suspicions. He had been so relieved to employ Evelyn, having found someone reliable to take care of her mother, and whom Lois had immediately warmed to and seemed to trust. She didn't want to worry him unnecessarily.

After mulling these thoughts over in her mind, she decided to wait a few days and then tell her father as soon as there was an opportunity. He would know what to do, he might even think of an explanation.

* * *

Over the next few days Nell took advantage of some quiet time at home when she was not at college to revise for her mock 'A' levels which were fast approaching. She had still not mentioned the conversation with Jenny to her father; Patrick and her exams were uppermost in her mind at that time. Studying was usually more of a pleasure than a chore for her, especially English Literature; she had her father's diligence and ability to be single-minded and to concentrate on the job in hand. This time however she found her attention wandering, always to Patrick, thinking about their next meeting or their last one. Sometimes her mind pictured his home and family in West Cork, determined that she would go there one day and see for herself.

That thought led her on to thinking about bringing Patrick to meet her parents. She knew it could not be avoided for ever and she was relieved that they had not mentioned the subject so far. But it would be difficult. Her father was not a snob; he valued honesty, hard work and ambition above everything, and Patrick certainly had those qualities in abundance. His recent promotion to foreman would go in his favour. Neville would no doubt give Patrick credit for trying to better himself, but he would have concerns.

Her mother would not be so easy to impress. Unwittingly, Lois had inherited a small degree of class superiority from her mother. This was rarely evident because circumstances seldom arose in her day-to-day life which would cause her to question anyone's status or social standing. Their circle of friends was small and tightly knit, and Lois never strayed beyond those boundaries. Meeting Patrick would undoubtedly bring any prejudices to the surface.

But I have three weeks to think about this and prepare, she thought. She was not sure whom she needed to prepare more, Patrick or her parents. In the end she decided, with wisdom beyond her years, that Patrick should just be himself, which was after all was the reason she had fallen in love with him. Her parents' reaction would be whatever it would be; she doubted that they would stop her seeing him. And once the initial meeting was over, things would surely settle down. With that reasoning, she banished all thoughts of it and resolutely turned back to Jude the Obscure.

Purely by chance, Lois and Evelyn, sunbathing on the terrace in Solibrio were having a discussion on the same topic.

Lois had been delighted with the accommodation. The travel agent and owner had been true to their word; it was comfortable and convenient in all aspects with large rooms, tasteful décor and furnishings, and thankfully full air conditioning which even in June was essential during the heat of midday. The apartment was stylish, with beautifully patterned floor tiles throughout, occasional furniture carved from dark wood, and sumptuous sofas with soft cushions. There were bright woven rugs on the oak floor and some elaborate hanging tapestries on the internal walls. Evelyn had remarked on the modern contemporary kitchen, and the bathroom had a low-level shower, ideal for Lois to manage independently. The double patio doors led out onto a stone terrace with Jacaranda trees still sporting some of their purple spring blossoms, and date palms lining the edge of the road like sentinels. From the shady dining area, the curve of the bay could be seen with its strip of almost white sand, pine trees clinging to the rocky golden cliffs beyond, and further still the deep opaque blue of the Mediterranean. It was breathtaking.

Evelyn cooked simple light meals each evening. Lois had a small appetite, and Evelyn was a believer in quality rather than quantity, so this suited them both. Only once had they eaten out in a restaurant and although the tourist season was not yet at its height, Lois still shunned crowds and busy places so after that they were content to dine back at the apartment with an omelette and salad and some delicious fruit Evelyn had bought from the local market. This had not been planned as a sight-seeing holiday, but on the second afternoon they caught the bus into Nerja for Lois to visit an open-air art exhibition. Decades before, she would have enjoyed this and would have wished to spend time gazing at each canvas and maybe talking to the artists who were always willing to discuss their paintings in the hope of a sale, but the trip was abandoned after half an hour; Lois became ill at ease and anxious to return to the apartment.

On the third day of the holiday, they were lazing on sun loungers on the terrace, which was secluded but within view of the sea. It was not yet midday but already the temperature was climbing. Evelyn, ever mindful of Lois's health had suggested they retire to the cool dark salon, but in fact Lois was coping with the heat better than expected, feeling inclined to stay outside or even go for a short stroll during the hottest part of the day, which Evelyn advised against. The warmth helped her muscles, Lois insisted, like having a constant heat lamp on her body, loosening the stiff joints and giving her a feeling of well-being. She wished she could bottle the sensation to take home and bring out during the cold winter days.

As their friendship grew, the ladies exchanged confidences. Evelyn had been widowed five years previously, and with her only son now living in New Zealand, she told Lois how nursing had become therapeutic to her and had helped her through the early months of bereavement.

They had been dozing in the sun for nearly an hour when Evelyn broke the silence.

"Have you met Nell's young man?" she ventured, more in the way of making conversation than out of curiosity.

"He's not really her young man", replied Lois, reaching for her glass of iced water. "I don't think there's anything serious there. I doubt that we shall ever meet him".

This denial piqued Evelyn's interest. "She sees a great deal of him, you know, several times a week at least. And it's been that way for quite a few months now". Evelyn was persistent. "Why not ask Nell to invite him home one evening after the holiday?"

Lois had come to trust Evelyn's opinion on most things, and did not regard this as interference, but with a sudden shock she realised that Evelyn noticed far more about Nell than she did herself, in fact she was keen to know a great deal about most things, and the thought was slightly uncomfortable. In a way she thought Evelyn might be right, that she should meet Nell's friend Patrick soon, and that as her mother she should take more interest in her daughter's life. It was easy to think that way here, she reflected, detached from reality, feeling warm, relaxed and free of pain. Easy to think about matters other than herself when she was experiencing the blessed relief of remission which had thankfully coincided with this holiday.

"I'll talk to Neville when we get home and see what he thinks" she said at last, putting on her sunglasses against the glare. "Perhaps you're right, Evelyn, maybe we should meet him".

The subject was closed at that point, and the ladies went on to discuss the evening's menu and plans for a short walk along the beach when the temperature was cooler.

After a further week, the holiday was already achieving its aims, Lois visibly benefitting from the sea air and the restful comfort of her surroundings. She looked better than she had done for over a year, with a pale golden tan and a glow that was less to do with the weather, more due to the absence of pain and total relaxation as she allowed herself to unwind from the mental strain of her illness. It was as though her body was responding by being capable of feeling normal again at times, despite her condition being life-long and incurable. But she was aware that this was a fortunate period of remission; the thought of the inevitable return to chronic fatigue and suffering was pushed to the back of her mind.

* * *

A few days after Jenny had told her of Evelyn's visitor, Nell asked her father if she could talk to him for a little while about something serious. At first, she was going to suggest she brought Patrick home to meet them as soon as her mother returned from Spain but decided that the matter of Evelyn was more urgent.

Nervously she related her conversation with Jenny.

He listened carefully and looked puzzled. When she explained Jenny's theory that Evelyn had been looking for house deeds, he laughed.

"Well, I certainly don't keep my house deeds lying around loose in a drawer for one thing" he said. "They are lodged with the bank and kept in their vaults. No one can get at them without my say-so. If that's what she was looking for then she will have been disappointed. The most she will find in my desk are a few old exam papers, some star charts and a paper I had started to write on the use of astronomy in the modern world. I don't think we need worry too much. She may be a nosey parker but that's not a crime. I will ask her who her visitor was though, that does seem strange. It can't have been an estate agent, that's just too nonsensical".

Neville was delighted with the improvement in Lois's health on her return, and felt vindicated that the trip to Spain, which after all was something of an experiment, had been a success. He thanked Evelyn for taking such good care of his wife and for overseeing such a change in her. As Lois went to rest after the journey, his mind subconsciously returned to the words of the travel agent; the owner wished to sell the apartment. Should he put in an offer? This could be a solution – it would enable regular trips to a familiar place where Lois felt at home and secure, and which had already brought about a transformation in such a short time. Neville tucked the thought away to be returned to later. Perhaps he would discuss the idea with Nell. He was realistic enough to know that Lois's present improvement would be short-lived; there would be some difficult days ahead and she could experience a relapse into troubling symptoms at any time.

* * *

Months previously, Patrick's friend Joe had warned him against becoming too attached to Nell. The differences in their situation were just too great for anything to come of it, he said. But contrary to his predictions, two weeks after Lois's return from Spain, Neville suggested that Nell should invite Patrick in to meet them on the next occasion when he called for her. This came as a surprise to Nell who had been trying to work out in her mind how to broach the subject and more importantly how to manage her parents' reaction to meeting someone who would likely differ so much from their expectations.

A date was arranged on an evening when Patrick and Nell had planned to go out together afterwards. As Patrick followed Nell through the tiled hallway into the breakfast room where

Neville and Lois were watching TV, he was momentarily overwhelmed by the scale and grandeur of Nell's beautiful home, the size and number of rooms, and remembered how he and his six brothers and sisters had squeezed into two bedrooms back on the farm in Ireland. Once again, he was aware of the huge gulf between his life and Nell's and wondered how he could ever really become part of her world.

If Neville and Lois were surprised that their daughter had brought an Irish bricklayer home to meet them, they were too polite to show it. Neville shook Patrick's hand and asked about his work, knowing a little about the Council contract Patrick was working on. Lois enquired about his family in Ireland and listened as he told her about his parents' farm and his brothers and sisters. It was a stilted, constrained conversation at times, but Patrick behaved impeccably, standing to open the door when Nell appeared with a tray of tea and taking it from her. Somehow, they found things to talk about for a further thirty minutes; Patrick went on to tell Neville of his plans to have his own business eventually, and Nell felt that if nothing else, they had been able to break the ice. When he and Nell left for the cinema, Patrick breathed a sigh of relief and felt that he had conducted himself well; Nell agreed that the meeting had been successful.

"It was your Irish charm" she said happily, sliding into the passenger seat beside him and squeezing his arm.

But when she was next alone with her mother, the inevitable questions came.

"Nell, I know you say you like Patrick and he's a nice enough lad, but you have nothing in common with this young man, nothing at all. He is Irish so I suppose he is a Catholic?". (This was a rhetorical question; religion had never been an issue for Lois and Neville, so Nell was surprised that her mother raised it now). "What can you possibly see in him? There is no future in this darling so don't get hurt. He will probably disappear back to Ireland all of a sudden and leave you wondering whatever happened. Try and find a nice local boy, why don't you?".

This was the first time Lois had paid any serious attention to her daughter's life outside of the home, and Nell was torn between welcoming her mother's interest in her and feeling fiercely protective of her relationship with Patrick.

Neville, discussing the situation with Lois later, was more conciliatory. "Lois let's leave them be for now. She's a sensible girl, it will probably fizzle out, but in the meantime let's not interfere. He seems a decent enough chap; he is Nell's first boyfriend, and she will no doubt have many more before I walk her up the aisle".

Neville was to be proved wrong. The friendship between Nell and Patrick blossomed and became more intense. They couldn't bear to be apart, and each counted the hours until they were together again. Sometimes they just sat in his tiny bedsit and chatted, Patrick always mindful of the time so as not to keep Nell out too late; he was terrified of upsetting her parents in case they forbad her to see him.

Nell often referred to her lonely childhood and difficult relationship with her mother; she felt she had missed out by not having a brother or a sister. She said that in the future she would like a big family.

Patrick found this encouraging; he hoped that by this statement Nell was saying that someday she would like children with him.

One rainy Sunday afternoon, when the weather was too wet to go for a walk, they sat in his bedsit and relaxed in the warmth of each other's arms. Patrick had lit some candles, and their soft light seemed to transform the shabby room. The radio was playing quietly in the background; the atmosphere between them was tranquil and comfortable yet somehow heightened with expectation.

Patrick's lovemaking was tender, slow and gentle, realising Nell's nervousness and conscious of his own lack of experience. Afterwards, as they lay there together, both feeling that they had taken a step from which there was no way back, Patrick tentatively asked Nell if she had any regrets.

"Of course not" she said contentedly, cuddling up to him. "How could I regret it? You make me so happy".

"I love you so much" he said simply and meant it. Never before had he been so certain about anything. When Nell told him that she felt the same he was overjoyed, and both felt that life could not get any better.

"What is Irish for 'good night'" Nell asked. They had lain there together for hours, as the room darkened, and the streetlights came on outside.

"Oiche mhaith is goodnight" Patrick said, explaining the pronunciation. "And Acushla means 'darling'. But no one really says Acushla now, not where I live anyway. I think I only remember my granda saying it".

"I must get you home" he said, suddenly realising the time. Both felt that they didn't want to be parted from each other after what had taken place between them that afternoon, but it wouldn't do to make Nell's parents anxious.

They said little on the way home, but the silence was full of unspoken words, with the feeling that their love was stronger than ever and that they were now committed to each other with a bond that no one could break.

"Oiche mhaith, Acushla" said Patrick, as he kissed her goodbye.

Of course, after that day there was no going back to how things had been before. Two months later, Nell realised that she was pregnant.

Chapter Nine

October 1979

Patrick had insisted on being with Nell when she told her parents. "I'm responsible for this situation, and I'm responsible for you now" he said, holding her close as they made plans about how to break the news. "You're not facing this on your own, you will never face anything on your own again. I love you. And you will never be lonely again, I promise".

Despite her trepidation at the thought of her parents' reaction, Nell felt a surge of happiness that whatever happened, Patrick loved her and would never let her down.

A few days previously, he had proposed to Nell, and with delight and no sign of hesitation she had accepted.

Lois's reaction to the news was a little puzzling. She said little, and was visibly shocked, as expected – perhaps her shock was due to the fact that Patrick was responsible for Nell's pregnancy rather than the pregnancy itself. There was no hint of excitement at the thought of a grandchild, which might have gone some way to alleviating any concern she felt. But Nell detected some other unspoken emotions in her mother's face; was it envy, worry.... or even fear? Privately, Nell put aside those questions to think about at another time. Evelyn, who was invariably present when family matters were discussed, was tight-lipped and disapproving, as though Nell's announcement was a personal insult sent to annoy her. Clearly, she did not want anything to disrupt her hold on the routine of the household.

Neville was more pragmatic. "Motherhood at such a young age was not what I had hoped for, for my daughter" he said to Patrick sternly. "Nell had so much ahead of her, her studies, her career, her chances. I hope you realise the consequences of your actions". He paused, waiting for

Patrick to speak, but almost imperceptibly his mind took him back to the time when his own carelessness had resulted in a disastrous outcome for Lois, also for them as a family, and his view of Patrick softened slightly.

"I am sorry if you think I have deprived Nell of those things, sir" Patrick said desperately, floundering for words. "All I can say is that I love your daughter, I will look after her and I will always do the right thing by her" and summoning up courage "I would like your permission to marry her".

"Hmmm". Neville stepped away, silent for a moment and looked out of the drawing room window at the thick carpet of leaves on the lawn. Those would need sweeping up later, he thought.

In a way he blamed himself. He had done everything he thought was right as a father; Nell had wanted for nothing, but somehow, he had failed her. The realisation hit him. He had allowed Nell to become too isolated, too solitary, he had not done anything about her loneliness. If he was honest, he been too distracted by Lois's problems and later her illness and had immersed himself in his work or had shut himself away with his books and telescope when he should have been spending precious time with his daughter, encouraging friendships, sports, hobbies, anything except sitting in her room reading endlessly, keeping out of her mother's way. Small wonder that she had needed a soulmate and had found that in Patrick.

"I am not going to give you an answer to that right now", he said at length. "I shall discuss this with your mother, Nell and we will all talk again in a few days' time. In the meantime," this to Patrick, "I suggest you give some thought as to how you propose to support Nell, where you will live and what your immediate plans will be, supposing I agree to this marriage".

"He can't stop us marrying. I'm eighteen" said Nell as they drove away later.

* * *

85

It had taken Neville quite some time to process Nell's momentous news, and it wasn't until a few days later that he remembered the strange conversation about Evelyn. He asked to see her the following afternoon while Lois was having a nap.

"Evelyn, I'd like to ask you about your visitor, the man who came here before the holiday".

She was visibly shocked, and Neville could see the disbelief on her face while she racked her brains for a reply. She stalled.

"Visitor?"

"I think you know who I mean".

"Oh, that visitor. Mr ...I can't remember his name"

"I hear he was taking measurements in the drawing room".

Evelyn looked more discomfited.

"Well..." she hesitated again. "I...I asked him round to see if he could fit an orthopaedic bed in there. Your wife may need to live downstairs in time.... I was just looking into the possibilities".

"Hmm. Well in future please refer to me before making enquiries of that kind. I will make any decisions of that nature, thank you".

She left the room, looking angry but at the same time puzzled.

Neville was not convinced by her explanation but did not know what to believe. He was a fair man. Without firm evidence of anything untoward he did not feel it was right to accuse Evelyn of anything. For now, she must have the benefit of the doubt.

For several weeks Evelyn was mystified. She had taken great pains to ensure the utmost discretion over the matter of her gentleman caller and had been equally certain that no one had witnessed it. What was more perplexing was that the expected letter, detailing the estimated value of Moongarth and the agent's willingness to accept instruction, had not arrived. Before the holiday she had checked daily through the bundle of letters left on the desk in the hall, and on a couple of occasions after their return she had ventured to ask Jenny if any post had arrived for Mrs Garth during their absence; this was met with an emphatic denial. But Evelyn had to be careful; too many enquiries would arouse suspicion. A surreptitious phone call made to the agent's office confirmed that the valuation had been sent out. Unsure of what had happened to the original letter she dared not ask for a duplicate. Instead, she would take time to decide her next step.

* * *

Patrick felt that he had got off lightly; he had expected far worse from Nell's father. Back in Ballymere such news would have sometimes resulted in fisticuffs between families, even if later the wedding plans were settled over a few pints of Guinness and a glass or two of Irish.

In the end Neville and Lois reluctantly gave their blessing; reluctantly because they had both, for different reasons wished for a better future for their daughter. But the prospect of Nell bringing up a child as a single mother was not to be contemplated and Neville consoled himself that Patrick was an honest man, a hard worker and that he really did seem to love Nell very much. The wedding was arranged for the following month.

Patrick telephoned his mother Bridget the next day.

"I can't believe you have got yourself into this mess Patrick". Bridget was appalled at his news. "How do you think this is ever going to work?". He had previously told his mother about Nell, this lovely, beautiful, clever girl he had met, how she was an only child, her father had an important job, she lived in a big house and her parents had welcomed him into their home. But none of this cut any ice with Bridget. "She's a Protestant no doubt, that will not go down well with Father Donovan. What were you thinking of?"

"Mam, I love her, it's as simple as that, and we are going to be married. We both believe in the same God, if it's anyone's business. And it's got nothing to do with Father Donovan".

"Don't blaspheme, Patrick. I don't like this at all, and your father will be furious".

"Will you come to the wedding, Mam?"

"I will not. And I hope you're not thinking of bringing her here". With that she ended the call.

Patrick made light of this conversation to Nell later, telling her that his parents could not leave the farm at such short notice, even for their wedding. He knew that his father would not be furious, and his mother's opposition would be short lived; no one could help but love Nell.

It was a discreet, quiet wedding in Kirchington Registry Office four weeks later, followed by a formal dinner at the Golden Lion Hotel. There were very few guests; Neville and Lois, Evelyn, and Jenny and her husband Phil. Caroline Brooke was Nell's maid of honour and Joe Clancy was best man. Patrick's brother Connor and his wife Gráinne had travelled over from Ireland, his mother still adamant that she and her husband Dermot would not attend, yet part of her wanted Patrick's family to be represented (and to report back to her, Patrick thought). He knew his mother so well.

Nell wore a cream knee length lace dress with a wide-brimmed hat in a matching colour and carried a bouquet of ivory roses and orchids. Under normal circumstances it would have been customary for Lois, as the mother of the bride to take a major part in helping choose a bridal gown and trousseau, but with this being a hastily arranged marriage, Nell had made her own decisions; Lois had not wished to be involved, and Evelyn had advised against any excitement. The pregnancy showed only slightly, and Nell's lustrous dark hair hung loose over her shoulders. She looks like an angel, Patrick thought, his heart missing a beat as Nell walked towards him on her father's arm, smiling. He felt he was the luckiest of men, and that with Nell by his side he could conquer the world.

As he made his marriage vows to Nell, he added a silent promise to make her the happiest woman. He was also determined to prove himself to her father and somehow to win over her mother. The latter would not be easy, he realised. He did not really understand Lois and she did not encourage conversation or familiarity.

So it was a small party that sat down to dine, Lois as always uncomfortable in company. Patrick and Joe would have liked to join Connor at the bar first, Dutch courage being in short supply, but they were aware of the need to be on their best behaviour. Nell tried to make conversation with Gráinne, who seemed warm and approachable; there was a hope of a future friendship there, Nell thought, acknowledging that it was Gráinne's first visit to England and she was bound to be shy in a room full of strangers. Patrick noticed the exchange and was grateful that Nell was making an effort with his family, it's not easy for anyone here, he thought, no one can relax. He would be glad when he and Nell could leave the gathering and go up to their room; they had booked to stay overnight in the hotel.

There was no wedding cake, but Connor took a great many photographs, and later Neville ordered some bottles of champagne for a toast. Neville, Patrick and lastly Joe made short speeches but as only Neville was used to speaking in public, the latter two consisted mainly of thanking everyone, with Patrick in particular thanking Neville and Lois for the gift of their daughter, which everyone including Lois agreed was as simple and sincere an expression as anyone could wish for. After a respectable interval, Patrick and Nell thanked everyone again and took their leave.

It was with relief that they closed the hotel bedroom door behind them – it was an ordinary double room; Patrick could not afford the honeymoon suite – but they didn't care, just to be alone together was all they wanted. They collapsed exhausted onto the bed and Patrick took Nell in his arms. "How does it feel to be Mrs Walsh?" he murmured lovingly.

"It's the best feeling in the world" she replied and meant it.

Chapter Ten

Not forgetting his promise to his father-in-law to support Nell and provide a decent home for her, and for the baby they were expecting, one of the first things Patrick did after the wedding was to raid his modest savings for a deposit and apply for a mortgage in order to purchase a small flat in Kirchington. To Nell's delight, he was successful and as the previous owner was anxious for a quick sale, the process was completed swiftly, and they were able to move into the flat within six weeks. It was a major step up from the rented bedsit, and the fact that this was their own home and achieved without any help from Neville gave Patrick a sense of pride. In a few short months he had been made foreman at Keane Construction, had married a wonderful girl and he now owned property; he would soon become a father as well. Meeting Nell had transformed his life, he thought; he could hold his head up with her parents and show them that the assurances he had made to look after their daughter had not been empty words. His own parents would be impressed too; for a while it would be a grudging acknowledgement from his mother, he realised, but he knew that in time she would accept Nell as a daughter-in-law and would welcome her first grandchild.

And so began their married life; a huge step up for Patrick financially, socially and professionally. The prospects were different for Nell; she knew that by abandoning her studies she would give up her dreams of university, teaching or becoming a writer at least for a time, but the excitement of her new life with Patrick, a little home of their own and a baby on the way dispelled any doubts that she had.

There was no honeymoon; they were being cautious with money despite Patrick's promotion and although Neville had bestowed a significant lump sum to Nell on her marriage, she and Patrick felt it wisest to keep a rainy-day fund as his was the only income. Patrick insisted that Nell returned to college in a few months' time to take her 'A' levels – he did not want her parents to blame him for any further sacrifices Nell would make.

"I will take you on a wonderful holiday soon after the baby's born", Patrick promised her.

"I would just like to go to Ireland" Nell replied simply. "To meet your family, see your farm, live life in West Cork, even if just for a week or two. Your parents would surely like to meet their new grandchild?"

Patrick remained silent, conscious of the fact that introducing Nell to his mother would be equally as difficult as his first meeting with her own parents. His father's welcome would be more cordial. But he agreed in principle and was moved by her desire to know more about his homeland and to be part of his family, just as he had by some unbelievable chance of fate moved into her sphere. His mother would come round.

Although the flat was a considerable improvement on the bedsit it was still tiny in comparison to the spacious home Nell was used to, but she made the best of it. She found that studying for two 'A' levels was all she could manage, and she made the decision to drop French, hoping there would be an opportunity to take it sometime in the future. Her time was divided between revising, preparing for the birth of her baby and making the flat as comfortable as possible. Some unwanted furniture was brought from Moongarth and some brightly coloured cushions and favourite paintings and posters had been recovered from her old bedroom. Lois and Neville had given them a new washing machine and cooker; Patrick brought very little from his furnished bedsit, so the rest of their essentials were second hand or bought cheaply in the market in Kirchington. But they managed well; Patrick was careful with money and rarely went to the Bridge Tavern on Friday nights except at Nell's insistence – she did not want him to give up all his enjoyment for her. She in turn was determined not to ask her parents for help; she had made her choices and wanted to prove that despite being not much more than a schoolgirl she could make a success of her new life with Patrick and be a good wife and mother. So far it had been an easy pregnancy, all of her checkups had been what the midwife called 'textbook' and she was young and healthy. There was no reason to suspect a repetition of her mother's experiences.

The flat was in a good state of repair and in a pleasant area of Kirchington, close to shops, the river and a park. There was one large bedroom, a living room, kitchen and bathroom and a narrow hallway. Being situated on the first floor with no lift it was manageable for the two of them, but Patrick could foresee the difficulties for Nell hauling a pram up the stairs when he was at work. "Maybe this wasn't such a good idea" he said to Nell one morning, shaking his head as they discussed the practicalities. "I think we should look for somewhere more suitable as soon as we can. We have our foot on the property ladder now" he added proudly.

Nell, who had never even considered the matter of the stairs began to realise how much she had taken for granted in her life previously; the space and comfort of Moongarth and how privileged an upbringing she had had, despite the lack of emotional ties with her mother. Patrick by contrast was ever practical, thinking not only of the safety of Nell and the coming baby but of the limitations of their new home and how he might overcome them.

"The pram will have to stay in the hallway", he said at last. "That's ok, there's enough room there, it won't get damp". Once again Nell thought of all the empty space at Moongarth, the barely used storerooms, attics and outbuildings. She could not imagine how Patrick's large family had squeezed into a small farmhouse with few amenities and constant noise, queuing for the one bathroom and nowhere private to entertain or have friends round. No wonder he wanted to escape to England, she thought. Yet somehow the thought of that way of life appealed to her. She longed to see for herself the rugged coastline of West Cork, the wild scenery and the perpetual greenness of the fields and pastureland, but most of all she wanted to meet his family, and experience for a while how it would be to live amongst lots of siblings in a busy and noisy household, things she had missed growing up in the quiet seclusion of Moongarth. Father has a sister somewhere in Canada whom he has never met, she recalled suddenly. How sad that must be, to grow up without ever knowing your sibling, perhaps worse that having no siblings at all. How complicated family life can be. Nell was lost in thought for a moment.

She had liked Gráinne despite only having had a brief chance to chat to her at the wedding, and Patrick was obviously close to his brother Connor. Surely Patrick's mother would welcome her. Nell had deliberated over this many times; Patrick had voiced his reservations.

"You need to understand Ireland a little before you go there", he said at last, "and when you understand the country you will begin to understand the people too. It may be only seventy miles across the sea but it's not like going into just another county of England. It's different, so different in its ways from your life here".

He went on to explain, trying to put it in a way that Nell would make sense of, without alarming or worrying her.

"To begin with, it's not so modern as England. Dublin maybe. The fact is some parts are decades behind England. Change comes very slowly. Ireland has been oppressed for centuries" (he decided against adding 'by the British' because he thought that might be too hard for her to grasp). "Land, and owning land is everything to the Irish. They have long memories" he continued. "There aren't any Irish alive now who remember the Great Hunger, but stories have been passed down through the generations. The Irish are great storytellers, some are made up, of course" he added with a wink. "But the stories about the bad times are never forgotten. The Seanchai, they're like historians, they will sit in a bar and tell anyone who'll listen, and you can learn a lot from them. Sometimes they're invited to people's homes to entertain, but it's a serious part of Irish culture.

And then there's religion. We are mainly Catholics in the South. The Catholic Church is very involved in peoples' lives. The local priest is like one of the family. He knows a great deal about you, he visits every week or so, he is very respected. Many people go to Mass every week, some go every day. And to Confession when they feel the need to go". Patrick paused, as if wondering to say any more.

"In the past, the Church was very hard on women who got pregnant outside of marriage if the father wouldn't do the right thing. A lot of them didn't even know the facts of life. Many of their babies were taken away at birth and the women were forced to give them up for adoption. It went on for years, it was cruel. It happened to Mam's older sister Angela, her baby son was taken, she tried but never traced him. She never got over it".

Nell shivered. She placed her hand on her rounded stomach; soon, she was told, she would feel the 'quickening' – the baby's first movement. Their baby. Another time, another place, that could have been me, she thought, and her eyes filled with tears. She had a glimpse of why Patrick's mother might be less than pleased to meet her; it might bring back difficult memories of her sister's suffering. It was just fortunate that Patrick and I were able to marry. What would have happened to me otherwise? she thought and began to realise that despite having had the best education, how little she knew about life and the world, the injustice, the unfairness.

Patrick endeavoured to lighten the mood. "But the people are friendly and kind, they'll give you their last penny if they have it to give. Ireland isn't known as the land of a hundred thousand welcomes for nothing. My family will love you, Nell, and our baby. But being accepted as one of them, as a local takes years. Just be yourself and don't expect too much too soon. Mam takes time to adjust, but she always does in the end".

It was a great deal for Nell to take in. She began to realise that in the weeks and months to come she would not only be learning to adapt to life as a new mother, but if she did visit Patrick's family, she would need every ounce of understanding, awareness and effort if she were ever to become a part of it.

* * *

Working life as a foreman was very different for Patrick. He was now giving instructions to the workforce instead of receiving orders. This could have been the cause of difficulties as he had previously worked with Joe Clancy on an equal basis, but Joe, being good natured about his friend's success, held no grudges and without it ever being planned, became Patrick's unofficial right-hand man.

Patrick soon discovered how much there was to learn, but he began to understand how to work to plans and drawings, how to calculate the quantities of materials required for a phase of the work and how many man hours would be needed to complete it. The site manager and project co-ordinator treated him with a new respect and spoke to him differently. Sometimes there were matters beyond his control; bad weather could hold up parts of the job for days and occasionally men did not turn up for work or would walk off the site. He knew that delays cost money; deadlines were all-important, and he had to juggle so many problems. But he was gaining in knowledge and confidence and felt that in time he could go further. He could gradually learn enough to run his own company – there was enough construction work to go round, but he also knew that starting a business would need investment and would involve a certain amount of risk. That was a decision for the future, he concluded; for now, he would concentrate on being a good foreman.

* * *

Christmas was fast approaching. At Moongarth the preparations were understated; there was no tree and very few decorations. Jenny brought in some greenery and placed jugs of holly, laden with glossy red berries in the hall and the drawing room, and some special groceries were ordered from a delicatessen in Kirchington. But there was no excitement, no anticipation; Evelyn's disapproval of any change of routine was unmistakable.

Lois liked to pay Jenny each week in cash, and two weeks before Christmas Lois and Neville always gave her a generous bonus. Neville arranged to draw cash from the bank each week in time for Lois to make the payment and left it in an envelope in her dressing table drawer. It was the one small act of financial independence that Lois had retained, and she enjoyed handing Jenny her weekly wages. When it was time to pay the Christmas bonus along with the wages, Lois and Jenny would sit down for a chat with a glass of sherry and a mince pie and make a little occasion of it. It was almost a ritual, and one small, familiar social custom to which Lois looked forward in the safety of her own home.

On the day when the bonus was to be handed to Jenny, Lois struggled up the stairs and went to fetch the envelope from her dressing table as usual.

It wasn't there.

She hunted through every drawer, every cupboard, checked her handbag and even Neville's desk in the observatory room. There was no sign of the envelope. She came downstairs in a flurry of embarrassment.

"I'm so sorry Jenny, I think Neville must have forgotten or he's put it in a different place. It's most unlike him. I will ask him when he gets home, and he will bring it round to you later. So disappointing. It's never happened before". Lois was mortified.

Jenny was less concerned about her wages at that moment, for Lois's distress was plain to see; she realised Lois was trying to save face, to explain away the reason why the envelope was not where it should have been. She doesn't want to accept the idea that she may have misplaced it; she is hoping that Neville has forgotten. She doesn't want to blame herself in case she is forced to admit that her memory is at fault. All these thoughts went through Jenny's mind. Then an unwelcome possibility struck her. Was someone else to blame, someone who for months now had been behaving in a suspicious manner? If that were the case, it was a cruel act to create doubt in the mind of a vulnerable woman, quite apart from the fact that the envelope and its contents seemed to have vanished. Once again, she agonised over what to do, and in the end decided to talk to Neville when she next saw him.

Neville was equally puzzled. He most certainly had drawn out the money and put the envelope in its usual place. He tried to make light of it to Lois who was still upset, and for her sake decided to let her think he had mistaken the day and that he would deal with the matter; she was not to worry.

The following evening Neville visited Jenny and apologised for the delay with her wages. Jenny could be outspoken and by then was convinced that Evelyn had either hidden the money or stolen it. But Phil advised against making accusations, she had no proof. He still didn't know she had taken the letter addressed to Lois and would have been angry with her. Neville was trying to be philosophical. "It's a mystery, Jenny, I don't know what's happened. I think Lois must have moved it and forgotten, it will probably turn up in some unlikely place but until then there's not much we can do. We may have to have a different system for paying you in future though, it's a worry if Lois has become forgetful about money".

Jenny agreed and said she would look out for the missing envelope when doing the cleaning. No more was said, but she could see from the look on Neville's face that he was greatly concerned; whether that was more about his wife's memory lapse or the unpleasant prospect that a theft had taken place was hard to tell.

* * *

Nell tried to brighten up the flat for Christmas; she bought a little tree and adorned it with some cheap decorations from the local market and a string of fairy lights. One evening Patrick came home from work with a surprise – he had been invited along with Nell to represent Keane Construction at a Christmas gala dinner hosted by Kirchington Chamber of Commerce. The project co-ordinator was unable to attend, and Patrick was to go in his stead. He was nervous but excited – the mayor, the local Member of Parliament and other business leaders would be present. It was a great honour for Patrick, and he had never dreamed he would be included in such a gathering. Once again, he realised how far he had come with Nell's support and encouragement. He rarely gave himself credit for his own hard work and determination.

Nell was doubtful about the dinner at first; her pregnancy was clearly visible now. "I have nothing suitable to wear" she said despondently. "Nothing fits me, I can't get into any of my nice clothes".

"We can surely run to a new dress for you". Patrick so badly needed her by his side at this important event. "We'll go shopping in town, I'll buy you something. It will be my Christmas present to you".

They had never been shopping together for anything as glamorous as outfits for a special occasion. Although she had never been to one herself, Nell knew enough about the academic dinners her father had attended (usually alone) to know that Patrick would need formal wear as it was a black-tie event. A dinner jacket and shirt for Patrick was easily tracked down; they had decided to hire those items, but a suitable dress for Nell proved more difficult. Noticing that Nell was almost too tired to look any further, Patrick was about to suggest that they try another day, but then Nell spotted a shop down a side street that she hadn't seen before. Gracie's looked expensive and classy, probably way above their budget but Nell looked at the gowns in the window display with renewed energy.

After trying on three dresses, Nell opted for simplicity. The one she chose was not a maternity style but if she bought it in two sizes larger than usual it would fit perfectly. The dress was full-length and sleeveless, in midnight blue velvet, softly draped, with a boat-shaped neckline. The colour brought out the deep grey of her eyes.

When she emerged from the changing room to show him, Patrick's expression said it all. "Wow" was the only word he could manage. He gulped when he saw the price ticket, but Nell insisted on paying half out of her savings. "The dress will be an investment" she said, pointing out that she could always have it taken in if there were any opportunities to wear if after the baby was born.

The following day Patrick confided in Nell that there was still one thing worrying him: the matter of dinner table etiquette. He had never been to a formal dinner in his life and was terrified of making a mistake, using the wrong cutlery or glasses and showing them both up. Nell tried to allay his fears by telling him just to copy other people, but the next day she walked to the local library and borrowed a reference book entitled "Essential Etiquette". They pored over it that evening, both laughing at some of the more extreme examples, but Patrick relaxed visibly after that, realising that normal good manners and respect for others would be sufficient to carry him through the most demanding moments of the gala evening.

When Nell told her parents about the invitation, Lois was, as always, slow to give praise but she seemed pleased; the upset about the missing money seemed to have been forgotten for now. Nell detected something else in her mother's eyes. Was it wistfulness, she wondered? Was Lois seeing in her daughter a glimpse of how her life might have been if circumstances had been different?

Neville was impressed that Patrick and Nell had been invited to such an important local event. "This is an opportunity for you to make contacts in the business world, Patrick. It's called networking – you never know where it might lead. Always a good idea to get yourself noticed for the right reasons".

And noticed they certainly were. A week later, as they walked into the foyer of the council offices and were offered pre-dinner drinks, the local press was very much in evidence and many eyes turned towards this little-known young couple. Patrick's looks and colouring were eye-catching and the beautiful young woman on his arm, unable to disguise her pregnancy, looked radiant. After they had been presented to the mayor, some councillors and other civic dignitaries, a man approached them, having overheard the introductions.

"Hi. I'm Ray Darrington, how do you do? I'm familiar with Keane Construction, we've used them on several of our contracts. I have a property development company" he added. "Darrington Design". He spoke as though they ought to have heard of it. His eyes appraised Nell, his gaze lingered a little too long, Patrick thought, and somehow the man made him feel uncomfortable. For the sake of politeness Patrick exchanged a few more words with him then a moment later they were alone again.

"He was a bit creepy" whispered Nell. "I hope we don't have to sit near him at dinner".

After a while a middle-aged couple who had been standing nearby offered to show them to the lounge area so that Nell could sit down. "They look nice" thought Nell, as they introduced themselves. "Jonathan and Barbara Grant. Good to meet you. But don't I know you"? said Jonathan, looking at Nell. "We're you at Kirchington College? I'm an accountant, Cunningham and Grant, but I lecture at the college once a week. Business Studies".

"Of course", said Nell, realising she had seen this man occasionally around college. "This is my husband, Patrick Walsh. I'm Nell Walsh now but I was Nell Garth. I was at college until recently. English and History. I shall be going back in the spring to take my 'A' levels".

"I've met your father", said Jonathan. "I think we were at a conference together once".

They sat down and sipped their drinks. Patrick was feeling a little left out, but Nell tried to bring him back into the conversation. "My husband is a foreman at Keane Construction" she said proudly. Jonathan turned his attention to Patrick. "Keane Construction is doing very well I hear. There's plenty of work about at the moment".

Barbara started chatting to Nell, and Patrick found himself talking easily with this pleasant, fatherly man who was essentially a stranger, telling him how he had come over from Ireland to look for work, had recently been promoted, and of his ambition to start up his own company in time. A year ago, I wouldn't have dreamed I could do this, he thought. He knew he had Nell to thank for most of it.

"There's a new housing development planned for Wharnden Meadows, permission has just been granted last week," said Jonathan. "Work will probably start sometime next year. They will be looking for sub-contract bricklayers. If you do think about setting up on your own, give me a call, I may be able to help". He gave Patrick his business card, and after a few more minutes they were called into dinner.

Patrick now understood what his father-in-law had meant by networking.

"Well how about us, rubbing shoulders with all the top brass" Patrick whispered to Nell as they got up to leave and thank their hosts. He needn't have worried; the dinner was a little less formal than expected and many of the company had drunk a great deal by the end of the evening, so the atmosphere was relaxed and convivial. Just as they moved out into the foyer, Nell smiling happily on her husband's arm, the photographer from the Kirchington Evening Echo stepped forward and took their photo, glad to capture a shot of such an attractive young couple.

The next day, two important things happened.

A write-up of the gala dinner appeared on the front page of the Echo, along with a colour photograph of Patrick and Nell.

And almost without knowing what it was – a sensation so slight but not imagined – Nell felt the baby move for the first time.

Chapter Eleven

Kathleen Buckley slammed her till shut and went to place the keys on a hook in the storeroom. "I'll be off now, Mrs Byrne" she called, and was met with a grunt in reply. It was not quite one o'clock but there were no customers, and she wanted to get home on time. She was more than ready for a cup of tea or an early glass of wine and a sandwich, and to put her feet up for half an hour.

Serving part time behind the counter at Byrne's General Stores in Ballymere was to her mind the most boring job possible, but it was the only work that she had been able to find. It was made just about bearable by the local customers, most of whom were friendly and liked to stop for a chat – that was unless Mrs Byrne, the proprietor didn't appear with one of her disapproving looks that seemed to say, 'why are you laughing and enjoying yourself in work time?'

It looked like rain as she left the shop, huge black clouds were piling in from the west. Reaching for her umbrella she strode out for home, which was only three hundred yards along the village street. She should make it before the downpour started.

She was surprised to see her father's Land Rover parked outside her house, with her mother sitting in the driving seat. This was unusual; Bridget was not in the habit of coming out at lunch time, there was always so much to do at the farm that she rarely took any time out to see her daughter during the working day.

"I'm glad I caught you; I wanted to show you something". Bridget closed the door of the Land Rover and waved an envelope at Kathleen.

"Let's get inside Mam and put the kettle on first". Kathleen was not too pleased to see her mother; she had promised herself a quiet afternoon in front of the TV before Michael arrived home. "You won't be stopping, Mam, will

102

you? I want to see the next episode of Harmony Road, and then there's Quick Quiz".

"You're always so grumpy Kathleen" said her mother, taking off her coat. "I'll make the tea". She looked round the untidy room despairingly, noticing the overflowing mountain of ironing on the dining table, piles of magazines cluttering the easy chair, and through the door into the kitchen she could see stacks of dirty crockery awaiting washing up and a waste bin in need of emptying. "If you ask me, you'd be better off taking an afternoon to do some housework instead of watching soaps all the time. No wonder Michael spends every evening drinking at O'Malley's".

"I didn't ask you, Mam. Are you going to make that tea or what?" Kathleen's expression was sulky but defiant.

With the tea poured, the two women sat side by side on the worn sofa and Bridget picked up the envelope again.

"This letter has just arrived from Patrick" she said, unfolding a single sheet with a newspaper cutting tucked inside and handing it to her daughter. "They went to some big business dinner" she continued. "The newspaper reporters were there, and they took their photo. What do you think of that?"

Kathleen opened the folded piece of paper and stared at the colour photograph of her brother in a dinner suit with his pretty wife in a shimmering blue gown, her pregnancy showing unmistakably, and the caption 'Local couple Patrick and Nell Walsh shine at the Chamber of Commerce Business Gala'.

"Very nice" said Kathleen dismissively, passing the letter and its contents back to her mother and turning her face away.

"Oh come on now Kathleen, surely you can be pleased for your brother? He seems to be doing very well I must say".

"You've changed your tune Mam" retorted Kathleen with obvious irritation. "You didn't have a good word to say about him when he told you his last piece of news".

"Well I know" admitted Bridget, "but I've thought about it a lot since then. I really do think he is making a go of his life out there. And Nell does seem to be a decent enough girl. Gráinne said she was very nice to her at the wedding".

"And so she should be, coming from a big house, plenty of money, best of everything. And all brides are nice to people at their wedding. What I don't understand is what she sees in Patrick? A bit of rough, is that it?"

"Don't be coarse Kathleen" reproved her mother. "You never have a good word to say about anything these days. Well, I'll be off, there's no talking to you when you're in one of these moods. I'll see myself out". Kathleen made no move to leave the sofa as her mother picked up her coat and closed the front door behind her.

She sat there for a long time after her mother left, staring into space, not even bothering to turn on the TV. Yes, she was jealous. And bitter, she acknowledged, she felt trapped in a dull job in a small town with no money, no prospects, no hope of things ever changing. She was only twenty, but she felt old and tired. Tired of living the way she lived.

She thought of the photograph of her brother and the sister-in-law she had never met, radiant and beautiful with every possible advantage life could offer her, and for the thousandth time she reflected on how unfair things were.

Connor would have the farm. Sean was in the United States, no doubt doing all right for himself, they hardly ever heard from him now. Patrick – well he had fallen on his feet for sure. Aidan was clever, he was likely to carry on with his studies, maybe train as a priest, although fewer men did that these days. Orla – well as soon as she leaves school, she will realise there's no future here for her, just like I've had to. And Niall is too young to worry about it yet, but he will end up going abroad for work like Sean or Patrick. The boys have all the opportunities, she thought angrily, there's nothing for girls here except to get married and have children. She thought about her hasty marriage to Michael last year, rushed because of a pregnancy scare which turned out to be a false alarm. That was a blessing in the end, except that she was now tied to a man whom she felt little for and who couldn't wait to get away from her to O'Malley's bar or to the betting shop. Everything in her life so far had been a disappointment, she concluded, family, school, marriage, her job.

Her mother had been right. Their home was a shambles, there was no money to make any improvements. They could barely afford the rent; Michael spent any spare cash on himself. She earned a pittance at the shop, just enough to cover their grocery bill. Kathleen was so full of self-pity at that moment that she couldn't see that it would cost nothing to make things better for herself – for them both – such as cleaning the house, putting things away, tidying the back yard. She lacked the motivation to do any of those things, she could only dwell on the negative thoughts and the feeling that everyone else had a better deal than her.

The wild beauty of West Cork, the peace and timelessness of the countryside where she lived completely escaped her. She could only see the things it lacked, excitement, opportunities, glamour. There was no way out for her, she was sure of that. Once, while she was still single, soon after Sean had left, she had approached her parents. "I'd like to go to America, to New York, maybe next year. Why shouldn't I go? I could save up for the fare. What's to stop me?"

Dermot had laughed at first, and her mother looked incredulous. Then, seeing that their daughter was serious, Dermot became angry. "I never heard of such a thing Kathleen. What do you think you could do in New York? Sean can turn his hand to most things, he'll earn good money. You'd be in the gutter within a week. I'll hear no more of this nonsense".

Miserably, remembering that conversation, Kathleen accepted that her father had had a point. What could she do in America, or anywhere for that matter. The only girls she knew who had emigrated had gone to train as nurses in England. That wasn't the lifestyle she hankered for. Her other sister-in-law Gráinne worked in a bank and wore smart clothes to work, she had brains. But unlike Gráinne she had left school without any qualifications, well none that would get her very far anyway. The inequalities, even within her own family were undeniable. Boys could always make a living in the building trade, even those with no skills could find work as labourers and get taken on anywhere, here or abroad, or so she thought. There was nothing for girls unless you were clever or if you married someone with a bit of money. Kathleen felt that she had failed on both counts. So much for the twentieth century, she thought. It feels like women are a hundred years behind the times here.

She turned her mind to the woman in the newspaper cutting, her new sister-in-law at a glittering occasion with her brother, drinking champagne with all those important people, attended by the press. What a busy social life they must have, Kathleen thought. She had only glanced quickly at the photograph but grudgingly Kathleen had to admit that apart from being stunningly beautiful, the girl did look nice, and something else.... kind? Friendly? More than that even, she couldn't quite put her finger on it. It was only a photo after all. Perhaps I was too hard on her, I shouldn't judge someone I have never met, she said to herself. But it was so difficult not to, Kathleen had been given a glimpse of a world which she longed for, yet to which she could never aspire. Tears pricked at her eyelids.

Of course, the grass is always greener on the other side of the fence. Kathleen had no way of knowing about Nell's sad and lonely childhood and that if only they had known each other then, there might have been times when Nell, despite all the trappings of a privileged upbringing would have willingly swapped places with her.

Chapter Twelve

Arthur Dermot Walsh was born at 4.17 on the twenty sixth of April 1980 at St Catherine's Hospital, Kirchington. He arrived red-faced, crying loudly, punching the air with his tiny fists. Already showing the early signs of red-gold hair like his father, he left no one in any doubt of his presence in the world. At just over nine pounds he was a healthy, hungry baby.

Nell's pregnancy had been straightforward but occasionally she had been puzzled that her mother had not been more interested in her progress, although in the end had decided against broaching the subject. The labour had been long and at times frightening as she battled wave after wave of intense pain, constantly wondering if this amount of suffering was normal and how much more she could endure. Fortunately for Nell, husbands were actively encouraged into the delivery room to support their wives and to have the earliest opportunity to bond with their new baby. But as with most new mothers, the memory of the pain faded as soon as her son was placed into her arms. Patrick was the epitome of an anxious expectant father; he had often wondered how it would feel to meet their child for the first time, but nothing prepared him for the surge of love he felt for both Nell and his little son as they spent those first special moments as a family. It was as though he had in a few hours taken another leap forward in his life. He was now a father, a family man; together he and Nell had created this perfect new human being. Nell felt it too despite her exhaustion, but Patrick was euphoric.

He had been unsure about the name Arthur at first. During the preceding weeks they had considered dozens of boys and girls names; Arthur was Nell's choice, and he did not object to it, but when she reminded him of the legendary warrior king, he agreed it was a good strong name. Later when she suggested Dermot after his father as a middle name Patrick was touched and said how delighted his father would be.

Arthur was a contented baby as long as he was fed regularly. "Just like his father" Nell commented, laughing as she bathed him for the first time.

"Happy mum, happy baby" said the midwife in a brisk, matter-of-fact way, watching her.

* * *

The first few weeks of life with a new baby was a huge adjustment for both Nell and Patrick. The lack of sleep, the seemingly endless routines of feeding, changing, bathing and laundry which barely left them with any time for themselves or each other were harder than expected. Patrick took a few days off when Nell came home from hospital; it was all he could manage, but he was a devoted husband and father, determined to take his share of the chores and the pleasures of fatherhood too.

All too soon Patrick returned to work; his hours were long and the work physically hard. Often, he was exhausted by the time he returned home at six o'clock. But somehow Nell coped. Arthur was doing well, gaining weight and sometimes sleeping through the night after a few weeks, which was bliss for his parents as they caught up on uninterrupted sleep themselves. During the long days alone with him, Nell established her own routine of caring for Arthur, playing with him, constantly talking and reading to him, trying in some way to give him the best of herself as a mother without really recognising what unnamed force was driving those compulsions. She had been used to spending time alone when not at school or college, but it was strange at first to have one-sided conversations with a small baby who did little except watch her intently and occasionally gurgle. Her old school friend Caroline Brooke visited regularly; she was a lifeline to Nell on the days when fatigue and the demands of motherhood overwhelmed her. It had been decided that Caroline would spend two afternoons looking after Arthur while Nell sat for her 'A' levels. Nell was reluctant to leave Arthur, and she was not confident about the exams; she wondered if she had done enough revision during the last few weeks of her pregnancy, and now she felt indescribably tired; concentrating for long periods was difficult. Still, I will give it my best shot, she thought, as she filed into the examination room, already feeling strange amongst the other students in her year. Some of them smiled and waved at her but she was aware that somehow things were different; I'm not one of them anymore, she realised, my life has moved on in a different direction to theirs.

On other days, Caroline happily looked after Arthur while Nell took the opportunity to catch up on sleep for an hour or so, tidied up or peeled potatoes for their dinner. Over many cups of tea, the friendship was strengthened. This led Nell to thinking about Arthur's christening; when that should take place and whom they might ask to be godparents. Caroline and Joe perhaps. But maybe they should involve Patrick's family as well. Nell decided to talk to Patrick about it soon.

Sometimes Nell pushed Arthur in his stroller to the park or to feed the ducks, occasionally chatting to passers-by or parents out with their children, then returning home to prepare a meal or to finish chores before Patrick came home. She had learned to cook basic meals, and Patrick always praised her efforts even when they didn't turn out quite as planned. Their little flat was easy to maintain and keep clean; the lack of space being the only thing that tried her patience. As time went on, life with Arthur became easier, mothering seemed to come naturally to Nell; how that just happened was a mystery as she could hardly remember the times when her own mother had shown maternal feelings towards her. But her love of literature and writing was never far from the surface – there were days when she read a chapter or two of a favourite book or a new title she had borrowed from the library.

Lois visited now and then, always with Evelyn whose presence as her constant companion now seemed non-negotiable. Neville came less often as he was now headmaster of Kirchington Grammar School and was invariably busy. To Nell that was a sign that he trusted Patrick to look after her and Arthur, and that his own role as her father had changed. Evelyn was generally disparaging and seemed uninterested in Arthur's progress; if things had been different Nell would have welcomed her medical knowledge. Lois also was reluctant to get involved, often remaining passive and rarely offering to hold Arthur or play with him. It was heartbreaking for Nell to witness her own mother keeping her first grandchild at a distance, but realised why this was and knew it could only make matters worse if she challenged her about it, however sensitively.

One evening after Arthur was settled and she and Patrick had finished their meal, they sat down together in an exhausted heap on the sofa. Instead of turning on the TV, Patrick took Nell's hand.

"I've been thinking some more about starting up in business Nell. Joe and I had a chat today, he has offered to come in with me".

"What – a partnership?"

"Yes, except it wouldn't be entirely equal, not at first, anyway. It takes money, and most of my savings went on this place. But Joe has something put by, it would be enough to get us started. Once we are up and running, I would pay him back".

"What about our nest-egg from Dad? Couldn't we use that?"

"No". Patrick was emphatic. "That's our rainy-day fund. Your father didn't give it to us for me to start in business. I don't want to involve your parents".

"Is there enough work Patrick? Enough to support us?" Nell was already anxious; she could see only the pitfalls. To her it seemed like a huge gamble.

"There are plenty of opportunities out there if you know where to look, new plans are being given the go-ahead all the time. Kirchington is a growing town and even Lamberham has some small developments in the pipeline. If the worst came to the worst, we could always go back to Keane's. But I'm sure that wouldn't happen though".

"Would they have you back if you'd been setting up as the competition?"

"We wouldn't really be the competition. Joe and I are only thinking about bricklaying at first. Keane's covers all types of building work. But anyway, we're not going to make any decisions yet. I've decided to have a chat with that fellow we met at the dinner, that accountant. I have his card somewhere. It won't do any harm to get some advice".

The following week Patrick and Joe arranged to have a meeting at Jonathan Grant's house in Kirchington to discuss the prospects of going into business. Jonathan rang him back shortly afterwards to invite Nell and Arthur as well; Barbara wanted to meet Nell again and sent her congratulations.

They arrived at the Grants' home at seven o'clock on the following Thursday evening. Nell was unsure about disrupting Arthur's bedtime routine, but Patrick said it wouldn't matter just this once. Apart from the help he was hoping for from Jonathan he thought Nell might make a new friend in Barbara despite their age differences.

The Grants lived in what could only be described as a show home – a contemporary detached house with huge rooms and a great deal of glass and chrome. They were shown into a comfortable sitting room on two levels with stylish furnishings in pale, understated colours. A large conservatory adjoined the room and through the wide patio doors could be seen an immaculate garden. It was sumptuous and elegant. Patrick found himself wondering again how he had suddenly become part of a world inhabited by wealthy people in big houses and how far removed this was from rural Ireland.

But Jonathan and Barbara were not a pretentious couple – they welcomed their guests with genuine warmth, and after drinks had been offered and poured, Patrick and Joe followed Jonathan into the conservatory where the meeting was to take place. Barbara sat down with Nell and admired Arthur who was sleeping peacefully, unaware of his new surroundings. After a while he woke, and Barbara asked if she could hold him. As she did so, all the while gently crooning and supporting his head, Nell couldn't help comparing Barbara with her own mother who had no desire to cuddle her own grandson yet here was a complete stranger holding him with such longing and affection. Barbara had two grown up sons, only one of whom was married, and there was no sign of any babies yet, she said regretfully. "But I keep hoping" she added, clucking at Arthur who fixed his gaze on her and gave the beginnings of a smile.

After they arrived home and put Arthur to bed, Patrick sat down with Nell. "Jonathan thinks we can do it. I think we can. He has given me some names and Joe and I are going to put out feelers. We have the skills, there are contracts to be had. But there's a great deal to it, a lot of legal stuff. Partnership Agreement, capital, insurance, tax, cash flow. We will need a business plan; Jonathan will help with that. But I won't go ahead unless you're happy about it too".

Nell nodded. She was not completely reassured and part of her thought it was too great a risk. But this is also about trust, she realised. She must trust her husband to make the right decisions; she knew he would not gamble with their financial security, and he had taken advice from a qualified person. She must not stand in the way of his ambitions. She took a deep breath and mentally crossed her fingers.

"I think you should go for it, Patrick. Talk it over with Joe again and make another appointment with Jonathan. It could turn out to be the best move you will ever make".

Patrick took her in his arms. I promise you we won't regret it, Nelly". He often called her that when he was especially happy. "I really do want to do this. We'll make a success of it, you'll see".

A week later, after further discussions with Jonathan and some tense meetings with the small business manager at the bank, the partnership agreement was signed. That same evening Patrick took Nell to the window of the flat and pointed at his van parked in the street below. On the side was written in bold lettering: 'Clancy and Walsh, quality brickwork'. Joe had wanted the names the other way round as the idea had been Patrick's, but in the end they agreed that 'Clancy and Walsh' sounded better.

Patrick kissed her. "In a few years it could be 'Walsh and Son' "he said excitedly. "I think we should open a bottle of wine tonight, to celebrate".

Chapter Thirteen
June 1980

Patrick and Joe decided that they would leave Keane Construction on the tenth of June, have a break for a fortnight or so and start their new business on the first of July. This seemed like a good opportunity to take a trip to Ireland. Patrick had promised Nell this holiday; it was the best time of year to travel, his family could meet Nell and of course get to know Arthur while he was still less than two months old. A few doubts remained about introducing Nell to his mother, but her letters had been more friendly of late; she was looking forward to meeting Nell one day, she said, and especially her new grandson.

The announcement about the holiday put Nell in a panic. She was nervous of course; meeting Patrick's big family was something she had very much wanted to do but all of a sudden, she felt unsure of herself. Was she becoming like her mother, she wondered, then dismissed the thought. All would be well; Patrick would be with her.

Nell had never travelled abroad before and had no passport but the helpful lady at the Post Office in Kirchington assured her that identification such as her Student Union card with her photo would be accepted for Ireland.

On the twelfth of June they sailed on the ferry from Fishguard to Rosslare harbour in County Wexford. They travelled in Patrick's van; it was their only means of transport but fortunately had plenty of space for the ever-growing amount of baby equipment they needed to take. Joe travelled with them, he was also overdue for a holiday back home, he said. He and Patrick took turns to drive. The actual crossing was only about four hours but the journey to Fishguard from Sussex took five. All were very tired by the time they drove off the ferry at Rosslare, and they had several more hours driving before they reached West Cork.

"I am going to learn to drive when we go back to England," said Nell. "Just so that you can have a break now and then. Joe won't always be travelling with us".

Patrick and Joe exchanged conspiratorial glances and Nell, sitting in the back of the van was about to ask which one of them would give her lessons, but at that moment Arthur woke up and her attention was diverted. She had fed him during the ferry crossing but the van bumping down the exit ramp had woken him again. She cradled him on her lap and quietened him as the momentum of the van and the regular throb of the engine noise lulled him back to sleep.

One of the first things Nell noticed as they drove away from Rosslare was the intense greenness of the countryside. She had grown up in rural Sussex so was used to the gentle colours and chalk downland of her native county, but the landscape here was dazzling. No wonder they call it the Emerald Isle, she thought.

They left Joe at Kent Railway Station in Cork city; he would then travel onward by train to his home in Killarney and make his way back to meet them for the return journey at the end of the holiday. They were to stay with Connor and Gráinne in their house which was half a mile from the Walsh's farm near Ballymere but would join the family at the farm for meals. Bridget had decided that until she knew Nell better, she could not expect her to stay in the overcrowded farmhouse even though nine people had lived there together a few years previously.

But their first stop was the farm. It was dark by the time they arrived, so Nell had little chance to take in the surrounding countryside or the coastline. She couldn't wait to see it in daylight. She climbed out of the van stiffly and instinctively looked up at the sky. It was cloudy. "No stargazing tonight" Patrick laughed, watching her. Hearing the van draw up, Bridget opened the front door to greet them, with Dermot a step behind her.

Bridget threw her arms around Patrick and hugged him, then stood back, looking at Nell and went to shake her hand. It was an awkward moment as Nell was holding Arthur in her arms but then they both laughed.

"You're so welcome Nell. I'm pleased to meet you. And is this Arthur? He's grand. What a little treasure". She looked down at the baby with real fondness. Again, Nell could not help but be amazed at how everyone except her own mother adored him at first sight.

Dermot also shook her hand and gave Patrick a half-hug.

"You must be tired, come in and take a seat. Here's Orla, she's been longing to meet you"

A lively, smiling girl of about fifteen ran into the room and hugged her brother. She had Patrick's red curly hair but wore it long over her shoulders. "I've missed you Pat" she said laughing. "It's so good to have you home". She turned to Nell and was suddenly shy. Nell smiled at her and held out her hand. When Orla saw Arthur on her lap she was entranced. "My nephew" she said, looking down at him. Nell nodded. "Yes, you are the first auntie he has met".

A slight, fair-haired boy, a little younger than Orla had followed her into the room. He went over and punched Patrick playfully on the shoulder. "Good to see you back, Pat" he said, and looked a little self-consciously at Nell and Arthur as the introductions were made. "This is Niall," said Bridget. "Aidan will be back at dinner time, and you'll meet Kathleen at the weekend. Connor will come down to fetch you later. Dinner will be ready in half an hour, Patrick, show Nell round. Orla will mind Arthur, won't you?" She spoke quickly and Nell quickly realised that as the head of a large family Bridget was used to organising everyone.

After a tour of the house, which took very little time, Nell, seeing that Arthur was quite contented on Orla's lap, went into the kitchen. "Can I do anything to help, Mrs Walsh?"

"No dear, it's all under control. And call me Bridget".

"I suppose we're both Mrs Walsh now, aren't we?" Nell was trying to make conversation.

"Well yes, and there's three of us when you count Gráinne". They both laughed. Patrick, listening from the sitting room where he was chatting with his father, heard the laughter and felt a sense of relief that the ice was broken.

When Aidan arrived and more introductions were made, they all sat down at a long table to a hearty stew, accompanied by mashed and boiled potatoes. Arthur slumbered peacefully in his carry cot despite all the laughter and noise. Nell thought suddenly, this is what a real big family feels like. Seven of us sitting down to a meal together. This is what I have been missing all my life. She looked at Patrick, sitting opposite, and he winked at her. I feel at home here already, she said to herself.

* * *

The following day Nell felt very tired after the journey and was relieved when they did not venture very far from the farm. The weather was drizzly; "Typical Irish weather to welcome you" said Gráinne, making toast and coffee on the first morning. Patrick and Connor had gone out early to do the milking and the two women sat chatting in the kitchen while Arthur slept after his first feed. Nell had switched him to formula feeding during the daytime; he continued to gain weight and was already growing out of newborn size clothes.

"We're hoping to try for a baby soon" said Gráinne, pouring Nell a second cup. "If that happens, I'll still have to work part time afterwards. The farm doesn't pay very well, we need two incomes".

"Patrick told me that you work in a bank. It must be nice, working with a lot of people".

"There's not that many of us, it's only small branch. But yes, it's ok, better than a lot of jobs around here. There's no transport, so I have to cycle. Not much fun in bad weather".

"I've never had a job" said Nell, then immediately wished she hadn't disclosed that, it made it sound as if she had no need to work, which was not the case at all, but Gráinne didn't seem to construe it that way. "I mean, I was at college until recently. I've only just taken my 'A' levels. I get the results in August" she added with a wry smile.

"I have to get off to work now," said Gráinne. "Sorry to abandon you. We will meet later and talk some more. I'm so glad you've married Patrick, you're well suited. I can see that he loves you so much".

Nell was touched by her sister-in-law's kindness and not for the first time felt that despite her misgivings she was beginning to fit in and feel part of the Walsh family.

The next day the weather was clear and bright, the previous day's mist having lifted with a change of wind blowing in from the southwest. As it was Saturday, Patrick was to take Nell out for a drive along the coast to Ballymere and to the nearest town.

Arthur was to be cared for by Bridget with help from Orla who already doted on her little nephew. Nell had not wanted to impose on her mother-in-law and was reluctant to leave him, but Bridget waved away her objections.

"Haven't I brought up seven of my own now? He will be grand, don't worry about him, go and enjoy yourselves".

"But you're busy with the farm…"

"Not today, Aidan is here, and Patrick is going to help bring in the cows later when you get back".

Nell thanked them both, ensuring they had supplies of nappies and bottles and went to join her husband. This is the first day out for just the two of us in such a long time, she thought happily. As they drove along the track Nell was struck by the isolation of the farm, although she knew Ballymere was less than three miles away. Apart from the farmhouse and outbuildings, and Connor's house further down the laneway she could see no man-made structures at all. It seemed a long way before they joined a metalled road. Nearer to the coast the landscape was not so green; the terrain was rocky and bleak, the banks covered in brambles and thorn, but along the verges were huge clumps of orange montbretia and scarlet fuchsias, lending some vivid colour to their stony backdrop. Nell remembered her father buying similar plants at Lamberham Garden Centre – here they grew wild in profusion. There were very few trees. The remains of broken-down stone walls were visible here and there, and as they drove over an uneven stone bridge above a gushing torrent of water it reminded her of the amount of rainfall here and the wet climate of West Cork. They parked the van at the side of the road and walked a little way. This is not a place where I should want to get lost, Nell thought, and shivered. They had so far not passed one other vehicle; she couldn't even see a signpost. Yet there's a certain wild beauty here, she acknowledged. There was something ageless, almost primeval about the landscape which she found hard to define. The only sounds were the rush of wind, water and the cry of a gull, and as she stood there taking in the scenery, she was conscious of the fact that nothing had changed in these surroundings for hundreds of years.

They moved on for a few miles and stopped again at Roaringwater Bay. It did not live up to its name that day; the sea was rhythmically pounding against the rocks at the shore and white crests could be seen further out in the ocean, but Patrick said it would be far rougher during the winter storms. The coastline was beautiful but rugged, and had it not been for the bright sunlight the atmosphere would have been brooding and almost formidable.

If Nell had been a photographer, she would have been taking endless reels of film and exclaiming over the next shot she couldn't wait to capture. But instead she was silent, absorbing every detail and aware of a compulsion that somehow, while all these images were fresh in her mind she must write about them, commit them to paper, to be returned to as holiday photos are pored over time and time again as souvenirs; her writing would be a permanent reminder of everything she had experienced here in this place; even if no one else ever read it, this would be a memory she alone had created. There was something enduring about the written word that reached across centuries. To her it held more resonance than a speech or a photograph.

Patrick watched her intently, fascinated by her reaction. He could see that she was emotional, moved almost to tears by what she saw around her.

The ambition to write was nothing new; she had often hoped that she would become a writer someday. Throughout her short life Nell had loved stories, books, literature; as she grew older it had become more than enjoyment, it was a means of escape, deliverance from the sadness of her circumstances. But the sudden inspiration came as a surprise. She stood there for a long time, thinking of how she would open her notebook later and jot down everything she remembered before it faded, in case she never returned to that spot again and witnessed its beauty. It was as though the landscape was whispering to her, telling her to hold on to that moment.

They continued on for nearly an hour, then stopped at a village called Crookhaven. The air was crystal clear, and the sea was rougher here, the wind tangled Nell's hair as they stood on Barleycove Beach, looking out across the water and the rocky crags. Patrick pointed out the Fastnet Lighthouse on the horizon. "The Teardrop" said Nell quietly. Patrick nodded, touched that she had remembered. Afterwards they had lunch at O'Sullivan's Bar, which was said to be the furthest in the southwest of Ireland, nicknamed 'the pub at the end of everywhere'. Here they enjoyed some fresh shrimps with warm crusty bread, accompanied by a half pint of Guinness for Patrick and orange juice for Nell, as she was still breast-feeding Arthur at night.

They drove back through the deserted countryside. Some stretches of landscape seemed barren compared to the lush pastures surrounding the Walsh's farm. But the little towns they passed through were colourful and bustling, some buildings decked with window boxes and bunting, the houses and shops painted in bright shades of blue and terra cotta. Knots of people were talking together here and there, everyone seemed to know one another. On a street corner a busker was singing, accompanying himself on guitar.

After another half hour's drive they came to Ballymere, the little town nearest the farm. In comparison it seemed dull and drab. There was a church, a school, a bank, a butcher's shop and Byrne's General Store, interspersed with a row of narrow terraced houses, their front doors opening onto the pavement. Here, only a few were brightly coloured, the rest were in varying shades of faded cream or grey. A couple of the buildings were boarded up.

At the end of the street was O'Malley's Bar, the only building which seemed to have benefited from a recent lick of paint. The overall impression was one of poverty and deprivation, and Nell felt a sense of disappointment. There are such contrasts here, even within a few miles, she thought. But she said nothing, this was where Patrick had grown up after all, it was the place he loved and it was not for her to comment or criticise, she still knew very little about this welcoming but complicated country.

"That one is where Kathleen and Michael live" said Patrick, pointing out a house with a paint-chipped front door, not far from the shop.

"Shall we call in on them Patrick" asked Nell. "Kathleen is the only one of your family I haven't met, apart from Sean of course".

"No, Kathleen would not want us to visit without warning" he said carefully. "She is.... well.... things are difficult. She'll come to the farm tomorrow; you'll meet her then".

Nell did not press the point but guessed there was more to this than Patrick had let on and resolved to ask him more later.

"He's been no trouble" said Bridget as they returned to the farm a little while later. Nell picked up Arthur from his carry cot and was rewarded by his first real smile, and Nell realised how much she had missed him, even having been parted from him for less than a day.

After another substantial family meal, Nell pushed Arthur in his stroller around the farm. It was hard going because of the mud, and after a while she gave up but just stood and watched Dermot, Connor and Patrick bringing in the cows for milking at the end of the day. She was amazed to see a different side to Patrick; she had only known of his skills as a builder but here he was, marshalling seventy head of cattle into the milking parlour and linking them up to the vacuum pumps as though he had done it all his life. Which of course he had, she recalled suddenly, apart from a few months' bricklayer training the farm was his life before he met me.

"What breed are these cows?" she asked Dermot

"These are Holsteins", he told her. "They give the best milk, and the yield is good. But a lot of it is down to the grass here, and the climate. And they graze outdoors most of the year".

"Do they all have names?"

"Not really, only one or two. But they all have their own personalities, you get to know the ones that are always pushing to the front and which ones are lazy or slow".

"It's a shame Arthur isn't old enough to take notice. He would love to see the cows when he's older" Nell thought of how he would be in a year's time.

"There's plenty of time" said Dermot, and he looked down at his grandson affectionately. "You'll be coming back again, for sure".

After breakfast the next morning the family prepared to attend Mass at Ballymere. Nell detected a slight tension in the air, knowing that this was going to be difficult and wondered what to say. Patrick had mentioned that he would go to Mass along with the others but as he'd said nothing further, she realised he expected her to stay at the farm with Arthur.

She took a deep breath. "Can Arthur and I come to Mass, Bridget?" she asked her mother-in-law nervously.

To her surprise, Bridget looked pleased. "Of course you may come, dear. And Arthur too. You cannot take Communion, but you will be very welcome at the service".

Everyone visibly relaxed after this conversation; Nell began to understand how important their faith was and that by extending an olive branch to Bridget over such a tricky subject she had started to build more bridges with this family.

Nell followed the Mass easily enough and to her relief only a small part was in Latin. Surprisingly, the priest spoke in a very informal way to the congregation, mentioning particular events in their lives, praying by name for those who were ill or in difficulty, and giving thanks for good news or improvements in the town. Arthur was content, just whimpering occasionally. The church was full, and she was struck by how friendly people were to her, even though she was very aware of being an outsider and not a Catholic. She was introduced to Father Donovan at the end, and many of the women came up to her and congratulated her on the birth of her son. Clearly the Walsh family were well respected and news of one of their sons marrying an English Protestant girl had been a source of interest. This is a real community, Nell thought. I know it would take time, but I think I could fit in here. She was glad that she hadn't rushed to judgement during her brief visit to Ballymere the day before. These were good people, that was what mattered.

On the way back, Patrick turned to her. "That meant so much to Mam, you coming to Mass today" he said seriously. "The Church is really important to her. She likes you very much, you know. But you have made a lot of effort, and I know she can be difficult". They both laughed. "Well, I'm getting to like your Mum – your Mam – too," said Nell. "And she's very fond of Arthur already".

As if wanting to join in the conversation, Arthur gave a squawk from his carry cot, reminding them that he was ready for his feed, and they lost no time in returning to the farm for a delicious cold lunch that Bridget had prepared before they left. "I shall never lose my baby weight" said Nell ruefully. "Your Mam is such a good cook".

"That's one thing about Mam and Dad, they never let us go hungry, even when money was tight". Patrick looked thoughtful and Nell wondered if the history of hardship and hunger still lived on in the minds of the people of West Cork.

Kathleen and Michael came to dinner that day. Michael said very little to anyone and settled down with a newspaper while the rest of the family gradually assembled. Kathleen was completely different in looks from her sister Orla, having long straggly black hair, thick dark eyebrows and pale skin, and her eyes were a deep piercing blue. But she seemed sullen and unfriendly compared with her brothers and sister which detracted from her looks somehow; she gave only a half-smile to Nell when introduced and barely looked at Arthur. There is a very unhappy woman, said Nell to herself, unsure of whether to try to make conversation and risk rebuff, or whether to respect Kathleen's obvious reluctance to join in. I wonder why they have come at all, was Nell's next thought, then realised that Bridget probably insisted on having her family all together on Sundays.

Later, while Nell was feeding Arthur, she spotted Patrick and Kathleen walking outside together, deep in discussion. Kathleen seemed to be angry and although Nell could not hear what was being said, clearly it was a matter of some importance.

"I saw you walking with Kathleen". When they were alone back at Connor's, Nell decided she would ask Patrick what was going on with her sister-in-law.

Patrick looked troubled. "She was asking me for money", he said at last. "I was going to tell you. I know Michael keeps her short. He likes a drink, well they both do, come to that and I don't think he treats her very well. But Kathleen's her own worst enemy, she could manage better than she does. She's asked Connor many times and he's started saying no. And Aidan doesn't have any money".

"Will your parents help her?"

"They won't when they think anything they give her will end up in the till at O'Malley's".

Nell sighed. She could tell that Kathleen was suffering, but it seemed an impossible situation, and one she did not dare to give an opinion on; she still felt like an outsider when it came to such deep-rooted problems.

"Will you give her some money Patrick?"

"I've agreed to this once, but I've told her not to ask again. The thing is", he paused and looked sheepish. "She thinks that now I've married you, we must be well-off and can easily afford to help her".

"What, she thinks I'm an heiress to a family fortune or something?". Nell was incredulous.

"Something like that. Anyway, I've put her straight. If she asks again, I shall refuse. I don't want to be paying good money for Michael to prop up the bar either". He paced around the room a few times. "It's not just the money though. Kathleen is very unhappy. She hates her life, and she doesn't know how to change it. She only married Michael because she thought she was pregnant, Mam and Dad insisted they marry but then it turned out she wasn't pregnant after all. Michael felt she had trapped him and has blamed her ever since. They had no opportunity to save up for a proper home, their house is a feckin' disgrace and they owe money everywhere. No one knows what to do about her".

Nell was silent. It was unusual for Patrick to swear even mildly, and it showed unmistakably his strength of feeling. She didn't know what to say or suggest. Not for the first time she realised how fortunate she was and how sheltered she had been from other peoples' struggles. All families have their secrets, she decided, but I'm a Walsh now and Patrick is trusting me with details of this darker side of his family situation. Despite her concerns for Kathleen, it was another step forward. It occurred to her that perhaps there might be ways to help Kathleen other than money, but that would need a great deal more thought. It would not be right for her to interfere, however well intentioned.

Chapter Fourteen

The next morning Nell pushed Arthur in his buggy along the boreen to the farm. It was a warm, still morning with hardly a breath of wind. Patrick was helping his father and Connor work on a tractor and Gráinne was at the bank, Orla and Niall were at school. She was going to ask Bridget if she could prepare the vegetables for the evening meal while Arthur slept, but she spotted Aidan reading on a bench in the garden.

"Do you mind if I join you?"

He nodded shyly and put down his book. Unlike his brothers and sisters, he was quiet, softly spoken, with short brown hair, deep set blue eyes and long dark eyelashes.

"What are you reading, May I see it?"

"The Celtic Twilight, by W B Yeats. It's about Irish folklore".

"I've heard of him but not read any of his work. I've been studying nineteenth century literature for 'A' level. Hardy, Austen, Keats, Wordsworth".

Aiden was interested. "Who is your favourite author? Mine is Yeats".

"I suppose it has to be Emily Brontë. I've read Wuthering Heights dozens of times".

"Do you find that with some books you can find something new however many times you read them?"

"Exactly! Or it makes you look at something in a different way each time". Nell was excited that she had found a kindred spirit.

"And also depending on your stage in life. Reading something at eighteen will not be the same as if you read the same book at the age of twelve ".

Nell had never thought of it that way but realised he was right. "Are you studying for anything in particular? Patrick said you might enter the priesthood".

"It's possible, but I doubt it. I'm more likely to go into teaching".

"My father's a teacher, he's a headmaster now, but he started as an assistant during the Second World War and worked his way up. He's always said it's the most worthwhile thing you can do, to educate children".

"Yes. For some it can be life changing. Round here there aren't many opportunities. Having some qualifications helps".

Arthur started to whimper, and Nell picked him up and rocked him for a moment. Aiden watched her.

"It's been lovely to meet you Nell, I've enjoyed our chat. We should compare notes more; you could give me some book recommendations. We have a lot in common".

As she put Arthur back in his stroller, she thought again how this family never ceased to surprise her

On the Wednesday evening after dinner Patrick announced he was taking Nell to hear some live music. She had listened to some traditional Irish music back in England and often longed to sit in a bar and experience it first hand, knowing it to be an important part of Irish culture and often spontaneous.

"Where will we go? O'Malley's?" she asked.

"No, Conroy's at Lanreagh is the best round here. It's a bit further but that's ok. Mam and Orla will babysit, I've asked them".

Connor and Gráinne were going too, Connor drove so that Patrick could have a few drinks.

The four of them settled at a table near to a makeshift stage. Connor bought a round of drinks, Patrick and Gráinne were drinking Guinness and Nell was persuaded to try some although she was still strict about avoiding alcohol. After a few mouthfuls she pushed it away, saying she thought she could get used to the taste if she stayed in Ireland long enough, but for now she would stick to soft drinks. The others laughed.

The first musicians, a guitarist and fiddle player duo tuned up and started singing a selection of songs by the Furey brothers, some of which Nell recognised, and she found herself joining in with 'Come by the hills". They went on to perform some of their own compositions. The second one was a moving account of The Great Wind of 1839. She asked the others about it during the interval.

"It's a true story. It was the most terrible storm ever to happen in Ireland. Many people perished, and thousands of homes were destroyed, ships were wrecked off the coast. It happened further north. Of course we were all one country then. West Cork escaped most of it, but it was a catastrophe". Connor's face looked grave as he told her. Nell reflected again how much disaster and hardship had befallen this country and its people.

Another round of drinks was bought and the mood lightened for a while. The bar was noisy and crowded, the atmosphere friendly and relaxed. The second half of the entertainment began, and a girl with a pure soprano voice sang 'She moved through the fair'. This was unaccompanied but many of the audience joined in quietly. Then a young man appeared and performed some instrumental pieces on a whistle. Another man came forward with a bodhran and provided some rhythm accompaniment. It was all very informal. Then after a while the musician picked up an instrument which Nell didn't recognise. "Those are Uilleann Pipes", Patrick told her. "Irish Bagpipes. They're quite different from the Scottish ones".

The young man began to play and the whole bar fell silent. Not even the clink of a glass could be heard. Nell thought it was the most hauntingly beautiful sound she had ever heard; plaintive, mournful yet evocative. She felt that the music reached right into her soul, and somehow it spoke to her of everything she was beginning to learn about Ireland. She turned to Patrick with tears in her eyes.

"Hey, is this how you are on a night out?" he teased. "I think we'd better get you home. Let's drink up".

As usual, Arthur had been contented and happy with Bridget and Orla. When Nell and Patrick got back, Orla was giving him a bottle feed with her mother's supervision. She beamed when she saw Nell. "He's been grand, I love him so much" she said, handing him to Nell. "I shall miss him when you go back to England. I shall miss you too" she added.

"Well hopefully we will be able to come back again before too long," said Patrick. Turning to his mother he said "I shall be busy for quite a few months, setting up the business. But if all goes well, we will be able to take another holiday soon".

The days passed quickly. For Patrick it was a working holiday at times, there was always plenty to do on the farm and Dermot and Connor were glad of another pair of hands. But he took time off as well; they sometimes left Arthur with Bridget who insisted the farm could manage without her now and then. He took Nell souvenir shopping in Glengarriff, then they ventured further, driving for miles up the Wild Atlantic Way and back along the coastline of the Beara Peninsula and Mizen Head. The scenery was breathtaking, and Nell thought she could never see enough of its beauty.

The following Friday Nell asked Patrick if he would drive her into Ballymere and look after Arthur for a few minutes while she called into the shop.

"I thought I'd ask Kathleen if we could meet up for a cup of coffee or something", she explained. "I need some baby milk, and it will be an opportunity to chat to her"

"You're wasting your time" said Patrick resignedly. "I doubt if she'll give you the time of day. But don't mention money, that's off limits now".

Nell promised to keep off the subject and leaving Patrick and Arthur in the van, crossed over the street to the store.

There were no customers waiting. Kathleen was reading a magazine but looked up when she saw Nell.

"Well, here's a surprise" she said, not in an unfriendly way but sounding slightly sarcastic.

After Nell had paid for her purchase, she took a deep breath. "Kathleen we never had much chance to chat on Sunday. How about we go for a cup of coffee before I go back to England?"

"And what might we have to chat about? Babies? Posh dinners? Books?"

Nell persevered. "We're in the same family now, surely we could get to know each other a bit more?".

"Why would I want to do that?" Kathleen's tone was hostile.

"I just thought it would be nice if we could...well...get together"

"Nice? I'll tell you what would be nice. You could feck off back to England and leave me alone".

Nell said no more and turned to leave, feeling completely crushed. Patrick had been right, this was pointless. But as she opened the shop door, Kathleen called after her.

"I'll tell you what. Meet me at O'Malley's at seven o'clock this evening. We can have our 'chat' there". She emphasised the word 'chat' in a derogatory way, leaving Nell in no doubt of her contempt, and returned to her magazine.

This was not what Nell had had in mind, but she realised her sister-in-law had somehow thrown down a challenge. When she told Patrick about the plan he was concerned.

"I'm not happy about you going there, O'Malley's is a rough place. She knew I wouldn't approve, that's why she suggested it".

"I'll only be an hour or so, I'll be fine. And it looks like it's the only opportunity I'll get".

Bridget was tight-lipped when she heard about the arrangement but agreed to look after Arthur while Patrick drove Nell to Ballymere and collected her later.

As Nell walked into the crowded bar, the conversation ceased for a few moments and all heads turned to look at her. Michael was standing at the bar, talking to some other men and nodded to her, then said something to his companions who laughed. Suddenly she felt horribly exposed and vulnerable and for a moment she wished Patrick was with her. She shouldn't have come. Then she caught sight of Kathleen seated at a side table and made her way over to meet her.

Kathleen was nursing a half pint of Guinness and Nell saw that a glass of orange juice awaited her. She looked at Kathleen in surprise and stammered her thanks. She had not relished the thought of going up to the bar.

"I knew you'd come, you just couldn't resist it, could you?" Kathleen's tone was scathing.

"I don't know what you mean...."

"Coming in here, all high and mighty, just to see a bit of how the other half live, then you can go back to your nice life in England and think how lucky you are".

Suddenly Nell was angry, angry at Kathleen's spiteful words, at being misjudged and that her efforts at friendship were being thrown back in her face.

"Kathleen, I don't know why we've got off on the wrong foot. Let me remind you that it was you that suggested O'Malley's. I'm doing my best here to get to know your family, to fit in, I've been worrying about meeting you all for months. I like your family and I'm getting to love Ireland, what I've seen of it so far, good and bad. Mostly good. You can say whatever you want but you won't put me off coming back, I'm a Walsh now whether you like it or not".

Did she imagine it, or did Kathleen look at her differently following that outburst? Perhaps she was one of those people who respected straight talking and who would exploit anything she saw as weakness.

"And just for the record, in case you have got this wrong, we live in a tiny flat on the first floor, I have a baby and no job, Patrick is putting everything on the line to set up in business and it may all come to nothing. Don't go thinking I'm some sort of princess".

To her surprise, Kathleen burst out laughing.

"You don't hold back, do you? Well then, hear me out. You might think Ireland is something special but let me tell you, green fields and nice scenery don't do much for me. I hate it here. I've always hated it. Do you want to come and see my house? It's a tip. My job is humdrum, I can't afford to go on holiday and my husband would rather be here in this bar with his mates than sit with me. That's for starters".

Nell didn't know what to say. Any reply would sound trite or condescending. They sat in silence for a while, but the buzz of conversation at the bar became louder and a glass smashed on the floor. There was laughter followed by a few expletives. Nell turned to Kathleen.

"I know you said you can't afford a holiday. But would you like to come over to England sometime and stay with us? Just for a change. For a break. You never know, it might help to get away for a while".

Kathleen seemed speechless for a moment. "Do you really mean that? You're inviting me to stay with you? What about Patrick?"

"Yes, why not. You leave Patrick to me. Have a think about it. Maybe wait a few months until the business is up and running, but I'm sure we can work something out".

Nell was about to take her leave, but suddenly Kathleen stood up and faced her.

"Thanks Nell. For the offer, I mean. I would like to come to England. Once I thought of going to America, but Dad soon put me straight on that idea. I've never been anywhere".

"Well let's see if we can make it happen. Good night, Kathleen".

"I'll see you again before you leave. Good night, Nell".

It seemed like a breakthrough. Nell felt she had done the best she could, Kathleen was certainly a very troubled woman. She decided to wait a while before telling Patrick of her suggestion to his sister, it might not come to pass but somehow, she could not walk away without offering some sort of help. Patrick would understand, she was sure of it.

The last few days of their holiday went by in a flash. On their last evening the family all assembled for a farewell meal, and even Kathleen seemed a little more sociable.

After dinner, as Nell and Orla cleared the table, Niall and Patrick strolled up the boreen to watch Connor and Dermot bring the cows in.

"Pat, I want to ask you something. Can I come and work for you in England? Now you have your own business?"

"You're only fourteen Niall; you're still at school"

"I mean, when I leave school, when I'm sixteen"

Patrick looked at his younger brother with affection.

"You'll probably change your mind about what you want to do loads of times before you leave school. It's far too soon for you to be making those sorts of decisions"

Niall persisted. "Well, if I do still want to when I'm sixteen, will you take me on?"

Patrick sighed. "My business hasn't even got going yet, Niall. It may never get off the ground, and I'll be back working on the cards".

Niall looked dejected. "I don't want to work for Dad or Connor. I'm not cut out for the farm. There's not much else here I want to do".

"Don't be thinking it's an easy life in England. There may be more choices over there, but construction work is hard, very hard everywhere. It's long hours, it's hard graft. You need to grow some more muscles first" he said jokingly.

Niall looked imploringly at his brother.

"Well when I'm sixteen then?"

"I'll tell you what. When you're sixteen, if Mam and Dad agree, and if my business is doing ok by then, you can come and give it a try for a few weeks. If that works out, we'll see about an apprenticeship for you. That way you'll learn a proper trade, otherwise you'll just be a labourer all your life and there's no future in that"

Niall beamed and gave his brother a hug. "Thanks Pat. I shan't change my mind"

Patrick smiled at him. "We'll see. Let's leave it at that for now".

Joe Clancy arrived early the following morning to travel back with Nell and Patrick on the return journey. Nell pushed Arthur in his stroller round the farm one last time and then went to say her goodbyes to the family. As it was Saturday, everyone was there to see them off except Kathleen who was at work.

Bridget embraced Nell and told her to come back again soon. To Nell's surprise, Bridget's eyes were misty. Nell herself was on the brink of tears. "I've had such a wonderful holiday Bridget", she said, feeling somehow closer to this woman whom she had known only a fortnight than she felt to her own mother. "Thank you for everything".

Orla hugged her too, and kissed Arthur. The men all shook her hand and wished them a safe journey. "Slan go foill" said Dermot.

The crossing back across the Irish Sea was rough that day, but Nell didn't notice the seasickness; she felt that she had left a little part of herself in West Cork and that somehow it would always be home from home.

Chapter Fifteen
July/August 1980

The first few weeks of starting in business were not easy. Patrick began to realise what a huge risk he had taken; apart from his own family finances, he was gambling with Joe's savings and livelihood. They had taken Jonathan's advice and followed up the contacts he had given them and had pursued several leads of their own. So far none had borne fruit. When they were not telephoning contractors or visiting sites, they spent time sorting out tools and buying in small quantities of materials, enough to go ahead with work as soon as they were offered any. Joe rented a lock-up garage nearby which they used for storage.

It was an anxious time. July stretched into August, and no money was coming in. Patrick tried to conceal his worries from Nell, but she could tell how troubled he was, and she felt she could do nothing to help except to keep their home running smoothly and to look after Arthur. Almost at his wit's end, Patrick was on the point of conceding that they might, after all, need to dip into their rainy-day fund, and in desperation he said as much to Nell one evening.

"Well Patrick that's what it's there for. Perhaps this is a rainy day. And if it makes you feel better, just borrow from it, and repay the money when things look up. Don't let's get behind with our bills when we have savings". Nell was trying to be positive; it wouldn't help if she became anxious as well.

Patrick kissed her. "If you're sure you're ok with that, we may have to. It will just be a temporary loan". He tried to sound more certain than he felt.

The next morning, as if in answer to their prayers, the phone rang. It was a company called Armstrongs, the main contractor involved in the building of a care home in

Kirchington. They needed bricklayers urgently, another firm had let them down, could Patrick attend a meeting?

Patrick's first thought was to telephone Jonathan. The last thing they needed would be to work for a company that might be financially unstable or who might fail to pay them. But his fears proved groundless; after a short time, Jonathan phoned back to say yes, Armstrongs were a reputable firm and his advice was to go ahead, subject to the contract and terms being agreed.

The work would last about three months, long enough to get them started. It was fortunate that the contract was in Kirchington as this kept their costs down. But even from the first week, Patrick turned his mind to what would happen when the job was finished, and they both came to realise the importance of continuity of work as any gaps would mean loss of income. Joe suggested they take on minor jobs as well, such as garden walls, repairs and repointing, or even house extensions, sub-contracting to small building firms. This would give them some bread-and-butter income in between bigger contracts and would also make their name known in the local area. They advertised their services in the Kirchington Evening Echo and soon, offers of work came flooding in. Clancy and Walsh had their first foothold in business.

During this time, Nell had not forgotten her promise to herself to write an account of her experiences in Ireland. She had made many notes at the time but had taken it no further while they were on holiday; she needed quiet time to sort out her thoughts and structure her writing. But now, with Patrick busy at work, and the flat being easy to keep clean and tidy, she took time while Arthur was having naps to give her creative talents free rein.

Writing was something she found immensely rewarding; it was like satisfying a yearning, obeying an instinct. She began to understand how artists felt compelled to paint, or why the great composers could lose all track of time when creating a masterpiece. Not that her work could by any means be considered a masterpiece, she thought ruefully, but it was important for her to record all the sights and impressions of her trip, particularly about the countryside and everything she had learned about the local culture and history. It occurred to Nell that she and Patrick had both made new beginnings that month; Patrick with the business, and she having taken the first small steps to fulfilling her writing ambitions.

She visited her parents as soon as Patrick was back to work; she had been reluctant to call on them while there was no work coming in as she wanted more than anything to be able to say with certainty that the business had made a successful start. Lois's condition was stable; there was no further physical deterioration that Nell could detect but her mother was vague and enigmatic. She seemed pleased to see her but didn't really notice how well Arthur was doing and asked very little about their time in Ireland. Evelyn took no interest in their holiday, her attitude was hostile and unwelcoming, it was as though she resented anyone else's presence in the house. Her behaviour to Jenny was at times unpleasant, and always unfriendly. There was something strange about her demeanour; she was very protective of Lois, and Nell had no opportunity to talk to her mother alone. Nell couldn't help thinking of the suspicion surrounding Evelyn, and she was equally concerned about her father's reluctance to challenge her over the missing money; that was still unexplained.

By contrast, Neville was keen to hear about the Walsh family in Ireland and could see how his daughter had benefited, not just from a change of scene but from a completely different way of life. He realised how being married to Patrick was transforming her and bringing her out of her shell. To be plunged into a large family in a land with different cultures and traditions when she herself was a new wife and mother would have been daunting even for those more confident and well-travelled. She had done well to cope with all that, he thought. He was keen to hear about Patrick's business and that work was steady; Patrick had impressed him with his desire to improve their fortunes and that the results of his efforts were already becoming evident.

Nell wanted to describe the West Cork landscape to her father. "Daddy you would love the countryside where we stayed. It's so remote, very few buildings and you could look at the stars there to your heart's content. It's really dark and clear, the skies and the horizons are very wide".

Neville remarked that it sounded ideal and thought wistfully of the prospect of a stargazing holiday on his own in such surroundings. Instead, they were to take a holiday in Spain later that month. He had recently completed the purchase of the apartment, having gone as far as he could in arranging for surveys, searches and other legalities whilst never having visited the property himself. He had relied on Evelyn's information; she missed nothing and was able to give Neville a clear account of not only its advantages and convenience but also to confirm that the apartment was in a good state of repair with no obvious defects.

Evelyn was to accompany them; Lois seemed unable to function without her. At times, when his wife was in remission from her illness and underwent small improvements day to day, needing less help, Neville wondered if Lois had become almost addicted to the constant attention that a paid companion gave her. She has become totally dependent on Evelyn, he realised. Of course, he never voiced this, but occasionally he felt it to be an unhealthy development, and it also meant that he and Lois were unlikely ever to be just a couple again. He tried not to let this thought depress him; it must be enough; he reflected that she is coping with her symptoms and still able to find some enjoyment in life.

They departed on the eighteenth of August, eagerly anticipating a fortnight's relaxation in the sun. Surprisingly, for a middle-aged man, this was Neville's first real holiday away from home – his journey from Canada as an eleven-year-old boy was now a dim memory. The high temperatures in Spain during the height of the season concerned him a little, but recalling how well Lois had not only coped with but welcomed the heat during her holiday the previous year reassured him. They would take no chances with her health.

He had packed one of his smaller telescopes in the faint hope that there might be opportunities to study some different constellations from the Spanish coast, but realising how well-lit and populated the area was likely to be, he knew this might prove disappointing. He would need to venture further away into the countryside to find the darker skies like the ones Nell had described.

Clancy and Walsh as a company were doing well. The care home contract had another couple of months to run, and Patrick and Joe were taking enormous care with their work, knowing that first impressions were all-important, and that reputation was everything; their future would depend on it. They attended to the small things as well; clearing up and leaving everything tidy at the end of each day, ensuring they always arrived at the site on time or a little early and staying late when they needed to finish a section of the work. In August the weather was invariably fine and the evenings light, but Patrick remarked one day that it would be a different story on cold wet winter days when it grew dark early, and frost and freezing temperatures could slow down operations considerably. They must make the most of the good conditions while they lasted, especially during this crucial first year.

Nell had become used to long days on her own. She didn't mind too much; she spent lots of time with Arthur, who was now four months old and becoming more alert and interesting every day. She took every opportunity to catch upon her reading; her account of the West Cork holiday was now complete, but she was determined not to let motherhood overtake her to the exclusion of all else. On the day a large buff-coloured envelope arrived, she took it and sat down at the breakfast table with trepidation. She guessed it was her 'A' level results.

Patrick had already left for work; Arthur was gurgling in his carry cot.

Why am I so nervous, she asked herself. Whatever the results, it won't make any difference now. My life has changed, I'm not worrying whether I have the right grades for university.

A in English Literature, B in History.

Nell stared down at the piece of paper. It was better, much better than she had dared hope. She had sat the exams when Arthur was less than a month old, she had been breast feeding, sleep-deprived and physically exhausted, so much so that she had almost decided it was too much effort, it was the wrong time, and she had been tempted to give up at that point. But it was worth the struggle, she thought. I did this. I succeeded. Whatever happens, I have these results for always and no one can take them away from me.

When Patrick arrived home and heard the news, he gave a whoop of delight and picked Nell up and spun her round. "You're amazing, do you know that? My clever brainy wife. Arthur take note, you have something to live up to here" He looked down at his son and gave Nell a long loving kiss. "We ought to go out to celebrate".

"Well we can't. Who would babysit at short notice? And anyway, you're tired and it's been a long day. Let's just have fish and chips and a glass of wine at home". Nell was happy just to share her happiness with Patrick; she didn't need to have a night out to do that.

"We're doing ok, aren't we?" Patrick turned to Nell as they sat together on the sofa later sharing a bottle of wine. "Yes, we are. Things are looking up for us at last". Nell said. "It's been quite a day".

Chapter Sixteen

One Saturday afternoon, Nell told Patrick about the offer she had made to Kathleen about a holiday with them in England, and they had their first real argument.

"What were you thinking of Nell?" He was almost shouting. "You've seen what she's like, you know she's bad news. There's no helping her, God knows enough people have tried".

"Surely you can't just write your sister off like that? I just wanted to try to do something for her. She told me how unhappy she is. I don't think she's really had a chance"

"She's had the same chances as the rest of us".

"Well maybe, but I can tell she has a miserable life. Look Patrick, you're doing ok, we all are, I know most of it is through your hard work and effort, but can't we spare a little of our good luck to help Kathleen? I think it would mean a lot to her".

"I can't understand why you're so keen on this idea Nell". Clearly Patrick was still furious. "She wasn't very kind to you, was she?" Nell realised that he had guessed there was more to their conversation in the shop than she had let on. "If she did come here for a couple of weeks, what then? She'd go back to Ireland even more discontented, and we'd have made matters worse. I don't want to hear any more about it. And anyway, there's no space here to have anyone to stay. Let that be an end to it".

He left the room, slamming the door behind him. A moment later she heard his footsteps running down the stairs and the roar of the engine as the van started up. That's the first time he's gone off in a temper like that, Nell thought, and her eyes filled with tears. As if in sympathy, Arthur started to cry. He was teething and had been grouchy that day, which was unusual for him. She was at a loss to know how to make amends with Patrick and knew even less how to withdraw the invitation to Kathleen. It would be worse than never having made the offer in the first place. What a mess. She picked Arthur up and rocked him; he snuggled into her. She had only wanted to do the right thing, but she had misjudged the situation badly and it had backfired.

Two hours later, Patrick returned with a bouquet of flowers and took her in his arms. "I'm so sorry, Nell, I shouldn't have shouted at you. I never meant us to quarrel"

"I'm sorry too Patrick, I should have asked you first. I was only trying to help, and I went about it the wrong way. But you're right, there's no room here for visitors to stay"

"I know you meant well, Nell. Let's leave it for now, we'll have a think about it another time"

The subject was closed, and Arthur, red-faced and grizzly took their attention, so they decided to go for a walk in the September sunshine. After feeding the ducks at the lake in the park, they sat down on a bench together hand in hand, their differences forgotten.

"Remember when we once sat on a bench together, by the river?" Patrick winked at Nell.

"Yes, that was our first date"

"Think how far we've come, Nell. And we're only just getting started". She nodded in agreement.

After a while they walked home by a different route past the care home which was under construction. Patrick pointed out the section he was working on which was just visible through the scaffolding. "I don't see your business signboard anywhere" Nell said, peering through a gap in the hoarding.

"That's because we're sub-contracting to Armstrongs" he explained. "When we work on our own contract one day soon our name board will be there for all to see".

But there were times when that day seemed a long way off. The care home contract was completed by the end of October. There was sufficient work coming in to keep them going after that but as autumn advanced and the nights drew in, Patrick and Joe were forced to accept smaller jobs further away which sometimes only offered enough money for them to break even. In addition, many contractors were due to close down operations for two weeks over Christmas and individual customers postponed work in their homes until after the festive season was over. On a few occasions they worked separately if there was not enough to keep two men occupied on the same job, but they really worked best as a team as they shared a common goal – to make a success of their partnership and to make their name as a reliable, trusted local business.

They decided to take a full week off over Christmas. It was the longest time Patrick and Nell had spent together since the holiday in Ireland, and they were determined to make the most of this first Christmas as a family. Arthur was now eight months old, sitting up unaided and alert to everything going on around him, gazing at the lights Nell had strung along the shelves and reaching out at the shiny ornaments and decorations. Nell served up a traditional Christmas dinner and Patrick commented later how much her cooking had improved in a year. "Well, I have to live up to your Mam's standards now" she retorted, throwing a tea towel at him.

There had been no invitation from Nell's parents over Christmas, but on the day after Boxing Day Nell and Patrick decided to visit them anyway. Evelyn answered the door, and immediately Nell could sense some hostility. Unwillingly, Evelyn invited them in. "Your mother is resting" she said defensively. "She shouldn't be disturbed. Your father is in his study".

Daddy doesn't call it that, thought Nell. It was always his observatory. It was in a way a small thing yet somehow, she felt an overwhelming resentment that Evelyn had taken it upon herself to change the name of something so fundamental in their home. Calling it a study was to diminish her father's passion for astronomy after which the house had been named. She has no right, thought Nell fiercely. Another thought struck her. Why was Evelyn here, surely she would have gone home for a few days over Christmas? Leaving Arthur with Patrick she rushed past Evelyn up the first flight of stairs. Pausing on the landing she peered into each of the rooms.

There was no doubt; Evelyn's belongings were evident in Nell's old bedroom. She's moved in, thought Nell incredulously.

After running up the next flight of stairs to the attic rooms, she calmed herself and knocked on her father's door. She had been instructed to do that as a child; some habits were hard to break.

Neville embraced his daughter and seemed almost emotional to see her. They exchanged pleasantries about Christmas, and he asked after Patrick and Arthur, then Nell came straight to the point.

"Daddy is Evelyn living here now?"

He didn't answer for a moment; the silence was uncomfortable.

"Well yes, she is, as a matter of fact. I'm not happy about it, actually I put up a lot of objections, but I was overruled. Your mother has insisted that Evelyn lives in now. She gets so agitated if I disagree with her about anything, especially where Evelyn is concerned. I don't like to upset her, but the truth is, I'm in a bit of a bind over this. You see, she became used to having her there all the time on that first trip to Spain, and now she's taken it into her head that she will always need a resident nurse".

"Daddy this is your home. It seems like Evelyn is taking over. She is your employee when all's said and done, you decide the terms. And is it good for Mummy to rely on her to this extent?"

"You're right, but I'm in an impossible position. Please try to understand. There are times when I wish she'd never come here. It worked well at first, but it's all gone too far. I just don't know what to do."

He sat down at his desk with his head in his hands. He looks defeated, thought Nell. Poor Daddy. He's looked after Mummy through so much, he's always done what he thought was best and now that they should be enjoying life together there are still so many problems.

"Can I do anything to help, Daddy?"

"Not really. You have enough to do with looking after Arthur, and Patrick has his business to take care of. I think it's down to me to sort this out, I will find a way. It won't be easy, I feel completely outmanoeuvred". He forced a smile. "But please don't let this stop you coming here. It's been lovely to see you. You belong here, you know" he added suddenly. "This is your home; it always will be". Neville kissed his daughter and followed her down the two flights of stairs to see Patrick and Arthur. Evelyn had not offered them tea, and shortly afterwards they took their leave, promising to visit again soon.

During the drive home, Nell explained the situation to Patrick. He could see how worried Nell was and tried to reassure her. "But really, it's for your father to decide what to do. If you interfere it could make it worse. Let's just visit him more often, we won't let Evelyn put us off. At least if we know what's going on we can take action if ever we need to".

Nell had to be content with that, but she was very quiet for the rest of the journey. Her father's last words came back to her suddenly: 'This is your home; it always will be'. Why had he said that, she wondered. And why now? It was puzzling. But perhaps there was more to this situation than she knew. The answers will come, she thought, I will just have to be patient.

Chapter Seventeen

1981

It rained constantly until the first week of February. Some of the construction sites were flooded and many men were laid off. Patrick and Joe felt themselves fortunate that they had booked in some indoor work after Christmas; enough to keep them going; laying bricks was often out of the question so they turned their hands to anything they could find; sometimes small painting jobs, and now and then fitting cupboards or wardrobes as Joe had learned some carpentry skills from his father. Later that month the weather improved, and they were able to start work on a hotel extension in Lamberham. This was a large-scale renovation and the first contract they had bid for independently. It would last them at least until the summer and they both felt a sense of relief that they had come through the worst of the winter without having to down tools.

Their friendship with Jonathan and Barbara had gone from strength to strength, despite the age difference. Nell sometimes pushed Arthur in his stroller round to their house in the afternoon if the weather was fine; Barbara was always pleased to see them both and took an interest in hearing all Nell's news. Nell found herself able to talk to Barbara about anything, she was a good listener. She told Barbara about her concerns for her parents, Evelyn's increasing presence at Moongarth, and when she explained the quandary she was in regarding Kathleen and the tense, strained relationship with her sister-in-law, Barbara looked thoughtful.

"I can see your predicament" she said at last, gazing down at Arthur who had fallen asleep on her lap. "But Patrick is right, sometimes it's hard to help people, even when you can tell how much they are suffering. What do you think Kathleen would want to do, if she could choose? I mean, how would she like to change her life?"

"Probably to leave Ballymere, find a different job, something more interesting. And I know she is unhappy with her husband. That might be the most difficult thing of all to solve; Bridget, her mother is a strong Catholic, and anyway divorce is not an option in Ireland".

"Mmm. It is a difficult one. Leave it with me for now, I might have an idea, but I need to think about it".

Nell was open-mouthed. "Barbara, I didn't expect you to solve my problems! I only told you because, well, because I knew you would understand. It's just nice to be able to get someone else's point of view".

"I know that. But Jonathan and I struggled when we were young; we started out in rented rooms with no money, Jonathan was studying. But we had a lot of help to get where we are now, life hasn't always been easy. We've often said that if we can help other people out, we should. Pop round next week and I'll maybe have a suggestion for you".

She kissed Nell and Arthur, and they took their leave. Nell could not stop herself thinking how kind people could be; Jonathan had given Patrick and Joe a great deal of help to get started in business, and now here was Barbara trying her best to help her through another dilemma. Things have a way of working out, she thought.

Just as Nell turned round the corner, the heavens opened and she hurried home, trying to escape the worst of the rain. I must learn to drive soon, she said to herself. She had planned to do so ever since the trip to Ireland and it didn't matter that she could not afford a car of her own; it was another step towards adulthood, she thought. One afternoon when Caroline came round for a cup of tea, Nell mentioned the idea to her friend.

Caroline, who was by then halfway through her nurses training, was all in favour. "Have proper lessons with a driving school like I did" she suggested. "I could stay with Arthur if you arrange the lessons when I'm not at work".

Nell told Patrick later and said that with his agreement she would find the money for some lessons out of their savings.

She was very conscious of having no income of her own but surprisingly he offered to pay for the first ten lessons for her. "We're doing ok", he said. "It's important for you to learn and I haven't really the time to teach you myself".

March came. Their lives had become so busy that the plan for driving lessons had been shelved for the time being and she had given very little thought about Evelyn moving into Moongarth. I must go and see Daddy about this again soon, she thought. But today her plans were to visit Barbara.

"Jonathan and I have had a chat about your sister-in-law", she said, taking Nell's coat and helping her lift Arthur from the stroller.

When they were seated and Barbara had poured them some coffee, Nell said "It's so kind of you to be concerned. But...."

"It's ok. Here's a suggestion, it's just an idea. Jonathan will need someone to work in the office later this year, answering the phone, some reception work, do a bit of filing. Susanne is due to go on maternity leave in a few months' time and in any case, they are moving away. How about if we offer the job to Kathleen? Would she be able to do that?"

"She's only ever worked in a shop. She's not got many qualifications. I think she would jump at the chance, but I don't know if she would be suitable...." Nell's voice faltered; it was a wonderful offer from Barbara, but could Kathleen fit in? She could be so sullen, so unfriendly; a receptionist needed to be smiling, engaging, professional. "The other thing is, we would need to find her somewhere to live. There's no room at the flat".

"We've thought about that as well. We have an annex here, it's self-contained. We were expecting Jonathan's mother to come and live in it but sadly she passed away last year. It would be a low rent. What do you say? Why not talk it over with Patrick and see what he thinks?"

Nell was overcome with gratitude and sheer amazement that Jonathan and Barbara had made this offer. She couldn't wait to tell Patrick later.

At first, he was slightly annoyed that she had confided in Barbara about his sister. "It's a family matter Nell" he said, and for a moment she thought he was going to lose his temper with her all over again. But when Nell explained Barbara's proposition, he was astonished.

"It's really good of them to make that offer". Patrick was completely taken aback. "Why would they do this? They've never even met her. If they had they might not be so keen" he added with a wry smile.

"They're good people, Patrick. They have this vacancy, and they've offered it up for Kathleen, knowing she wants to come over here. It could be the making of her. It would be wrong for us to deny her this chance without even asking her about it".

"Could she do it though? She would have to smarten up her act, show a bit of initiative, keep off the booze and stop feeling so sorry for herself. And if it went wrong, it would look bad on us". At that moment Patrick could see only drawbacks to the plan.

"Let me write to Kathleen and see what she thinks. From what I know about her she will jump at the chance and make it work. But it's up to her how she deals with Michael and your Mam. Those are things we can't sort out for her".

In the end Patrick agreed, and for the next hour or so he was unusually quiet. As Nell sat writing to Kathleen that evening when Arthur was in bed, he looked at her fondly. "You're the best woman in the world, do you know that? I knew my luck was in the moment I saw you that day at college. And you can tell Kathleen I'll send her the money for the ferry".

* * *

Kathleen met the postman the following Friday morning as she walked to work. She rarely received handwritten letters, but it made a change from bills, she thought ruefully. The letter had come from England, but she did not recognise the handwriting. She had dismissed the conversation with Nell about a holiday; she had become so used to disappointments that she no longer believed in promises.

There was a queue forming outside the shop and as Mrs Byrne unlocked the door at half a minute to eight, no earlier, Kathleen realised she would not have time to read the letter until later. As luck would have it, the shop was busy all morning and Mrs Byrne came out of the storeroom to serve customers with her, so there was no opportunity for Kathleen to open it until she went home at lunchtime.

She sat down in her cluttered sitting room with a cup of tea and unfolded the sheets of paper.

As she read, her eyes widened in astonishment and her mouth dropped open. It was not about a holiday. Nell had found her a job! A job in England as a receptionist! This couldn't be right, there must be some mistake; that sort of good luck didn't happen in real life, not in her life anyway. Her eyes quickly scanned the letter, and she became suspicious. But here it was, in black and white, Nell's friends were offering her an office job, starting in September. Something worthwhile and interesting, not mundane like pricing boxes of cornflakes and selling packets of tea to people who said the same thing to her, day in, day out. Her next thought was that as a receptionist she could wear smart clothes and makeup to work like Gráinne instead of the dull brown tabard she was used to putting on every day. She could mix with important people who would be polite to her and treat her with respect. Then she brought herself back down to earth. It couldn't be true. It must be a joke, a cruel hoax.

She read on. It was not a joke. Nell's friend also had offered her somewhere to live, an annex, whatever that was. This was even better, it was unbelievable. And in the next paragraph she read that Patrick would send her the fare to England. They had thought of everything. All she needed to do was decide whether to accept and to let them know as soon as she could make arrangements.

Her tea grew cold and was left untouched. For an hour, Kathleen sat lost in thought. Miracles do happen, she said to herself. My life can change. All I have to do is take this chance.

Her mind went back to Nell and suddenly Kathleen was overcome with remorse. It was an emotion she had rarely experienced, but she suddenly remembered her unkind and vindictive words to Nell in the shop and in O'Malley's. Nell had not deserved that treatment, and she, Kathleen certainly did not deserve this life-changing opportunity that Nell had found for her. Kathleen realised that Nell had been better than her word and had done this because she cared. Cared enough to give her a chance despite all that had happened between them. Her mind went back to the day when she saw the newspaper cutting of Nell and Patrick at the dinner. She had been jealous then, she recalled, even before meeting her sister-in-law, but also remembered seeing something in Nell's expression in that photo, something she could not define then and even now she could not characterise. She is a very special person, she thought, to do this for me. Already, Kathleen was determined to accept the offer but had no idea how she would ever be able to thank her sister-in-law.

She wondered what she would say to Michael, but it struck her that probably he would not really care if she announced that she was leaving him to work in England. He might not even believe her, he would just laugh and think she was joking. That didn't matter so much, she had long realised that there were no feelings on either side, there never really had been, but the conversation with her parents might not be so easy.

* * *

March went by in a flash. It was Arthur's first birthday at the end of April; he had already started to pull himself up to a standing position and take a few wobbly first steps. Later the following month Nell realised she was pregnant.

When she told Patrick that there would be a new baby soon after Christmas, he looked stunned and more than a little concerned.

"Don't look so surprised, you surely know what's caused it" she joked. They both laughed and he took her in his arms.

"Well, we did want more children, it's just a bit sooner than I thought", he murmured, kissing her. "But we will be even more cramped for space here. I think we will need to move before the baby's born".

Business as always was at the forefront of Patrick's mind. He and Joe often worked on Saturday mornings as well as long hours through the week; time was money, and they had both agreed to reach a certain financial goal by the end of the first year. He was conscious of the fact that they could not stand still; at this stage they were only as secure as the next contract. They needed to have some reserves, and the business would need investment if it were to grow. He realised that although they were doing well and work was coming in regularly, buying a bigger home was going to place a strain on their finances; it was something he and Nell had discussed but they had decided they could manage for a while longer. A new baby on the way had changed that. Somehow, he would need to find a solution before Christmas.

Chapter Eighteen
1981

It was late July before Nell decided to tell her parents about the pregnancy. In fact, they told Barbara and Jonathan and Joe and Caroline as soon as three months had elapsed, but Nell felt a curious reluctance to give her own mother this news, knowing it would not be received with great enthusiasm and could be a source of further unhappiness to her, possibly causing her a return to earlier sadness and painful memories.

She went to find her father first. He was alone in the garden at Moongarth, carefully tying up some delphiniums. The flowers stood in a tall clump of deep blue at the far edge of the border, a vibrant bank of colour against the darkness of the hedge. Neville hugged her and offered his congratulations, shook Patrick by the hand and seemed genuinely happy for them both. He took Arthur from Patrick for a moment and Nell saw real affection in his eyes for his grandson. "We are off on holiday again in a week's time" he said. "It's the only time I can take three weeks off. But actually, I've decided to retire. I shall be leaving Kirchington at Christmas, well at the end of next term, possibly earlier. I have my reasons, and I've made some decisions".

Nell looked at her father sharply, but it was clear that he wasn't going to go into details there and then. I wonder if this is to do with Mummy or Evelyn, she pondered.

"Don't tell your mother, about the baby I mean. I'll tell her later. Sometimes you must pick your moments for these things. But I'm so pleased for you both".

Nell and Patrick went into the house to see her mother who was busy packing with Evelyn. Lois ignored Arthur and was too preoccupied to notice that her daughter had put on a slight amount of weight, but Evelyn looked at her quizzically. Nell wished them a pleasant holiday and said that she would visit them again on their return from Spain. She went to kiss her mother and would have liked to stay longer but Evelyn looked at her with hostility, and Nell felt uncomfortable. "Your mother's busy" she said disapprovingly.

"She's up to something, that Evelyn" said Patrick as they drove away. "I wonder if she has her eye on your father?"

"Surely not". Nell was stunned by the suggestion but once again she felt that Evelyn's behaviour and motives were suspicious. "Daddy would never look at another woman, he loves Mummy so much"

"Well, she definitely has some sort of control over your mother. It's almost as if she's trying to isolate her from the rest of the family. I don't think your mother looks any worse physically since I last saw her, but she seems to be away with the fairies a lot of the time".

"She has taken away a lot of Mummy's independence. I had high hopes of Evelyn when she first came, and so did Daddy, but it's not turned out how either of us expected. She is totally reliant on Evelyn now, Daddy can see it, but I think he's frightened to do anything about it in case she leaves. Then there's the question of that money that went missing. He shouldn't have let that go. It was quite a surprise that he's decided to retire early. He's sixty-one, so I suppose he can retire at any time. I just thought he would carry on for a few years yet. He loves teaching so there must be more to it".

"It's a puzzle" agreed Patrick as he parked the van. "But not ours to solve, we've enough of our own to be going on with".

Later that day he found Nell in tears in the bedroom. "What is it Nelly", he asked, taking her in his arms.

"It's Mummy. Well Evelyn really. Mummy didn't want anything to do with Arthur, and Evelyn more or less asked me to leave and said Mummy was too busy to talk to me. How dare she! How did things ever get to this, Patrick? Now I'm not even allowed to speak to my own mother. Evelyn's turned her against all of us, including Daddy. And there's more to it, I think she is trying to swindle them somehow. But Daddy is so naïve and trusting. And there's nothing more I can do about it".

Patrick did not know what to say or how to comfort her.

* * *

As expected, Kathleen had lost no time in accepting the offer of a job working for Jonathan. Patrick met her at Fishguard early one Sunday morning in September and was surprised to see that she had made a huge effort with her appearance, even for travelling. Her hair was trimmed stylishly into a neat bob, her trousers and jacket looked new, and her fingernails were manicured. "I nearly didn't recognise you" said Patrick, thinking what a difference he could see in her.

"Well, when I left Byrne's, I found I had some holiday pay owing to me" Kathleen explained. "So I thought, start as you mean to go on, I will need to be smart for this job. I'm thinking I shall have to have an interview first, and I splashed out on some new clothes".

Patrick thought privately that despite the outward transformation, Kathleen would need to show a better attitude than she had in the past and adopt a more friendly manner than he was used to seeing if she were to succeed in this new position. Is she capable of changing her ways, he wondered. But if Jonathan and Barbara are prepared to give her a chance despite knowing her situation, then so must I. How many people would offer someone a job without even having met them? There is no doubt, they are very special people.

Kathleen's first impressions of Wales and then England were all positive ones; she liked the look of the busy bustling towns with large shopping centres and crowded streets. "There's more life here" she said, catching a glimpse of a fashionable department store and later looking on in amazement at the three lanes of traffic on the motorway. "This is nothing – you should see it at eight o'clock on a Monday morning" Patrick laughed, and glanced at her,

155

noticing her surprise, and realised just how narrow her life had been until then. "You forget I've never even been to Dublin" she reminded him. Cork is the biggest city I've ever seen".

When they stopped for refreshments at a motorway service station Patrick was relieved to see that Kathleen asked for tea and not for alcohol. So far, so good. He ventured to ask his sister how her plans for working in England had been received by the family; the subject can't be avoided forever, he thought.

"If you want to know the truth, I think Michael was glad to see the back of me" she said, her tone defiant. "It was a mistake, you know, him and me. We should never have got married. Well, you know the rest". She sipped her tea. "Mam, well that's a different matter. It all came as a bit of a shock to her. She was pleased that you and Nell had found me this job and somewhere to live, in fact she didn't believe it at first. Neither did I, when I read Nell's letter. I thought someone was playing tricks on me. Anyway, Mam understands that it wasn't working out with Michael, she's known that for a long time, but she was quite understanding in the end. She seems to be ok with us living apart for now. As far as I'm concerned, we will never get back together, but divorce, well that's not going to happen, is it".

Kathleen looked round her and leaned in towards her brother. "I'd like to buy Nell a present" she said, remembering with embarrassment how badly she had treated her sister-in-law. "And something for Arthur".

"Nell won't expect anything," said Patrick. "There's no need". But Kathleen insisted so they wandered into the shop and bought some flowers for Nell and a fluffy rabbit for Arthur. "We have another baby on the way" said Patrick, as they left the service station and joined the motorway again. "Due early next year".

Kathleen was delighted and murmured her congratulations. She really does seem different, happier, thought Patrick. Perhaps Nell had the right idea after all. But it's early days yet, he reminded himself. As they drove on, she asked him about the Grants, their house and where she would be living. "Kirchington's a grand place to live. It's quite a busy town, decent shops and restaurants, a bit of night life. Not that Nell and I see much of that" he added jokingly. "There's a river and a park, a theatre and a cinema. The Grants live a little way out of town, it's a nice area. But you'll be able to walk to work, and it's only a short bus ride away from our flat".

They stopped at the flat first. Nell was equally astonished at the change in Kathleen and was surprised to see her sister-in-law make a fuss of her nephew who gurgled happily as he reached out for the rabbit. After sitting down together for an early dinner, Patrick took Kathleen to meet the Grants. She felt suddenly shy, but they gave her a warm welcome and over a cup of tea asked after her family and the journey from Ireland. Then they took her to see her accommodation and to get settled in.

The annex was attached to the main house but had its own front door. It was ideal for one person, comprising a living room, bedroom, kitchen and bathroom all on one level. In keeping with the rest of the house it was tastefully decorated with comfortable furnishings and modern accessories. To Kathleen it was sheer luxury; like a dream come true – she had only ever imagined how it would be to live in such a place. I shall love living here, she said to herself; even cleaning will be a pleasure.

How did this happen? For the first time in her life she felt that the tide was turning, that here she had an opportunity to make something of herself. By some miracle she had been given a second chance.

Chapter Nineteen

Kathleen made a promising start at Cunningham and Grant. Susanne stayed on for a week to give a 'handover', as she called it, so she was able to show her the filing system, the partners' diaries and how to book in appointments. Callers in person were easy, she said, if they don't have an appointment fit them in with Jonathan there and then if you can, otherwise arrange for them to come in on the next available date. Mr Cunningham is out with clients most of the time, she added, so he won't see anyone who's not booked in.

"And don't worry, you won't need to know anything about accounts", Susanne reassured her, laughing at Kathleen's horrified face as she tidied up a stack of papers, the contents of which looked to her like a foreign language.

Kathleen took special note of Susanne's pleasant manner with clients, how she smiled and welcomed callers and asked them to sit down and offered them a cup of coffee while they were waiting. She learned how to transfer calls into the partner's offices and when to arrange a call-back. During quiet moments she was expected to open the post and link it up with client's files, clear the filing at the end of each day, water the plants and generally keep the reception area tidy. It all seemed straightforward when Susanne explained it, but Kathleen felt very nervous at the thought of facing clients without anyone there to help her. Working together side by side that week was a plan thought up by Barbara, knowing that this was a huge change for Kathleen. On her first morning, as she sat alone behind the reception desk before clients started to arrive, Jonathan came out of his office to chat to her.

"I'm so pleased to have you on the team, Kathleen" he said warmly. "If there's anything you're not sure about just ask Fiona, my secretary, she's in the office next to mine. And if you do make the odd mistake, well it can always be put right, you know. It's been a pleasure working with your brother, he's quite a family man now, isn't he, and the business is doing well".

Kathleen nodded and thanked him, and thought to herself how different it was going to be from working at Byrnes.

The day went quickly; the office was busy, being a Monday and there was a steady stream of people calling in, some to deliver papers, some to make appointments or attend a meeting. Later in the afternoon a young man who was a delivery courier stopped to chat. "You'll get to know me, I'm Andy" he said, seeing that Kathleen was new to the job. "I call in most days. I can take your post if you have it ready for mailing".

The telephone system gave her the most difficulty. On the second morning she failed to put a call through to Jonathan correctly and Fiona came out to show her again. But it was not a disaster, each day things became easier. She began to enjoy the job and to recognise regular clients. I used to serve the same customers day after day in Ballymere, she said to herself, but somehow this is different. Occasionally they said how much they liked hearing her Irish accent. Kathleen had never really thought about it before; it was something she took for granted but at times it was very strong. On a day when a client failed to understand what she was saying, she realised she might need to modify her speech a little. I shall take notice of how Nell and Barbara speak, she decided. Here it's important work, it's not the same as when people used to come into the shop for a pint of milk. Jonathan had spoken seriously to her at the beginning about how everything she saw and heard in the office was confidential. I'm trusted with information now, she reflected, and the for the first time in her life she felt valued as a person. She looked forward to going home at night as well; stopping off at the local supermarket to buy something nice she had chosen for her dinner, and then to cook in that beautiful kitchen and watch what she wanted on TV. She was able to please herself now and felt truly independent. She had hardly given Michael a thought since arriving in England.

Sometimes Kathleen went window shopping in her lunch break. She had brought a small amount of money with her from Ireland but had to make it last until pay day, so she resisted the urge to buy anything she didn't need. Barbara had said she could start paying rent at the end of the month which was a great help.

Everything seemed perfect. What was that phrase she had read somewhere in a magazine? Living the dream? Kathleen really felt that she was.

* * *

One Wednesday evening towards the end of October Nell and Patrick were surprised to be invited to Moongarth at short notice and not altogether pleased.

Nell was nearly seven months into her second pregnancy and feeling particularly fatigued after a difficult day with Arthur who was teething again, walking unsteadily and bumping into everything around their tiny flat. He was normally a placid child but that day he had been grizzly and cross. Patrick was working long hours to ensure that the final stage of the hotel contract was completed on time, ready for inspection. He was tired, stressed and under pressure, as was Joe; he was looking forward to a shower, a hot meal and a beer, and to relax with Nell for a couple of hours after Arthur was settled.

As it was, they rushed their meal and left for Drover's Cross soon after seven o'clock. Nell always tried to keep Arthur to a bedtime routine so was not happy to bring him out into the cold autumn evening but something about her father's summons sounded urgent so could not be ignored or declined.

Neville answered the door and ushered them in to the drawing room where Lois was sitting. She smiled at them uncertainly. Evelyn was nowhere to be seen at first but a few minutes later she came into the room and sat down beside Lois. Neville looked angry at the interruption; he had intended this to be a private family discussion. As usual, he said nothing, but his frustration was plain to see.

After the usual pleasantries and deciding against allowing Arthur to crawl or totter round the room, Patrick lifted his son onto his lap. Neville cleared his throat and addressed his daughter and son-in law.

"I expect you're wondering why we've asked you here tonight?"

"Well yes Dad, it sounded important on the phone".

"So, you know your mother and I are planning to go to Spain again, soon after I retire?"

"You told us you'd decided to retire at the end of term. I didn't realise you were going to Spain for Christmas? But that will be lovely for you both (Nell emphasised the word 'both' deliberately), you will have some winter sunshine".

"Yes, well......." Neville got up and walked around the room, looking slightly awkward. Lois, who until then had said nothing, suddenly spoke:

"It's not for a holiday. Your father has decided that we will move there permanently".

Neville looked at his wife with slight impatience.

"We've decided" he said firmly.

Nell was astonished. "You mean for good? Not just a holiday?"

"No, we've made up our mind to live in Spain".

Lois forced a smile and Nell wondered if there was a touch of resignation or defeat in her expression.

"We've all known for some time that your mother does need a warmer climate and to live somewhere more suitable. She can't manage here any longer".

"We will be leaving on the fourteenth of December," said Lois. "Evelyn is coming with us". She looked at Neville, now with a touch of defiance. "A lot of our packing has been done and there are a few more arrangements to be made, but we are more or less ready".

"You've kept it very quiet, Mum" said Nell, still reeling from this announcement. "Yes of course I can see that the warmer weather has helped you so much, it makes sense to spend more time there…. but what about this house, is it going on the market?"

Neville stood with his back to the fireplace. "That's what I was coming to. We are offering you Moongarth, lock stock and barrel. Unencumbered, no mortgage, no strings attached. It will belong to you and Patrick. I have drawn up the Deed of Gift with my solicitor. All you have to do is accept". He let his words hang in the air.

Nell and Patrick were speechless. Lois's expression was inscrutable. The only sound was from Arthur, murmuring and wriggling on Patrick's lap.

After a few moments, Neville continued. "Of course, I have an ulterior motive. My dearest wish is for Moongarth to remain in the family. Arthur, and your baby, when he or she arrives, will be the fifth generation of our family to live here". He looked at Arthur with fondness. "But obviously I want you and Patrick to have a decent home, and you do need somewhere larger".

Patrick felt slightly put out at the last remark. His eyes met Nell's, and something told her to defer to her husband over this matter. She knew he had been trying to find them a larger flat or a small house soon after they knew about the pregnancy, but he had taken his eye off the ball just recently. There was so little time lately for him to do anything except work and sleep. But Patrick resented the inference that he was neglecting his responsibilities to Nell and his growing family, and now it seemed as though his father-in-law was riding to the rescue with a grand gesture with which he could not hope to compete. Deciding that he needed to assert himself before Neville put him at any further disadvantage, he spoke at last, respectfully but firmly:

"Thank you, sir. It's a very generous offer you have made there. But if you don't mind, I'd like to talk to Nell later about this. There is a lot to think about. We can't just give you an answer immediately".

Neville looked a little surprised. "I would have thought you would have jumped at the chance. You're not likely to get another offer like this, you know. But of course, you two have a chat and we'll see you.... let's see, time is short.... this weekend?"

Evelyn had listened attentively to all that was being said. To Nell's astonishment, she seemed to agree with Patrick. "Of course it's an unsuitable plan. Patrick will want to make his own arrangements for his family. Young people need to make their own way without accepting handouts. He will wish to be independent and move somewhere more modern, closer to the town. I'm surprised you suggested it Neville".

Neville was visibly furious at Evelyn's intervention. Clearly it was taking every ounce of his self-control not to remind her that this was a family matter and one on which she had no business in offering an opinion. But Lois nodded as if Evelyn had every right to comment.

The atmosphere became tense and for a while no one spoke. Nell felt irritated that Evelyn had forced her way into the conversation and that no one seemed willing to challenge her or point out that this matter did not concern her. There was a long silence, and it soon became clear that nothing more was going to be said; it was as though Evelyn's unsolicited remarks had stifled any further debate.

Patrick could see that Nell was looking exhausted and quite overcome by the turn of events, and as Arthur had by then dropped off to sleep in his arms, they made their excuses and left, Patrick agreeing that they would meet Neville a few days later to discuss the proposition further.

Patrick was very quiet on the way home and neither of them spoke a word until Arthur was settled in bed and they had sat down with a cup of tea.

"That's a grand offer your father has made us" Patrick said at last. "I don't know what to make of it at all".

Nell said nothing. If it had been up to her alone, she would have accepted in a heartbeat. She could see immediately

163

the advantages of living back in her childhood home; plenty of space for them all, safe gardens for the children to play in, lots of outdoor buildings for Patrick to store tools, vehicles, materials. It would be perfect. And of course, she had a sentimental attachment to Moongarth which was hard to fight against. But Evelyn's words had disturbed her; it was worrying to contemplate how much influence she might have on such an important subject.

But it was not solely Nell's choice to make. Patrick was a proud man, despite his humble beginnings. This was what marriage is really like, she thought. Compromise. Considering each other's needs and points of view. Sometimes giving way to the other. We are a team, not just two individuals. The realisation made her hold back and wait for Patrick to continue.

"I'm not completely happy about it, Nell. I know it's a fine house, and we would be set up for life. I could never have dreamed of living in such a place, let alone owning it". His voice became earnest, and his accent became more pronounced as it always did when he was tired or anxious. "But can you understand, I would always feel under an obligation to your mother and father, that it wasn't through my own efforts, it was because my wife had rich parents. I'd feel less of a man...." His voice tailed off.

"I do understand Patrick ". Nell said, putting her arms round his neck. They were silent for a moment. Then she placed his hand on her bump. The baby was kicking now, as it often did in the evening.

"He's a fine strong fellow" laughed Patrick, momentarily distracted.

"Let's go to bed and sleep on it. It's been a long day, and it's a big decision, not one we should be making when we're both tired".

Patrick murmured his agreement and no more was said. They switched off the light, checked on Arthur and settled into bed. Nell often found it difficult to find a comfortable position but this time she fell asleep immediately. Patrick laid awake for an hour, mulling everything over in his mind, unable to come to any conclusions. Nell was right, it was too late to think clearly. The answer would come in the morning.

Surprisingly, it did.

Chapter Twenty

After Nell and Patrick had left Moongarth, Neville was very quiet. Evelyn had gone to bed, and he and Lois remained in the drawing room alone; this was a rarity. He sat preoccupied for half an hour with a glass of whiskey, not a usual nighttime habit for him but sometimes it helped him think. Finally, he said to Lois:

"Do you know, I'm worried that I might have offended Patrick".

She looked up from her magazine.

"Yes, I think you did, Neville. He probably thought you were being patronising. You made him feel a failure by offering him the house in the way you did". Lois could be perceptive at times, but seldom offered an opinion unless asked, except on the subject of Evelyn. "Put yourself in his shoes. He's come here to England with nothing, a few pounds in his pocket and only his hard labour to offer. Then he meets our daughter and suddenly he's pitched into a different world. Of course he's offended. He wants to do things his way, and he's working very hard at his business to make that happen".

This was a long speech for Lois, and Neville, surprised at her reproving tone, immediately took notice. He realised that any disapproval she once felt for Patrick had gone; but he sensed something else at work, something more subtle. Maybe by giving in to his wishes about Spain and his plans for Moongarth she was trading this for his acceptance of Evelyn in their future. The games some women play, he said to himself. He had never thought of Lois as devious. But he brought his mind back to the matter in hand.

"What do you think I should do?"

"Go and talk to him, man to man. Apologise. Find out what he really thinks about the offer. And don't be upset. This isn't all about what you want".

So, on Thursday evening, Neville telephoned Patrick and asked him out for a drink at the Bridge Tavern the following Saturday.

Patrick arrived first and ordered a round; a pint of Guinness for himself and a local craft beer for his father-in-law. Being early gave him a slight edge, he felt. He never seemed to have the upper hand with Neville although on most levels their relationship was genial.

After a few minutes Neville arrived, and they made their way to a corner table.

"Cheers" said Neville, sipping his drink.

"Slainte" replied Patrick, raising his glass. The two men sat in silence for a moment.

"I've come to apologise" said Neville after a while, removing his raincoat and laying it over the back of a chair. "What I said the other night was clumsy and insensitive. I should have gone about this differently". He took another sip of his beer.

This visibly took the wind out of Patrick's sails. "No need to apologise, sir" he said gruffly. "I'm just a little unsure about the whole thing, to be honest. But I can't accept such an offer. I don't need charity. I can provide for your daughter and grandchildren you know".

"Yes Patrick I do know that, and I respect you for it. You'd rather do things your way. I just wanted to make life easier for you, that's all"

There was a few more moments silence while they drained their glasses.

"So, I have another proposition for you. You have many skills, a great deal of experience in the building trade. Moongarth is long overdue for modernisation. Of course, Lois and I did a great deal to it when we were first married, and structurally it's as sound as a bell, but it really needs another facelift now. How about if you take on some major renovations instead of repaying me? A complete restoration?" He surveyed his empty beer glass and paused, then continued. "You could take out a mortgage to finance the work once you have ownership. You may even make a little profit on the sale of your flat. Then, as the work is completed or even during the transition, you could use the house as an example of your workmanship for Clancy and Walsh, you know, showcase the project, a portfolio, free advertising. So it wouldn't be just a gift from us, it would be a business asset – long term, I know, but at the end of it you would have added thousands to its value, and your skills, your vision, your hard work would be your investment. And a tremendous boost to your business. What do you think?"

Patrick didn't know what to say for a moment. He realised suddenly that this was more than a gift; Neville had thrown down a challenge. He would have responsibility for a huge project, it would give him prestige and status in the area and could create untold business opportunities for him. He could take on more men; electricians, plumbers, plasterers, and provide them with the security of long-term work. He could perhaps bring in his brother Niall as an apprentice. Plus, it would be a wonderful home for them all.

"Thank you, Neville," he said at last. It was the first time he had used his father-in-law's first name, but it gave him a sense of being on an equal footing with him; however generous this offer, Patrick refused to feel beholden. "I do like the idea of this being a business opportunity rather than a hand-out. It's a grand house now but it would be an honour to be in charge of such a project and redesign it. But I have Joe to consider, he is my partner; how will he fit into this plan? I want to talk to him about this, and Nell and I will discuss it some more later. I shall also need to consult my accountant. Perhaps you can come with us? I'm sorry, I know you are keen to have matters settled but if I'm going to take this on, I need to have the right advice. Let's just say I agree in principle for now".

Neville looked slightly disappointed; he had wanted to have matters decided there and then. But he felt a sense of admiration for Patrick; clearly, he was intent on doing things properly and fairly and would not be rushed; that in itself was a sign that he could be trusted with this undertaking.

With that, the two men shook hands, and Neville ordered another round of drinks. After a while they took leave of each other; Neville took a taxi back to Drover's Cross and Patrick walked back to the flat with his head in a whirl.

When Patrick told Nell of her father's idea of total modernisation of Moongarth and that he, Patrick would be in charge of it as a business proposition rather than as an outright gift, she was careful to moderate her reaction. Inwardly she was overjoyed at the prospect of moving back to Moongarth and the difference it would make to their lives in so many ways. But mindful of Patrick's sensitivity on the subject, she focused on the business benefits that it would bring, and how he would have a free hand in the design and control over the whole project. But Joe must also agree, and she realised that could be problematic. He was a partner but would not have legal ownership. Perhaps Jonathan could find a solution. Patrick explained the idea to Joe the following morning, and he agreed that it was a wonderful chance for them both if his own position in the business could be safeguarded.

Two days later the three men sat in the reception area of Cunningham and Grant, having been greeted by Kathleen. Patrick was astonished at her transformation; is this really my sister, he wondered, watching her announce their arrival to Jonathan, find their file and offer them coffee. Neville said how pleased he was to meet her and that she must come for a cup of tea at Moongarth before they left for Spain. What a kind man Nell's father is, she thought as she showed them into Jonathan's office.

Jonathan listened while Patrick and Neville outlined the plan. He asked several questions, made some notes and was careful to ask Joe his views. He could see no problem in applying for the finance with Moongarth as security and the day-to-day business income supporting the repayments. But the sticking point would be that Clancy and Walsh could only provide one year's accounts; any lender would need more than that. Their business forecast for the coming year would help but Jonathan could see some difficulties ahead.

"You would need to offer up any profit you make on the flat to be included as your investment in the project" he said to Patrick. "But I think most banks would expect more". He turned to Neville. "Would you be willing to act as guarantor?"

There followed a discussion on what that would involve. Neville pointed out that he would be a pensioner very soon, albeit his teacher's pension would be generous. "But I have stocks, bonds I could assign" he said at last. "I am willing to stand as guarantor if that will satisfy the bank". Patrick studied his father-in-law for a long moment. He really is putting everything on the line for us, he thought and suddenly understood just how much it meant to Neville for his daughter and son-in-law to become the next owners of Moongarth.

Joe's position in the scheme was equally difficult to resolve. He was by law a business partner, but Moongarth would belong to Patrick and Nell. Joe had been pleased to hear about Patrick's extraordinary piece of good fortune and wanted to continue to work with him but found the situation complicated.

After a while, Jonathan had a suggestion. "You could dissolve the partnership" he said thoughtfully. "Patrick can repay your initial investment out of the bank loan. He can form a new company or start again as a sole trader for the duration of the project, and you could either form your own company and work with him or become a salaried employee of Patrick's new business. That way you will have no liability for the bank loan, but you can still work together".

At that point Neville, having made the offer of his commitment to the plan could see that it would be prudent to leave the others to discuss the matter without him so took his leave, reminding Kathleen as he left about the invitation to tea. After agreeing to tell Jonathan of their decision later, Patrick and Joe made their way to the Bridge Tavern, and two pints of Guinness later came to the decision that they would take Jonathan's advice and Joe would work for Patrick as contract manager. It need not affect how they worked together day to day, but it would clear up the legal and financial position. Joe would also be able to oversee the other building work currently in the pipeline and help Patrick tender for new contracts.

As they sat there, deciding against a third pint as it was lunchtime, they both reflected on their first meeting on the ferry from Ireland less than three years ago, when they were just hopeful of finding any paid work and making a modest living. Now here they were, in business together, talking in terms of a major contract with a huge budget. "And a lot of debt to the bank, if it all goes ahead" said Patrick with a nervous laugh.

At the weekend Nell and Patrick paid another visit to Neville and Lois, and Patrick thanked them again for the opportunity they had given him and said that they would be pleased to accept. Evelyn was present as usual; this time she said little but had an air of anger and extreme disapproval which Nell found hard to fathom. But she dismissed her concerns; today was a turning point in all their lives and she felt a huge debt of gratitude to her father for presenting the idea in a way that Patrick had felt able to accept. The agreement was sealed with a bottle of champagne and orange juice for Nell, while Arthur slept on Patrick's lap. Plans were made to put the Kirchington flat on the market and to arrange to move to Moongarth within the next few weeks.

A few days later, Caroline looked after Arthur while Neville, Lois, Patrick and Nell attended the office of Dawson and Gould, solicitors in Kirchington to sign the Deed of Gift, and then went on to the Golden Lion for a celebration lunch. This time, to Nell's relief Evelyn was not with them. They had not been there since the wedding two years previously and all of them commented on how much had happened in that time. Lois seemed well and did not complain of pain, but Nell was shocked to see her mother using a wheelchair and wondered if this was due to Evelyn's instruction and that she was encouraging her mother to consider herself more ill than she actually was. Yet Lois managed well with Neville's help; things are so much better without that woman, thought Nell, and despite the use of the wheelchair she was encouraged to see her mother looking more relaxed than she had been for months. Perhaps it is the prospect of going to live in the sun, Nell said to herself, as she looked out on the bleak, overcast November weather. Or was Lois content because she had insisted on Evelyn accompanying them to Spain and her father had capitulated. She decided to give the matter more thought later.

Neville was as good as his word and invited Kathleen to tea the following weekend. He decided to ask Patrick and Nell to bring her; she might find it difficult to come alone as she had only met him briefly at the accountant's office. And a small child will always break the ice in any situation, he thought.

Kathleen had once been scathing about Nell, coming from a big house with lots of money, as she put it, and had voiced her ill-informed opinion to Bridget on more than one occasion. There were still times when she struggled with guilt about how badly she had treated Nell during that visit to Ireland, and how wrong she had been about her. But Nell had proved herself to be a true friend to her sister-in-law and the two women had become closer since Kathleen had arrived in England. She could not believe how her fortunes had changed so much in a few months and had begun to make the most of every opportunity that presented itself. Realisation had dawned on Kathleen that her jealousy of Nell was borne out of desperation because she could never see herself moving in the same circles and could only think about how unfair life was. As she approached the front door of Moongarth she reflected that she was now stepping over the threshold not just of a house, but into a lifestyle that she never thought she could be part of.

As her brother had done two years previously, Kathleen gazed around her in awe at the spacious tiled hallway, the beautifully decorated and furnished rooms, and the view of the immaculate flower beds through the French windows of the breakfast room, still showing some late autumn colour. Nell made the tea, and Patrick carried the tray through to the drawing room. Kathleen was suddenly shy; she did not know how to make conversation with Neville and Lois but felt she was on safe ground by admiring the house and garden. Evelyn's presence, as always, created a tense atmosphere at first and Nell wished that just some of these family occasions could take place without her. Neville, sensing Kathleen's shyness, came to the rescue by asking how she was liking her job at Cunningham and Grant, and had she settled into her accommodation. The mood became more relaxed after that, and Arthur captivated everyone's attention, wriggling out of Patrick's lap and tottering around the room under Nell's watchful eye. Only Evelyn remained silent and stony faced. Surprisingly, Lois seemed to take to Kathleen and was interested to hear about Barbara's annex and its style of décor.

Kathleen knew that Neville and Lois were about to depart for Spain and asked about their holiday home. Here, Lois seemed to become animated and described the apartment, the secluded terrace and the quiet beach where she bathed in the warm Mediterranean waters. She went on to say how much her health had improved since making regular visits.

"You must come out to Spain to stay with us one day"

Lois's words to Kathleen were met with speechless astonishment by everyone. It was almost unheard of for Lois to issue any kind of invitation, let alone an invitation to a virtual stranger for a visit abroad, and no one, including Neville, quite knew what to make of it. Was this a genuine offer or was Lois just being polite, he wondered, but Lois didn't seem to notice anyone's reaction. Kathleen, however, took it at face value and thanked her warmly for the offer. Patrick was equally amazed, partly at Lois's suggestion but also at the change in his sister who was listening excitedly to Lois as she spoke about the comfortable and easy-going life in Solibrio.

"Your parents are so nice" said Kathleen on the way home. "It was kind of her to invite me to their home in Spain. I would love to go" she added wistfully.

"You're very honoured, we've never been invited!" laughed Nell. Privately she was still puzzled by the proposition and wondered if it was seriously meant or just mentioned as a passing comment, but she did not want to disappoint Kathleen so said nothing more. How little I know my own mother, she thought to herself.

"I don't think Evelyn likes me at all though". Kathleen remarked. Nell and Patrick exchanged glances. Kathleen has noticed the hostility as well, Nell said to herself. She was at a loss to know what to do about the situation. Soon her parents would be leaving, Evelyn accompanying them and there was nothing Nell could do about it.

Chapter Twenty-One

December 1981

On the morning of their departure to Spain, Neville woke very early. He lay awake for some time, thinking about Lois, Moongarth, the move, and his life here in Drover's Cross. He realised with a shock that he didn't want to leave; apart from a few years living in Kirchington this house was all he had known. Everything important to him was here – people, memories, family history. He could barely remember his childhood home in Canada.

He looked at Lois, still sleeping peacefully beside him. Lois, his first and only love, with all her shyness, awkwardness and complexities. Fate had dealt her a double blow, he thought sadly. Firstly, the miscarriages and the tragic loss of their baby Laurence, then the rheumatoid arthritis which had struck just when he thought she might have started to recover from all the anguish of those sad times. He had to make the change for the sake of her health, he knew. And Moongarth would remain in the family, it would be in good hands. But one thing still troubled him. Evelyn.

There had been several occasions recently when Neville's doubts about Evelyn had become more serious in his mind, and he blamed himself for allowing her to become such a dominant presence in their lives. It was even more of a dilemma because Lois was quite happy with Evelyn taking such an essential position in the household, in fact she encouraged it. In his efforts to provide excellent care and companionship for his wife, and to spare Nell from having to take on the role of her mother's carer, Neville had become blind to the surreptitious control Evelyn was exercising until her involvement was firmly established, and by then it was too late to change things. But when he had been discussing the possible transfer of Moongarth with Nell and Patrick, he was inwardly furious that Evelyn had given an unsolicited opinion, voicing her views unequivocally, saying that it was not a good idea; young people should find their own way and not be offered such handouts. It was good for them to struggle in the early days, she had insisted, and Neville and Lois would regret taking this decision. She had stated her point of view forcibly, as though she were a member of the family whose wishes should be considered. At the time, Neville had mustered all the forbearance and politeness possible but later told her in no uncertain terms to mind her own business. Her interference reinforced the doubts that had gone through his mind about her mystery visitor, and the disappearance of the money envelope. Could it be the case that Nell and Jenny could see far more in the situation than he? Was Evelyn attempting to perpetrate some kind of fraud or deception on them? She was overly interested in all matters to do with their family finances and property.

When she became aware that Neville had rebuked Evelyn for meddling in their affairs, Lois was angry with him. Not for the first time, he realised that she was terrified Evelyn would leave if things did not go her way. Personally, Neville felt this to be unlikely, but he did not wish Lois to become agitated so once again he decided to let the status quo remain for the time being. He reproached himself for the umpteenth time for his failure to be more assertive, yet he felt he was in an impossible position. However, he made sure that any future discussions about money or family matters took place when Evelyn was not present.

Lois had been most insistent that Evelyn was to accompany them to Spain. She could not manage without her, she said, and Neville could see that having persuaded his wife to make the move, another battle was looming if he disagreed with her over this. At first, he had liked Evelyn, he had trusted her medical knowledge and experience and for a while had been grateful for her support to his wife; life would have been even more difficult in the early days of Lois's illness without her.

But now, something about her nagged at him; he could not quite explain it, even to himself. And if he was honest, he resented her constant presence and the fact that she and Lois were so close. Neville could not help but wish that this new chapter in their lives could have been for he and Lois alone.

He became more and more convinced that Evelyn had an ulterior motive. She had been quick to accept the prospect of a move to Spain with her patient; perhaps a little too eager, he thought. Neville recalled that Evelyn had been the one to recommend the benefits of a warm climate. He would have to re-negotiate terms with her; she could not be allowed to regard this as an indefinite free paid holiday in the sun, however indispensable she had made herself to Lois.

He dressed quickly and silently and went downstairs. On an impulse he decided to go into the back garden and walked to the edge of the field. It was still dark; there were not yet any streaks of dawn in the east, and the moon had dipped below the horizon. The air was sharp and dry, his breath visible as he huddled slightly against the cold, and his feet crunched on the frozen grass. The sky was completely clear and amongst the thousands of stars he could see the spiral arms of the Milky Way. He recalled a time one Christmas when he had stood on this very spot with Aunt Phoebe and his brother Henry, pointing out the constellations in that winter sky so many years ago. His thoughts went to his little brother who had lost his life only a few hundred yards from where he was standing, and as he gazed up at the heavens, he felt Henry's presence close to him, so real that it seemed he could almost reach out and touch him. It was as though his brother was standing there beside him in solidarity, understanding his dilemma.

And then he saw it. A phenomenon so rare that only a few people in the whole world had ever witnessed it or even knew that it existed. He had looked for it many times, but it was elusive and fleeting.

The Venus Shadow.

Venus was by far the brightest object in the sky at that moment, so bright that on that clear, still morning it cast a subtle translucent shadow on the sparkling ground.

It was a sign; he was sure of it. He was not a religious man, but he had heard of Jesus being referred to as the Morning Star.

Suddenly he remembered reading in an astronomy book, or somewhere in his science studies long ago that most of the elements of the human body were formed inside a star. We are all children of stardust, he thought whimsically. It comforted him to think of Henry as a star now. Henry was surely up in heaven, yet on this last morning that Neville spent at Moongarth, he knew with certainty that for a few moments, Henry had been there with him.

* * *

Later that morning Nell and Patrick came to say goodbye to Neville, Lois and Evelyn as the taxi arrived to take them to the airport. It was an emotional farewell, especially for Neville as he took a final look up at Moongarth and he hugged Nell close, shook hands with Patrick and gave a last fond look at Arthur. More than anything, Nell was sad that her mother had said only the most perfunctory of goodbyes to them, and had not asked how she was, despite being in the last month of her pregnancy.

"We will be coming back from time to time" said Neville "so we will see you in a few months, I expect".

"It may be a building site by then, if all goes to plan". Patrick warned him light-heartedly. "I shall be taking photos of how the house is now, you know, before and after. But after may be a long way off, there's a huge amount of work here".

"Let me know how what happens when you have the meeting at the bank, and if I can be of any further help. Plus, I'd like to see a copy of the drawings when they are ready". Neville was anxious that the final stage of the agreement, the financing of the project should run smoothly. He would be keeping track of progress, but he felt a slight pang of regret that he would not be more closely involved. I must let go now, he thought, as they drove off. It was a defining moment.

Chapter Twenty-Two

Perhaps it was the excitement or maybe she had overdone things, but Nell went into early labour on the day of the move.

Their modest possessions from the flat had been brought in a van and were unloaded into the hallway alongside the remaining items belonging to Neville and Lois. Arrangements had been made for these to follow on to the apartment in Spain over the next few days. Nell had resigned herself to living in a muddle for some time but as all rooms were functioning and comfortably furnished, the move did not present any immediate problems. Patrick had been impatient to get started with plans and designs for the refurbishment of Moongarth, but as so often happens, circumstances prevented any changes happening for quite a few months.

Henry Patrick Walsh was born prematurely on the sixteenth of December and due to his low birth weight and some breathing difficulties was transferred to the Special Care Baby Unit in St Catherine's for the first few days of his life. Nell came home from hospital after two days and still needed to rest, so Patrick took some time off work, delegating as much as possible to Joe, who as an employee was now responsible for overseeing the contracts currently in progress.

It was a difficult time. Naturally, Nell wanted to be with their new son in hospital and visited every day, so Patrick took charge of looking after Arthur, who at nineteen months was too young to understand what was happening. Caroline called in whenever she could between nursing shifts to lend a hand. Despite knowing every inch of Moongarth and sensing a huge amount of relief in moving out of the flat, Nell felt unsettled; there had been so many changes in such a short time. There was also Christmas to prepare for and in some ways, she had never felt less like taking on extra shopping, cooking, and decorating the house. But when she brought home their tiny new baby, life at Moongarth took on a different routine. She made a brief telephone call to her parents' apartment; to her dismay Evelyn answered, and Patrick had to insist on Neville being brought to the phone. Nell was near to tears by the time she spoke to her father, but he was delighted to hear that he had a new grandson and overjoyed at their choice of name. It meant so much to Neville that they had thought of his brother.

During this time, Patrick visited the bank along with Jonathan. Securing the mortgage had not been as easy as Neville had anticipated. To begin with, it was far more than the amount Patrick had borrowed to purchase the flat. Secondly, the circumstances were not straightforward. It was unusual for someone of his young age to come into ownership of such a valuable property, and investigations had to be carried out to confirm the title and satisfy the legalities. A further complication was the lack of several years' accounts, added to which the partnership no longer existed, and Patrick was in effect starting a completely new business with no history. His ability to service such a large loan was questioned in depth, and he could not help worrying what would happen if he were to be refused – where would that place him with the agreement he had made with his father-in-law and his plans?

But two days before Christmas the business manager at the bank telephoned to say that their enquiries had been completed and with Neville acting as guarantor, the mortgage was agreed.

There was no chance to celebrate with the demands of a premature baby and a toddler, and with Christmas almost upon them Nell wondered how she would find the time or energy to make it anything other than an ordinary day. She was feeding Henry every three hours, trying to look after a lively nineteen-month-old and there was still unpacking to be done. Added to that she felt exhausted and physically drained, having barely an hour's sleep at a time. How will I ever cope, she asked herself.

But help came unexpectedly. On hearing that Nell Garth (as the local people still thought of her) had returned to Moongarth with a toddler and a tiny newborn, there was a steady stream of neighbours to their door bringing home made cake, mince pies, casseroles and presents for Arthur and Henry. Becky, Jenny's niece brought along a small Christmas tree and decorated it for them.

Nell was touched and accepted all offers of gifts without hesitation. Her situation as a new neighbour, albeit a returning one had prompted a great deal of interest in the community – whether this was out of kindness, genuine friendship or just curiosity did not matter. Patrick was relieved to see how the neighbours were rallying round and although he did not have an opportunity to thank them all, he was grateful for their help and felt that he, too, was accepted without question as the new owner of Moongarth. By nature, he was a modest man, but it was impossible for him not to feel a sense of pride and achievement.

Christmas came and went; this time Nell was glad when it was over, and a normal routine could be established. Arthur took more interest now in what was going on around him but aware of the change in his surroundings and the fact that Nell was preoccupied a great deal with Henry, became fretful. Henry had regained his birth weight and was growing stronger, but Nell was still fatigued and tearful, finding everyday chores overwhelming.

Patrick had planned to take only two days off despite the building trade traditionally shutting down for a fortnight until the new year, but the weather was against them. Instead, he and Joe spent time preparing tenders for new contracts, costing materials and organising the outbuildings at Moongarth which would be used to store machinery, supplies and tools. It meant that Joe would no longer need to rent the lock-up, which would save money. One morning in early January Patrick went off in his van on a mystery errand, returning two hours later.

"Come and have a look outside" he said to Nell, taking her hand and leading her out onto the driveway. Miraculously both children were asleep for a few blissful moments. "Look". He pointed proudly at the van, which now bore the lettering 'Walsh and Sons'. "I had that done this morning. We now have a family business as well as a family home".

Normally Nell would have been excited and enthusiastic. She managed to summon a wan smile, but her weariness defeated her at that moment. Patrick was disappointed at her reaction, then concerned. "I'm worried about you Nelly," he said, taking her in his arms. "I think we need to see about some help for you, just for a while".

"I'm just not having a good day, Patrick. And we can't really afford paid help, I know money is tight".

"We're doing ok. Let me worry about that. If the worst comes to the worst, we can use some of our savings, it's for emergencies. Remember you said that to me once before when I was just starting out". He made Nell sit down and rest for a few minutes while he made tea for them both. After lunch he went off again, saying he had something to sort out. Nell picked up Henry to feed him and Arthur snuggled in beside her. After half an hour she had almost drifted off to sleep but was awoken by a familiar voice.

"It's ok, the cavalry's here".

"Jenny! How lovely to see you!"

"I thought I'd come up straightaway. Patrick said you could do with another pair of hands, and I have some time to spare so it's all agreed, I'm going to pop up for a couple of hours every morning, longer if you need me. And Becky will look in on her way home from school in the afternoon in case you need to put your feet up for half an hour".

Nell was near to tears. It could not have been better timed, and there was nothing she would like more than Jenny's calm, friendly presence in the house. Jenny was pleased too; the departure of Neville and Lois meant that her job had come to an end, and despite her discomfort about Evelyn, this had been a huge disappointment to her. Patrick looked at Nell and winked, and she smiled back at him; the relief on her face was unmistakable. "Thank you so much" she said, both to Patrick for arranging the help and to Jenny for agreeing to it. He had decided they could afford to pay Jenny a small wage, and she was only too happy to come back to look after a new generation of the Garth family, as she still thought of them privately.

Jenny set about preparing vegetables for their evening meal, cleaning the kitchen and loading the washing machine. Nell immediately felt that a huge burden had been lifted and that just the thought of being able to catch up on sleep and that someone else would take care of the chores while she attended to her children was comforting. Most new mums have their own mother or a sister to help them when they have given birth, she thought sadly and wondered for a moment how Bridget would have acted in this situation; practical, kind, reassuring. How come she knew this much about her mother-in-law after only one meeting? Yet she felt that she did. But now I have Jenny, Caroline comes when she can, and Barbara is going to visit soon. And Becky will call in after school. I have everything I need; the most wonderful husband who works so hard for us, two beautiful sons and now we own a family home. I told Patrick on our wedding day that I thought I was the luckiest woman in the world. Well now I know I am.

Chapter Twenty-Three
1982

As the weeks went by, Henry thrived and by March the health visitor told Nell that in most respects he had caught up with growth and development as if he had been born at full term, but in fact he had arrived only two weeks early. Nell was reassured; she had been anxious at first. Arthur was now nearly two and unmistakably like Patrick with a crop of red hair and a sturdy build, whereas Henry was fairer and seemed to have inherited Nell's fine bone structure and grey eyes. She had only ever seen one faded, grainy photograph of her Uncle Henry as a boy but there did seem to be a slight family resemblance, she thought, but of course it's far too early to be sure, and in any case, babies change so quickly.

With the arrival of spring, plans for the refurbishment of Moongarth began to take shape. It was going to be a formidable amount of work and hugely disruptive but exciting too. Patrick, mindful of Nell's attachment to the house and out of respect for Neville, consulted her extensively. Nell had her mother's eye for style and design, but she deferred to Patrick's knowledge of construction and relied on him to explain what was possible. In addition, it was vital that some rooms and functions were always available, even if somewhat rudimentary.

"The kitchen is the most important room Patrick" she said, after studying some of his rough drawings and hastily sketched plans. "It needs to be done first, and then the main bathroom. The other rooms are less urgent, some will just need redecorating".

"Think carefully how you want it, make sure to include everything. We need to get this right first time, there's no going back and making changes later". Patrick was emphatic.

"And it will have to last; we won't be doing all this again any time soon".

Together they took measurements and decided on the number and location of units, appliances and – essential for Nell – a modern kitchen range. "The kitchen could be extended to include a walk-in larder" Patrick suggested; "a kitchen can never be too big. The old butler's pantry can become a utility room".

They had so far only planned a couple of rooms but already Nell was beginning to understand the scale of the project. Our everyday lives will have to fit around all this disturbance for months – years – to come, she thought, and at that moment the prospect overwhelmed her once more. But we must focus on the long-term goal, she decided, remembering the tiny kitchenette at the flat; a few weeks inconvenience would be worth it for the benefits of a modern contemporary kitchen with plenty of workspace and storage. Before the children came along, she had enjoyed experimenting with cooking, but since Henry was born and Arthur was being weaned the meals had been more basic. This was one thing she hoped to improve; Patrick liked his food and the thought of them all sitting round a table together in a newly refurbished dining room enjoying a home cooked meal was an appealing one.

Once all the structural changes to the house had been agreed on, a professional architect was engaged and at the end of April, just after Arthur's second birthday, work began in earnest. Patrick took on two men to start the demolition. Walls were knocked down, floors ripped up and debris seemed to surround them for a while. Jenny was a tower of strength to Nell throughout all the upheaval and mess; housework became pointless, such was the level of plaster dust and fine powder that seemed to pervade every inch of their home. But somehow, they managed; the most important thing was to keep Arthur out of the way of the builders and anything dangerous. He was walking confidently now and could always move more quickly and reach further than Nell expected. "See, he's taking an interest already," laughed Patrick. "Give him a few years and he'll be wielding a trowel and laying bricks like his dad".

Patrick had successfully bid for other contracts in the area and Joe was now in charge of the work. They had taken on three more men to work on the Lamberham site and two in Kirchington. Company signboards for Walsh and Sons were being seen in the area and their reputation was spreading. Their work now encompassed general building instead of just brickwork, with sub-contractors taken on when required. The development at Wharnden Meadows had been delayed but was now getting started and Jonathan suggested that they tender for it. It would mean subcontracting even more workers and Patrick had moments of panic when he thought about all the men who were depending on him financially, but Jonathan arranged a further meeting with the bank to show evidence of how the business was growing. This resulted in a separate overdraft being agreed. Patrick was relieved at having his cash flow problems solved but tried not to think about how much money he owed. "A great many businesses run on overdraft most of the time" Jonathan reassured him. "When we do the next accounts, they will show you are in a good position".

The work at Moongarth and out on site was helped by a dry spell, and good use was made of the light evenings and fine summer weather to make progress. By the following autumn the kitchen and ground floor bathroom were completed, work had started on the attic shower room and Nell was pregnant again.

* * *

In Solibrio, the first real battle of wills between Neville, Lois and Evelyn presented itself.

It was only Neville's second visit to the apartment, and his first since they had taken ownership. Completing the purchase after just one brief holiday was, he admitted, not without risk, but he was pleased with the apartment, its suitability, comfort and proximity to the sea. He had relied on Evelyn after her first visit with Lois to give him a good description of the apartment, and by way of courtesy he remarked on this again to her as they settled in after their journey. She received this praise with a blank stare as if it was no more than she deserved. She really doesn't like me, he said to himself. But I've never done anything to offend her except to put her in her place over the business of Moongarth and I was within my rights to do that.

The following day he approached her while Lois was resting on the terrace. The weather was warm enough that day for sitting outdoors.

"Evelyn, now that Lois and I have moved out here, it's time that you and I discussed the terms of your employment". He was careful to state 'Lois and I'; it would not do for Evelyn to view the arrangement as a permanent threesome.

"Oh?"

"Yes, we should have sorted this out back in England but now is as good a time as any".

She was silent, but Neville could sense some underlying hostility.

"I've been paying you a salary and of course I shall continue to pay you for your care of my wife, but there will be a reduction in the amount, to reflect the fact that you are living here rent free, you have full board and lodging and no outgoings to speak of".

"Have you consulted Lois about this?" Evelyn looked furious.

"This is nothing to do with Lois. I pay your salary; this is between you and I. There is no need to involve her".

"There's every need. But anyway, you're wrong, I do have outgoings. I have a home in England to maintain. That costs money".

Yes, and I wish you'd go back there, Neville thought despairingly.

"I'm a widow you know, I have no one else to support me".

"I do know that, Evelyn. I will still be paying you a fair wage and you are very comfortable here. But I shall be paying you less from the end of next month. That's a reasonable period of notice".

Evelyn stamped out of the room in a temper. Neville guessed that would not be the end of the matter and that despite his request, she would immediately tell Lois who would beg him to reconsider. Evelyn was relying on that, he thought. Divide and conquer. Well, I refuse to be blackmailed. Such an ugly word, he reflected, one I never expected to use about my own wife.

Sure enough, later when they were alone, Lois asked him about his decision. She was angry, he could see, and fully expected him to give in.

"Lois my mind is made up. I've been reasonable about this. I'm on a pension now, in case you've forgotten. And I am being more than generous".

"But Neville what if she decides to leave?"

As always, this was the dilemma Lois presented him with. Nothing must interfere with her dependence on Evelyn. Evelyn whom he was certain had some nefarious purpose in maintaining this hold on his wife. Suddenly all became clear. Quite possibly she had financial benefits in her sights; that was why she made her opinion known so strongly over the Deed of Gift. She had inveigled her way into the household; charming and helpful at first, then once her position was secure, she started to turn the situation to her advantage, knowing that here was a vulnerable woman and a husband who would do anything to safeguard his wife's health and happiness. He realised he had done no investigation into Evelyn's background, relying totally on the agency and one letter of reference. That could have been forged for all he knew. He had been too trusting. His previous doubts were now coming back to haunt him. He wished Nell was here to talk to about it; he knew that she had had suspicions about Evelyn for a while.

"Then she must leave".

Lois looked at him with horror.

"Neville you can't mean that?" she said incredulously. "You know I can't manage without her. We went through all this before we left…."

"Yes I know, but we didn't agree anything about her salary. I should have explained this to her sooner, I'll admit, but it's done now. You must see I'm being reasonable"

"I do not see that"

"Anyway, we could manage, just the two of us. You are so much better here, with the warmth and the sea bathing. And such an easy apartment, no stairs, an accessible bathroom. We could have a cleaner two or three times a week. I could learn to cook. We will have a lovely retirement; it would be perfect. But I am not going to change my mind over this ".

Lois gave a sob and left the room. She has gone straight to Evelyn to complain about me, he realised sadly.

Neither Lois or Evelyn referred to the matter again within his hearing although he suspected they discussed it a great deal when he was not present, but Neville was resolute, and Evelyn's salary was adjusted the following month. He began to think that he had won a battle, if not the war, then felt ashamed for thinking in such adversarial terms about Lois. But it is Evelyn who is driving this, he thought, she has influenced Lois so much and set her against me. His plans for a contented retirement with his wife seemed a distant prospect all the time Evelyn stood between them.

But almost as if Evelyn had been biding her time, another dispute arose a few months later.

There were three double bedrooms in the apartment. He and Lois shared one, Evelyn had another and in the third, which had the most uninterrupted view to the horizon, he had positioned his telescope in front of the window, arranged his reference books on the shelves and set up a desk with a reading lamp.

One evening as they were getting into bed, Lois said, out of the blue: "Neville, I would like you to move out of this bedroom and sleep in your study from now on". She had started to call it a study in the same way as Evelyn had changed the name of his observatory room at Moongarth.

Neville was aghast but immediately guessed what was behind the request. It was another attempt by Evelyn to separate him from his wife; clearly the privacy of their bedroom was the only place where she had no control.

"No" he said firmly. "I'm not moving out, Lois and that's an end to it. We agreed I would have a room for my telescope and anyway this is the only place where you and I can spend time alone. I am not giving that up".

She began to cry and turned away from him, refusing to kiss him good night as she usually did. Where did this all go so wrong, he wondered as he switched off the bedside light. He resolved to sit down and write to Nell in the morning; perhaps setting out his worries on paper would help. There was nothing that Nell could do but he had no one else to turn to. And she would be upset if things were not working out and he didn't tell her.

He tried to sleep but his mind wouldn't relax. He hated to see Lois so upset but it would be even worse to allow Evelyn to have any more power in their household or over their relationship, of that one thing he was certain.

Chapter Twenty-Four
1982–1983

It was a busy household during those first years at Moongarth; time was short, demands were many and the work on the house seemed never ending, each stage taking longer than expected. Nell was always relieved when five o'clock came and the builders went home so that she could have some respite from the constant noise and activity. The children sensed her disquiet and at times became crotchety, so the easiest solution was to push them out for a walk in the double buggy when the weather was fine. Often, she took them into the garden or down to the edge of the field where they might see rabbits, and occasionally a fox or a deer. Nell sometimes pointed out buzzards circling overhead, soaring on the wind currents then swooping down to seize on unsuspecting prey. By early October Henry was sitting up and paying attention to everything around him, and Arthur, excitedly watching the animals was talking well, remembering their names and pointing to pictures of his favourites. At bedtime Nell made up stories for them about the creatures that lived in the field at Moongarth and this gave her an idea; one day she would write a children's story, maybe just for her own little boys. If she ever had time to herself again, she thought despondently. Her third pregnancy had been confirmed; it had come as a shock and not altogether welcome at first; the timing was all wrong, Henry was not yet a year old and she had enough to cope with already. Although she and Patrick had both agreed that they wanted a large family, having three children in little more than three years was not part of the plan, especially with Patrick's business demanding every spare moment of his time and the interminable work on Moongarth taking so much of their attention and energy. But she resolved to manage as best she could; she was fortunate that she still had

Jenny's help every day and friends who visited, despite her home resembling a builder's yard.

"I need to learn to drive soon, while I can still fit behind the steering wheel". Nell's plans for taking lessons after Arthur was born had been shelved; Patrick had offered to pay, but there were just not enough hours in the day. Even now she did not know how she would find the time. But she realised that soon she would be stuck at home a great deal otherwise; public transport in Drover's Cross was limited at the best of times, walking any distance would not be practical with three children and she could not always expect lifts from other people.

Over Christmas Nell discussed the subject with Patrick. He agreed that she needed to learn but simply did not have time to teach her himself. But once again she called upon the help of her friends and in January a rota was devised. Barbara, Caroline or Jenny would look after the children while Nell had formal lessons with a driving school three times a week. Once she was sufficiently experienced, Barbara would take her for drives in her car for extra practice. Over the next few months this arrangement worked well. Nell was extremely motivated because time was short; she knew carrying on with lessons after the birth of her baby would be almost impossible. Mr Norton, her instructor at L-amberham School of Motoring was impressed with her progress and following his advice she booked a driving test for late May. Nell soon found that knowledge of the Highway Code was different from revising for her 'A' Levels; driving discipline was more factual with so much of it based on the law; there was no room for her own interpretation or opinion. But she prepared as well as she could.

On the twenty seventh of May, feeling more nervous than at the birth of either of her children, Nell was driven by Mr Norton to the Test Centre outside Kirchington after a final hour's practice. If the examiner was surprised to see that a young woman who was so heavily pregnant had entered for her driving test, he was too polite to say so. Privately he had concerns about Nell's level of concentration, speed of reaction and whether she could manoeuvre sufficiently well under the circumstances. But his doubts proved groundless; she had shown herself to be more than capable, and the examiner had no hesitation in giving her a pass certificate.

"Pity I can only celebrate with a cup of tea" said Nell later, as she told Patrick her good news. "Oh no, now I suppose I have to buy you a car" he teased, hugging her. "Well done, Nelly, I'm so proud of you".

"I'd like to do something for the girls to thank them. I couldn't have done it without their help".

"Well let's get you a car first, then you can take them all out for a meal or something one evening. While I still only have to babysit two children". They both laughed.

That weekend they went to a second-hand car showroom in Kirchington and after listening to endless sales talk and looking at several cars of varying degrees of suitability, they decided on an estate car which was five years old with low mileage and a warranty. "This will be the most practical for you and the children, you can fit a double buggy and all your shopping in the boot," said Patrick. After a test drive, with the salesman sitting worriedly beside her in the passenger seat, Nell agreed it would fit the bill and was told that she could take delivery the following week.

Patrick's time was divided between his business, overseeing the work on Moongarth and trying to carve out some time for family life. Joe Clancy, being Patrick's right-hand man was a stalwart support. There were many evenings when he would sit down with Patrick at the table in the breakfast room, trying to make sense of invoices, bank statements and estimates. Patrick had always been the practical one out of the two; he preferred being out on site, directing his men, checking their handiwork and always noticing which of them were more skilled or who took greater care. He always put his best bricklayers to build the corners of any building, knowing that if the corners were strong and true, the courses of bricks in between would be secure as well. However,

Patrick had less of a head for figures and his weakest point was tendering for contracts. Too high and he would be undercut; too low and there would be insufficient profit margin. But here Joe, who had more of an aptitude for the financial side of the business came into his own. Together they were a powerful team and their reputation for fair business practice and solid workmanship was assured.

Joe had met Ruth Adams, a local girl, and they had become engaged. Sometimes he brought her to Moongarth in the evening and she and Nell would sit and talk, Ruth would help with the children or make tea while Nell tidied up, loaded the washing machine or just sat with her feet up.

Nell had received a worrying letter from Neville and the fact that her suspicions about Evelyn were confirmed gave her even more anxiety. She knew he did not expect her to have any answers, but her heart went out to her father who had given Lois every possible comfort, understanding and medical help over the years, had coped with her strange moods and insecurities and only wanted to spend precious time with her in peace and contentment. Daddy has had just as difficult a life as Mummy in a way, she thought sadly. He left his parents to come here to England and never saw them again. He lost his little brother in a terrible accident; he lived through a world war and then just when he hoped for some happiness with Mummy everything went wrong in their lives. And now this.

Soon after receiving the letter, she confided in Jenny one morning.

"My father is in such a predicament about Evelyn. Her behaviour is getting worse and so is her control over my mother. He's at his wit's end, I think. He knows how worried we were about your money that time, and I told him about that man you saw visiting. He tackled Evelyn about it, you know, and she made some excuse, so he let that go as well. He never should have done".

Jenny looked pale.

"Nell, I need to tell you something. I should have told you ages ago, but I kept hoping all of this would go away. But now things are getting worse, I must tell you what I did. It's unforgivable and you may decide to sack me". Jenny was clearly upset.

"Jenny nothing you could ever do would make me want to sack you. Whatever is this terrible crime you've committed?"

"You know I was very worried about that man that visited Evelyn, that time I hid?"

"Yes, behind a bush in the garden". Nell smiled at the recollection.

"He said he would send her some figures, some information through the post. Well, a few days later, when Evelyn and your mother were packing for their holiday, a letter came, addressed to your mother. I took the post in. I knew your mother never received business letters, and I just thought it was too much of a coincidence. So...." Jenny faltered, "I took the letter and kept it. I never opened it, but I still have it. I'm so sorry Nell; I've had nightmares about it ever since. It seemed the right thing to do at the time, but I would never normally hide anyone's post. It was wrong of me; you have every right to be angry with me". She gave a sob.

Nell was silent for a few moments. She didn't know what to think. But somehow, she knew that Jenny, who was loyal, faithful and always trustworthy would never have taken such a course of action without good reason.

"Jenny, I think I understand why you did this. It may prove to be the best thing anyone could have done. But without seeing it we don't know what it contains, or what value it may be to us. It could be vital evidence. Where is the letter now?"

Jenny went to fetch her handbag. "It's in here. I've carried it around with me every day since I took it". Nell took the envelope from Jenny and looked at her as though they were co-conspirators. Her hand shook slightly as she opened it and unfolded the single sheet. It was creased at the folds but still legible.

Charles Dalton, Independent Valuer and Surveyor. The address was in Trentingham, more than forty miles away, and the letter was dated June 1979.

Evelyn had been cunning; she had not approached a chain of local estate agents, Nell thought. Inviting an unknown private valuer had enabled her to cover her tracks; far less likely to be traced or checked up on if anyone suspected. "Dear Mrs Garth" it began.

She read on. There was a detailed description of the whole house, all four floors, including outbuildings and grounds. Goodness, Evelyn must have shown him over every inch of the property.

Her eyes scanned to the bottom few lines. "….in its present state of repair, etc etc, would benefit from early decoration and modernisation…… current value freehold: £38,000".

The letter continued: "…thank you for your valued business and for taking the time to show me round your excellent property. I look forward to receiving your instructions as soon as you are ready for me to place your house on the market"

Yours sincerely,

Charles Dalton.

Wordlessly, Nell passed the letter to Jenny to read.

"Jenny whatever the letter had said I would not have blamed you for doing what you did. But the letter proves that your hunch was right, Evelyn was posing as my mother, and she was having the house valued with a view to selling it. But how did she think she would get away with it?".

Jenny shook her head, and she too was speechless; relieved in one way that her action in intercepting the letter had been vindicated but horrified that someone her employers had trusted implicitly had hatched such a daring plan and was prepared to go to any lengths to cheat the family she had looked after and loved for so many years.

Nell sent Jenny home early, knowing that she was feeling equally overwhelmed by the morning's revelations. She needed to tell Patrick, to hear his advice, feel his reassurance. But it was not until she had settled the children for sleep that evening and cleared up the dinner things that she sat down with him and showed him the letter.

He was as dumbfounded as she had been. "What a good thing it was that Jenny did this. We always thought Evelyn was up to no good but here's the proof, in black and white. She's a fraudster, a swindler. And this was carefully planned, it wasn't a spur of the moment act. The police should be told, she must be stopped".

"But Patrick how did she think she could have pulled this off? It's one thing to have a valuation done on the quiet but surely an actual sale couldn't have gone through without my parents' knowledge?"

"I don't know, it doesn't seem possible.... but she's very clever, very crafty. Who knows what might have happened.... of course! It was the Deed of Gift that stopped her! When your parents transferred the property to us there would have been change of ownership at the Land Registry. She couldn't possibly have gone ahead when we had only just been registered as the new owners. No wonder she tried to persuade your father not to do it. All that rubbish about young people shouldn't have it so easy....". Patrick was fuming, remembering Evelyn's unsolicited comments at that family meeting.

Nell couldn't sleep that night; her mind was in turmoil. She must tell her father. It would mean a long letter of explanation and somehow tomorrow she must find the time and enough peace and quiet to compose it. By four o'clock she was beginning to doze off when another thought struck her as suddenly as a lightning bolt.

Evelyn had been trying to separate her parents – permanently. She had made herself so essential to Lois over time that her mother was blind to it. That part was nothing new. But if she had been trying to convince Lois to divorce her father, then persuade her to claim Moongarth as a divorce settlement, it was then a small step for Evelyn to prevail upon her naïve, trusting mother to name her, Evelyn as a joint owner. And then, if anything happened to her mother, (and that was something Nell could not contemplate at that moment), Moongarth would be hers.

Except that her father had decided to transfer Moongarth to his daughter and son-in-law by Deed of Gift, and that had scuppered Evelyn's plans.

But it seemed Evelyn had not given up. She had been foiled in her plan for Moongarth but was she now setting her sights on the holiday apartment in the same way?

It was a great many ifs and maybes, but the more Nell thought about it, the more convinced she became that she was not that far from the truth.

'Dear Daddy' she wrote back

'It was lovely to hear from you and I am missing you very much. It doesn't seem possible that you've been in Spain for nearly a year now, and I hope you are enjoying the sunshine and the peace and quiet. It must seem strange to be retired after so many years teaching. What is the stargazing like in Solibrio? Don't forget that one day we will go to West Cork, and you will see for yourself those clear dark skies where you can observe so many more stars.

The situation with Mummy and Evelyn sounds very worrying and seems to have got worse since you left England. It is almost as if Mummy is being brainwashed by her or is scared of her in some way. I think you are doing the right thing to stand up for yourself; please don't be bullied into doing anything you feel is wrong. Surely Evelyn will get the message in the end. And it may be necessary for you to call her bluff. It might be the best thing all round if she did leave. When you read on, you will see why. I know Mummy will be upset at first, but she will get over it after a while and there may be other help that she can have.

I have long since felt that Evelyn had some reason for worming her way into Mummy's good books and for trying to turn her against you – and the rest of us. Patrick and I both noticed this a while before you left, and we didn't know what to do about it. But yesterday I received an extraordinary piece of knowledge, and this has left us in no doubt that Evelyn has been trying to defraud you in the most devious and unscrupulous way.

Jenny came into possession of a letter addressed to Mummy, soon after the unknown man visited Evelyn. The letter was from an agent who had been invited to Moongarth to value the property. Clearly Evelyn had posed as Mummy for the purpose of the valuation, and obviously she had intended to go on to put the house up for sale and somehow receive the proceeds. How she would have been able to do this is beyond me; I am sure she must have had a plan. But Daddy you had a better one, although you didn't know it, because soon afterwards you transferred Moongarth to Patrick and me. This stopped Evelyn in her tracks. I have the letter now, it is proof of her evil intentions; Jenny was a witness to the visit, and there is no way Mummy could have been involved in this.

It's up to you now Daddy what you decide to do; whether to confront Evelyn, involve the police or report her to the agency. I know it's a lot to take in, and you must think about how Mummy will cope with this news. None of this is easy.

Be strong, Daddy and give Evelyn her marching orders. Don't forget that if you and Mummy want to come home for a break you can stay with us. The work on the house is going well so we are living in a building site, but you will always have a home here. Do you remember you said that to me once?

Arthur is growing bigger every day and talking well. Henry is sitting up now and loves watching his brother, it will be lovely when they can play together soon. One other piece of news is that I am expecting another baby in June. It was a bit of a surprise, but we have got used to the idea now. I am keeping well and have lots of help so don't worry about me. I have passed my driving test too!

Patrick sends his regards, and I hope to hear from you again soon,

Your loving daughter,
Nell'

When Neville received the letter, he took himself off for a solitary walk, firstly along the beach then turned inward to follow the winding street that led uphill into the town. The morning air was fresh, but the sun was warm on his back as he climbed, then he sat down on a bench, surrounded by tubs of bright red geraniums and looked down at the view of the harbour as he opened the envelope.

The shock he felt at reading Nell's words was palpable. For a while he sat in silence, taking in the contents of the letter. As the reality hit home, he shook violently and became slightly breathless. Then he shivered, despite the warmth of midday. Nell and Jenny had been right all along about Evelyn; they had seen the warning signs; he had been blind to those signs or had chosen to ignore them. And he and his family had so nearly paid a terrible price for his lack of action.

He stayed out for several hours, pondering what to do. He didn't feel hungry but stopped at a coffee shop for a black coffee to help him think. He was a little taken aback by the news that a third grandchild was on the way, and his next thought was of concern that Nell's health might be compromised by having three babies in such quick succession. But he trusted Patrick to ensure that she had enough help and rest. Lois, relaxing on the beach with Evelyn was silent when he gave her the news later; any mention of pregnancy and babies always disconcerted her, and seemed to remind her of her own traumatic experiences. Neville detected a look of anger in her face, clearly directed at him. Should I not have told her, he wondered to himself. Yet how could I not? There are enough problems between us without keeping secrets as well. Evelyn looked shocked and disapproving, as though it were a further inconvenience sent to annoy her.

For the rest of the day, he reflected on the contents of Nell's letter. How he missed her. His daughter was so perceptive, so clear-thinking; her words crystallised many of his own thoughts, and right now he needed her perspective on his dilemma. Yet he felt for the first time in years that he had the upper hand with Evelyn now; he had right on his side – the woman was no doubt a swindler, if not an actual criminal. It was only by sheer chance, the timing of the Deed of Gift that she had been thwarted. Nell was right; what was the worst that could happen if he did dismiss Evelyn? Because he now had no choice but to do that. The woman herself would have plenty to say, probably she would accuse him of unfair treatment. She might even threaten to take him to court, but the evidence was stacked against her. In any case there was no formal contract, only a verbal agreement with no end date, no specific terms other than the salary which had been the subject of their recent argument. In any case he would give her an acceptable amount of notice. That in itself could be a problem, he realised; she could inflict a great deal of damage during that time out of sheer spite. A clean break might be better, with salary paid in lieu. More concerning was how the dismissal would affect Lois; it would undoubtedly make her angry, upset, panic-stricken, frightened even. Neville thought through all the possible scenarios. But much as he did not want his wife to experience such distress, he concluded with some certainty that it would not adversely affect her health. This was a myth that had been perpetrated by Evelyn to strengthen the hold she had over her patient, and Lois had willingly fallen for it, so much so that she firmly believed that Evelyn alone was essential to her comfort and well-being.

By late afternoon, Neville had made up his mind; he would ask Evelyn to leave. Not immediately – but soon. Now he had indisputable proof he would bide his time. Undoubtedly there would be a crisis or a situation of some kind in the near future which would give him an opening. He would manage the fallout somehow. What was that old saying? The end justifies the means. Maybe. The long-term gain would be worth the short-term pain. Another cliché. But he firmly believed that for the sake of Lois and their future together, it would prove to be the right course of action. The relief he felt at having come to a decision was enormous. It was as though a huge weight had been lifted. He felt almost cheerful as he accompanied Lois and Evelyn on their evening walk.

Chapter Twenty-Five

A daughter was born to Nell and Patrick on the twenty fourth of June 1983. The due date had passed by several days and the baby weighed over nine pounds, crying lustily from the moment she made her entrance into the world.

Nell had secretly hoped for a girl this time but as with all new parents was happy that her baby was healthy and been delivered safely. She and Patrick had discussed a few names and were still undecided, but Nell had an idea that she would like to name their daughter after one of her favourite writers. The Brontë sisters, Charlotte, Emily and Anne came to mind, but Nell could not decide between the three. Then the answer came to her suddenly: they would call her Brontë.

Patrick was against it. The name was too unusual, it would need too much explaining, he argued. The disagreement would have led to a more serious quarrel except for the fact that Patrick did not want to risk Nell becoming agitated so soon after giving birth. But when Nell told him that the father of the literary sisters was Patrick Brontë, an Irishman, he was persuaded, and when she suggested Elizabeth as a second name, this being his mother's second name also, the matter was settled. "I'm choosing the names for the next two", he said jokingly, holding his new daughter in his arms and sending up a prayer of thanks for her safe arrival.

"Oh, and what makes you so sure there will be any more?" quipped Nell, half laughing, half serious. "We have our family now".

"But you always said you wanted a big family". Patrick could remember the time and the place where she said that, and he recalled how he had hoped she meant that she would love to have his children.

"Yes, I did say that" admitted Nell. "But perhaps within three hours of giving birth isn't the right time to think about it".

Brontë Elizabeth Walsh was brought home from hospital after two days to a house full of noise, dust and disturbance. The first-floor family bathroom and attic shower room were in progress, but to Nell's relief the en-suite in the master bedroom had been completed. The window had been replaced by full length glass doors leading on to a Juliet balcony which was just wide enough to accommodate a couple of small seats and some plant pots. Nell was thrilled with the transformation and thought how pleasant the bedroom would be with the doors open during the hot summer months.

Everything took longer than it was supposed to, there were delays in materials arriving, endless waiting for newly plastered walls to dry out, and occasionally the workmen had to be redeployed on other contracts. Why did we ever agree to all this work, wondered Nell, shutting the bedroom door for the umpteenth time to escape the noise and to protect Brontë from breathing in plaster dust as she slept. But we are committed now, there's no going back. One day I shall tell myself it's all been worth it. She picked up Brontë who had begun to whimper. All three of our children are so different, she thought as she cradled her daughter. Arthur is the image of Patrick already with his colouring and stocky build. Henry is slighter and fairer but definitely has his father's smile. And Brontë, well perhaps it's too early to say but I think she will have my dark hair and pale skin.

Barbara called in to see her the following week with gifts for the children and flowers for Nell. She sat down in the breakfast room with Nell and asked if she could hold Brontë for a few minutes. Arthur and Henry were playing on the floor, and for once the house was quiet, the builders were having a tea break.

"Someone Jonathan knows at the Echo has been in touch" she said, smiling down at Brontë who had dropped off to sleep. "Jonathan would have come himself to ask you but he's extra busy this week. Anyway, the features editor has heard about your project here and is interested in writing an article for the weekend supplement. A sort of before and after theme. He would like to come round with a photographer".

Nell was interested. "It would be good publicity for Patrick and Joe" she said thoughtfully. "My father always intended the building work to be an opportunity to showcase the business. Patrick took a great many photos before the work started; they might want to use them. But I shall need to ask him, it's not just up to me".

"Tell Patrick there's a chance of sponsorship if your suppliers agree to advertise with the feature. It could be a win-win. The Echo would arrange all that. Moongarth is an unusual property, but it has history and a local interest angle as well. People love to read about that sort of thing, especially when there's a young family with a new baby involved".

Nell promised to ask Patrick to telephone Jonathan later. The newspaper could be a useful contact, especially if they wanted to return in a few months' time and report on the progress.

Patrick was excited at the prospect and after conferring with Joe, he called Jonathan to give the go-ahead in principle. He started to look out the photos they had taken soon after moving in. "Some of the rooms don't look any different now" commented Nell.

"They will, just give it time. We will be over the messy stage soon. It will all change once we start decorating and having new carpets laid, you'll see".

Patrick had something else on his mind, Nell could tell. Business was going well, she didn't think there were any problems there. But he had received a letter from his mother a few days previously and she wondered if everything was all right at Ballymere. One evening when the boys were settled and she was feeding Brontë, she asked him what was wrong.

"I wasn't going to bother you about this, not just yet anyway. But it's Mam. She's worried that none of the children have been baptised"

That was not what Nell was expecting.

"I did think about it after we had Arthur. We didn't do anything about it then, that was partly my fault. But when we went to Ireland, I realised that your Mam would like to see Arthur baptised in the Catholic faith, and as I'm not a Catholic I didn't know where I stand with it all. I suppose we ought to have some advice".

"So you're not against it? Having them baptised as Catholics?"

"No, not really. I'm C of E, I suppose, I was christened as a baby, but my parents never took me to church after that. Except that I can just remember going to my little brother's funeral." A shadow crossed Nell's face. "Strange, I've never really thought about it that way before but Dad and I both had younger brothers who died. Of course, I never knew my brother Laurence, he was still born". Patrick sat down beside her and placed an arm round her shoulders. They looked down at Brontë lovingly, both somehow realising how lucky they were.

"How about if we all go to Mass one Sunday, we could have a chat with the priest afterwards".

Nell agreed, and a week later they attended Mass in Lamberham. There were fewer people there that morning than she remembered at the church in Ballymere, and not many families with children. Afterwards they introduced themselves to Father Egan who welcomed them warmly.

He explained that Nell need not be a Catholic for their children to be baptised there, but he would like to see them at Mass occasionally. It would be her decision how big a part to play in the ceremony and suggested that they might wish to involve other family members, possibly as godparents. He gave them a booklet to read and asked if he would be able to visit them at home to make arrangements.

A date for the baptism was fixed for late August by which time Brontë would be two months old. Patrick was hugely relieved, and Nell could tell he knew how much this would mean to his mother.

On the way home, a thought occurred to her.

"Do you think your parents would like to come over to England so that they could take part in the baptism, Patrick? They could stay with us. I don't think they've had a holiday for years"

Patrick was unsure. "It's a nice idea, but I don't know if Dad could leave the farm" he said at last. "Mam would love it though. She's never been out of Ireland in her life, only to Northern Ireland just the once. I wonder if Connor and Aidan could cope without them. Niall could lend a hand as well".

Nell had a suggestion. "What about the side-rooms, Patrick?" She was referring to the ground floor extension. Those rooms were rarely used because they could not be accessed from within the main house and were being used as temporary storage while the building work was carried out. "We haven't really made any plans for those rooms yet, but they could be made into a lovely guest suite for your parents. Could you fit a bathroom in there? Would there be time before the baptism?"

Patrick laughed. "No pressure then! I don't know, I'll have to talk to the others. It may be possible, and you're right, it would be nice to have self-contained rooms for guests. Not that we have that many. Guests, I mean".

"One day we might, Patrick. Don't forget, this is a long-term project".

He agreed and they turned their attention to whom they might ask to be godparents.

A week passed and they heard nothing further from the Echo. Then early one evening Patrick received a phone call. Toby Stannon, the features editor wanted to arrange a date to interview him and to take photographs of the building work. It would be what he called a human-interest story, and completely informal. Work should carry on as normal, but he would like to fit in as much information as possible during the visit and include all the Walsh family. A date was agreed for the following Wednesday, so Patrick arranged for Joe and the whole team of builders to be present on site that day.

Nell tried to tidy up some of the rooms as best she could, but Patrick reminded her that this was unnecessary, the feature was to show work in progress. Toby and his photographer, Rick Hargreaves arrived at nine o'clock and Patrick showed them over the house and garden, explaining the plans for each of the floors, including the basement. The photos Patrick had taken eighteen months previously were examined and Toby asked if he could borrow them. He made extensive notes, and the interview with Patrick and Joe was recorded on a Dictaphone.

After a while, Nell brought in a tray of coffee while Jenny minded the children for a few minutes, and Toby turned to her.

"I'd like to hear your story, Nell" he said, explaining that readers would like to know how she managed with two small boys and a new baby amid all the disruption. While Patrick and Joe went back upstairs with Rick, Nell began to tell Toby how this was her childhood home, and that several generations of her family had lived here before her, starting with her great-grandfather Geoffrey who had founded the Garth Brick and Clay Company two hundred years previously. Toby said he had heard of it; he was making a great many notes. She didn't disclose anything about the Deed of Gift or how the project was funded; that she felt was private. But she went on to mention the help she had with the children from Jenny and her friends.

After he closed his notebook, they went on to talk about the neighbourhood. Nell told him that she had attended the village school, then went on to Lamberham High School and took her 'A' levels at Kirchington College. He commented how much local knowledge she must have. Then somehow, she found herself telling Toby of her love of literature and how much she enjoyed writing. "But doing anything in that direction will be a long way off" she said ruefully, hearing Brontë starting to cry and then noticing that all went quiet again as Jenny picked her up. "That's off the record" she said firmly. "Please don't include that in your article". He nodded and paused, but clearly, he was interested.

"Would you have time to write the occasional short item for the Echo? I mean, just a commentary about local village life. Four or five hundred words? You know, your observations, any events going on, clubs, activities, that sort of thing. People always like to read about places they know."

Nell was silent. It was a great opportunity but could she do it?

"Why don't you write a specimen article and send it to me to have a look at, no obligation on either side. We can take it from there. Do give it a try Nell. I'm always on the lookout for something new, and if we can link your name up with the Moongarth feature, so much the better".

Nell agreed to give it some thought. At that moment the men re-appeared, and Rick wanted to take various shots of Patrick and Joe, the workforce and some of Patrick with Nell holding Brontë and the two little boys at their feet, and one more including Jenny, whom Nell was determined would not be left out.

Nell couldn't wait to tell Patrick about Toby's suggestion, but he was full of excitement about how well the interview went and what good publicity it would be for the business. It was to be a three-page colour spread in the weekend supplement and suppliers connected with the work would be advertising alongside it. He would receive a fee for the feature and the Echo had negotiated some discounts for Patrick from local firms who wanted to be associated with the project. The newspaper had a wide readership, and Patrick was hopeful that the article would generate interest in his business and the prospect of more work.

Early on the following Saturday morning, Patrick went into the village and bought six copies of the Echo. They spread out the supplement on the breakfast room table and pored over the article. Toby had been as good as his word; it was a well-written and factual account of the house, its history, Nell and the children and the renovations so far.

An update with the Christmas edition was promised. He had used the best of the photographs which really showed how far the work had come since the early days. They looked eagerly at the one of the family. "There we all are" said Patrick proudly. "Walsh and Sons. And wife and daughter. We're famous now". He took her in his arms and whirled her round. Suddenly Nell decided she wouldn't mention just yet the offer she had received from Toby about a village feature. Patrick was so happy about their success with the newspaper article, and she didn't want to take the edge off his excitement. She would give the matter some more thought and tell him later.

Chapter Twenty-Six

1983

Patrick wrote immediately to his mother and father, enclosing a copy of the newspaper supplement. Bridget was interested to see how the work on the house was taking shape and exclaimed over the family photo, but when she read in his letter that they had decided to have the children baptised at the Church of the Blessed Virgin Mary at Lamberham on the twenty eighth of August so would Bridget and Dermot like to come to Moongarth for a holiday and take part in the service, she was delighted.

She immediately went to ask Dermot if they could manage to take some time off to visit Patrick and the family in England. It won't be easy, she thought, but surely the boys can manage without us just this once? Surprisingly Dermot agreed with her. "They'll have to cope one day when we retire", he said, realising how much this trip would mean to his wife. "And we'll be able to see how Kathleen's doing".

Bridget lost no time in accepting the invitation, and this time Nell wrote back to her, saying how much she was looking forward to their visit and suggesting that they stay for a fortnight. Dates for the holiday were agreed so Patrick booked the ferry crossing and sent them their tickets. He was to meet them at Fishguard on the twenty fourth.

Converting the side-rooms, as Nell called them had put Patrick and his men under a great deal of time pressure, but she had been quite insistent that the self-contained extension should be completely ready for his parents including an en-suite bathroom. The rooms must be decorated, carpeted and furnished in good time for their arrival. Some of the work on the attic rooms had to be delayed as a result but that could not be helped. Nell was determined that Patrick's parents would enjoy a comfortable stay and that she could repay their hospitality.

* * *

In Solibrio, Neville had been wrestling with his conscience. At the beginning of July, he had received another letter from Nell announcing the birth of her baby daughter. They had a granddaughter! Inwardly he was excited, and his first instinct was to tell Lois, but something held him back. She had not welcomed the news of Nell's pregnancy and Evelyn had been scathing. After much deliberation he decided to delay telling Lois until after the baptism. He replied to Nell's letter, sending his congratulations and enclosed a cheque for christening gifts for the children. He had long suspected that Patrick would prefer them to be brought up in the Catholic faith, and personally he had no view one way or the other; it was the parents' decision. But Lois might use this as one more barrier against the rest of the family.

Kathleen and Joe were to be godparents for Brontë, and Barbara and Jonathan had agreed to be godparents for Arthur and Henry. There had been a visit from Father Egan, who had explained the commitment in some detail but suggested that in the circumstances it would be asking too much to have one set of godparents for all three children.

It had been Nell's idea to choose Kathleen. They had thought about asking Caroline, but she was about to move to London to take up a post as staff nurse, much to Nell's sadness. "But Kathleen's changed so much, Patrick," said Nell. "She is more responsible; she is happier, and I know she would take it seriously. Sometimes you just have to give people a chance".

After a great deal of thought, Patrick had to agree that Nell had a point. Kathleen was delighted to be asked and felt that at last, here was a way she could repay her sister-in-law for helping her change her life, which was exactly how she saw it. She had settled in well at the office job and made friends, in particular with the courier Andy Collins who had taken her out several times. She loved living in Kirchington; she enjoyed shopping, walks in the park and by the river, coffee in Markhams with Fiona and best of all, her lovely little flat which she couldn't wait to go home to every night after work. Now she heard that her parents were coming to visit for the baptism, and she thought how proud she would be to show them not just where she lived, but how she lived. She would do her best to be a good role model for Brontë, she said to herself, and to be someone whom Brontë could come and talk to, or confide in. She recalled how despite being one of a large family she had never had someone like that, and Aunt Angela had always had so much sadness in her own life that she had been her godmother in name only. Kathleen was determined to do better for Brontë.

It was hard to say who enjoyed the holiday fortnight more: Bridget or Nell. Bridget was overjoyed to meet her two new grandchildren and to see how much Arthur had changed – he was only two months old when Nell and Patrick had visited Ireland. She was astonished to witness the transformation in her eldest daughter; not just in her appearance but how she had almost re-invented herself. The difference in the way Kathleen spoke was evident; she had retained a noticeable Irish accent, but her diction was clearer now and her tone more professional. When she showed her mother round the annex, spotlessly clean and with not a thing out of place Bridget could not help comparing Kathleen's beautiful new home with the neglected chaos of her old house in Ballymere and stood open-mouthed in disbelief.

When Patrick gave his parents a tour of Moongarth, explaining what changes they had made and what work was still to be done, they were overwhelmed. They both found it very hard to take in the fact that less than five years ago their son was barely skilled as a bricklayer and had left the family home to try to make a living here in England. Now he was a family man, an owner of this impressive property, had designed all the details for its restoration, and had his own business employing several men. They were touched that Nell had specially arranged for the guest rooms to be made ready for their stay and had never known such luxury. Dermot loved the garden and spent many hours exploring, strolled around the little orchard and the field and took himself off for walks up Hasker's Hill into the woods. When Nell told them of the accident that had befallen her father's brother very close to where they lived, she noticed that Bridget's eyes filled with tears. She realised how close she had become to her mother-in-law despite only having met her once before and could not help thinking how far-removed Bridget was from her own mother, who had not even written to her or sent a card when Brontë was born.

For Bridget the highlight of the holiday was the baptism of her three grandchildren, and Patrick could see how important this was to his parents but especially to his mother. He said as much to Nell when they were alone for a few moments after the service, and how he hoped she did not regret having them received into the Catholic Church.

"Why would I? We worship the same God, when all is said and done" she replied.

Curiously, Patrick remembered saying the same thing to his mother several years before when she had voiced her disapproval of his intention to marry Nell, a Protestant. How things have changed, and all for the better, he said to himself.

Nell had decided that having a christening party at Moongarth was impossible while so much work was taking place, so Patrick had hired the function room at the Golden Lion in Kirchington where a buffet tea had been laid on. Apart from the family and the godparents, there were few other guests, Caroline, Jenny and Phil, Becky, Jenny's niece and Joe's fiancé Ruth. Bridget found herself chatting with Barbara as if she had known her for a long time, and Dermot and Joe had put money behind the bar, so it was a lively, convivial atmosphere and Nell felt that everything had gone well; there was just one thing missing – her own parents. If only she could see a way to healing that situation. But the more she thought about it, the less she could find a solution. I shall just have to give it time, she thought to herself sadly, then turned her attention to feeding Brontë who had begun to cry.

Patrick took two days off after the baptism to spend some time with his parents, and to show them around Kirchington, Lamberham and the market town of Rivenden where they stopped for a pub lunch. The next day he drove them up into the South Downs and to one of the seaside towns where they ate fish and chips on the beach and walked along the promenades, exclaiming at the number of holiday makers making the most of the last few days of summer weather. He realised how much busier and more crowded this part of Sussex was in comparison with rural Ireland and that this was his parents' first proper holiday. Sometimes Bridget pushed Brontë in her stroller into Drover's Cross to do some errands for Nell and enjoyed chatting to the people in the village stores. But at other times she and Dermot were happy just to sit in the garden at Moongarth with a tray of tea and watch the children playing on the lawn.

Nell felt emotional saying goodbye to them. Their visit had brought back to her some of the essence of Ireland that she had missed during the last few years when she and Patrick had been so busy with the house and the children. She promised that they would come to West Cork again soon and waved them off, feeling somehow bereft.

They made good time to Fishguard, and while Bridget and Dermot were waiting for the ferry to dock, Patrick said suddenly:

"You can tell Niall that if he still wants to join me in the business he can come over and stay with us for a few weeks soon, just to see if he takes to the work. He's sixteen now, so I guess he's just left school. That's if it's all right with you both?" It occurred to Patrick that maybe Niall hadn't told his parents that he did not want to work on the farm, but Dermot seemed to have accepted this.

"I think he is just waiting for you to offer," said his father. "When I give him your message, he'll be on the next boat over here". They all laughed, and Patrick said he would send his brother the fare.

Everything is working out for us, thought Patrick as he began the return journey and joined the motorway through South Wales. Everything except for Nell and her parents. He was still thinking about that as he crossed the Severn Bridge into England and could not see any way out of the dilemma.

Chapter Twenty-Seven

Solibrio was scorchingly hot, even for early September. It was too uncomfortable to sit on the beach or the terrace in the heat of the day, so Lois and Evelyn rested in the cool salon where the air conditioning gave some welcome relief. They had been conferring in whispered tones but stopped whenever Neville entered. After a while he retreated to his observatory room and tried to read. But he could not concentrate.

The heat was making all three of them short tempered and irritable. This was unusual for Neville who was normally placid and easy-going. He sat for nearly an hour with his book open but after a few paragraphs his mind wandered. Then he shut it with a snap. Now's as good a time as any, he thought, and went out to the salon.

"Evelyn, could you leave us for a few minutes please? I'd like to have a chat with my wife".

Lois looked annoyed but wordlessly Evelyn stood up and left the room.

"That was unnecessary. There's nothing you can possibly have to say that needs to exclude Evelyn"

"I disagree. But anyway, I thought we could share some family news, just you and me. You can tell Evelyn later, if you wish".

"What news?" Lois sounded impatient.

"We have a granddaughter. She was born at the end of June. Her name is Brontë Elizabeth".

There was a long pause.

"Why are you telling me now? We're in September, how long have you known? Have you kept this from me? And what a ridiculous name, whose idea was that?"

The questions were fired at Neville in quick succession, without waiting for answers.

"I have known for several weeks. The reason I haven't told you before is because you were very unwelcoming about

218

the news that Nell was pregnant when I told you back in October. So, after that I thought it best to keep off the subject for a while. But if you'd given the matter any thought at all you would have surely worked out that the baby would have been born by now. Yet you didn't refer to it or even ask if I'd had any news. Do you have no interest at all in your daughter or your grandchildren?"

Lois said nothing but looked at him in disbelief.

"You never want to hear about Nell or the children these days. I know, of course I know better than anyone what you went through years ago, I went through it as well, remember? But you've let the past turn you against the present. Or someone has encouraged you to do that". He let the last remark hang in the air. "Nell is the only family we have. Why do you think she is so happy with Patrick and having children with him? Because she missed out on so much as a child. No siblings, hardly any friends, no fun. She is not blaming us Lois, but she is just making up for it. Can't you see that? Have you any idea how hurt she is, that you more or less ignored her and rejected Arthur whenever they came to see us? And you did not even write to her when Henry was born. Surely you can be happy for her and be thankful that we have three lovely grandchildren now, grandchildren that you will never see or get to know unless you start taking an interest and let go of the past?"

Lois stood open-mouthed with shock. It was so rare for Neville to criticise or to find fault that she could not believe what she was hearing. Neville was always gentle, understanding, so considerate. In all the years of their marriage he had never spoken to her in such plain terms.

"Get out!" She almost spat the words at him.

Neville got to his feet. "I'll leave you to think about that. And just for the record, Nell chose the name Brontë because of her love of the work of the Brontë sisters. Something else you didn't know about her".

Neville strode out and shut himself in his room. He was shaking. Had he gone too far? Maybe. But it was as though a dam had burst, and all the things that had needed saying for months – years – had come tumbling out of his mouth and once he had started, he could not stop himself. Perhaps he had made things worse, or was that even possible? But one thing was certain, his outburst had brought matters to a head. He put his head in his hands and wept.

* * *

Two days passed. The heat outside was unbearable and the tension inside the apartment unmistakable. Towards the end of the third day a thunderstorm broke over the bay but instead of the longed-for downpour, only a couple of light showers of rain fell, not enough to provide relief or cool the landscape.

Neville could tell that his firm words had been the subject of some heated conversations between Lois and Evelyn. Lois had barely spoken to him for three days and left the room whenever he walked in. Evelyn did likewise. This is becoming childish, he thought angrily. In bed at night, unable to avoid him she turned away resolutely, even refusing to say good night. On the evening of the thunderstorm, he once again insisted on talking to Lois on her own. She looked mutinous and defensive.

He heard the front door slam as Evelyn left the apartment.

"Lois I am not going to say any more about Nell and the grandchildren. I hope you've given the matter some thought but right now I want to talk about us. I have decided to give Evelyn notice."

His wife looked at him in horror. "Neville you can't mean that! It's not possible…you know I need her; I should have thought that much was obvious. You cannot dismiss her; I won't let you. How shall I manage? I shall always need her." Lois was beginning to tremble, whether it was with anger, shock or fear, Neville could not tell.

"You will always need some help, I agree. But not from Evelyn. Not anymore. She has done untold damage to us Lois and you just can't see what is in front of your eyes. We were happy before she came along, happy in our way. Oh, I know we had our problems, even when you were diagnosed, but we faced them together, we weren't at odds with each other like we are now, we had an understanding. But if things don't change soon, it will be too late. I can't go on like this any longer, being shut out, being an outsider in my own marriage". Lois gasped, but he continued. "Surely you can see that's what she's done. She's poisoned you against me, and against Nell too, why I can only imagine but I suspect her motive is financial gain. I had a feeling about it before we left, she never wanted Nell and Patrick to have Moongarth. As if it was any of her business. And she was very quick to accept the chance of coming out here. I think she was hoping I would disappear quietly, and she would have you and our money and our property to herself, and you would assign everything to her because she had made herself indispensable. Well, I can see through it, even if you can't, and I'm not about to let this situation continue."

"Neville surely you're not serious?" Lois looked at him in horror, too astonished even to give in to tears.

"If it was just me thinking this, I would have questioned myself. But Nell and Patrick have been worried about Evelyn's behaviour for months, and how this has affected us. Even Jenny noticed and was concerned enough to mention it to Nell. There have been several occasions where her actions have been – well – more than suspicious, downright wrongful, and potentially criminal, and as a family we came very close to losing Moongarth. I will explain more later. We have been blind, Lois and I am to blame for not intervening sooner. But we can salvage something out of this, something for our future. Darling, please try and see. I love you, and I want us to share our last years together with some peace and happiness".

There was a long silence.

"You have no proof, about Evelyn, I mean?" Just for a moment, it seemed that Lois was listening.

"What I have seen with my own eyes would have been proof enough, and Nell has felt uncomfortable about her for some time. But now I have indisputable evidence, evidence that would stand up in court if necessary, and a reliable witness. Evelyn has been deceiving both of us, she has attempted to defraud us in the worst possible way. If only you could see this objectively you would realise. But I am not going to risk the situation getting any worse".

Another long pause.

"Lois please will you think about what I have said. I know it's a lot to take in, and it's been a shock. But don't discuss it with Evelyn, just try to take some time on your own and we will talk again tomorrow.".

Neville said nothing more, but when Evelyn returned from her walk, he noticed that Lois told her that she was going to retire early and did not need any help to get ready for bed. Evelyn looked suspiciously at him but said nothing.

The following morning the weather was fresher, and the atmosphere seemed to have cleared. Lois asked to speak to Neville while Evelyn went to the market.,

"I'm still struggling to understand some of this, Neville". She looked pale and exhausted; Neville knew that she had hardly slept. "But I didn't realise that I have upset Nell so much, and of course I want to hear about our grandchildren. It was just that every time there was talk of babies, it made me so unhappy, and those awful years came back to haunt me. The only way I could cope was to shut out the memories. It was painful to think about Nell having babies one after another without any problems, it was so unfair and well… cruel. Evelyn's advice was to avoid Nell and Arthur as much as possible. Perhaps that was the wrong advice, I'm beginning to see that now".

Neville felt an overwhelming sense of relief that Lois was at last confiding in him.

"We can't change the past, darling, we have to accept what happened all those years ago. I do understand, better

222

than anyone. But we can enjoy the future if only you will allow us to".

She nodded but looked completely bewildered.

"This is what we are going to do, Lois. We shall shut up the apartment and go back to Sussex for a while. My idea is to stay in a hotel in Kirchington so we are not far from Nell and the children, and you can start to build bridges with her. We will make an appointment with Mr Clifford so he can assess your progress and review your medication. Then we will make some decisions about what help you need and come back to Spain for the winter before the weather in England gets too cold for you. I shall explain to Evelyn that we will no longer need her services".

Lois still looked aghast at the prospect of managing without Evelyn, and clearly there was some trepidation in her face at the thought of Evelyn's reaction. She still has such a hold over her, despite everything I've said, thought Neville sadly.

"You can leave everything to me now. I am going to book taxis and flights, and we will be on our way soon. Perhaps going home for a while will be our new beginning after all".

Chapter Twenty-Eight

Sometimes when Kathleen thought about her old life in Ballymere, she wondered if that life had belonged to another person. Everything was so different now; where she lived, where she worked, her friends, her outlook. She had changed. She had more confidence; she had taken a new job in a new country and made it a success, and she had impressed her parents whom she knew had almost given up on her two years ago. She was able to go out and enjoy a glass of wine with friends without drinking to excess and making a fool of herself. And best of all, she had been asked to be a godmother to her little niece, an honour that showed that she was now trusted by Nell and Patrick to fulfil an important role. I can go on to do more things, there may be more opportunities, she thought, there are so many more possibilities here. Knowing the right people helped, she acknowledged. That part has been down to sheer luck and Nell making it happen. I can never thank her enough. Then she realised that seeing Kathleen content with her new life was all the thanks Nell needed.

One thing troubled Kathleen, and she didn't know what to do about it. She had been seeing Andy regularly for quite a few months now. What had started as a friendship had developed into a relationship and had recently become more serious. She had become very fond of him. But she was married. Andy was aware that she had a husband Michael in Ireland and that she had been living apart from him for over two years. But Kathleen knew that in Ireland divorce was against the law. How that affected her now that she lived in England was not clear. She decided that if Andy ever popped the question, she would have to take some legal advice. That may never happen though, she thought sadly. Perhaps we will just end up living together. Somehow, she didn't want to settle for that. In a way it made her feel worse. I made one mistake, she thought, just one. No matter how hard I try I can never change that. Will I have to pay for it for ever?

* * *

At Moongarth, arrangements were under way for Niall to visit for six weeks. As expected, he was excited at the prospect of his first visit to England and at the opportunity to work with Patrick and maybe learn a trade. Nell wondered if she should offer him the guest rooms, but Patrick was against that idea.

"He's sixteen. He's used to sharing with Aidan. He'll be more than happy just to have his own room. He can have one of the attic rooms, the biggest if you like, and there's a functioning en-suite bathroom up there now".

Nell agreed but went to some trouble to make it ready for Niall, adding some bright cushions, a couple of football posters and a second-hand desk "just in case he needs to study" she said, thinking of a time in the future when he might have college work if he took an apprenticeship. "Aren't you getting a bit ahead of things?" asked Patrick in amusement. "He may not even take to the work and be on the next ferry back to Ireland".

* * *

Having made known to Lois his major decisions and immediate plans, Neville allowed a few days for her to take in the seriousness of his words and the implications for their future. He put no further pressure on her but watched her reaction and behaviours carefully. She was very quiet and withdrawn, but he detected a marked lessening of her closeness with Evelyn and that Lois spoke to her only when necessary and then with a perceived coolness of tone that had not been there before. Neville was not sure whether that indicated acceptance of the situation as he had explained it to her, and that Lois was now feeling nervous of the woman she had trusted implicitly for so long. Or was it due to her apprehension of the inevitable repercussions which would follow when he confronted Evelyn and gave her notice. He could not tell. But either way, he observed a change in Lois that signalled an acquiescence to his judgement, and that was tremendous progress in such a short time.

Neville was meticulous in his planning and had told Lois of the arrangements in the briefest of terms. She had not demurred. Two days later he caught the bus into Nerja where he went first to a travel agent and purchased a one-way air ticket from Malaga to Heathrow. He then continued on to his bank, where after some initial explanation with the bank cashier in his stilted Spanish, he drew out a large amount of cash. On the way home he picked up a couple of business cards from local taxi firms. When he arrived back at the apartment, Lois greeted him anxiously. He smiled at her reassuringly and went into his observatory room and closed the door. After a few moments thought, he reached for his pen and wrote out a letter of notice to Evelyn, setting out his reasons. He was careful not to defame her or to mention his suspicions. Although he was convinced of her dubious motives, he did not want to risk putting them in writing. Instead, he thanked her for all her help to Lois and for accompanying them to Spain. He referred to the improvements in Lois's health and how much she had benefited from her holidays. But their plans had changed; a return to England to spend time with family was imminent and that they had no further need of a nurse with immediate effect. He apologised for the short notice, but he had compensated for this by giving her a generous sum in lieu. He then placed the letter, along with the ticket and a personal cheque in one envelope, and a bundle of cash in another. A short time later he opened the door and asked Evelyn to step into his room.

Neville asked her to sit down, then handed her the envelope containing the letter.

"Please read this" he said, feeling at last that he had the advantage.

She opened the envelope and after reading the letter, looked up at him in disbelief.

"You can't do this. You have no right. I have a permanent position here. Your wife needs me".

"You do not have a permanent position Evelyn, you never have".

"This is breach of contract...."

"There is no contract".

"Well, there was an understanding, I was to be nurse to your wife for as long as I was needed".

She suddenly realised she had talked herself into a trap.

"Exactly, for as long as you were needed. Well because of circumstances, you are no longer needed. You will see from the cheque that I have paid you three months' salary in lieu, plus you have your air ticket back to England, and to assist you I am giving you a sum of cash as well". He handed her the second envelope. "This is more than I am required to do in the absence of a contract, but I'm sure you will agree I am being extremely fair".

"I agree nothing". Evelyn's face was twisted with anger and shock. "What about your poor wife? Who will look after her?"

"My poor wife, as you put it, will do perfectly well, and it is no longer any of your business Evelyn. Remember this. I am not as blind as you think I am. I know things about you, I know how you have attempted to defraud my family. Need I say anything more? But if you wish to argue the point, I will present my evidence to the police in England, and you can explain your behaviour to them. Now your flight leaves at seven-fifteen this evening. I suggest you take an hour or so to do your packing. I shall then call you a taxi to take you to the airport".

Evelyn continued to look at him in fury and amazement, her mouth opening and closing without making any comprehensible sound. But she grabbed the envelopes.

"You may go now. Oh and Evelyn" he beckoned her back for a second. "Please hand me your front door key before you leave".

She went out and slammed the door. Neville felt drained. It's done, he thought, it's over. His next thought was for Lois. He left the room and went looking for his wife. After a while he spotted her walking slowly down the road, leaning on her walking stick, obviously heading for the beach. She probably wants to escape for a while, he thought. Maybe she would find it too difficult to say goodbye to Evelyn, she's still coming to terms with the last few days. He had no wish to leave Evelyn alone in the apartment and knew that Lois would be making for her favourite shady spot at the edge of a line of palm trees. He would wait to see Evelyn safely off the premises and then meet his wife later for an evening walk. It would be just the two of them at last.

Chapter Twenty-Nine

1983

Nell was excited to receive a letter from her father telling her that they were to return to England for a while the following week. He explained in some detail the circumstances around his giving notice to Evelyn, wishing to spare Lois from having to listen to it again when they all met up again for the first time. He asked Nell not to refer to the matter and not even to mention Evelyn in front of her mother, for now at least. Nell felt a huge sense of relief that her father had at last taken such decisive and determined action, and hoped against hope that this would be the last any of them would hear of the woman who had come so close to destroying their family.

As she read on, she was overjoyed to hear that her mother was looking forward to seeing her grandchildren. Could this really be true, she wondered. Daddy has had such a hard time, dealing with Evelyn, explaining to Mummy how worried we've all been for so long and convincing her that Evelyn was up to no good. And now she seems to want to make up for lost time with us. The emotional turmoil that Nell had felt for so long about her mother was beginning to ease.

Neville and Lois were to stay at The Swan's Rest in Kirchington. It was a small, quiet hotel near the river, some way away from the city centre. This was perfect for Lois, and Neville had managed to book a ground floor suite of rooms for three weeks. Their homecoming was full of mixed emotions; they were glad to be back in England despite the fact that autumn was not far off, and were now looking forward to seeing Nell and the family, although Lois felt somehow nervous of their meeting and ashamed that she had so purposefully shut her and the children out of her life for so long. This was something she knew she would have to come to terms with over time. Both were still shaken that it had been necessary to dismiss Evelyn, and Neville was racked with guilt and regret that he had not been assertive enough to take action sooner, but he realised that the task would not have been any easier six months or a year previously.

There was to be a party at Moongarth to welcome the travellers. It would be just family, including Kathleen, Niall who had recently arrived from Ireland, and Jenny and Phil. Somehow, in between looking after the children, coping with the continuing disorder of the building work and running a busy household, Nell found time to shop and prepare a special buffet tea. She never stopped being thankful for the independence that passing her driving test earlier that year had given her.

It was an emotional moment for Nell when Lois hugged her awkwardly and asked if she could hold Brontë. Nell had for so long given up on that ever happening, and she knew it had taken a huge amount of effort on her mother's part to take that step. Arthur and Henry looked at their grandmother curiously as she spoke to them, and Lois realised with a pang that they regarded her as a stranger. Soon they returned to tipping their toys out of the toy box while Lois sat on the sofa with Brontë in her arms. Brontë was now over two months old and smiled and gurgled, reaching out at Lois's necklace. It was a milestone, and one which her husband and daughter had thought they would never witness.

"Elizabeth is my middle name too" Lois said, looking down at her granddaughter with tenderness, and then up at her daughter.

"I had no idea" said Nell and wondered why she had not known this simple fact about her mother.

Neville and Patrick exchanged glances, both wondering if they could believe what they were seeing. Kathleen took Niall off into the garden, ostensibly to ask for all the news from Ballymere, but realising that this was a time when the family needed some privacy. Jenny and Phil were busy in the kitchen making pots of tea and setting out trays, but after a while

Kathleen came back in and offered to help carry in the tea things, and Niall hung eagerly around the buffet table.

The atmosphere became more relaxed as the tea was poured, and everyone tucked in to the delicious food Nell had prepared. Conversation flowed freely. The transformation of Moongarth was discussed at length and after tea Patrick showed Neville around, mentally crossing his fingers that his father-in-law would approve of all the changes they had made. He need not have worried; Neville was delighted with the new look of the house, marvelling how Patrick had managed to achieve such a contemporary design whilst retaining the character of the family home. Lois was unable to go upstairs but Patrick had taken some photographs and had them printed a few days beforehand so that she was able to see how those rooms had been refurbished. She was impressed with the new extended kitchen and utility room, noticing immediately that it was now all on one level and that there was no longer a steep step down from the hallway.

"You could have stayed in these guest rooms, Mummy" said Nell, showing her how they had created the self-contained suite with a shower room on the ground floor. "But there is still some building work going on, there would be too much noise and disturbance for you. The next phase will be the basement, Patrick has an idea for making that into a playroom for the children when they're older".

Lois understood but pointed out that they were less than thirty minutes away in Kirchington and that they hoped to visit often during their stay. This is even better, thought Nell, it's not just a one-off visit.

They all assembled in the drawing room later for more tea, and any onlooker would have thought that this was a normal, happy family gathering; there was no visible sign of the strain and upheaval of the past few years. Nell had to remind herself that her mother had an acute condition that was life-long, for apart from her lack of mobility she seemed well and looked fit. She had a pale golden tan which had not yet started to fade, her eyes were bright, and she had put on a little weight which suited her. Perhaps the illness is in remission, Nell wondered. Then another thought occurred to her. Had Evelyn encouraged Lois to feel more unwell and more afflicted than she actually was, in order to increase her reliance and to reinforce her hold over her? It was possible, but hopefully that was all in the past now, and her mother would gradually regain a little of her previous strength and start to enjoy some independence again. She knew that was her father's dearest wish. She watched her chatting animatedly with Kathleen and Jenny about Solibrio; Evelyn's name was not mentioned, and Lois spoke enthusiastically about the comfortable apartment and the beach, and that there were hours of warm sunshine every day. Mummy is different altogether, Nell observed, it's like a miracle.

As Neville and Lois settled into their hotel sitting room later that evening, Neville asked his wife how she had enjoyed the day. She was clearly very tired by then, but she told him that she was so happy to have seen the family and met all her grandchildren. She had not referred to Evelyn since their homecoming, and although Neville felt sure that the events of the previous week were still very much on her mind, each day brings new hope of leaving that part of the past behind us, he thought.

"We will have to think about what help you will need when we go back to Spain" he said tentatively. "I could make some enquiries while we are here".

"There's no need" Lois was unexpectedly firm. "I have already thought about it. I should like to ask Kathleen".

Chapter Thirty

If anything, Patrick had underestimated Niall's reaction to the attic bed-sitting room that Nell had prepared for him.

Prior to Connor getting married and setting up home with Gráinne, and Sean and Patrick leaving Ireland, Niall had shared the largest bedroom at the farm with all four of his brothers. More recently he had just shared with Aidan who was out a great deal of the time, so even that was an improvement. But to have a room all to himself, comfortably furnished, a tiny shower room en-suite and his own wardrobe and chest of drawers was the height of luxury to Niall who throughout his sixteen years had been used to sharing every inch of space and fighting for every scrap of privacy.

To Niall, Moongarth was like a stately home. He had never imagined that he would live in such surroundings, and to be part of Patrick's family and to be treated like an adult was like a dream come true. He had visited Kathleen at the annex and seen her beautiful little flat, how she was enjoying life with new friends and had a more interesting job. England is so different, he thought. Small wonder that Patrick had no wish to return to Ireland permanently; Niall understood that those who had left still felt the pull of their homeland from time to time but realised that this was a sentimental attachment; there was little else to keep young men in rural West Cork these days.

The arrangement was for Niall to spend six weeks at Moongarth to work alongside Patrick or one of his men, just to have a taste of the rigours of the construction industry and to decide whether he would like to go on to be employed permanently. If he wished to train, Patrick would set him up with an apprenticeship, either in bricklaying, plumbing or carpentry, so that in time he would have a recognised trade and a formal qualification. Niall had already decided that he wanted more than anything to work in his brother's business.

The farm back at Ballymere was the only alternative but he had discounted that; England offered so many more possibilities. He could see how Patrick had made such a success of his life in a few short years and had taken every opportunity. Kathleen also had turned her life around and had never looked back; she certainly had no regrets and had made the most of every chance offered to her.

With Nell and the children, his brother now living with him and his sister only thirty minutes away, Patrick felt surrounded by family. It was hard to believe that less than five years ago he had come alone to England as a young single man, not knowing anyone except for Joe whom he had met on the ferry. He felt optimistic. His love for Nell grew stronger every day – her reconciliation with her mother had removed a huge burden from them both. The work on Moongarth was nearing completion and his business was doing well; they were financially secure. Could life get any better, he wondered.

* * *

Neville was astonished to hear that Lois was considering asking Kathleen to be her companion and to return with them to Spain.

"Do you really know her well enough, dear?" he asked, looking puzzled. "And she has no medical knowledge. She's a receptionist and before that she served in a shop".

"I like Kathleen, Neville. She'll be good company. She's very honest and she's been through a lot, I can tell. Her life was very unhappy until she came to England. She admits some of it was her own fault, she had a disastrous marriage that only lasted five minutes and then she lost heart with everything, I think she nearly gave up on herself. But she's done well over here. She sings Nell's praises, you know. And employing someone trained didn't end well, did it?" This was the nearest Lois had come to referring to Evelyn.

As usual, Lois was seeing things as she wished them to be, but Neville was used to that. It was remarkable that she had been able to move on from the crisis so quickly, and he was so relieved to see his wife becoming more positive and enthusiastic that he decided to give her suggestion the benefit of the doubt.

"Shall we ask her round to tea at the weekend and find out what she thinks? She already has a job at the accountants, she might not want to give that up. And there's that lovely flat that goes with the job...." Neville was doubtful. "Don't put your hopes up, my love. If this doesn't work out, we still have time to find someone else. But Kathleen is more or less family now, when all's said and done". He mulled over the idea for a moment. "But better to have someone we know, if she's willing". He reflected on the disastrous decision they had made with Evelyn, and he had no intention of repeating the mistakes of the past. This time he would set out exact terms and make it plain that he and Lois would spend some time alone.

Kathleen was surprised to receive an invitation to tea with Neville and Lois but accepted willingly. She had enjoyed chatting with Lois and she thought Neville was the perfect gentleman. He collected her in his hire car at three o'clock on the following Saturday and she sat in awe as a mouth-watering afternoon tea was wheeled in by the hotel room service waiter. She had never stayed in a hotel in her life, and until she came to England, she had only been out for a meal in a restaurant a few times.

There was small talk at first, but Kathleen was beginning to learn that often, this preceded something more important and wondered what it could be.

Neville spoke first. "We are planning to go back to Spain in a couple of weeks' time" he said, stirring his tea. "Lois cannot cope with the cold winter months in England and the weather in Solibrio is so much better for her". He took a sip of tea and continued.

"For reasons I won't go into, our previous arrangements with help for Lois have fallen through". He was still reluctant to mention Evelyn by name and had no wish to elaborate. "So, we are looking to find someone to accompany us back to Spain, to give assistance and companionship to Lois when required. She no longer needs a nurse. It will not be a full-time position as Lois and I plan to spend time together whenever we can". Neville wanted to make that clear from the very beginning.

Lois, who had been silent until then, turned to Kathleen.

"Kathleen, we are wondering if you would like to come to Spain with us? It will be a paid position, of course, we will discuss the salary later. You will have your own room, board and lodging and quite a bit of free time. We will pay your air fare. I told you about the apartment, it's very close to the beach, there are nice shops and restaurants, there's a bus into town every hour and the weather is always good".

Kathleen sat open mouthed. This just couldn't be happening. What was that English saying she had heard about London buses? You wait for one for ages and then two come along at once. She had been lucky enough to have one wonderful job land in her lap, and now here was another offer, out of the blue. She was utterly shocked and didn't know what to say. She sat speechless for several moments.

Neville came to her rescue. "Please take some time to think it over, Kathleen. We don't expect an answer now, and of course you will wish to talk to your employer. But I think Jonathan and Barbara will be understanding. Let's leave it at that for now, and perhaps you can telephone us, say Monday evening, with your decision".

"Thank you so very much. It's a grand offer". Sometimes when Kathleen was put on the spot or flustered, her Irish accent became more pronounced. "I would really love to come to Spain, but I will have to talk to Jonathan first. He's been such a good boss, and they were kind enough to offer me somewhere to live".

"Of course," said Lois. "We will talk again on Monday. Now, would you like more tea?"

* * *

The following afternoon, Kathleen sat with Jonathan and Barbara in their conservatory, and having made profuse apologies, explained nervously that she had been offered a post as companion to Lois in Spain and was unsure what to do.

Barbara smiled. "There's no need to apologise, Kathleen. It's a great opportunity for you".

"But I'd feel guilty, letting you down. You've been so good to me".

Jonathan was sanguine. "The main thing is, what would you like to do, Kathleen?"

"I would love to go to Spain. I've never travelled, you see, coming to England is the furthest I've ever been from home. I've never been on a plane, never visited a hot country. But I do love my job here with you, and my flat...."

"You wouldn't be letting us down. I won't deny we would miss you Kathleen, you've fitted in so well at the office. But I can ring an agency tomorrow and arrange for a temp. That's not a problem".

Barbara had a suggestion. "Why not ask Neville if you can take the post on a six-month trial basis? If it works out you could continue, if not you could come back to your old job. Jonathan will hold it open for you, won't you?" She looked at her husband, who nodded. "And all being well, the annex will still be available, or we will help you find somewhere else".

It seemed a perfect solution, and Kathleen thanked them once again for being so understanding. She had not been so excited since opening that letter from Nell back in Ballymere and knowing that her life was about to change. But Barbara turned to practicalities.

"Do you have a passport, Kathleen? You will need one for Spain".

Kathleen's face fell. She had only needed identification to come to England. "There won't be time to get one", she said, disappointment clouding her face. "Neville wants to leave in a fortnight. But I do have my birth certificate".

Barbara, always determined to overcome obstacles, said she would take Kathleen to the Irish Embassy in London to make her application, which would be quicker. "You would need to apply for an Irish passport, and there are procedures for people who need to travel abroad urgently" she explained. "I can countersign it as your employer". Jonathan agreed she could have the Tuesday off. "And while we're in London we can do some sightseeing and have lunch out".

Back in the annex, Kathleen was thoughtful. Why are people so nice to me? She had often wondered this to herself since leaving Ireland. I don't deserve it. Even my own mother thought I would come to a bad end. But that's all in the past, I have another wonderful opportunity now. On Monday evening she picked up the telephone and gave Neville her answer.

Chapter Thirty-One
1983–1984

"His name's Zacky" said Patrick, who had brought home a black and white border collie. The dog was looking round the breakfast room excitedly, his tail wagging and straining on his lead, eager to explore.

"He's from a rescue centre; he's in need of a good home. I could have brought us a younger dog, but I thought you wouldn't want all the extra work of training a puppy. Collies are working dogs; he can come with me sometimes. He has a lovely temperament; he'll be fine with the children".

By now, Nell was down on her knees stroking Zacky, who rolled onto his back as she tickled him. "I love him already" she said, "but you might have warned me! I had no idea you were even thinking about getting a dog. I have nothing here for him".

"It's ok, we'll go out this afternoon and get him a basket and a bowl. I picked up some dog food on the way home".

At that moment Arthur came running into the room and seeing the dog, started laughing and made straight for Zacky. Nell held him back. "Don't get too close darling, we need to let Zacky get to know us first. This is his new home; he has to get used to it. We'll take him for a walk in the garden after lunch and he will want to have a good sniff round and follow some scents. That's what dogs like doing". Henry, who had trailed in after his brother also tottered up to Zacky, who licked his hand. He looked up at Nell as if to say, is this all right? She picked him up and sat him in his highchair. "Lunch first, before Brontë wakes up" she said. "Then after I've fed her, we will all go shopping for doggy things. Arthur, you can choose him a toy".

The Walsh family had settled down after the whirlwind of surprises following the return of Neville and Lois. It wasn't until she really understood all that had taken place regarding Evelyn that Nell realised what strain she herself had been under. This was partly her own increasing anxiety for her mother's well-being but also due to the worry she had felt for her father to whom she was very close, and the knowledge of what a difficult position he had been in for so long. It was a relief that things had at last come to a head and that her mother had eventually realised that she was being used and exploited. The change in Lois's behaviour was remarkable. There were times when apart from her slow mobility and loss of dexterity, her mother's illness was less obvious; Nell began to agree with her father that Evelyn had encouraged Lois to think herself more needy, more seriously ill and therefore more dependent. This was a false premise, designed to gradually erode Lois's confidence. The constant attention Evelyn had given her, and the way in which incrementally she had isolated her from her family, had been for Evelyn's benefit only.

Patrick thought Neville should have reported Evelyn to the police as the evidence of Evelyn's deceitful intentions existed, but as she had not gone on to commit the crime, albeit she had been foiled in the attempt, that part could be hard to prove in court. Neville thought that he had frightened her sufficiently on the day of her dismissal into believing that he could have her charged, and this would ensure that she would be gone from their lives from now on and that they could make a fresh start.

The other bombshell was that Kathleen was to be Lois's new companion and was about to leave her job with Jonathan and travel to Spain the following week. Nothing could have been further from Nell's thoughts when Kathleen telephoned her to tell her the news. Within a few days, Kathleen had accepted the offer from Neville and Lois, had received her passport and Jonathan had given her an option of returning to her receptionist job if things didn't work out. But Nell, who had for a long time seen Kathleen's potential if only she were given the right chances in life, was wholly in favour of the plan and could tell that her parents were looking forward to this new arrangement with enthusiasm. Daddy just wants to enjoy his retirement with Mummy in peace and quiet without any more worry, she thought.

Patrick was stunned. Not for the first time he was astonished, not just in the change in his sister but how other people viewed her; as someone who could be trusted, who would conduct themselves well and be relied upon. He knew that his parents were equally amazed that their wayward and unmanageable daughter had not only turned over a new leaf but had gone on to make such a success of her life in two short years.

Nell had a sneaking suspicion that Patrick had brought a dog into the household in the hope that it would take her mind off her worries. She was right, Patrick had become increasingly concerned about Nell and had made plans to rescue a dog long before Nell's parents returned to Kirchington. But everything had fallen into place; her parents would soon be travelling back to Spain with Kathleen with the previous crisis overcome, and as well as Niall, they now had another addition to their family who was already making his presence felt.

So busy family life continued at Moongarth. Arthur had started at the Young Drover's Nursery in the village; Henry would join him the following year. Nell was keen for her children to have a head start in their education, and she made sure that she read to them every night at bedtime. The boys cuddled up with her on the bed to listen, with Brontë laying nearby in her carry cot. Arthur knew some of the books off by heart although he could not yet read, but could recognise some words and letters, while Henry pointed at the pictures. Sometimes Nell made up stories about animals or places they had seen during their walks or in the garden, and this gave her inspiration to write a children's book one day. When I have time, she said to herself, remembering that her first commitment was to the Kirchington Evening Echo and that she must do something about that soon.

Patrick, as always was busy. Walsh and Sons were in demand and from time to time he took on extra men in order to meet deadlines. Occasionally things did not work out, there had been one contract recently where payment had been delayed, which caused Patrick to dip into his reserves unexpectedly. This was a timely lesson and after taking advice from Jonathan he checked the credentials of companies more thoroughly.

As well as settling in well with the family, Niall had begun to adjust to life in the building trade. Getting up early and working long days were difficult for him at first, and Patrick had to explain to him very firmly that if he wanted to do a man's job, he would have to get used to a tough regime; out at the crack of dawn in all weathers, taking responsibility for his own safety and that of others; remembering that someone was paying his wages to work hard and finish a project on time. But his brother was a good role model and Niall recalled that not so long ago, Patrick was in his shoes and just starting out. Now he owned his own business and was leading a successful life. He adored his sister-in-law, often praising her cooking. At sixteen he was always hungry, and Nell became accustomed to catering for two grown men's appetites. Arthur and Henry were now eating the same food as the rest of the family, and Brontë was growing fast.

On the first Sunday each month, they all attended Mass in Lamberham. Sometimes they stopped for a cup of coffee after the service. Father Egan was always welcoming, and pleased to see that Niall came along too; unlike Ballymere there were very few young families in church. Nell knew that Bridget would approve and thought affectionately of her mother-in-law, realising with a jolt that they had not yet made the promised return visit to Ireland. Despite only having spent two weeks of her life there, Nell felt a yearning to go back and re-live the experiences of their earlier holiday. Their children were half Irish, after all; she wanted them to grow up knowing where their father came from and to learn about their heritage.

By spring the following year, the work on Moongarth was almost finished. All that remained to be done was redecoration and carpeting in the drawing room and dining room. The project had been a huge undertaking and at times Patrick had wondered if the budget, and Nell's patience would stretch far enough. When he thought of how much had been achieved, especially with three small children, a demanding business and all the worry about Nell's parents, he was amazed that they had come through it unscathed. But here they were, almost ready to invite The Echo back to do a further feature on the refurbishment. But Nell had stalled over this. She felt guilty that she had done nothing about the specimen article she had agreed to write and that contacting the Echo would prompt Toby to ask questions about its progress. But with the demands of her children and all the events of the past year she had had so little opportunity for writing; if she did manage to carve out any time to herself in the evenings, she was exhausted or wanted to spend it with Patrick.

As Brontë approached her first birthday, her routine became more settled and apart from occasional broken nights with teething she was a placid and contented baby. Nell became less tired as a result and her mind turned back to her books. She tried to spend at least half an hour each day reading; she still had a reading list from her 'A' level studies and decided to start with that, feeling the need to expand her mind beyond nappies, cooking and housework. Jenny was a star but even with her help there were never enough hours in the day. Nell was still only twenty-two and was determined to have a life as a person in her own right as well as being a wife and mother. But reading did not give her the satisfaction that it once did; she felt that familiar urge to write returning, to do something creative herself. Now is as good a time as any to tackle the piece for the Echo, she decided.

She made friends with Donna and Katy who ran the nursery school. Sometimes when she took Arthur she stayed to help, at the same time watching Henry tottering around and keeping one eye on Brontë and occasionally joined the leaders for a cup of coffee at the end of the session. They had not lived in Drover's Cross for very long and Nell found herself telling them about the history of the village, how she had grown up there and moved away then returned, now with a husband and three children. She realised she had a wealth of knowledge about the area and the two friends listened intently as she described the changes she had seen since her childhood, and the restoration project undertaken at Moongarth. On the way home, deep in thought, she formed some ideas in her mind. As soon as Brontë went down for her nap after lunch and the boys had settled at play with Jenny supervising, Nell sat at the table in the breakfast room and started work on her first offering to the Echo. As Toby had suggested, it was to be a roundup of village life at Drover's Cross. She spent an hour composing a snapshot of forthcoming weekend events, with some nature notes added. She tried to make it appeal to all age groups and to reflect her own experiences as a long-time resident of the village. In total it was less than five hundred words. She typed it out and enclosed it with a covering letter to the Features Editor, explaining that this was her first attempt, she could write a longer piece if required and would be willing to submit a monthly or weekly column if the first one proved popular with readers.

Almost by return of post, the editor wrote back, thanking Nell for her article and asking if she would be able to write a series of six weekly features, each of approximately fifteen hundred words. Deadline dates were specified and a fee of twenty-five pounds would be paid for each item. If the series proved successful then a permanent arrangement would be made under a formal contract.

And thus, the Kirchington Evening Echo began to publish Drover's Diary, written by Nell Walsh.

Chapter Thirty-Two

Nell didn't realise just how much work writing a weekly column would involve. There was plenty to write about; during her last trip to the village shops she had seen notices advertising the local book club, the fitness class, the wine-making circle and realised that the varied programme of the Women's Institute alone would fill a whole article. A wide range of events were held at the Village Hall; Nell could go on to mention the Amateur Dramatic Society, the Brownies, Scouts and Guides, the Shanty Singers and the Seniors Lunch Club. St Luke's Parish Church had its own calendar of activities, and The Herders pub on the village green held a weekly quiz night. She couldn't possibly write about so many but decided to visit one club each week and cover it in some detail with a brief mention of the others. The diary was supplemented by her own observations of her surroundings; the rise and flood of the River Haske in the spring; when she saw the first primroses appear along its banks; the date the swallows arrived. If she had enough space, she added a description of the village as she remembered it during her childhood when carrying out errands for her mother, and the flowers and insects she used to take for the nature table at school.

Patrick was so proud to see her name in print beside the title Drover's Diary. "We are both known in the community now" he said excitedly. "The Walsh name is being noticed". He knew how important this chance was for Nell, this little piece of independence. Nell realised with a shock that the fee from the newspaper was the first money she had ever earned. Never mind, everyone must start somewhere, she thought.

The following year, with the renovations at Moongarth fully completed, she came to a decision. One evening as she and Patrick were sitting alone, Nell with a cup of tea and Patrick with a glass of Guinness, she said suddenly:

"Patrick I would like one of the attic rooms for myself. A study – a space where I can write. Dad's old observatory room".

Patrick looked mildly surprised. "How much room do you need to do a bit of writing? You can sit in the breakfast room or at the kitchen table".

"Patrick it's more than a 'bit of writing' as you call it. It means a lot to me. And it's not just about the space, it's peace and quiet that I need, away from the children now and then, to concentrate. I really want to make a success of this newspaper feature; it could lead on to more things. I have an idea for a children's book as well".

"I don't see why not". Patrick drained his glass. "We can't really disturb Niall; he needs to have the room with the shower. But we should work out something about the bedrooms. Arthur and Henry won't always want to be sharing". Nell knew that he still remembered the overcrowding at the farm in Ireland and was determined that his sons would have their own space. "Brontë will need her own room before too long as well". He winked at her. "And it's high time that we had our bedroom to ourselves again".

"I mean it Patrick. I'm going to keep you up to this". Nell refused to be deflected from her purpose. "Just make sure that the front attic room is ready for me soon. I don't need much. There's already a radiator, a carpet and enough electric points. But I would like a desk, a lamp, a cupboard and a few shelves".

"Don't worry, it will be done. I'll try and get it ready for you in the next couple of weeks. Niall will help me. Mustn't interfere with the creative flow" he teased.

Nell was well aware that despite his attempts at humour, Patrick did take her request, and her writing seriously. This was payback time, and he knew it. She had never faltered in giving unswerving support to his business, even in the early days when their fortunes had been precarious. But he had done well, mainly through his own hard work although a certain amount of luck and meeting the right people had helped. The Walsh name was well known and respected, and he had never been short of work. In time he would go further. The refurbishment of Moongarth and the publicity it had brought him was a huge boost to his business as well, but it had come at a cost in terms of the strain on family life, the disruption and the sacrifices Nell had made. Living in a building site for several years with three under-fives was not for the faint hearted. But now she just wanted something for herself, something she had achieved through her own efforts that was nothing to do with her children, her parents or the history of the house.

Patrick was as good as his word. The following Saturday he took Nell into Kirchington to choose some office furniture and the rest of the items she needed, and later that day he and Niall assembled the desk and cupboard and put up three rows of shelves; fewer than in Neville's time but sufficient for Nell to accommodate all the books she had kept from college and her schooldays.

It had been agreed that twice a week Jenny would look after the children in the afternoon for an hour so that Nell could write. This was a luxury and would at last give her some uninterrupted time with which to formulate ideas and plan her writing diary for the months ahead. Some of her research in the village was done during the day when out walking Zacky, or on her way back from the school run, but many of the clubs were held in the evening so at those times she had to prevail upon Patrick or Niall to listen for the children.

As time went on, Nell started to flesh out some details for her first book. She had several themes in mind, all based on the stories she had made up for her children and were inspired by animals they had seen in the garden or on their walks in the countryside. She had five titles in mind:

The Lonely Frog
Fletcher the Pheasant
Bertie the Bashful Badger

Freddy the Friendly Fox
Dan the Dippy Donkey

She had also started thinking of a story about Zacky and his life before he came to live with them but had no title for it so far.

In the end it was Freddy that she decided on. They had often seen him in the field behind the house. Like most foxes he was bold and unafraid especially in his quest for food, and had become a frequent visitor, even venturing onto the lawn at dusk. They had named him Freddy; Arthur became excited to see him and often cried if he didn't put in an appearance. The story centred on how he made a home in a little girl's outdoor Wendy House, and she brought him food secretly every day.

Nell completed the first draft of the story very quickly but soon realised that she would need an illustrator; pictures in children's books were all important. It was something else she would have to research, and the rest of the titles would have to wait. More than anything she needed time, and this was always in short supply; she had already imposed on Jenny's goodwill as far as she could.

Toby Stannon and his photographer made their return visit to Moongarth that autumn, later than planned. Originally it had been intended as a Christmas feature the year before but the work on the house had over-run. Patrick wanted it to be finished in every detail before allowing the cameras back, and Nell had been relieved to be spared any reminders for the newspaper column. But a date had been fixed, and the interview was to take place in October, just before her twenty third birthday, by which time Drover's Diary had become a regular feature.

The photoshoot went well, and the house and garden were captured from every angle. Jason, the photographer was new to the Echo so had not seen Moongarth in its earlier stages of progress, but Toby was visibly impressed by how much had been achieved since his last visit. Nell and Jenny had taken trouble to clean the house from top to bottom, tidy away all the children's toys and arrange fresh flowers in the downstairs rooms. After they all met up for a cup of coffee in the breakfast room, Patrick took Jason down to photograph the basement, which was the last room to be completed, although still empty of furniture. Toby moved on to the subject of Drover's Diary. "It's gone down very well with the readers", he said, helping himself to a biscuit. "People like to read about local places they know, and many readers like your little snippets about how the village used to be".

"You make me sound ancient!" said Nell, and they both laughed. "Well, I'm talking about people of your own age who remember it" he explained. "We've had some lovely comments. So if you're agreeable, we will be sending you a year's contract shortly. There will be an increase in your fee, and we will review it annually".

Nell had been hoping that her diary could continue but to hear it confirmed directly from the Features Editor was a great relief; this was her first offering as a professional writer, and she had taken nothing for granted.

"It's the only piece of serious writing I've done since I wrote about Ireland" she confided.

Toby wanted to hear more.

"Where we were staying...some of the scenes we visited.... it was just the feeling those places gave me. There was a wildness, a desolation about the landscape and the coastline that I could only explain by writing. I couldn't have given a talk about it. It wasn't a typical holiday destination like you would see in a brochure. The atmosphere was...well...other-worldly. It really affected me. We were only there for two weeks but I made lots of notes and I wrote about it as soon as I came back to England". Suddenly she felt foolish in front of this seasoned journalist. But he seemed to understand.

"When you're writing a piece like that it's your impressions, your perceptions, even your feelings that readers want to hear about. Some might say it comes from your soul. People can obtain facts about a place from lots of sources.

But the writer's own observations, their own reflections are what will set your story apart".

Nell was silent but hung on to every word.

"We have a regular travel page in the Echo" he continued. "Would you like to submit your piece?"

"Please don't think I am an experienced traveller" Nell wanted to clear up that point quickly. "For reasons I can't explain just now, the trip to Ireland was my first proper holiday. I have never been anywhere else".

"That doesn't matter. I'd like to see your story".

Nell agreed to send it to him on condition that they would have a further discussion before any plans for publication went ahead. I will have time to do a proof-read and make any corrections, she thought, and felt a buzz of excitement that interest was being shown in her work, writings that she once thought would never be read by anyone else.

Hearing the others returning, Nell made a quick decision. "Do you know of anyone who might be interested in illustrating a children's book?" she asked. "I have a first one in draft".

Toby's eyebrows shot up. "Wow! You are a woman of many talents!" he said in surprise. "I might know someone. I'll make some enquiries and get back to you".

As the two men went to take their leave, Toby had one more question for Patrick. "How would you feel if we did a continuing feature on your family" he asked. "Now all the work on the house is finished, readers might like to hear more about you all. You're well known now, you know".

There was a pause, then Patrick spoke firmly. "I'm sorry but the answer must be no. I think we need a bit of time to settle down. It's been a busy few years, we've hardly had time to draw breath. Nell is enjoying writing her column and we will look forward to seeing the final feature on the house, but that's as far as it can go, I'm afraid".

Toby looked disappointed but said he understood. He had a young family himself.

After they left, Patrick turned to Nell. "That put me on the spot just there" he said. "I hope you think I said the right thing".

"Of course," said Nell, putting her arms around his neck. "We don't want to live in a goldfish bowl. We need a break from everything now".

I'll tell him about the Ireland article another time, she said to herself.

Chapter Thirty-Three

1985–1988

The weeks passed, another Christmas came and went; Henry turned three and Brontë was now eighteen months. Arthur was to start at the village school in the January term; he was not five until the following April but more than ready.

Drover's Diary was now a fixture in the Echo and Toby had put her in touch with an illustrator who said she would like to see the draft of Nell's first book so that she could decide if she could offer her services. Everything was going well; Niall had decided to take a carpentry apprenticeship and would attend Kirchington College one day each week from the following September, working for Patrick the rest of the time.

"That's the first place I worked when I came to England", Patrick told his brother. "And it's where I met Nell" he winked at his wife across the breakfast table.

"Yes, that place has a lot to answer for" she quipped. "Look at us now".

They heard from Kathleen regularly. She loved the life in Solibrio, she said, and was so happy helping Lois and making herself useful. Nell found herself wondering for the hundredth time how the unlikely pairing of Kathleen and her mother had ever happened, but she knew that both her parents were delighted with how the arrangement was working out. This was even more surprising after the near disaster with Evelyn; they could have been forgiven for being extra cautious but they both seemed to have moved on from the strain of the past few years.

Kathleen was still reeling from the turn of events, the second major change in her life in two years. Here she was living in Spain in a beautiful apartment by the sea with enough money in her pocket, board and lodging included and with plenty of time to herself. The weather was pleasant and dry, even in winter and she was looking forward to sunbathing on the beach during the hotter months, so different from in Ireland where she never left the house without an umbrella. There was some night life too; she had noticed some of the bars and clubs along the strand stayed open until late; the restaurants were affordable and offered a range of local dishes, although she observed that some holiday makers still asked for sausage and chips.

She was aware, without knowing the precise details, that Neville had fired Evelyn because she had let them down badly. This made Kathleen even more determined to do her very best in this new position as companion, and not to give them a moment's concern. She had become fond of Lois, whose demands were not so great; she helped her shower and dress in the morning, prepared the breakfast, tidied the apartment and did the laundry. The change in Lois in her holiday surroundings was striking; she underwent a transformation almost as soon as she stepped off the plane. Life here was relaxed and unhurried; perhaps it was the climate, Kathleen wondered, or maybe it was the absence of stress – that was certainly the case for Neville. He was insistent that he and Lois spent the afternoons and evenings together so after preparing lunch Kathleen was free to spend time as she wished. Sometimes she would run errands for them in the town or shop at the local market, occasionally stopping for a cup of coffee at a beachside bar, enjoying the view of the Mediterranean and indulging in her favourite pastime: people-watching.

Her only slight regret was leaving Andy. True, there had been no firm plans for an engagement and Kathleen realised that even if he had proposed, there were a great many legalities to be untangled before she could contemplate re-marrying. But they rarely exchanged letters now. On one level she missed him, but such were the distractions of her new life in Solibrio that each day she thought about him a little less.

* * *

Life at Moongarth was never dull. Arthur settled in well at school and with Henry attending nursery regularly Nell found she had a little more time for herself, but Brontë needed a great deal of her attention so once again the writing of children's books had been put on hold, with the exception of Freddy. Bryony Cox, the illustrator had presented a selection of drawings to accompany the book, and Nell had provisionally accepted them, but she had progressed no further towards having it published. Her weekly column continued to be popular, however. She had also submitted her piece on the holiday in Ireland which had been well received and to her delight, complimentary letters from readers were published regularly on the newspaper's contact page.

Each time Nell thought about that trip almost five years ago, she realised that they were no nearer to making a return visit to Ireland. It was not due to lack of money or intention, but mainly because Patrick was so busy. He works too hard, she sighed, knowing that he would never turn down work, never pass up a contract and was always willing to work late and put in extra hours at weekends to ensure that a certain stage was completed, or that a job was finished on time.

"It's just how it is when you work for yourself, Nelly", he said taking her in his arms one evening when Nell complained that she hardly ever saw him. "If you miss a trick, someone else will be ready to step in. It's only a few years ago that we were watching every penny. You don't want to go back to that, do you?"

"Of course not". Suddenly she felt guilty. Patrick is doing this for us, for our family, for our home, she thought. He doesn't want to risk us going without anything. He remembers how tough finding work was in Ireland, that's why he came to England. But if he hadn't, she would never have met him. "I just miss you, that's all. We all do".

"I'll have a word with Joe and see if I can take some time off soon" he promised, and Nell had to be content with that.

But it didn't happen that year, and two more years were to elapse before they were able to return to Ireland.

* * *

Can you see your younger self in your children, Nell wondered as she watched her daughter. As Brontë grew, Nell realised that she was going to be a clever child. At the age of four she was quick, attentive, curious. If it had been possible to remember herself at that same age she would have remarked on the similarities between them. Brontë had been a contented baby but had begun to show signs of the same insecurities as Nell had experienced as a small girl, but whereas Nell had been reacting against the years of trauma her parents had been through, for Brontë there was no such explanation. She was sensitive, often tearful for no obvious reason, constantly needing her mother's company and preferred being with Nell to playing with her brothers or other children.

"It will sort itself out when she goes to school" said Patrick, after Nell's third unsuccessful attempt to introduce her to nursery. "It will have to; she'll be five in a few months".

For a brief time, Nell had toyed with the idea of educating Brontë at home, but she was expecting another baby that spring. It had come as a surprise but a welcome one. Ronan Neville was born in May 1988 into a noisy boisterous household, and Nell's concerns about Brontë were set aside for a while, the decision having been taken to postpone her starting school until the following September. Nell did not want her daughter to feel pushed out because of the arrival of her little brother, although he was the most placid and undemanding baby she could have wished for. Patrick teased her, saying that Ronan knew he had to be good because he was at the bottom of the Walsh pecking order.

Patrick had been invited to join the Chamber of Commerce in Kirchington. He felt it was an honour, one that he had never expected to receive, and recalled how his own start in business had begun at the business gala held at Christmas many years ago by that same organisation. It was all down to networking, Neville had said. Patrick had never forgotten that. He felt he owed a great deal to the community that had helped him succeed, and if he could encourage other newly self-employed people by giving them the benefit of his experience, he should do so.

Nell was pleased for him and proud that he had been asked but realised that it would mean even more time spent away from her and the children, and made a promise to herself that she would keep him up to taking them away on holiday later that year.

But it was for the saddest of reasons that the family crossed the Irish Sea that summer. At the end of July, Dermot died suddenly.

Patrick was full of remorse when he first heard the news. "You were right, we should have gone to see them last year. I left it too late. I'll never forgive myself". It was the first time she had ever seen a man cry, and Nell's heart went out to him.

"Patrick don't blame yourself. Your Dad was so proud of you, of everything you've achieved. He loved you, you know, and they both had a lovely holiday with us that time. None of us realised he had a heart condition, he didn't even know himself". She tried to comfort him, and the children, realising something was wrong were quiet and subdued.

Hasty arrangements were made for the journey. Jenny agreed to call in to Moongarth each day and look after Zacky. A minibus was hired for the trip as Kathleen and Niall were to accompany them. Kathleen had not seen her father since her parent's trip to England and she too felt numb with shock. Unlike Nell's last journey to Ireland, which was full of excitement and anticipation, this time the mood was sombre and downcast, but as they drove off the ferry at Rosslare, she had the feeling of coming home, which was extraordinary, seeing as she had only spent two weeks in Ireland in her entire life.

Bridget and Orla rushed out to meet them as soon as they arrived at the farm, Bridget looking drawn and exhausted but overjoyed to see them all and to be introduced to her new grandson. Aidan held back but embraced his brothers and Kathleen; he had little to say but sadness was etched clearly in his face. Connor and Gráinne joined them for dinner, they now had a little daughter, Aisling, who was two. So it was a large family gathering that sat down to dinner that evening; happy to be together but feeling keenly the absence of Dermot, whom Bridget said was a family man through and through and would have loved to have been sitting round the table with them all.

It had been decided that Bridget would retire. She and Orla would swap houses with Connor and Gráinne who would take over the farm as planned. Aidan now had a house which went with his teaching job and Orla, now twenty-three was planning to get married later that year and move out; there had been many changes since Nell and Patrick had last visited.

During dinner there was a knock at the door. Patrick got up to answer it, knowing that his mother was not expecting anyone.

A tall red-haired young man stood there. The likeness to Patrick was unmistakable.

"Sean!" The brothers hugged and Bridget gasped in delight. Soon the whole family was in uproar. Although Bridget had managed to telephone her son in America to tell him the sad news about his father, she had not expected him to make the journey back to Ireland for the funeral and was overcome at seeing him for the first time in nearly ten years.

"I now have all my children and grandchildren under the same roof". It was a bittersweet moment for Bridget as she thought of the one person missing. Nell thought how much she could learn from this strong, brave, capable woman who even in the throes of bereavement was ever practical and making the most of having her family all around her.

Sean was excited to meet five new nephews and nieces and to be introduced to Nell for the first time. His Irish accent was much slighter than Patrick's and had a distinct drawl although they had both been away from Ireland for several years. Bridget would not leave his side and Nell realised with a shock that his mother had not expected to see him ever again and wondered how she herself would cope if she ever had to wave a final goodbye to any of her children.

The funeral took place two days later at Ballymere, and Connor, Patrick and Sean prepared the largest of the barns for the wake. Several of Bridget's nearest neighbours called with pies, ready cut sandwiches, rolls and cakes for the funeral tea, and helped Kathleen and Gráinne make it ready. Supplies of beer, wine and whiskey were brought in. Some dubious bottles of poitin, a local homemade beverage donated by friends stood on the table. Patrick shook his head. "Don't you be trying any of that" he said to Nell jokingly, explaining that it had been brewed in someone's garden shed, "unless you want the mother of all hangovers in the morning". His brothers laughed. A little bit of humour broke the tension somehow. But on the evening before the funeral, Dermot's body was brought back to the farm and Bridget and her sons sat up overnight in vigil.

Aidan had arranged for a local band with two fiddlers, a guitar and whistle to provide some musical entertainment. Nell, who to her own surprise had to admit that she had never attended a wake before and could hardly remember the funeral of her little brother, was amazed that it was not the sorrowful occasion she had expected but more of a celebration.

During the days that followed, there was plenty to do helping Bridget sort out her belongings in readiness for the move, and Connor and Gráinne were doing likewise. Work on the farm continued regardless but there were several extra pairs of hands, and this also gave the brothers a chance to spend time together, their first opportunity for many years. Nell did what she could to help around the house while Orla looked after the older children, but she was constantly tired as Ronan was still only two months old and not yet sleeping through the night. It was not a holiday in the usual sense and was anything but restful; the household was always busy, and Nell had a glimpse of how it must have been in years gone by when all the Walsh family lived there together. But Patrick was determined that they would have one day out together and leaving all the children including Ronan with Bridget and Kathleen, they headed out onto the Wild Atlantic Way. The coastline was different here, still dramatic and rugged but interspersed with mystical islands at times shrouded in mist, ancient buildings on the edge of the shoreline, and steep cliffs lashed by the powerful tides of the Atlantic Ocean. There were stunning views around every curve of the road, and the countryside seemed untouched by the twentieth century. They stopped for lunch at Ladies View overlooking the Ring of Kerry, so named after Queen Victoria's visit when her ladies-in-waiting admired the scenery. Nell was once again entranced by the breathtaking landscape. "I can never get enough of this beautiful country Patrick" she said with reverence. "I know why you came to England, but it must have been so hard to leave all this behind".

Later that evening, Sean took them by surprise by saying that he intended to stay in West Cork for a time, in fact he would like to come to stay with Nell and Patrick in England as well if they would have him. Patrick wondered privately if everything was working out for his brother in Boston but decided not to ask him until there was a suitable opportunity.

As they were together in the barn doing a final clear-up after the wake, Patrick asked Sean about his life in America. Sean hesitated.

"As a matter of fact, I'm not going back at all" he said at last. "I haven't told Mam yet; I only decided a short time ago".

"Have things gone wrong for you out there?" Patrick ventured to ask.

"No, quite the opposite, I've done ok. I've not made a fortune, but I've come back with something to show for the last ten years. I had a good job in a company that supplies materials to the building trade. I worked my way up, had several promotions. But the thing is", Sean looked slightly embarrassed. "I suppose I just missed Ireland and the family. The pace of life in Boston is too fast, too stressful. Yes, the money was good, but I began to feel I was just living to work because you get caught up on the merry-go-round and you can't get off. There's pressure on you to do more and more. I think my health was beginning to suffer, and I got out just in time".

"What will you do?"

"I'll say here on the farm for a while, help Mam settle in and give Connor a hand. But I was serious about coming to England. Could you put me up, just for a short time while I have a look around?"

Patrick, knowing Nell would welcome him as she had Niall, agreed and said he could come at any time. He felt sure there was more to Sean's request than he was ready to admit to. But that can wait, he thought. He had seen the strain on his brother's face and knew it was not just the grief at the loss of his father.

On their last evening together at the farm, there were fifteen gathered around the table. Bridget and Orla had cooked a special roast chicken dinner, and after three bottles of wine the atmosphere was cheerful and relaxed.

Bridget stood up. "I'm not one for speeches" she said, looking round at her family. "But while I have you all here, I want to say thank you. Thank you for helping me through this last fortnight, but also to say Maith thu fein to all of you. Connor is making a success of the farm; Sean has done well in America. Patrick has built up his own business, Kathleen has a job in Spain that she loves. Aidan is teaching, that was always his vocation, Niall has taken an apprenticeship, and Orla has trained as a nurse and is about to get married to Finn. Your father brought you all up to work hard and to do your best, and you have done. Here's to Dermot. Slainte".

They all raised their glasses in a toast and the next half hour was spent in sharing family memories and lively chatter until the children started to fidget and a wail from Ronan reminded Nell that he needed his evening feed.

There were some tearful goodbyes when Nell and Patrick left the following day. "Mam, you can come and stay again soon" said Patrick, hugging Bridget tightly. "We're only four hours across the sea, you know. And Gatwick Airport is not that far from us, you could fly from Cork and be in England an hour later".

Bridget promised to visit and waved her family off in the minibus, then turned her attention to packing up more of her belongings. Best to keep busy, she thought. And Sean is here, what a blessing. I'm a lucky woman.

* * *

"I think Sean has been on the verge of a nervous breakdown", said Patrick to Nell as they sat down on their first night back at Moongarth after the children had settled at bedtime. "Or a mental health crisis, or whatever they call it nowadays. I don't know what's behind it, but maybe he will open up a bit when he comes to stay".

Sean arrived three weeks later, promising that he would only impose on them for a short time but needed somewhere to use as a base while he was deciding what to do. Nell had offered him the side-rooms, as she still called the self-contained suite on the ground floor. "It will be more peaceful for you in there" she explained, conscious of the morning noise and chaos at breakfast time with a hungry baby and getting the children ready for school when the new term started.

One morning when Ronan had settled for his nap and the house was quiet, Sean sat with Nell in the breakfast room and after she had poured him a cup of coffee, he spoke about his reasons for leaving Boston.

"I met a woman out there. Natalie. If things had been different, we might have got engaged, at least I hadn't proposed, but perhaps there was an understanding. For a

261

couple of years, we were very close. But there was something not right, I couldn't quite put my finger on it. She wanted to start in business as a beautician and she had her eye on some premises, but she'd never run a business before, and I don't think she knew what she was doing. I tried to put her off and encourage her to look for a job as a beauty therapist but no, she wanted to run the show. Well, she couldn't get the finance. That sort of thing was beginning to get very tough in the US, and several banks turned her down. She became obsessed about it and talked about nothing else. Our relationship suffered and I started to dread seeing her, I did my best to avoid her, made all sorts of excuses about being busy, working late and so on but that made things worse. One day she came out with it, she wanted me to put up the money for her. She knew I had a bit put by.

Anyway, I said no. I wasn't prepared to take the risk, and I told her to forget it – in the nicest way. She was furious with me and tried every trick in the book to get me to change my mind, but I dug my heels in. Then I began to wonder, was this the reason she had started a relationship with me, in the hope that I would bankroll her? I lost all trust in her and started to look for a way out. She was enraged with me and her behaviour became completely crazy. Then her father came round one evening and accused me of all kinds of things, misleading her, letting her down, breach of promise, it was ridiculous but then he threatened me with a lawsuit. It went on for weeks, I think they were both just trying to wear me down so that I would give in. There was never any agreement, so he didn't have a leg to stand on but by this time I had had enough, it was all taking its toll on me. Then one day, Mam called and told me that Dad had died. I was on the next plane out of there, I never even said goodbye to Natalie or told her I was leaving".

He took a sip of his coffee and looked at Nell apologetically. "I'm sorry, I shouldn't be burdening you with all this. It's just such a relief to tell someone".

"It's ok, you need to do that Sean. I wish I could help but it sounds as though you did the right thing by getting out of that situation".

"Of course it came as a shock about Dad, it all hit me at the same time. I felt I was losing my grip on everything. Then on the plane on the way over to Ireland I suddenly thought, I don't ever have to go back to that. I may not have a job here, but I can live on my savings for a while and find some work, maybe in England".

"Patrick knows a lot of people now Sean, he's on the Chamber of Commerce. Let him help you. You can stay here for as long as you need to. And I do understand what you've been through. My own parents came close to being defrauded in this very house by someone they trusted. It's a horrible experience. But you will get over it, just give it time. Things will get better".

Later that evening Patrick and Nell sat outside at dusk with a glass of wine and watched a harvest moon slowly rising above the tree line at the edge of the field. Sean had given permission for Nell to explain everything to his brother, and sitting side by side on the bench, they fell into silence for a while, both lost in thought.

"It sounds as though Sean's had a tough time of it. But he's had a narrow escape I reckon," said Patrick.

"Yes, it wasn't going to end well". Nell was still thoughtful. "Will you be able to help him get back on his feet?"

"I don't think he'll need much help, Sean's a survivor and he's got some money to fall back on, enough to get him started, over here or back in Ireland. But I'll do whatever I can".

"We had lots of help, didn't we? Barbara once said to me that people gave them a leg up several times when they were struggling".

"We're so lucky, aren't we?" Patrick was equally serious. "The children, family, this house, the business, our friends.... each other"

"Yes, we've had our fair share of luck but a lot of it is down to your hard work Patrick, and we've always wanted the same things. Besides, we're only just getting started".

"I love you Nelly".

"And yourself" she replied with the faintest of Irish accents. He laughed and putting his arm round her, kissed her as the moon sailed higher in the clear sky and darkness settled around them.

Not since the time of Geoffrey Garth had Moongarth been so full of life force and energy or had so many plans been made, dilemmas faced or worries shared within its walls.

But the house and its occupants had not yet witnessed the last of its surprises or challenges.

∗ ∗ ∗

PART TWO

Chapter Thirty-Four
1997

Usually, at the beginning of September Nell liked to make the most of the last few golden remnants of summer when the weather was still warm and dry, the gardens were still showing a profusion of colour and the children returning to school could manage for a few more weeks without coats and scarves. The light was different; the early September sun was gentler, more mellow, the shadows slightly diffused and less distinct. At those times she would fling the windows of Moongarth wide open to welcome in the last of the mild breezes, allowing them to penetrate and freshen every corner of the house, always reminding her of one of her favourite Victorian poems:

'Shorter and shorter now the twilight clips the days, as through the sunset gates they crowd, And summer from her golden collar slips and strays through stubble fields and moans aloud'.

But this year it had rained incessantly from the last week in August and there was no prospect of any end in sight. The younger children, being deprived of a final week of good weather before term began were crotchety and irritable; Ronan, who was nearly always cheerful was not his usual self, and Patrick was worried about some serious flooding on a construction site and how much it would cost to have more pumps brought into use. Even the dahlias look droopy and bedraggled, thought Nell looking vainly through the breakfast room window for a break in the clouds. The garden is as tired of the rain as the rest of us.

"I shall need my leotard tomorrow for gymnastics" said Emer, turning cartwheels all along the hallway. Her long curly red hair swung round her in a tangle.

At eight years old, despite being the youngest of the Walsh family, Emer was undoubtedly the most self-assured, confident and strong-willed of all her siblings. Some of her friends complained that she was bossy, and adults sometimes found her annoying and precocious.

Nell had been very firm. "This baby is most definitely the last, Patrick" she said, after discovering that she was expecting again when Ronan was only ten months old. He had laughed at her then but realised she was being serious when a few weeks after Emer's birth Nell suffered from a spell of depression so profound that nothing seemed to help her. It was only when he began to understand the toll that five pregnancies had taken on her body, and that Emer was a demanding and fractious baby that he at last agreed that their family was complete, and from that point, Nell began to recover. The physical effects were overcome in time; she had very few grey hairs and had retained her slim figure and porcelain complexion, although sometimes she joked ruefully that having five children had aged her. But whenever he looked at his wife, Patrick still saw the seventeen-year-old girl he fell in love with all those years ago.

The autumn term was to start the following day at the Juniors, and the day after that for Brontë and Henry. For Nell the new academic year brought back memories of her own schooldays and her father's careful preparations for the new intake of boys at the Grammar School. Her own family were growing. Arthur, now seventeen had been working with his father for the last six months. He's the image of Patrick, she thought, with his broad build and red hair, and she realised with a shock that he was only a few years younger now than Patrick was when she first met him.

Henry was of slighter build but still had a strong similarity to his father. His red colouring was less pronounced than Arthur's, but he had Patrick's eyes and most definitely his winning smile. Nell felt sure that Henry had inherited her own father's aptitude for science, and he was undoubtedly clever. Next year he would leave Lamberham Comprehensive to study engineering at the Kirchington Sixth Form College and maybe go on to university. She allowed herself to dream for a moment, picturing a time and place in the future when Henry would walk on stage in gown and mortarboard to receive his degree. Patrick would be proud too, the only mortarboard he had known when growing up was the sort bricklayers used.

Nell brought herself back to the present with a jolt as she turned her thoughts to Brontë. She sighed. Even now Brontë had shut herself in her bedroom and refused to come out. She dreads going back to school, thought Nell, who remembered vividly keeping to her room as a child, the same room in this house that Brontë now occupied, but for such very different reasons. Nell was certain that her daughter had been bullied at school during the previous term, in fact she suspected that it had been going on for longer than that, but so far Brontë had refused to allow Nell to raise the matter with her form tutor, fearing that any intervention by her mother would make things worse. She had inherited Nell's pale complexion and abundant dark hair, normally worn loose over her shoulders or scrunched back in a ponytail. Sadly for Brontë, that was where the resemblance ended; instead of Nell's slender frame she had her father's stocky build and was inclined to plumpness. At the age of fourteen, to be even slightly overweight was a disaster, an affliction so cruel that she could think of nothing else and at school the teasing was merciless. During the summer break Brontë had relaxed a little, had joined in with the family sometimes and had even run errands for Nell in the village where she was sure to be able to avoid girls from her class. But now with the new term about to start, the same fears resurfaced, and she had hidden herself away. Nell and Brontë shared a love of literature; it was Brontë's strongest subject at school but instead of enjoying and making the most of the English classes she preferred to study at home, sometimes discussing the books with her mother but more often sitting alone in her bedroom or finding a solitary space in a corner of the orchard where she could read unnoticed. But this week the wet weather had forced her indoors and upstairs, and she had locked her bedroom door.

I just don't know what to do with her, thought Nell in despair. Perhaps I should get some advice. I'll talk to Patrick later. At that moment Ronan, now known as Ronnie, came running into the room, kissed his mother, grabbed a drink and disappeared again. Unlike his brothers and younger sister, he had his mother's dark brown hair and slate-grey eyes. Nell remembered that Henry and Arthur had set up a snooker table down in the basement and Henry was teaching him. Ronnie. Her mood lightened for a moment. Neither Nell nor Patrick had favourites among their children but they both agreed that Ronnie had the happiest, kindest and most carefree disposition of all of them.

Emer Jennifer – named for Jenny who had sat all night with Nell through a long and exhausting labour – well, everyone agreed that she was a handful and no mistake. Patrick always said Emer would have an argument by herself in an empty room, and at times Nell found her constant contradictions and antagonism wearying. Why are the boys so easy-going and both the girls so difficult, she wondered.

Knowing Patrick was under a great deal of pressure at work, Nell decided against mentioning the subject of the girls that evening. The next day it was still pouring with rain. Arthur and Patrick went to work as usual, and Emer and Ronnie ate their breakfast, Emer complaining bitterly about not being driven to school like other children in her class.

"You can walk it in ten minutes, it won't hurt you" said Nell firmly. "I used to walk to school in the village in all weathers. No argument".

"What's the point of you having a car if you can't drive me to school?" Emer whined. She looked a little like Patrick's sister Orla with her long curly red hair which Nell was struggling to plait.

"It's wasteful for short journeys. And you have two good legs, be thankful".

"Is it because I'm the youngest, I don't have a say in anything?"

"It's not. It's because the school is close by and I'm not getting the car out".

"But..."

"No buts. Off you go now"

She saw them off down the driveway, Emer lagging behind, still grumbling and Ronnie striding ahead, seemingly without a care in the world. It was only eight thirty in the morning but already Nell felt battle-weary. She knew she had another confrontation looming with Brontë about returning to school, she would have to face that later. She returned to the breakfast room and surveyed the morning chaos. Henry was eating a bowl of cereal and had slopped milk everywhere.

Is this my life now? Nell felt completely overwhelmed. All I want to do is what Brontë is doing, opt out and curl up with a book. Or do some writing. Nell thought of her little writing room in the attic which she had hardly been into recently. Everything is on hold. As fast as I sort out one problem for this family another one comes along.

Zacky looked at her downcast as if he understood there was no walk in the offing.

At that moment Jenny arrived and took one look at Nell. "Emer?" Nell nodded. "You look as if you need to go back to bed" she said, worriedly

"I wish".

"Well, why don't you? Go and have a rest for an hour and I'll bring you up a cup of tea later. I can take care of this lot and I'll walk Zacky when the rain eases up".

For the thousandth time Nell wondered what she would do without Jenny, who was like one of the family and knew and understood her so well. She lay quietly on her bed, trying to sort out her thoughts. In the end it boiled down to two worries – her daughters. One quarrelsome, truculent and full of self-importance, the other quite the opposite; introverted, withdrawn and depressed. But in so many other ways the family was fortunate. She resolved to speak to Patrick that evening about Brontë, that was urgent. Emer's behaviour was different, perhaps she needed to talk to the school. She drifted off into a deep sleep as the rain beat an incessant drumming against the glass. It was two hours later when Jenny knocked the door. "Thank you, Jenny. I didn't mean to sleep this long" she said sipping her tea, and feeling refreshed, went downstairs, and finding that the kitchen was spotless, and that Jenny was vacuuming the drawing room, she set about organising their evening meal. Then gathering her courage in both hands, she went up to Brontë's room.

It was a difficult conversation. As expected, Brontë was defiant, moody and refusing to go to school the next day.

"You must go to school Brontë, said Nell patiently. "You're not ill. I know you're unhappy but if you won't discuss it, I can't help you".

"Mum school just isn't for me. I could study at home; you could teach me".

"No, I couldn't Brontë. I'm not qualified for one thing, but whatever it is, you need to face up to it, not hide away".

Brontë burst into tears and Nell's heart went out to her. She sat down beside her on the bed and put her arms round her daughter.

"Let's make a plan. We will take one day at a time. You will go to school tomorrow and I will make an appointment with your Head of Year. If something or someone is upsetting you at school, they need to know about it and deal with it".

"It's not just one person. It's all of them. It never stops. They laugh at me, they call me…. Brontosaurus". She was sobbing now. "They pick on me all the time". Her sobs had become almost hysterical. "I can't live like this any longer Mum, I hate them….and I hate myself".

Nell was beginning to feel completely out of her depth and struggled to reply. "What about Rachel?"

"She's the only one who's nice to me. And she'll be in a different class this term".

"That's something, you can still see her at break times. It's a new term, there may be different girls in your class, some of the unkind ones may have moved".

Brontë was silent.

"This is what we'll do. You must go to school for now, and I shall speak to Head of Year, but if there's no improvement after say, two weeks, I'll talk to Daddy about changing schools or having some private tuition at home. Your GCSEs are coming up, they're important".

Brontë still said nothing; Nell knew that the only thing that would calm her daughter was to allow her to stay at home and not return to school, but she was not about to agree to this. For now, speaking to the Head of Year and reviewing after two weeks was the only compromise she could think of, and as she went downstairs, she felt that she had done her best in what seemed an impossible situation. Patrick would be less sympathetic, he believed Brontë should just stand up for herself and give back the same. Men always see things so simplistically, she thought.

They all had dinner together later. Nell had made it a rule that they sat round a table for the main meal of the day. It was their catching-up time, as she called it. But tonight, Patrick was troubled about something at work, Emer was whiney and tired after her first day back at school, and Brontë was silent. Niall, who still worked for Patrick but now had his own flat, often joined them for dinner on Tuesday evenings but was busy elsewhere that night.

Nell had cooked chilli con carne with rice which she knew they always enjoyed and hoped that a good meal would cheer them all up.

"I told them at school that my name's Emerald, but they keep getting it wrong". Emer as always had a complaint.

"Your name's Emer, not Emerald, and that's an end to it". Patrick was snappy, it was unlike him.

"But…"

"I won't hear any more".

Nell had agreed on traditional Irish names for her two youngest children as promised when they had named Brontë, but she had not bargained for it being a cause of great debate for Emer, one more source of discord that they could all have done without.

Brontë was pushing her food round her plate, eating little. Nell noticed but said nothing, all the time wondering if this was another symptom of Brontë's unhappiness – surely not the beginnings of an eating disorder on top of everything else. But Patrick saw that she had left most of her meal and turned to her.

"Eat your dinner. Your mother's gone to the trouble of cooking for us, now eat it".

"I'm not hungry Daddy".

"Eat your dinner". Patrick was losing his temper. He must have had a very bad day, thought Nell. Brontë swallowed a few more forkfuls and drank some water.

"You've given me too much, Mum".

Patrick glared at his daughter.

Ronnie, always the peacemaker, changed the subject.

"There's a man living in the bus shelter with a small baby" he said, clearing his plate.

"Don't be ridiculous, people don't live in bus shelters," said Patrick. Clearly the children were trying his patience to the limit that evening.

"But it's true" shrilled Emer, as always wanting the last word. "He's …"

"Enough!" shouted Patrick.

Nell wondered why mealtimes had become a battle ground lately. In a calm voice, she said to Ronnie:

"He was probably waiting for a bus. He can't be living there. Or perhaps waiting for his wife to get off the next bus".

"Well, he was there when we passed him on our way to school and he was still there when we came home. I think he'd been there all day". Ronnie was matter of fact.

"Yes, there was...." Emer began.

"I told you to be quiet" thundered Patrick.

"But it's not fair, no one ever listens to me".

"Stop talking Emer and come and help me bring in the pudding". Nell tried to distract her.

Peace was regained when Nell brought in the dessert, an apple crumble she had made with some early windfalls from the orchard. Arthur and Henry immediately asked if they could have Bronte's share, seeing that she had refused a helping. This reminded Nell that she would have to talk to Patrick about her. But maybe not tonight, there's been enough drama for one evening, she said to herself.

As the children left the table, she said quietly to Ronnie:

"If that man and the baby are still there in the bus shelter tomorrow, let me know. It seems very strange".

"Ok, Mum". He kissed her and ran down the basement stairs with his brothers.

After she had loaded the dishwasher, she poured a glass of Guinness for Patrick and some wine for herself and joined him in the drawing room. They sat in silence for a while.

Emer popped her head round the door.

"May I remind you that in my letter from Granny Bridget she says it's time Ronnie and I were baptised". She pirouetted around the room and back out into the hallway before her parents could reply. "I shall wear a long white dress and have flowers in my hair...."

"Something will have to be done about that child, she's getting impossible. I feel sorry for her teachers". Patrick drained his glass. "She's full on from the moment she opens her eyes in the morning". He looks shattered, thought Nell. There were a few strands of grey at his temples now, but the rest of his hair was still a vibrant red. "Where does she get it from?"

"I'll talk to her, or maybe I'll make an appointment with the school. I know how difficult she is, Patrick. I have one or two ideas, but they'll keep. You look all in. Is it the flooding?"

273

"Yes, that and two fellows left today, out of the blue. It's left me short". Patrick had secured a major contract building an extension to the Leisure Centre in Kirchington. "I'll have to have a word with Joe, he might have some suggestions".

"Let's have an early night," said Nell. "No, not that sort of early night" she added quickly. Patrick laughed for the first time that evening. "We've both had a day of it. Perhaps tomorrow will be better".

Nell lay awake for a long time that night, feeling Patrick's solid warmth beside her and listening to his gentle snoring. Nothing keeps him awake at night, she thought enviously, not even work worries. But our problems are small compared to some families, there's nothing really that we can't deal with. Most likely the girls will both grow out of these phases.

The rain which hadn't let up for days continued to drum insistently on the windowpanes and spatter on the floor of the little balcony. The wind was stronger now as well, reaching force seven, she had heard on the weather forecast. Slipping noiselessly out of bed she went to check the window catch and peered out into the blackness. It was a terrible night. Her thoughts turned to Ronnie's story about the man in the bus shelter with a baby. Surely, surely that couldn't be right. He wasn't an untruthful boy, he would never make up things like that, and in a way Emer had corroborated his words. There must be some explanation. She couldn't bear to think of a baby – or anyone – outdoors without a proper roof over their head on a night like this. She got back into bed, still pondering what to do. If Ronnie said that they were still in the bus shelter tomorrow, she would do something about it. Having made a decision of sorts, Nell drifted off into a troubled sleep.

Chapter Thirty-Five

Unusually, Emer was the first home from school the following day. "Ronnie's talking to that man" she announced, then immediately launched into the demands of the day. "Mummy can I have ballet lessons? Chloe is starting next week. I will need tights, a tutu, point shoes...."

"I don't know, Emer and I refuse to think about it just now". Nell was more concerned about Ronnie's conversation with the man in the bus shelter. At that moment he came running in, breathless.

"Mum, I've invited the man to dinner. His name's Denny Reid and the baby is called Arlo. He is waiting for someone to sort out a house for them or something. Can I go and play snooker now?"

An extra dinner guest put Nell on the spot for a moment, then she quickly peeled a few more potatoes and vegetables and took an extra pack of sausages from the refrigerator. That is typical of Ronnie, she thought. I only asked him to report back but now I have a stranger coming to dinner. But it's because he's a thoughtful boy, he has such a lovely nature. And she remembered how her mind had run on in bed the previous night when she had been worrying about an unknown man and a baby out in the elements. The least they could do would be to offer a meal. Surely Patrick wouldn't mind.

Denny arrived at six o'clock, Ronnie having given him directions. He was carrying a large rucksack over one shoulder, a hold-all in one hand and the baby, Arlo in a sling. Arlo, who looked about six weeks old was surprisingly clean and seemed none the worse for having spent some nights in the open, Nell dreaded to think how many.

Nell left them in the dining room, and when Patrick came in shortly afterwards and went to wash his hands, he asked her how come they had an extra person for dinner.

"It's Ronnie" she explained. "He's invited the man from the bus shelter. I expect he did it out of kindness, you know what he's like. It's ok, there's plenty".

"Do you think we can have one normal mealtime this week without arguments, bickering or visitors?" Patrick was still tetchy. But during dinner he and Denny chatted pleasantly and Emer had less to say for a change. Denny praised Nell's cooking. "It's only sausage and mash" she said, laughing.

"But it's been a while since I had a good hot meal sitting round a table. It's very kind of you, Mrs Walsh".

"Nell" she corrected, offering him a second helping. He seemed ravenous.

Arlo, who had been sleeping wrapped up in a blanket on the easy chair, began to whimper and Denny fished in the rucksack for a feeding bottle. "Would you mind if I heat this up?"

After dinner, as Denny fed Arlo, Nell couldn't resist asking questions.

"Arlo's mother and I have been living apart since he was born. She's not very well, she's been in hospital. I'm hoping we can get back together soon but I need to find somewhere for us to live first. I have a friend who is trying to help us. I'm seeing him tomorrow actually".

"Have you really been living in the bus shelter?"

"Only during the day. I managed to get into the church at night, it was unlocked. They don't seem to worry too much about security round here. It was warm, the heating came on for a while, so we've been spending the nights in there then we leave in the morning before the vicar comes for the early service. There's running water in there and toilets. I warmed his bottles by laying them on a radiator".

Nell didn't know what to say to that. It all seemed implausible, and the situation railed against all her instincts as a mother, yet she could not bring herself to challenge Denny or pry any further into his business.

Denny prepared to leave, wrapping up Arlo tightly before placing him in the sling. Patrick accompanied them to the front door. As he opened it, the full force of the gale and torrential rain hit them.

"Look, you can't go out in this. I think you'd better stay the night. Nell, is the bed in the side-room made up?"

Nell was relieved that the invitation had come from Patrick; in his present mood he would have been annoyed if she had suggested putting up their guests overnight.

"It's because of the baby" he said later, after showing Denny into the guest suite. "I wouldn't have offered if it had just been that fellow on his own. The baby will be warm and safe in there, Denny can take a shower and have a decent night's sleep, and they can be on their way tomorrow".

"Thanks, you've been very kind and I'm so grateful to you, Mrs.... Nell", Denny said the following morning, after Patrick and Arthur had driven off to work and the rest of the children went their separate ways to school. Brontë had been very quiet and had refused breakfast. Nell had heard her crying in bed overnight, and for the umpteenth time she wondered how things at school had become so intolerable for her and felt guilty that once again her daughter's troubles were being lost in the general chaos of family life. Not knowing what more she could do at that moment, she wrapped up some fruit and snacks in the hope that Brontë might eat something later.

"It's ok, I'm glad we were able to help" smiled Nell.

"Actually, I have one more favour to ask you. Would you be able to look after Arlo for a few hours while I go to see my friend about this house? It's only the other side of Kirchington. I should be back by mid-afternoon".

Nell was a little taken aback. "Well...I suppose it will be all right" she said at last. "Do you have spare nappies and formula; I don't have anything here I'm afraid".

"Yes, it's all in here". Denny pointed to the rucksack. Nell took Arlo from him as he put on his coat and picked up the hold-all. They exchanged telephone numbers. "I'll see you later. Thanks again Nell".

* * *

"It's not my fault, Patrick" Nell was trying to explain what had happened. "I agreed to look after Arlo just for a few hours while Denny went off to meet this man. He said he'd be back sometime this afternoon. I've tried to phone him but I'm only getting his voicemail. I've left a message so hopefully he'll get back to me in a while".

Patrick had just arrived home from work and was not best pleased to find the baby still very much in evidence. "I was hoping we could have a quiet evening for a change" he said crossly.

"I'm sorry Patrick, I know it's a nuisance but I'm sure he's been held up, that's all. He will probably arrive just as we sit down to dinner".

But Denny didn't arrive then, and the evening wore on without any word from him. Nell tried several times to phone him and each time she left a message. At ten o'clock she tried again in desperation.

'It has not been possible to connect your call'. The automated response sent a shock wave through Nell as she realised the position they were in. She turned to Patrick, white-faced. "We're in a fix, Patrick. There's something wrong, I'm sure of it. If there had been an accident or something surely Denny would have let us know. But we have no way of contacting him now. It's almost as if Arlo has been abandoned".

"That's impossible". Patrick almost laughed, and then saw that Nell was serious. "That sort of thing doesn't happen. Children don't just appear out of nowhere, it's the other way round, they go missing".

"Perhaps he is missing, perhaps Denny told us a pack of lies and his mother is going frantic somewhere looking for him".

"We should never have got involved, we know nothing about him. We don't even know if that's his real name". Patrick was thoughtful.

"Should we call the police?"

"Maybe not yet. If there's no news by tomorrow morning, then we'll do that. Let's have a look through that rucksack in case there's anything in there that might help"

But the rucksack yielded no clues and the two of them sat there, running out of ideas whilst Arlo slept peacefully.

"I only have enough nappies and baby milk for tonight," said Nell. "There are a few spare clothes in here, but they look as if they need washing."

Patrick had no choice but to drive to the late-night supermarket in Lamberham for these necessities while Nell bathed Arlo and gave him the last of the formula left by Denny. All the time various possibilities and questions were running through her brain. Had Arlo been abducted? Was he the subject of a custody battle? Was his mother really ill? Why hadn't Denny been in touch? Was he on the run, was the baby a hostage? It was like being in the plot of a book or a film. Now and then she tried Denny's number, but it was still unobtainable. She switched on the national news, half expecting a news report or an appeal for information about a missing child. But there was nothing.

When Patrick returned, Nell went up to one of the attic rooms where they stored unused items. Somehow, despite her determination to have no more children she had been reluctant to give away the last of Emer's baby clothes and toys. She soon found what she was looking for, a Moses basket, the mattress clean and usable, then stopped at the airing cupboard on the lower landing for some soft sheets and a baby blanket that had remained there on the top shelf for several years. She made up some bottles and after giving Arlo another feed, settled him in the basket in their bedroom, then she and Patrick fell into an exhausted sleep, hoping that the next day would bring some answers.

It didn't. Denny's number was still unobtainable. The family was in more of an uproar than usual at breakfast time; Patrick and Arthur were late leaving for work because of the general indecision about Arlo, Emer was as usual whining about having to walk to school, and Brontë was upset because

Nell had not yet made the promised appointment with her Head of Year. This had genuinely slipped Nell's mind with the events of the day before. Arlo slept throughout the commotion, only waking up when Nell lifted him out of his basket to change his nappy.

After everyone had left and Nell had explained the situation to an astonished Jenny, she sat in the breakfast room to telephone the police.

The police officer was sympathetic and listened carefully as Nell gave him details about the baby that had been left in her care and whose father had seemingly vanished. But he was surprisingly unconcerned. "I'm sure that this Denny Reid will turn up before too long, full of apologies" he said reassuringly. "There will be a simple explanation, there usually is, but I've made a note of everything you've told me. We would be the first to know of any missing children, either locally or nationally, that's always a priority. But there are no such reports at this time. Will you be able to look after the baby for the time being?"

"Well, yes...."

"I advise you to wait forty-eight hours, Madam. If you've heard nothing by then, please call us again and we'll investigate the matter. I'm not treating this as a crime, it sounds like the man has had a delay for some reason and hasn't been able to charge his phone to let you know. But in the meantime, if you have any concerns, you can contact Children's Services at Kirchington Council". He gave her the number.

Nell and Patrick sat together that evening as Nell gave Arlo his bottle, and she told him of the conversation with the police.

"I'm not happy about leaving things for forty-eight hours" he said at last. "Did you say he suggested ringing the council? I think you should do that tomorrow".

Chapter Thirty-Six

Rosemary Shaw, trainee social worker with Kirchington Children's Services had a heavy caseload and a punishing schedule. She was under huge pressure that day with a report deadline to meet and a case conference later that afternoon as well as several home visits.

One of her calls that morning was to a Mrs Walsh who did not sound like a typical client, but go carefully she said to herself, remembering her training, what is a typical client? Be prepared for the unexpected, don't take anything at face value, be curious, ask questions.

Despite this, Rosemary had partly made up her mind that unless anything really worrying presented itself, she would place Mrs Walsh and the child at the lower end of her priorities that day. Her caseload included children suffering from various stages of neglect and deprivation, often where parents were either absent or had serious addictions. There were children who were persistently missing school and families with chaotic and disorganised lives where every kind of problem was present. Some parents were well meaning but just struggled with life in general, and at the opposite end there were the most serious cases where physical abuse was suspected. The list went on....

So, as Rosemary turned her car into the driveway of Moongarth just after nine thirty and looked up at the imposing house with wisteria climbing over the front wall, tended flower beds and freshly painted window frames, the open barn with neatly stacked logs and bicycles, she had more or less decided that even without meeting Mrs Walsh there could be nothing of concern here, and that this might be her easiest call of the day.

"Miss Shaw? Thank you for coming to see me. I'm Nell Walsh, do come in".

Nell led the way along the tiled hallway, past the racks of coats, wellingtons and sportswear and into the bright, sunlit breakfast room. Rosemary's gaze took in the comfortable furnishings, with patterned cushions on the long sofa, shelves stacked with books and a desk at one end of the room with a lamp and a laptop. She could detect the smell of fresh coffee. A vase of colourful dahlias stood on the table and a dog was curled up next to the range in the kitchen next door. In the corner Arlo slumbered contentedly in his Moses basket, occasionally murmuring in his sleep.

"I didn't quite understand why you contacted us, Mrs Walsh" began Rosemary. "We have several temporary staff at the moment, I'm afraid the message I received was not very clear".

"The situation is that a friend of my son, Denny Reid – well, he's not even a friend, just someone he met in the village – seemed to be homeless with a small baby. Ronnie invited him here with the baby for a meal five days ago; they stayed the night in the end because the weather was so bad. The following day Denny asked if I would look after Arlo, the baby, while he went house-hunting. I agreed, thinking it would be just for a few hours. He left me his number and when he didn't return by late afternoon, I tried to ring him, but no one picked up. I left messages and kept trying several times that evening and the next morning, but the number was unobtainable by then. That was five days ago, and I've heard nothing from him since. We informed the police, and they took the details, but they seem to think there's just a delay for some reason, and it will all sort itself out. Of course I've been looking after Arlo, he's a darling, he's no trouble and we've been out and bought everything he needs for now, and I still have some of my daughter's old baby clothes, but the point is, Arlo should be with his mother, he's nothing to do with us, we just don't know what to do".

"Can I see Arlo please Mrs Walsh? It's a shame to wake him but I really need to check a few things".

Nell went over to the basket and lifted Arlo out gently. He waved a little fist and screwed up his face in protest as she placed him into Rosemary's arms. Rosemary noticed that the baby was spotlessly clean and smelled freshly bathed. His little legs were bare, his skin smooth and warm. She undid the poppers of his sleep suit and saw a few blemishes under his chin, nothing more, and that the cord had detached cleanly from his navel.

"I think the milk spots will fade within a few weeks" she said. "He looks perfectly healthy and happy".

Nell tucked Arlo back into his Moses basket, also immaculate, Rosemary observed, and she noticed with approval that Nell had placed him on his back.

"You said you have children of your own, Mrs Walsh?"

"Yes, I have five. The eldest is seventeen, he works with his father, the others are at school. It's not usually this quiet!"

"May I see where the baby sleeps at night, Mrs Walsh?"

Rosemary had already seen all she needed to see, but for the sake of providing more details in her report she thought some cursory facts might pad it out a little. I'm just being curious, she said to herself, but in fact she was keen to see more of this beautiful house.

Nell showed her up to the first floor and into the master bedroom. Rosemary looked with thinly disguised admiration at the stylish décor, pale wood furnishings and spied a luxurious en-suite bathroom through a door at the back of the room.

"Arlo sleeps in his Moses basket here beside our bed" said Nell, and Rosemary took note of a side table stacked with nappies, baby toiletries, changing mat and a bottle warmer. She wrote some more details in her notepad and followed Nell downstairs.

"Coffee?" asked Nell.

"Yes please, a quick one. I have a few more calls to make".

Taking the mug from Nell, Rosemary sat down at the table facing her.

"Mrs Walsh, what would you like me to do?"

Nell looked astonished. "Well, I would like you to find Arlo's parents and get him back to them. Arlo shouldn't be here".

"We're not a tracing service Mrs Walsh".

"No, but you are Child Welfare...."

"Yes, our remit is safeguarding, child protection and the best interests of the child. But I have no concerns whatsoever on that score. Arlo is healthy, contented and well cared for".

"But he isn't ours!"

"No, and I will make enquiries for you. This is an unusual situation, I admit. I haven't come across it before and I will have to consult my manager. I'll get back to you as soon as possible; in the circumstances we will need to carry out an assessment if you don't hear back from this man soon. But I tend to agree with the police, the most likely thing is that this Denny Reid will be in touch before too long, there will be an explanation and he will come for Arlo and take him to his new home, I'm certain of it".

"But he can't stay here!"

Rosemary put down her coffee mug and looked around at the cosy, bright room, the spacious hallway leading to several rooms which she had only been able to peep into, the modern kitchen adjoining with a dog curled up in his basket, and the beautiful garden with its lawn stretching down to a clump of fruit trees laden with apples.

"You don't work do you, Mrs Walsh?"

"We'll I don't have a job, if that's what you mean, but...."

"Can you look after Arlo a little longer, until I have had a chance to contact my police colleagues, check if there are any reports of missing babies or abductions? I'm not aware of any, such cases are rare, and they're always well reported in the media, but they may come up with something".

Nell was visibly shocked. "I was expecting you to take Arlo with you" she said.

Rosemary shook her head. "I think Arlo's best place is with you for the time being. You are an experienced mum;

you have lots of space here.... I could look into a contingency grant for you if you wish".

"This is nothing to do with money". For a moment Nell felt insulted but tried to keep the rising tide of anger under control. It would not help to alienate this woman.

"Here's my card". Rosemary fished into the depths of an untidy canvas shoulder bag crammed with papers and folders. "Someone will be in touch soon about the assessment. Please don't worry. You are doing a wonderful job looking after Arlo, he is so well cared for. This will all be sorted out, I promise you". Rosemary was already making her way to the front door.

"But I know nothing about him!"

Rosemary stopped at the entrance. "You know everything you need to know to keep him safe and well. Mrs Walsh, if you knew the situations I see all the time where children are so neglected, so poor, sometimes in homes that you wouldn't keep an animal in, you would understand why I am more than happy to leave Arlo in your care for a few more days".

Nell said nothing but suddenly a feeling of guilt came from over her. It was true, she had so much. She could surely offer something – some love – to this tiny, abandoned boy who for now was entirely dependent on her. She would face Patrick later.

"Goodbye" she faltered "and thank you for coming". Those were all the words she could manage at that moment. She watched Rosemary get into her car and drive away.

Nell returned to the breakfast room and lifted Arlo out of his basket, cradling him on her lap as he started to whimper. He will need feeding now, she thought as she saw the small face screw up and let forth a cry that left her in no doubt. She looked down at him tenderly. "Looks like you are part of this family for a while longer, little man".

After driving away from Drover's Cross, Rosemary pulled into a lay-by, wound down the car window and lit a cigarette.

The Walsh's situation was strange, unusual, she thought. But it was puzzling rather than concerning. She refused to contemplate anything other than a simple explanation which in time would reveal itself.

Convinced that she had asked all the relevant questions and made the right decisions, she resolved to write up her report later, discuss the case with her manager as soon as he had an opportunity to see her, and provided nothing adverse about the family showed up on police checks she would recommend downgrading the referral. She would of course make the necessary enquiries, but she doubted if they would lead anywhere. It was a mystery, but not a disaster, she told herself. That would have to be enough for now. The assessment, if needed would provide more facts and information.

With that, she turned her attention to the remaining visits on her list and thought of her forthcoming two weeks holiday in the Lake District.

* * *

The dismay on Patrick's face was clear to see when Nell told him about the social worker's visit.

"You should have been firmer with her, Nell. She could see that he was being well looked after, he was in no danger, and she thought, oh good, box ticked. Don't you see, you were an easy solution for her. Never mind where it leaves us, literally holding the baby. You will have to talk to her again, or perhaps the police will take it more seriously now that it's been five days and still no word".

Nell agreed. She felt weary. It was a situation that had come out of nowhere and was already the cause of discord in the household. That afternoon Brontë had been upset because Nell had again forgotten to make the appointment with the school and Emer was complaining that she could not invite her friend Chloe round for dinner. Even the boys were feeling that their mother's time and attention was taken up with Arlo; not just in caring for him but they knew she was constantly worrying about his family and why they had ever become involved. That evening, Ronnie sat down with Nell as she gave Arlo his bottle.

"Mum, I'm sorry". He tucked his hand through her arm.

"What are you sorry for?"

"It's all my fault, isn't it? I should never have invited them here".

"Ronnie, we don't blame you. I know you were trying to be kind, and that's how you've been brought up. None of us knew how complicated this was going to turn out".

Another problem was the timing. Neville and Lois had decided to come back to England for a few weeks as Neville had some financial business to attend to in Kirchington. Kathleen, who had remained in Spain for the intervening years as a companion for Lois, was taking the opportunity to return to see the family and was also planning to go across to Ireland for a few days. For two years she had been seeing a man she had met in Spain, and she was planning to bring Adam with her to meet them all. Patrick had been looking forward to seeing his sister and likewise Nell was hoping to spend time with her parents. Looking after Arlo indefinitely had somehow upset all these plans; the situation was unpredictable and there seemed to be no resolution in sight.

The next morning Nell made a list of things to do. Phone calls, make up bottles, prepare the guest suite for her parents, shopping, talk to Emer. Sighing, she picked up the telephone and dialled the number for Lamberham Comprehensive School. After making an appointment to see Mr Franklin, Brontë's Head of Year two days later, she sat down with a cup of coffee and ticked off the first item. At least she had done something constructive. Brontë had been even more withdrawn since going back to school and was beginning to look unwell, refusing to eat and looking even paler than usual. Once again Nell had heard her crying in her bedroom the night before.

She balked at the thought of phoning the police again. They hadn't been in touch since that first phone conversation; no doubt Miss Shaw had contacted them already and told them that Arlo was in good hands for the time being. She was dreading telling Patrick that there was no progress.

Fresh air, that's what she needed. And a walk. She wondered whether to push Arlo out in Emer's old baby stroller, recently recovered from the attic room, but decided against it, feeling unable to face the inevitable questions from neighbours and thinking how difficult it would be to explain the extraordinary set of circumstances under which an unknown baby was suddenly in her care. Asking Jenny to listen for Arlo, and promising that she would only be half an hour or so, she set off for the village. By some miracle it had stopped raining, but the countryside was sodden, the verges were muddy, and the hedgerows still dripped with raindrops.

She pushed open the door of the Post Office Stores and was surprised to see it so crowded. It must be pension day, she thought. Picking up a basket she made her way down the first aisle. She didn't need much, just some things for their meal that evening and a few toiletries. Several of the shoppers knew her; most said good morning, and some stopped for a chat. As she reached for a pack of nappies, something stopped her as she touched it and she withdrew her hand quickly, instead picking up a bag of cotton wool balls. But a couple of eagle-eyed ladies had spotted this and looked at her curiously. It will be all over the village that I'm pregnant again, thought Nell crossly. People miss nothing round here.

"How's your girl, Mrs Walsh? My Sally said she hasn't been well". The enquiry came from Mrs Dawson who lived at the other side of Drover's Cross in a steep row of cottages called Stephouses.

"Brontë? She's fine, thank you. Back at school now. It's an important year for her".

Nell paid for her purchases and left the shop, inwardly seething. Honestly, why do people think Brontë's been ill, she asked herself. If you as much as sneeze in this village the next day someone asks you how your cold is.

After returning to the house, she telephoned the police again and spoke to the same desk sergeant. She was kept on hold for a few minutes then a female police officer came on the line. "Hello, I'm WPC Tina Drummond. I'm afraid we haven't any news about Mr Reid yet" she said flatly. "We have made enquiries, but nothing has come up so far. But we've heard from Children's Services that you have agreed to look after the baby for now. We do need to come to see you soon, Mrs Walsh, I'm sorry I can't say exactly when, we're not treating this as a criminal matter at this stage".

Nell sighed. "Isn't there any progress on this at all? His mother must be out of her mind with worry."

"If that was the case all police forces in the country would be on high alert and it would be headline news. Usually in a case of an abducted or a missing child, people come forward very quickly, obviously the parents, but also lots of potential witnesses or people reporting a sighting. This case is different. A child has not been reported missing, he has been left with you". WPC Drummond paused, there was a great deal of background noise. "My advice is to keep the situation within the family and the authorities if possible. A baby who has been abandoned will attract a great deal of speculation, and you'd be surprised how many people might claim him as their own child for very suspect reasons. We must guard against that. So I strongly advise you not to approach the media, at least not without talking to us first. We may hold a press conference at some point and make an appeal for information if you don't hear from Mr Reid soon. But do keep in touch with Children's Services, they will be able to advise you if you have any other concerns about the baby. We will call on you soon".

Nell put down the phone in dismay. Disappointment didn't even come close to what she was feeling at that moment.

Chapter Thirty-Seven

"I'm glad you made this appointment Mrs Walsh as I was about to ask you to come to see me about Brontë".

Mr Franklin's demeanour was pleasant enough, but Nell could sense a steely firmness underneath the friendly exterior.

"I'm very worried about her, Mr Franklin, we both are, my husband as well. She's been unhappy at school for months and I've had such a struggle persuading her to go back this term".

"Hmm". Mr Franklin looked momentarily uncomfortable. "Mrs Walsh, what I am about to say is a matter of some delicacy. A rumour about Brontë has reached me and I need to clear this up one way or another".

"A rumour? I don't understand...."

"There's no easy way to say this, but I must ask you to be totally honest. Has Brontë given birth to a baby during the summer holidays? We are worried that she may have been concealing a pregnancy".

"What?" The shock hit Nell like a thunderbolt. For a moment she was rendered speechless, and it was several minutes before she recovered her composure.

"Mr Franklin I can assure you that Brontë has not had a baby. This is a cruel and malicious story dreamed up by some spiteful bullies here at the school. It's them you should be questioning. My daughter is innocent, she has never even had a boyfriend. Because of the unkindness of some of the girls in her class she does not want to go out of the house, let alone go to school".

"You must realise that we have to take any suspicions like this very seriously. Brontë is fourteen, she is underage which would make it a police matter".

"You have my word that she has not been pregnant and has not had a baby. And I would fight you and the police all the way to spare her the trauma of going through an examination to prove it, if that's what you're suggesting. But since you have brought up the subject, perhaps I can throw some light on how this rumour may have started". She paused.

The pieces of the jigsaw were beginning to fit together. Firstly, the bullying Brontë had experienced about her plumpness – yes, she had put on weight in the past year, that was a fact and had lost a little over the summer. And of course, then there was the arrival of Arlo in the household, although they had tried to keep this private, on the advice of the police. The timing. Mrs Dawson's thinly veiled enquiry in the shop 'how's your girl?' indeed. Of course, Sally Dawson had a younger sister Debbie in Emer's class. Nell could just imagine Emer, holding court in the classroom: 'we have a new baby at home'. Two plus two had equalled five, and the gossip had spread to Lamberham in no time. Nell took a deep breath and told Mr Franklin what had happened within the family during the last fortnight, reiterating that Brontë was blameless and that she would not have her accused in this way when there was no truth in the rumour whatsoever.

For a while, Mr Franklin looked as if he was struggling to believe Nell's story. But before he could interject, Nell continued. "I know it sounds far-fetched, but I have already reported the situation to the police and Children's Services. They are taking it seriously from the point of view that an unidentified child has been abandoned into our care. You are welcome to check with them. But the police are keeping this low-key because of the risk of spurious claims and connections with the child. They have to be careful".

Feeling fiercely protective of her daughter, Nell made a further appeal, anger giving her fresh courage. "I must request that you and the Head Teacher take whatever action is necessary to stamp out this rumour and to address the bullying and unkind behaviour that is going on at this school. By giving credence to this gossip, you are in fact fuelling it. I shall be keeping Brontë at home from now on and I shall be educating her myself or engaging a private tutor. Her future is too important for me to allow this sort of spite to ruin her chances".

Mr Franklin looked taken aback. "It wasn't an accusation, Mrs Walsh, but I had to ask you, to get to the truth. I accept your assurances about Brontë, and I shall be taking steps.... but I urge you to reconsider about keeping her from school. She is a very bright girl; her written work is excellent, and I've had very favourable reports about her in most subjects. But she is withdrawn, reserved in class, she doesn't put herself forward. It's such a shame".

"Well now you know why. She doesn't want to draw attention to herself, she is teased and bullied about everything she says and does. I refuse to put her through this any longer".

"But Mrs Walsh...."

"Please will you do as I have asked about the bullying and write to me when you have spoken to Mr Sutton. At least it may spare another child going through this torture. Consider it a wake-up call. As soon as I have discussed this with my husband, I will let you know how or where Brontë will be educated from now on. Thank you for your time, Mr Franklin".

Nell stood up and left the room, not remembering how she found her way outside. As she walked across the car park, she found she was trembling.

She sat in the driving seat for twenty minutes before turning on the engine, hot tears streaming down her face. Questions flooded through her mind. How did life get so difficult, so out of hand, where did all this come from? Then she thought of Arlo, left in Jenny's care – how could an innocent, defenceless baby only a few weeks old unleash such upheaval on her family? She dreaded telling Patrick; he would rightly be furious, but she longed to speak to her father, he would have some good advice. Thank goodness he was coming home for a while soon.

* * *

Patrick was incensed when Nell told him about her meeting with the Head of Year, and equally as dumbfounded as she had been when Mr Franklin had posed that horrifying question.

"It's a good job I wasn't there; I would have punched him". Patrick's anger knew no bounds.

"Well, that wouldn't have helped, would it? An assault charge on top of everything else".

"I know. What shall we do Nell?"

They sat for an hour in the drawing room, trying to decide on a plan. For a change, Emer was quiet, watching television in the breakfast room. The boys were all in the basement, setting up a ping-pong table. Brontë was as usual in her bedroom.

"I will talk to Arthur and Henry" said Patrick at last. "You can go upstairs and put Brontë's mind at rest about school".

Nell agreed. "But I don't want to involve Ronnie and Emer. Ronnie is already feeling guilty about bringing Denny here, and Emer is too young, she'll just ask endless questions without understanding any of it".

Later, Patrick took Arthur and Henry to one side in the garden. As expected, Arthur knew nothing of the gossip about his sister, being at work and away from the school rumour-mill. But Henry looked sheepish. "I did hear things being said about Brontë" he admitted. "I tried to ignore them, but when I was asked outright by a couple of guys in Brontë's class, I just denied it, told them it was a lie. One day I nearly got into a fight with Josh Upton about it, but Mr Kendall came along".

"Brontë is not going back to Lamberham" Patrick told them. "This business has done her a lot of damage; she needs a fresh start. And your mother has told Mr Franklin in no uncertain terms that they need to deal with the bullying. So if you hear any more being said about Brontë, I want to know about it. Understood?"

Nell knocked on Brontë's bedroom door and heard a tearful 'come in'. She sat down on the bed and took her daughter in her arms.

"I went to see Mr Franklin" she said, stroking Brontë's hair. "It's alright, darling, I know everything. I know all about the rumours and the gossip, and I've put a stop to it. But here's the thing, I've told him that you won't be going back there. Daddy and I are going to see about you changing schools, or whether we can afford a part time tutor for you. It's over, Brontë, you don't have to go through this anymore".

Brontë lifted her head up to face her mother. "Do you mean it; I can stay home?"

"Well maybe not stay home permanently. We can find a better school for you perhaps, that's one option. You do need to prepare for your GCSEs and get some good grades. But for now, just study at home, I can help you with some subjects. Not maths though", she added, laughing.

The relief that swept across Brontë's face was immeasurable. She could hardly speak through her tears. "Thank you Mummy" she sobbed. "I will work hard at home, I promise. I like most of my subjects. I just hate school".

"Well perhaps Lamberham isn't the right school for you just now. But darling we will need to work on this together. Avoiding people and places forever isn't the answer. You shall have a break from school for now and have some lessons at home, then after Christmas we will see how things are, maybe look at some alternatives".

On her way back downstairs, a thought went through Nell's mind. Kathleen was coming home soon. Brontë's godmother. Kathleen who had been through her fair share of troubles in her life, who had been the subject of bullying once, but who had overcome many difficulties and now led a happy and fulfilled life. Perhaps she had some wisdom to impart to Brontë. Something else to talk to Patrick about.

Chapter Thirty-Eight
1997

A couple of days later, four men met for a drink in the Bridge Tavern at Kirchington. Patrick had arranged it, wanting to explain to Sean and Niall in advance of Kathleen's homecoming and the arrival of his in-laws the strange circumstances by which Arlo had appeared in their household, and the worrying situation regarding Brontë. Arthur was included, although being seventeen he was drinking cola instead of Guinness. But Patrick felt that as his son was now doing a man's job, he was entitled to be treated as an adult and to be involved in important family matters.

"It's a weird situation altogether". Niall, now in his early thirties tended to lapse into a stronger Irish brogue when with his brothers. "And very tough on Brontë, to be gossiped about like that. No wonder you've decided to take her out of school".

"Unbelievable". Sean had struggled to follow the turn of events.

"Nell has the idea to ask Kathleen to talk to her. You know, to take her under her wing a bit". Patrick took a long sip of his drink. "She is her godmother. It might help Brontë, to chat with someone different. But what to do about this baby, I'm baffled. The police are saying they have no evidence of a crime, and they don't want any publicity in case the wrong people come forward. The Council are quite happy he's being well looked after. Where does that leave us? We're stuck with him. He's a dear little fellow, no question, but that's not the point".

"Bet you thought you'd finished with all that after having five of your own". Sean gave a wry smile.

Arthur, who had been listening carefully, said "I think Brontë will find it hard to get over this all the time Arlo is living with us. It's like a permanent reminder of all that bullying she went through".

"It's a good point. But it doesn't help us get Arlo back to his real parents". His father looked confused.

"No, but how about if Brontë could leave home? You know, go right away for a while".

"I can see how it might help Brontë", said Sean. He was impressed with his nephew's maturity. He didn't see him very often, but he agreed with Patrick, Arthur was now of an age to be taken seriously.

"She's only fourteen" exclaimed Patrick.

But Arthur had an idea. "Do you think Brontë could go and stay with Granny Bridget? Just for a few months? I know it doesn't solve the problem of Arlo, though" he added, downcast.

There was silence for a few moments while they all took in this suggestion.

"It's a possibility" said Patrick thoughtfully.

"Mam would love it" Niall could see the advantages. "She's lonely, you know, even with Connor and Gráinne close by. And Aidan would surely help find a good school for her. Maybe the Convent of St Teresa. They wouldn't put up with any bullying, Orla went there, she always said how strict they were".

"We'd have to get everyone on board with this idea, Nell, Mam and Brontë of course. It's no good unless they're all in agreement. I'll run it past Nell first and she'll probably want to ask her dad's advice".

Sean couldn't think of a solution about Arlo. "All I can suggest is that you keep going back to the council. He's surely their responsibility. If you ask them again and again, they'll have to do something"

Niall went to the bar to get another round of drinks, and the conversation turned to work matters. Sean was now a senior project manager for Lovells, a civil engineering company in Kirchington. There was some discussion about whether there was possibility for an apprenticeship for Henry.

"Except Nell has her mind set on university for him," said Patrick. "He's clever enough, no doubt about that but I'm all for him learning a trade as young as possible".

Niall returned to hear the end of this conversation. "Why not let Henry make up his own mind on that one. He's old enough to decide".

Sean had another thought. "Maybe I could arrange for a few weeks work experience for him. If you want me to, that is". Patrick nodded his thanks, and they turned their attention to the karaoke that was just starting up. "Time to leave, I think," said Sean. "I don't think I can cope with that tonight". The others laughed and quickly finished their drinks, then went their separate ways home.

* * *

The following weekend Patrick drove to Gatwick Airport to meet the flight from Spain. It was the middle of September; the weather was still warm although the days were growing shorter, and the leaves were just beginning to turn. When the travellers appeared in the arrivals lounge, he was struck by how well they all looked. He had not seen his sister for several years; she had aged only slightly and looked relaxed and happy. Beside her was a tall, fair haired young man, deeply tanned and with blue eyes as piercing as Kathleen's but a lighter shade. This must be Adam, Patrick thought, then shook his hand as Kathleen introduced them.

A few steps behind were Lois and Neville; Lois holding tightly onto her husband's arm as he pushed the luggage trolley. He did look older, his once dark hair was now white but nevertheless thick and springy, his complexion a deep mahogany. Although now seventy-seven he was still tall and upright, his bearing as distinguished as ever. Lois, by contrast seemed to have shrunk a little in height and was noticeably more frail than when Patrick had last seen her, but her eyes were bright, her skin, although showing a few more lines, was lightly tanned, her hair cut into a short, becoming style and she was impeccably dressed in a light trouser suit with a colourful scarf hanging loosely at her neck.

They stopped for a pub lunch on the way home. Patrick wanted to take the opportunity to explain about the situation back at Moongarth; the arrival of Arlo, the bullying and gossip that Brontë had endured, and the dilemma facing them about how to go about repairing the damage that these things had wreaked on the family.

Neville and Lois looked astonished at first; Kathleen was sympathetic for her niece and promised to do whatever she could to help. Adam listened but stayed silent, obviously feeling it was not his place to venture an opinion this early in his acquaintance with the family.

It was a great deal for everyone to take in, especially for Lois and Neville who for a while seemed bewildered. Patrick realised that coming from the safe, protected bubble of their holiday home where their lives were peaceful and untroubled and from which past sorrows and fears had been banished, they felt suddenly exposed, vulnerable to all the uncertainties of the outside world.

After a while Patrick could see that in Neville's concern for his granddaughter, his professional training and experience gained over many years had come to the fore; with Patrick and Nell's permission he would like to talk privately with Brontë and see if he could see a way forward with which she would be comfortable, but which would not compromise her education. The prospect of a stay in West Cork was discussed; he did not know a great deal about the Irish educational system although he felt sure that they would teach to the equivalent of GCSE standard. But that was for later; Neville felt the priority was for Brontë to feel secure within the family, and to have time and space to heal amongst people she trusted and who loved her.

"Both of our girls are a worry to us at the moment". Patrick went on to describe Emer's headstrong and challenging behaviour, her constant demands and answering back. "She's totally the opposite to Brontë".

"Do you think she's being bullied as well" asked Neville.

"No, quite the reverse. No one would dare to bully her, she's the most confident and outspoken child you could ever meet, she'll argue till the cows come home and tie the teachers up in knots. I don't know how they cope with her at school".

"You've got a lot to contend with there, I can tell. It can't be easy for Emer, being the youngest of five. What about the boys, how are they getting on?"

"It's strange, they don't give us a moment's bother. Not so far, anyway. Arthur works with me, he's doing well, he'll be my right-hand man when he's a bit older. Henry, well Nell says he takes after you in maths and science, he's going on to study engineering. Ronnie's a bit too young to tell but he is a caring, kind little boy, lovely temperament, in some ways he's wise beyond his years".

With the arrival of four guests, the household at Moongarth was even more busy than usual. Nell was overjoyed to see her parents for the first time in three years and there was a great deal of hugging, talking and catching up to do. Lois and Neville were to have the side-rooms, as they were still called, and Brontë had offered to move to the remaining spare attic room so that Kathleen and Adam could have her bedroom on the first floor.

"I can never recall a time when Moongarth was so full of life" said Neville, having taken a tour with Patrick to see the latest touches he had added to the house. "It's wonderful what you've achieved" he observed admiringly. Emer was at his side, jumping around to show him this and that. "I asked to have the en-suite room on the top floor because I need privacy now that I'm eight". She hadn't stopped talking since the visitors had arrived and her grandfather could quickly understand why her parents found her exhausting. He remembered a time when he taught a class of thirty boys only a little older than Emer, none of whom would have been so direct or opinionated; such behaviour would have been considered impolite or disrespectful. How things have changed, he thought, then realised that his other four grandchildren were all well-mannered and courteous; Emer was the exception, and the reasons were difficult to fathom.

Lois went for a rest before dinner; she was glad to be back in Moongarth but the journey and the introductions had tired her. Nell could see that her mother was overwhelmed by all the noise and activity. Clearly, she was perplexed about the appearance of an unknown baby in their lives, and Nell realised how anything to do with babies or pregnancy still affected her deeply. Leaving Kathleen to look after Arlo for a few minutes she took her mother a tray of tea and helped her unpack. "It's so lovely that you've come home, Mummy" she said. "I hope you'll be comfortable in here. It's a big adjustment, coming from your quiet apartment to a houseful of people. Let me know if it gets too much, I will send the children down to the basement to give us some peace".

Lois smiled. "Your father's right, it's how it should be" she said. "I'm so sorry darling; it didn't work out that way when you were a child. I realise now how lonely you must have been. But you have a lovely family now, you have these wonderful young people instead of brothers and sisters".

As she prepared dinner, having settled Arlo after his feed, Nell reflected on her mother's words. It was a breakthrough of sorts, and it had taken over thirty years. Perhaps it's as near as it can ever be to Mummy coming to terms with all she went through, she said to herself. We must be content with that. She turned to Kathleen who had been preparing vegetables. "Tell me about Adam. Where did you meet him? He's very handsome".

Kathleen told Nell of how her friendship with Adam had grown over the last two years in Solibrio. He owned Martina's, a nearby café bar which she often frequented when walking back from the market. A cup of good coffee sitting at an outside table in the sunshine, looking across at the Mediterranean was one of her greatest pleasures. She had made the acquaintance of several local people and sometimes Adam joined her at the table when he was not too busy. He was an Australian, a widower, his late wife had been Spanish and together they had set up the café bar before she had become ill. He had thought about returning to Australia after Martina died five years previously but had decided instead to stay on and run the business in her memory. Adam had met Lois and Neville many times, often doing small jobs around the apartment for them or occasionally joining them for supper when he could leave the bar. He and Kathleen had become close; six months ago, he had asked Kathleen to marry him, and she had accepted.

"It all seems to have worked out, Nell. Last year divorce was made legal in Ireland. Michael and I have lived apart for more than fifteen years. We have no children or property; it should be straightforward. As soon as my divorce comes through, Adam and I are getting married! Hopefully next summer".

Nell was excited for Kathleen and hugged her, giving her congratulations. "We must have a toast to you both later" she said. "It's wonderful to have some good news for a change".

"I've been thinking about Brontë," said Kathleen. "Can I take her out next week? Just the two of us, so that we can have a chat. I know it's a weekday, but we will only be here for a short time".

Nell agreed and told her of Arthur's suggestion that Brontë should go to live in Ireland for a while. Kathleen looked thoughtful. "Don't say anything to her yet, though" added Nell. "I will need to find out whether your Mum would be willing to have her, and what my dad thinks about the idea. I don't want to put her hopes up when it may come to nothing".

Patrick and Adam were getting to know each other. Over a couple of beers Adam talked about his life in Spain, and how happy he was to have met Kathleen. Knowing that Adam owned a bar had given Patrick a twinge of concern; hoping against hope that Kathleen had not reverted to her previous drinking habits, especially as she was now in a position of responsibility with Lois. He recalled a time when his sister had been a great deal too fond of alcohol and that without the change in direction that leaving Ireland had afforded, that fondness might have spiralled into addiction. But there was no suggestion of this; clearly that behaviour was in the past; she had left it behind along with her disastrous first marriage. She was now a fulfilled, responsible and caring person and had made a success of her life. Her friendship with Adam had grown and developed into romance, and they had become engaged earlier that year.

It was a lively party of eleven that sat down to dinner that evening. Arthur and Henry carried in a garden table from the shed to provide some extra places. Niall and Sean had joined the family, eager to see their sister. Nell could not think when she had ever seen her mother so happy and relaxed. At the end of the meal Neville produced several bottles of champagne and stood up to ask everyone to join him in a toast for the happiness of Kathleen and Adam, and Nell thought back to the time when her father had made a similar speech at her own wedding. It was probably the last time her parents had drunk champagne; she reflected. He proposed another toast for Nell and Patrick, their family and congratulating Patrick on his successful business and the transformation of Moongarth. Emer was unusually quiet, the large gathering of adults posing more of a challenge that she was used to. A whimper from the Moses basket in the corner of the room signalled that Arlo was ready for his next feed, and was a sobering reminder to all present that despite the joviality of the occasion, none of them were any nearer to finding answers to the strange circumstances under which he was suddenly a part of this family, or knowing what to do about it.

Chapter Thirty-Nine

After breakfast the following morning, Neville asked Brontë to show him round the garden. For a while he talked to her about the time he stayed at Moongarth as a young boy with his brother during school holidays and later when he moved there permanently after he married Nanny Lois. She listened to every word, knowing about Uncle Henry's terrible accident but didn't refer to it directly, realising how distressing it must be for her grandfather even now. She wondered how he could bear to have lived for so many years near a place of such sadness. Feeling that she could trust him, she talked about her favourite subjects at school, but that school itself was a source of unhappiness to her. Instead of trying to persuade her, Neville told her of her uncle's first few months at boarding school, how homesick he was and that he found it hard to make friends, but how things had started to change after a few months. He knew that Nell had taken Brontë out of school and why, but not wishing to go into detail, asked her what she would like to do next. Would she like to have a home tutor, a new school or maybe explore other options? He was trying to test the water about her leaving home for a while without being specific about Arthur's idea.

To his surprise, Brontë replied that she would like to move away from Drover's Cross. She loved her family and her home she said, but found the household too busy and noisy, especially now that there was a baby as well. She knew she was too young to leave home and so she would have to work out how to cope with things as they were, but sometimes she wished she could have a quieter life. Neville thought sadly that it was the sort of thing a much older person might say, not a young girl on the cusp of womanhood. His heart went out to her. Putting an arm round her shoulders, he agreed that maybe school was not the right environment for her just now, and promised to have a chat with her mother about how she could complete her education in a way with which she would feel more comfortable.

They returned to the kitchen to find Emer arguing determinedly with her mother. She had discovered that Brontë was to go out with Kathleen later that morning, but being Monday it was a school day for Emer as usual.

"It's not fair, I want to go out with Auntie Kathleen"

"I'm sorry Emer, you must go to school. Brontë is not going to school for a while".

"Why not? I want to have a day off school too".

"It's nothing to do with you Emer, I'm sure you will be able to go out with Auntie Kathleen another time. Now go and brush your teeth".

"But I want to go today" whined Emer.

"You can't. Now do as you're told".

"Why do I always have to suffer like this just because I'm the youngest?"

"You don't know what it means to suffer, be thankful. Now teeth!" Nell ushered Emer towards the bathroom. "Welcome to the school-day madhouse, Daddy. She's such a prima donna; we have arguments about something every day. It wears me out".

"What's a prima donna?" Emer put her head around the door, then disappeared again quickly, seeing that her mother was becoming angry.

Neville, having witnessed what had taken place, put his hand on Nell's shoulder. "I can see she is very hard work" he said sympathetically. "She is trying to assert herself, and it is probably because she's the youngest. I don't really have any suggestions as to what to do, except perhaps to give her some responsibility, something she is in charge of herself. Let's have a chat about it while I'm here".

Later that morning when the house was quieter, and Arlo had been bathed, changed and fed, Nell settled down to telephone her mother-in-law. Bridget was so far unaware of the arrival of Arlo and the bullying Brontë had experienced, so Nell had given a great deal of thought as to how she would explain the bizarre situation the family had been plunged into.

Bridget listened, firstly in disbelief, then in horror. She took time to understand what Nell was saying. "It does feel as if we are living in some kind of weird film plot at times," said Nell. "I almost don't believe it myself. But we have two dilemmas: how to find Arlo's parents and what to do about Brontë. You see, I have taken her out of that school, she was so terribly unhappy, and I didn't feel that they were dealing with the bullying very well. We haven't come to any decisions, but we do have an idea. Brontë needs to get right away for a while; emotionally she is very fragile. Bridget, what I am ringing to ask is, can she come and stay with you for a while? Maybe go to school in Ballymere? I think the change, the peace and quiet and the slower pace of life would help her just now."

There was a long pause at the end of the phone, and for a moment Nell wondered if Bridget was going to refuse. Then:

"Poor little soul. To think of what she's been through, and none of it her fault at all. Of course she can come and stay, for as long as she likes. I would love to have her, provided she knows there's no entertainment here, she might get bored – as you know, we're at the back end of nowhere".

"I haven't asked her yet Bridget, I wanted to run it past you first. But if you're happy about it, Patrick and I will talk to her later. I'm so grateful to you, I can't thank you enough".

"Sure, won't it be company for me too? I shall love having her to stay".

* * *

Nell had offered to lend Adam her car so that he could take Kathleen and Brontë out for a couple of hours in Kirchington. She had suggested avoiding Lamberham as it was where Brontë had so recently attended school, and anyway there were many more shops in Kirchington.

Adam, knowing that Kathleen would like some time alone with Brontë, said he would like an hour or two on his own. He was going to take a walk along the riverbank and maybe spend some time looking round the church. After looking in the windows of Fullerton's, Kathleen noticed that her niece was quiet. "I don't really enjoy shopping" Brontë confided. "Nothing looks right on me; the clothes I like are never in my size".

"Let's go and have a cup of coffee". Kathleen suggested. They made their way to Markham's, which was quiet, even for a Monday morning.

"This is where Mum and Dad went on their first date" said Brontë, sipping a diet cola whilst Kathleen poured a cup of tea from a white china teapot.

"Talking of dates, Adam and I are going to be married next summer," said Kathleen. "Our wedding will be in Ireland, and we're going to start making arrangements this week when we go over to see Mam and the family. But what I wanted to say was, I would like you to be my chief bridesmaid. I shall ask Emer and Aisling as well, and maybe Orla. What do you say?"

Brontë looked excited for a moment, then her face fell. "I would really love to, Auntie Kathleen. But I would worry about a dress. I don't look nice in anything. I don't suit anything fussy or frilly. I would let you down".

Kathleen spoke gently. "Of course you wouldn't let me down. We have plenty of time to think about something you would feel right in, it doesn't need to be anything too girly if you wouldn't like that. How about if I choose a colour and let you choose a style, or we could have something made?"

Brontë nodded but still looked doubtful.

"Let's go and pick up a couple of bridal magazines, we can look at them when we go home and maybe we will get some ideas."

Kathleen felt sad for her niece. Clearly, she was still self-conscious and scarred from the cruel jibes she had received in school, and this had really damaged her self-esteem. She thought back to her ill-fated first marriage, there had been no white gown or fancy trimmings, she had worn a plain dress that Aunt Angela had made and an unattractive hat. She had not felt special as brides should on their wedding day, it had all been rushed and done on the cheap. This time it was going to be different, and she was determined that Brontë, with whom she felt a growing affinity, would enjoy being a bridesmaid and would wear something that made her feel good about herself and help build some self-confidence.

By the time they arrived back at Moongarth it was lunchtime. Arlo had been grizzly that morning and surprisingly, after they had finished their meal, Lois offered to push him around the garden a little way in his stroller to settle him. Nell was doubtful as to whether her mother could manage but she said she would not go far, and in any case pushing the stroller would help give her balance. Pleased that Lois was feeling strong enough, and noting her willingness Nell agreed, reminding her to call for help if needed.

Nell had already told her father of the outcome of her conversation with Bridget but as they sat down for a cup of coffee with Kathleen and Adam, she explained again to the three of them.

"I know Patrick is in favour, but I'm going to talk to him again this evening. I shall call Brontë down now and we can see if she would like to stay with Granny for a while".

Neville mentioned what Brontë had said earlier that morning, about wanting to leave home one day because she found the household too boisterous, too rowdy. "It was a curious thing to hear from such a young person, but she was being honest. That may be another reason why she dislikes school, but I agree with you, she needs to come to terms with this, she can't always avoid things she doesn't like".

Nell nodded. "I know, but for now I think she does need to get over what has happened. Ballymere would be a complete change for her. Living with Bridget would be ideal, it's so peaceful there. It may only be for a while until she has overcome this. It would be like…. healing".

Kathleen had a thought. "I know this is short notice, but if Brontë likes the idea, how about if we take her with us on Wednesday?" Adam nodded in agreement. "I could settle her at school while we're there. St Teresa's has small classes, it's run by nuns. Orla always said it was strict, but they were very kind; I think Brontë would prefer that. She's been baptised a Catholic, but in any case, I'm sure they would take her".

Brontë was a little overwhelmed by the plan at first but then became visibly more enthusiastic. It was such a sudden suggestion, coming out of the blue, and the prospect of staying with Granny Bridget whom she remembered only slightly was, for a moment a daunting one. But the thought of moving right away from Lamberham School and the people there who had caused her so much torment felt like a blessing; even the realisation that it meant leaving her family for some months was something she could face with equanimity. She liked the sound of St Teresa's; its quiet discipline and rural location would be just what she needed. "Yes please, I would love to go to Granny's. Thank you so much" she said, tears of relief pricking at her eyelids. Nell hugged her, thankful that they had reached a solution but feeling that parting with Brontë even for a few months was a high price to pay for her daughter's recovery.

Chapter Forty

Preparations for Brontë's departure were well underway by the following day. She completed her own packing then set about cleaning her room; normally Jenny would have done this, but Brontë insisted that she would do it herself. "It will be good practice for me when I'm at Granny's" she said. Nell had told her daughter that she must be responsible and help around the house during her stay in Ireland; Bridget was by no means elderly, but it would not be fair to give her extra work. That morning, Nell telephoned St Teresa's and spoke to the Head Teacher, explaining that Brontë would be staying with her grandmother in Ballymere for a few months and that they did not want her education to fall behind while she was there. Would St Teresa's have a place available immediately?

If Sister Francis was surprised to receive such an urgent request she was careful not to comment and said that yes, they would be able to accept Brontë into the fourth form for the remainder of the school year but that they could not guarantee that they would be teaching the same curriculum as in England and would she be able to adapt? Nell quickly confirmed that Brontë was willing to change to St Teresa's syllabus and in any case, she had only spent one week of the current term at her last school. An application form would be put in the post that day, to be returned as soon as possible. A list of school requirements would accompany the form; Nell realised that would be difficult but wondered privately if she might prevail upon Gráinne to purchase any extras if they sent the money.

Later Nell sat down with Brontë and told her that she would be starting at St Teresa's the following week. "I explained what happened at school here, Sister Francis was very understanding".

"You didn't say anything about.... you know" Brontë faltered, not wishing to put the worst of the gossip into words.

"I just told her that you had experienced serious bullying at your last school and that we've been so concerned that we have removed you from the school and you are staying with Granny while you recover. That's all they need to know".

At her mother's suggestion, Brontë sat for an hour and wrote out details of her current course work, her set books and the subjects she had planned to take for GCSE. This would give her new teachers some idea of the standard she had reached. In some ways she felt nervous, it was like going into the unknown, but she would be staying with Granny who was kind and warm-hearted; other family members would be close by, and it could not be any worse than the agony she had suffered at the hands of her classmates.

When he arrived home from work Patrick was surprised to hear how much had been arranged during his absence but was relieved that St Teresa's could accept Brontë and that she was happy with the plan.

"We'll miss her, I know" he said, and took Nell in his arms, realising what a wrench it would be for them to say goodbye to their daughter for a while. "But I'm sure we're doing the right thing, she will be grand out there, and it may be the best thing that can happen after all she's been through".

Emer was about to make demands in no uncertain terms when she heard that her sister would be going to live in Ireland for a while, but fortunately Kathleen, with great diplomacy asked her if she would like to be one of her bridesmaids the following summer, and that she could wear a very special dress. The prospect had the desired effect of diverting Emer immediately; after dinner she waltzed around the house excitedly and talked of nothing else for the next hour.

"How would St Theresa's be funded?" Neville asked Patrick, as they all sat together with a cup of coffee after dinner. Nell was busy bathing Arlo and supervising Emer's bedtime.

"The Church mainly, I think" replied Patrick. "And charitable donations".

Neville took out his cheque book. "It's the least I can do to help things along for Brontë" he said. "Perhaps you can enclose this when you send off the application form".

"That's really kind of you, Neville. You always know the right thing to do. Perhaps I should do the same. It's not easy, parting with your child".

He realised too late that the remark was ill-judged. Lois looked up sharply but said nothing; Neville did not seem to take it the wrong way but nodded as if in sympathy.

* * *

"Arthur that was a master stroke, your idea of Brontë going to stay with Granny" said Patrick who had gone down to the basement for a game of snooker with the boys. "It's all arranged, she's leaving on Wednesday with Kathleen and Adam".

"Wow, that was quick" said Henry, overhearing the conversation. "It's a shame she has to go; this has all been too much for her, hasn't it".

"Well, we will be going out there in the summer, won't we," said Arthur. "For the wedding, I mean. The time will soon pass. In a way I wish I could go".

"Hey…. I jumped through hoops so I could leave Ireland to come here," said his father. "Go one day for a holiday, but don't be thinking there's much out there for young men. That's the reason I came here, and then I met your Mam". He winked at the boys. "She's the best thing that ever happened to me. If you can both find someone like her one day, you'll not have done too badly".

Much of the following day was spent in last-minute tasks and checking all was in order for Brontë in readiness for her trip. The plan was for her to travel by train with Kathleen and Adam from Kirchington to the ferry at Fishguard. From Rosslare they would take another train to Cork City and hire a car from there. She had a few last-minute nerves, but these were soon forgotten in the excitement of the new adventure on which she was about to embark.

With all her packing done, there was nothing more to do in the afternoon. Kathleen and Adam drove into Lamberham for some last-minute shopping and gifts for the family, and Lois and Neville sat down with Nell and Brontë in the drawing room for a cup of tea. Arlo was sleeping peacefully in the corner and the house was quiet for an hour or so before the youngest children came home from school. Lois produced a small photograph album.

"We had quite a few days out together in Spain recently; it's something we wanted to do, to get to know the area further afield. The beach is wonderful and we're still happy with the apartment, but it's been nice to travel a little way as well".

She passed the album round. Nell was astonished; it wasn't many years ago that her mother would have been horrified at the thought of going anywhere unknown, where there might be crowds or strangers. But here was the proof; photos taken by passers-by or opportunistic photographers of her parents following the tourist trail in Nerja, looking as relaxed and devoted to one another as if they were on honeymoon. There was a photo of them sitting at a beachside café, sipping what looked like sangria, one with them watching a flamenco dance display, another with Lois sporting a beautiful frilly red Spanish shawl and mantilla, her father wearing a distinctive Cordobes hat, and several shots of them feeding donkeys at an animal sanctuary.

"We drew the line at watching bullfighting though" said Neville, anticipating Brontë's question. "It's still legal in some parts of Spain but it would have been a step too far for us".

"These are lovely photos, Mummy" said Nell, still amazed at the transformation. "I'm so pleased you've been doing more travelling". She felt a lump in her throat at the memory of how close her parents had come to disaster only a few years previously.

"It's worked out so well having Kathleen. She's been a godsend. But we've had to accept that things will change when she gets married, we can't expect her to live in after

STARS FROM THERE TO HERE

that. It's just as well that we have a few months to decide what to do. We're so happy for her though, aren't we Neville, Adam is a fine chap, we're very fond of him as well".

Nell prepared Brontë's favourite dinner that evening; fish pie with lots of vegetables, and lemon trifle. It was to be their last meal together as a family for some time, but Nell tried to hide her sadness, knowing that by parting with her daughter she was helping her to move on from the trauma of the last year and embrace a new life for a while. It was a noisy gathering, but Lois seemed to enjoy the hilarity, laughing at Henry's jokes and joining in with one or two of her own. If only I wasn't about to say goodbye to Brontë this would be perfect, thought Nell. For once no one minded Emer's incessant talking and everyone felt at ease with each other. Even Arlo gurgled contentedly in his basket, unaware of the changes and dilemmas his presence had created within the family.

As they settled into bed later that evening, Patrick turned to Nell and put his arm round her lovingly. "Looks like one of our chicks is about to fly the coop" he said, then seeing that Nell was very quiet and on the brink of tears, he added: "it won't be long before we visit her. You could take a flight out to Cork on your own for a week or so if it comes to that, we could manage here. And I've been thinking, we could all go out for a long holiday in the summer for the wedding. And maybe while we're there, Ronnie and Emer can be baptised. Lots to look forward to".

"Yes, you're right Patrick, I'm sure it will all work out. This is the first step, at least it may be a new beginning for Brontë. But I've been thinking about Emer too".

Patrick groaned. "What is it this time?"

"Just something Dad said. You know Emer has been asking about having a pony?"

Patrick sat up in bed. "No!" he said forcefully. "Definitely not. Talk about rewards for bad behaviour. Just think about it. Ok we have the land; we could fix up a stable. But it's feed, vets' bills, then we would be paying for proper lessons, next thing I would have to be buying a horse box, we'd be ferrying her around to this and that every weekend. She would never stop pestering. The answer's no".

"Wait, Patrick, hear me out. Dad wondered if she behaves like she does because she's the youngest, she always has to assert herself. He suggested giving her something that is her own, something she's responsible for. Anyway, I was looking at some photos Mummy brought from Spain. There was one of them with some donkeys at a rescue centre. Do you think we could do that, re-home a donkey for Emer? It would teach her to look after an animal and maybe take her mind off her own self- importance. It wouldn't mean taking her here, there and everywhere, the donkey would stay here in our field. Ok, there would be some vets' fees now and then but if it's through a charity they might cover some of the costs. Donkeys are such gentle creatures, perhaps it would calm Emer down a bit".

Patrick laughed. "They can be stubborn too, Emer would have met her match. Maybe it's not such a bad idea. I'll think about it".

They kissed goodnight; Patrick fell asleep straightaway, but Nell lay awake for a while, thinking about both of her daughters and hoping against hope that everything would go to plan. And we're still no nearer a solution about Arlo, she realised as she drifted off to sleep.

* * *

Neville, anticipating that his daughter would be emotional and upset at waving goodbye to Brontë, had booked to take her and Lois out to lunch at the Swan's Rest in Kirchington on Wednesday and had asked Jenny to take care of Arlo for a few hours.

Nell did her best to hold back tears as she and Patrick watched the taxi drive off down Hasker's Hill to take Kathleen, Adam and Brontë to the railway station. The family had all assembled on the front lawn to see them off, then

Patrick said he and Arthur must be leaving for work, and the other children went off to collect their belongings ready for school.

"I hope we haven't forgotten anything" said Nell as Patrick climbed into the driver's seat of the pickup.

"Stop worrying. She has enough money, ticket, ID, clothes, books, and a list for Gráinne. And your letter for Mam. It will all be fine. See you later. Oh, and while you're in town can you pick up a driving licence application form for Arthur. He needs to start learning soon". He kissed her and drove off, the tyres crunching on the gravel.

Back to reality, thought Nell as she made her way indoors. She felt empty, numb and as though nothing would ever be right again. But it's for the best, she told herself, as she went and helped Jenny clear the breakfast debris and load the dishwasher. After a while she went upstairs, put on some makeup and changed out of her jeans ready to go out with her parents. Next, I need to work out what to do about Arlo, the realisation returning to her that somehow, they must take action soon. That situation was not going to resolve itself.

Chapter Forty-One

By coincidence, two police officers called at Moongarth the following evening. Emer and Ronnie had just gone to bed, Emer under protest, Ronnie obediently, saying that he was going to read. Arthur and Henry were watching television in the breakfast room and Arlo was in his carry cot in the drawing room, awake but murmuring contentedly.

WPC Drummond and PC Finch introduced themselves to Nell and Patrick and nodded towards Neville and Lois. Nell explained that her parents were staying with them.

"Would you like us to leave you?" Neville asked Nell. "We can go and sit with the boys if you like".

"No please stay, Dad, it's important that we all hear what the police have to say"

"We spoke on the phone" said WPC Drummond to Nell. "I'm sorry it's taken a while for us to come and see you. How is the baby?"

"He's fine" said Nell gesturing towards the carry cot. The policewoman walked over and looked down at him. "He looks bonny. You're obviously looking after him well".

"The thing is, we shouldn't be looking after him at all" said Patrick, wanting to make this point clear from the very beginning. "What progress have you made with tracing his family?"

PC Finch took out his notebook. "So far, we've drawn a blank I'm afraid. We've made enquiries of all the maternity wards within a fifty-mile radius and followed up on all the new mums who've had babies within the last two months. All their babies are accounted for. We were fairly certain of that beforehand because any missing child is reported very quickly, but we had to be sure. We've been in contact with Children's Services to see if they know of any families in the area where there might be an unwanted pregnancy. That came to nothing. We've also searched for Denny Reid, but he seems to

316

have disappeared into thin air. He is not known to the police, at least not by that name. He could be going under a false name of course. While we're here we need to take a detailed description of him, and we may ask you to come into the station to see if he matches with any of our photo fits. But we're clutching at straws a bit, the only witnesses to him living in the bus shelter are eight and nine years old. We're not minded to carry out house to house enquiries unless we are certain that a crime has taken place. Without further evidence and in the absence of firm clues, there are two options: To continue in the hope that Denny Reid will soon return and claim Arlo with some sort of explanation, or if it does prove to be a case of abandonment, that would place it firmly in the hands of Children's Services. But we really need a breakthrough soon, it's been more than three weeks since you reported the baby being left with you."

"The thing is, it's normally the other way round. Children do go missing occasionally and as I said, when that happens, we have procedures to follow. But abandoned babies, well that rarely happens, I've never known a situation like yours since I've been on the force".

He paused. Patrick looked dismayed.

WPC Drummond continued. "As I said to you on the phone, we're not treating this as a criminal matter. Not yet anyway. I'm not saying this is case closed, but until we have more to go on we may not be able to take it any further".

"But surely abandonment of a child is a crime?" asked Nell despairingly.

"Well yes, but who are we going to charge? We don't even have anyone to question. I can assure you that if we track down Denny Reid, or anyone fitting his description we will bring him in for questioning immediately. At that stage CID may take over. But until that happens......" she shook her head.

PC Finch took down every detail of the description Nell and Patrick were able to give. "This description could apply to thousands of young men. Can you remember any distinguishing features? Anything that would make him stand out?" WPC Drummond made a further appeal. "Are you sure there's nothing else we should know? You're not covering for anyone? It's important that you tell us everything you can".

Nell shook her head and Patrick looked angry at the suggestion. "We have told you absolutely everything we know. Why would we do otherwise? We want his parents found as soon as possible".

At this point Neville, who had said nothing until then, addressed the police officers. "I can assure you that my daughter and son-in-law are co-operating fully and are telling you everything possible that will help reunite this child with his parents" he said sternly. His years as a head teacher had given him a natural air of authority, and his age and gravitas reinforced the seriousness of his words. He did not appear to the police officers as someone who would easily be taken in. "May I ask if you have considered DNA testing? Surely that would be one hundred per cent conclusive proof of parenthood?"

"As a matter of fact, we were going to ask you if we could take a mouth swab from Arlo while we're here" said WPC Drummond, producing a testing kit. "But I should explain, it's a very long shot. It will only be of value if it matches a DNA record already on the database. If the parents' DNA is not on the database, then there will be nothing to match it against. But if, in the future, a DNA sample were to be taken from one of them and entered, then a match would come up. But of course, that may never happen, or it may not happen for a long time".

Nell sighed, but Neville nodded as though he understood.

"You say Denny stayed the night?" asked PC Finch while his colleague was taking the swab. "It's possible that his DNA may be on the bedding or in the bathroom".

Nell realised with a sinking heart that she had asked Jenny to strip the bed, wash the sheets and clean the bathroom on the morning of Denny's departure. She explained this to the officers. "At that stage I had no reason to think there was anything wrong" she faltered. "I never expected any of this to happen".

Patrick had an idea. "He left his rucksack with us. Could any trace of him be left on it?" He went off to fetch it from the utility room and came back a few moments later. "We'll take this with us if that's all right" said PC Finch, "Forensics may be able to test it for hairs and fibres. It's the only material link with him now".

"So where does this leave us?" asked Patrick. He had a feeling that he knew what the police were going to say.

"Well, we will continue with our enquiries and arrange for the testing," said WPC Drummond. "If a match comes up, then happy days! We will then have the breakthrough we need. But as I said, don't put your hopes up. If you think of anything else that might help, then let us know straightaway. In the meantime, our advice is to contact Children's Services again. They will want to monitor the situation; they may decide to arrange a temporary foster placement for Arlo" She stood up and put on her hat. "Thank you for your help, Mr and Mrs Walsh, we'll be in touch. We'll see ourselves out".

After the police had gone, Patrick poured them all a whiskey. Lois, who had been silent throughout the conversation, accepted although she rarely drank spirits.

"There's only one thing for it" said Patrick wearily. "Back to Miss Shaw, I think. What other options do we have?"

A wail from the carry cot signalled that Arlo was awake. "He's become one of the family now" said Nell, picking him up. "I know we didn't want that to happen but somehow it has. What else were we supposed to do? I love him already; I just can't help it. I can't forget that for some reason that we may never know, his parents didn't want him. It would be too cruel for us to reject him as well".

Patrick looked at his wife as if to object, then stopped himself, realising for the thousandth time the reason why he loved her.

Chapter Forty-Two

Bridget had made a brief telephone call late on the Wednesday evening to confirm that the travellers had all arrived safely, but Nell was hugely relieved when on Friday lunchtime a call came through from Brontë and they were able to have a longer chat.

"Everything's fine here Mummy" she said. "Granny has been so kind. I have a lovely room with a wonderful view of the fields and a place to study. I'm to start at St Teresa's on Monday. Gráinne is going to take me into town this weekend and buy everything I need. How is everyone at home?"

"We're all ok but we're missing you". It was true. The family had never before been split up and it was a reminder to all of them how close they were. "Nanny and Grandpa send their love. Daddy's thinking of re-homing a donkey for Emer. If that happens, I'll send you some photos".

Brontë laughed. "She'll love that, she'll be able to boss it about".

"We're hoping a donkey may calm her down a little, but we'll see. Let's talk again after you've started school. I'm looking forward to hearing about it. Tell Granny to reverse the charges".

"Will do. Love you Mum".

"Love you too". They rang off.

* * *

At Nell's request, an appointment had been made the following week for a member of the Child Protection Team to visit the Walshes. Patrick decided to take the morning off work to be with her at the meeting, mainly as a support for Nell but also to ensure that they presented a united front if any decisions were made.

Helen Kimber introduced herself as the Team Leader and showed them her council identity card. She was a mature, pleasant woman, friendly but professional. She opened a slim folder which contained a few typed sheets of paper and some handwritten notes.

"Now, how is Arlo and how are you all coping? I should like to see him while I'm here but first tell me what's been happening".

Nell and Patrick explained that very little had happened since Rosemary Shaw's visit except that the police had paid them a call to report a lack of progress in finding Arlo's parents. "The case is still active, in that they're continuing to make enquiries" said Patrick "and they took a DNA sample but told us not to expect too much of that, it may not come up with a match".

Mrs Kimber nodded. "Yes, we are keeping in touch with the police on this matter, we are both in agreement that it's a very unusual set of circumstances". Nell was glad she had not referred to Arlo as a 'case'; that would have seemed so impersonal.

She glanced at her notes. "I have Rosemary's report here. She was satisfied that Arlo was well looked after and that you have brought up – oh – five children of your own, one of whom works with you, Mr Walsh! You have an extremely comfortable home here, and that you did not need any financial assistance".

Patrick looked slightly impatient. "Yes, well that's all correct but she promised it would all be sorted out soon. She hasn't come back to us...we left a couple of messages for her".

"Well soon after that meeting Rosemary went on leave, and she has now transferred to another borough. I think she may have explained to you that because you were taking such good care of Arlo, the situation was not considered urgent enough for us to take immediate action, other than to keep in contact with the police in case they could report anything useful. I think she did mention that a formal assessment would be necessary if the situation continued, but she was obviously of the opinion that everything would sort itself out and that the baby's father would return soon enough. I apologise that she didn't get back to you, she was under a great deal of pressure at the time; we had a serious case review to conduct which always takes priority, then she went on holiday, as I said".

Nell was trying to understand and looked questioningly at Patrick. It seemed that although the presence of Arlo in their family was of the utmost importance to them, it was not treated with the same urgency by the social work team.

"The police mentioned that you might be able to find a foster care placement for Arlo" said Patrick hopefully.

"Yes, that is the only other option we have, I'm afraid, unless his parents come forward. But that may take time; there's a shortage of good foster carers and so much need. There are children of all ages needing families to look after them, sometimes we have to place them outside the borough. Anyway, please may I see Arlo?"

Nell showed Mrs Kimber to the breakfast room where Arlo was sleeping. She introduced her to Jenny who was working in the kitchen.

This time Mrs Kimber did not ask to undress him; she could see that he was clean, contented and well-fed. But without making official notes, she took in every detail of the safe and comfortable surroundings, the spotless kitchen visible through the doorway, the warm temperature of the house, the dog curled up on his bed, the outside space and most of all the happy and homely atmosphere. There is domestic help here as well, she noticed.

"If Arlo has actually been abandoned, it was very lucky for him that he was left in such a beautiful home and with a lovely family like yours" she said. They returned to the drawing room and sat down. After a few minutes Jenny appeared with three cups of coffee on a tray.

"Mrs Walsh, returning to the subject of foster care, have you considered fostering yourself?" Mrs Kimber took a sip of coffee.

"No, I've never thought about it at all. I love children, obviously, we are a very close family. But our youngest is eight now, we never imagined...."

Patrick looked concerned. "Until Arlo arrived, we thought we had left nappies and night feeds behind. Nell and I were looking forward to more time together. Three of our children are teenagers, one works with me. The younger ones are growing up. Nell had some worries about her parents for a while but that's sorted out now, we were hoping for a more carefree time".

"Yes, I do understand. I just wondered. But do give it some thought. You have every advantage here. Rosemary mentioned in her report that you don't work outside the home. This situation is somewhat back to front I admit; normally foster carers must undergo training and a great many background checks before any child is placed with them; that can take months. In a way it's strange, there are no such checks when people have children of their own. But I urge you to consider fostering. Arlo may only be two months old, but he's already had one major upheaval in his short life. Finding another placement would be a further disruption, and it could mean a succession of carers. I know you aren't concerned about the financial side of things, but foster carers receive a generous allowance these days as well as out of pocket expenses".

Nell was silent but the look she gave Patrick spoke volumes. "We would have to give that a great deal of thought" he said noncommittally.

"I suppose your other four children are in school?" asked Mrs Kimber.

"Yes, two are at the village school, one is at Lamberham but he will be moving to Kirchington next year to do his 'A' levels, said Patrick. "Our eldest daughter is in Ireland at the moment, staying with her Granny".

"Oh? During term time?" Mrs Kimber sounded surprised.

Nell attempted to explain. "She will be going to school in Ireland. There were a few problems at Lamberham school during the last year, she suffered some terrible bullying, and we were very worried about her. For a time, we considered home-schooling but in the end, we found her a place at a small convent school near to Patrick's mother's. We decided that would be better for her. It's only for a while until she takes her GCSEs or whatever the equivalent is over there".

"That must be very difficult, her being so far away. How old did you say she is?"

"She's fourteen".

"Well, I know bullying is a problem at some schools. But it's quite an extreme solution, to send her out of the country. What did Lamberham School have to say?"

"I complained about the bullying and of course they knew we'd decided to take her out of school. They don't know about Ireland yet, but I shall be writing to them. I expect they will need to know for their records".

"Mmm. Well, I hope it all works out". Just for a moment Mrs Kimber gave Nell a long, hard look. "Anyway, do think about the fostering. I'll be in touch in a couple of weeks, and I'll let you know if the police come up with anything. They may contact you first, of course". She put away her file.

Patrick held the door open for her and she moved into the hall. "Thank you for looking after Arlo. Not everyone would take care of an unknown child so well. It's a very special thing that you are doing".

She took her leave and Nell and Patrick watched her reverse her car and drive off.

"Well! What do you make of that?" Patrick looked baffled. "I don't think we're any further forward at all".

"No. But did you hear what she said about how Arlo's future might be if his parents aren't traced? One set of foster carers after another, different placements, moving him around like 'pass the parcel'. Poor little chap, he never asked for any of this. It's so unfair on him". For a moment Nell looked angry. "How could he do it? How could that man just leave him with us without a thought? We could have been anyone.

He just didn't care. If I ever meet him again, I'll...." Words failed her.

"I know. It's cruel to leave your child with a stranger and just disappear, whatever the reasons. No decent person would ever do that. We will have to have a think about, you know, what she said.... fostering".

Nell looked at him, trying not to let her mind race ahead. She had learned many things about Patrick over the years, but importantly she knew that if there was an idea, a plan, it was more likely to succeed or be taken seriously if he had decided on it himself. He would never ignore her wishes; they discussed everything important, and he would always listen to her point of view, sometimes coming round to it. But he did like to have the last word, and at times she wondered if Emer had inherited that trait. For a moment, talking to the social worker, it had occurred to her that they might take on the role of foster parents to Arlo, but if that were to happen, Patrick must suggest it. And he had done exactly that – well, he had not ruled it out.

She tried not to sound over-enthusiastic. "Yes Patrick, it's something we should consider. I meant what I said the other night, I have come to love Arlo, it's only been a few weeks, but he's become one of us, and to be honest I would find it hard to part with him now. I may have to, of course". There was a note of sadness in her tone as she put the possibility into words.

"Yes. We are all fond of the little fellow. But I meant what I said too, we were looking forward to some time to ourselves. Plus, we have five children of our own, two of them with problems. Do we really want to take on anymore? There's no let-up at work, as it is I don't have as much time for family life as I'd like".

"Perhaps, because we have all that experience with our own children it's a reason why we might be good foster parents? I don't know, Patrick. As you say, we do need to give this a great deal of thought. I suppose there's no harm in finding out more from Mrs Kimber?"

"Let's talk to your parents about it as soon as we can. Your Dad has so much common sense and he knows a thing or two. He'll help us look at it from all angles".

At that moment Jenny put her head round the door to say she was popping down to the village shops, so Patrick left for work and Nell returned to the breakfast room and sat for a while, watching Arlo in his Moses basket. He was awake now, alert, looking all around. When he saw Nell, he smiled at her in recognition. He thinks I'm his mother, thought Nell, realisation dawning. "I won't let you down, little man" she said softly. "This is your home, for as long as I have any say in the matter".

Chapter Forty-Three

One of the reasons for Neville and Lois to spend some time back in England was for Lois to attend an appointment with the neurologist at Kirchington . Mr Clifford had retired two years previously; his successor was Mr Paul Ferguson, a much younger man whose credentials were impressive. He had a more relaxed, informal manner than his predecessor and shook hands with them warmly.

"Mr and Mrs Garth, it's a pleasure to meet you both. Mrs Garth, I've spent some time reading your notes, you've been through a great deal over the years, haven't you? But I see that since your diagnosis you've only returned for one appointment with Mr Clifford?".

This was true and Neville realised with a stab of guilt that he had been guided by Evelyn on these matters. It was one more measure of control she had exercised over them; she had convinced them that she knew enough about Lois's condition to render further consultations unnecessary. Of course, it was a ploy to encourage Lois to take a more pessimistic view of her health and thus increase her dependency, whereas Mr Clifford might have observed an improvement or a lessening of her symptoms. But Neville did not want to explain all this to Mr Ferguson.

"The thing is, we've been living in Spain now for several years. We don't come back to the UK very often. And my wife has been so much better since we moved to Spain; the climate suits her and the warmth really does seem to make a difference".

"Well, it's good to hear that your symptoms are less troublesome. Mrs Garth, tell me how you are feeling day to day. What gives you the most difficulty?"

Lois went onto describe the mobility problems she still experienced, the stiffness and weakness in her joints and hands and the general fatigue but explained that the level of pain was much more manageable even during flare-ups. She felt that overall, her condition had stabilised; she rarely needed her wheelchair and certainly felt no worse than when she first attended Mr Clifford's clinic all those years ago. In many ways she felt better, but whether this was due to the medications, the warm weather in Spain or the wonderful care she received from her husband and companion she couldn't say.

"That's really good news, Mrs Garth. We could arrange for some further tests if you wish, but I appreciate you're not staying in this country for very long. As you're so much improved, that could wait. But may I examine you now, while you're here?"

Mr Ferguson asked her some more questions, watched her move around the room, asked her to demonstrate her difficulty picking up things or grasping objects. He carried out an eye examination and tested her reflexes. "I would really need more specific tests to be carried out before I could say for sure", he said thoughtfully. "But from what I can see, I agree with you, there appears to be no further deterioration. It's quite remarkable. Normally with a chronic condition these things worsen with age, but you have done well. In fact, I would go so far as to say that if you wish, you could reduce the frequency of your pain medication, or we could try you on a lower dose during periods of remission. You could self-regulate this; you are so well attuned to your symptoms that I have no concerns about your judgement on this".

Neville and Lois left his consulting rooms in a buoyant mood, both relieved that after eighteen years the illness had not progressed, in fact there was every reason for hope that even if there were no further improvements, at least the situation might not worsen. The prospect of adjusting her medication to suit her own needs was an encouraging one for Lois; she liked the thought of being trusted to make her own decisions, thus giving her more control over her own body; a body which in the early days she felt had betrayed her.

"This calls for a celebration. Let's go and have a nice lunch at the Swan's Rest. We haven't booked but I'm sure Marco will find us a table". Lois agreed enthusiastically, and not for the first time Neville thought how much he was enjoying every minute spent with Lois, the ability to make spontaneous plans like this, but most of all the pleasure of them being a couple with no one interfering or intruding in their lives. There had been moments in the past few years when he thought these days would never come again.

* * *

Brontë knew from the first moment that she stepped inside the cool, tranquil corridors of St Teresa's Convent School that her parents had made the right decision.

Sister Francis had been welcoming but asked several questions about Brontë's last school and touched on why she had left. Brontë had been expecting this; without referring to the unpleasant rumour, she answered honestly and explained that as well as the bullying, she disliked the large classes, the noise, the fast pace and endless activity, the peer pressure and the expectations to fit into a certain mould which she felt was wrong for her. To her surprise, Sister Francis seemed to understand. "You will find it quite different here, Brontë. We have classes of ten, occasionally twelve or fifteen girls, no more. The school serves a very small community here. There is a strict daily routine; morning Mass, followed by half an hour's quiet contemplation in the classroom. We find this puts the girls in the right frame of mind for learning. Then the lessons begin".

Brontë thought this sounded perfect.

"At the end of the school day the girls and Sisters all attend an assembly and evening prayers before going home. Sometimes one of the girls will lead it. Father Sweeney comes in to take a service on Fridays. Because of our low numbers we are a close family in this school. I do not tolerate any bullying or spiteful behaviour, and you will find everyone to be friendly, so I do hope you will be happy here. I have assigned one of the girls in your class, Kitty to be your mentor for the first couple of weeks, but if you have any worries at all, please come and see me or ask Sister Mary Luke, your class teacher".

Brontë nodded, feeling hugely relieved. "Thank you, Sister".

"I have read your mother's letter, and I see that you have gained good marks in most of your subjects up to now". Sister Francis continued. "I am placing you in our Second-Year class which is right for your age group although you may be above average, we'll see. You will be working towards your Leaving Certificate".

"I've written down everything I've been studying in the last six months". Brontë passed a folder to Sister Francis. "Maths and Science are my weakest subjects I'm afraid. But I do work hard, I just didn't fit in with my last school somehow".

"No matter. Try to forget about that and concentrate on your studies now, and to embrace our way of life here. I'm sure you will find your feet very quickly." She stood up and went to a door which opened into an adjoining room where the school secretary was typing. "Mrs O'Shaunessy, please will you ask Kitty to come here and take Brontë to her classroom".

One of Brontë's greatest fears, if it could be described as a fear was that her new classmates would all be stick-thin, trying to look like super-models and competing for hairstyles and makeup. When she was introduced to Kitty Devlin any worries disappeared, she was a pleasant-looking girl of about her own age, also amply built with a fair complexion and auburn hair tied back neatly in a ponytail. Kitty led her on a tour of the school; they did not enter rooms where lessons were taking place, but Brontë took in the peaceful atmosphere of the school chapel, the quiet gardens where one of the Sisters was seated, lost in thought, and a small playing field of no more than half an acre where some girls were doing some physical exercises.

"I hope you'll like it here" said Kitty shyly. Her accent was very pronounced. "The Sisters are strict, but they are fair. Sister Mary Ruth, she teaches maths, now she can be a bit stern but underneath she's very kind. Sister Catherine takes us for music, she's a lot of fun. If you do your best here, you'll be grand".

Brontë learned that makeup and hair dye were not allowed and that normally, silence had to be maintained between lessons and in the corridors. She liked the sound of this discipline; it was not overly austere but appealed to her need for peace and quiet. The uniform was modest; dark blue pleated skirt, kilt-style, knee length and no shorter; matching cardigan, white blouse, and navy socks. Flat shoes were compulsory; no high heels were permitted. Sportswear consisted of navy shorts and pale blue t-shirts. It was a simple regime; the school had to allow that many of the girls were not from wealthy families and that parents had sometimes struggled to pay for the uniform as it was.

Sister Mary Luke introduced her to her classmates at the beginning of the next lesson. The girls looked at her curiously, but all seemed friendly and excited to welcome a newcomer with a very different accent and an unusual name. One of them asked what it meant. "Would you like to explain to the class, it's a name they've never heard". Just for a moment the Sister had put Brontë on the spot but she took a deep breath and told them that her mother had chosen the name in honour of the Brontë sisters. These were writers in Victorian England whose work her mother admired. She went on to tell the class that in order to be taken seriously their books had to be published under male pennames because female writers were frowned upon in the nineteenth century.

"This is very timely" said Sister Mary Luke, who took English as well as being the class teacher. "We shall be studying Jane Eyre by Charlotte Brontë later this term".

Brontë felt encouraged by the thought that she had already read Jane Eyre several times so in one subject at least she would be ahead.

The first week passed smoothly enough and without realising it, she adapted to the school's routine and felt that at last she could enjoy her studies and not once feel mocked or persecuted. By Friday she had made another friend, Cora, and despite missing her family, Brontë had begun to settle into her new life.

Chapter Forty-Four

Since Dermot died, Bridget had become used to a solitary existence in the house that was previously occupied by her eldest son Connor, his wife Gráinne and their daughter Aisling, who was now eleven. Her life had changed from being the busy wife of a farmer, working with him day to day, helping with the dairy herd and bearing him seven children to a quiet retirement, living alone with her thoughts and memories. She saw Aisling most days when she cycled past on her way to the village school in Ballymere, but Bridget was rarely needed for babysitting, Connor and Gráinne now lived at the farm, but they seldom went out in the evenings.

After she had recovered from the shock of Nell's request for Brontë to stay with her for a few months – and more to the point having struggled to understand the reasons behind it and the trauma that her granddaughter had been through – Bridget began to look forward to having her company and thought about how she might help Brontë to recover from all the upset.

As well as Brontë's visit, her daughter Kathleen and her new fiancé were going to spend some time in Ballymere. Bridget had mixed feelings when she heard that Kathleen had applied for a divorce and that it was uncontested; this had come about due to a recent change in Irish law, and she was not entirely comfortable about it. But she had to concede that the marriage between Kathleen and Michael had not been made in heaven; it had been a mistake on both sides and for nearly twenty years Kathleen had lived with the consequences, never expecting to be free from the wrong choices she had made when she was still only a teenager. Now that her daughter had fallen in love with someone she had met in Spain, Bridget could not deny her the happiness she herself had known in her long marriage to Dermot. But even the new laws would not permit Kathleen to remarry in church as Michael was still alive; it would have to be a civil ceremony.

The wedding was to be held the following summer, and Nell had mentioned in her letter that while they were staying in Ballymere for the celebrations, they would like Ronnie and Emer to be baptised. This had the effect of distracting Bridget from any uncertainties she still held on to about the divorce; she had been hoping that Patrick's two youngest children would undergo this rite of passage into the Catholic faith but for that to take place here after the wedding was another family occasion to look forward to. So there was much for Bridget to plan for, and the fact that Nell and Patrick had trusted her to look after Brontë for a few months made her feel useful again. However, she had not reached the age of sixty-four without acquiring some wisdom, and the information Nell had shared regarding the horrifying rumours about Brontë was something she would keep to herself; the fewer people who knew about that the better.

It was purely by chance that Bridget's elder sister, Angela and her husband Fergus had recently decided to move down from Limerick and open a guest house. The property they had purchased was an empty house situated outside Ballymere, not far from the farm. Work was still being carried out to convert the building, but they hoped to have a few rooms ready in time for Christmas when many of Ireland's sons and daughters scattered around the globe returned to their families for the festive season. As soon as Bridget heard about the wedding plans she made a plea to her sister to keep several rooms free for the last fortnight in July when she hoped that Sean, Niall and their partners would visit along with Patrick, Nell and the children, and that it might be possible for some of Adam's relatives to make the journey from Australia, although this was by no means certain.

Bridget, together with Kathleen, Orla and Gráinne thought that it could never be too early to start planning for the wedding; dresses, cars, flowers, cake and photographers were all discussed in detail and decisions made as to would do what. Yet feeling slightly superstitious, and not wishing to create a hostage to fortune, Kathleen and Adam decided not to book the Registry Office just yet until that important piece of paper, her Decree Absolute was in their hands. But Kathleen had not forgotten her promised to Brontë about a bridesmaid dress and the following Saturday Adam drove them into town, where the two of them spent several hours in bridal shops so that Brontë could find a dress she liked and that she would feel happy wearing. After finding nothing suitable at the first place they tried, they stopped for a cup of tea before making their way to the second shop. Brontë was discouraged by the name above the door: 'White Lace', fearing that it would offer only very fancy or overly feminine styles. But she was pleasantly surprised; she tried on a simple sleeveless dark green shift dress in a crepe-de-chine fabric, full length and with a matching stole. It had no embellishments except a discreet white scalloped trim around the neckline and hem. When Brontë looked at her reflection in the long mirror in the fitting room she suddenly felt a surge of happiness; the dress made her look taller, slimmer, more sophisticated and grown-up. She would look forward to wearing this, and her worries about feeling out of place or letting Kathleen down simply melted away.

Kathleen was delighted when you saw Brontë step out of the cubicle. "You look fabulous! That colour is perfect on you, it has a slight sheen but it's not too glossy. We will look for the right shoes to go with the dress, and you needn't wear a head-dress if you'd prefer not to. I think we made a grand choice, don't you?" She could go shopping for Emer's dress in Kirchington when she next visited Drover's Cross and would come back into town with Gráinne for Aisling's dress another day now that she had decided on a colour palette. Knowing Brontë to be extremely self-conscious it was important to spend one-to-one time with her in order to find a dress that was exactly right. After leaving the shop they met up with Adam for a much-needed cup of coffee, both satisfied that the afternoon had gone well.

* * *

It had been nine years since Brontë came to Ballymere with her parents and she could barely remember that visit, which was at the time of her grandfather Dermot's funeral. She had been five years old; her brother Ronnie was a small baby, her sister Emer not yet born. But Nell had so often described to her the wild, breathtaking scenery of West Cork, the rugged coastline and the remote, isolated countryside that somehow it felt familiar to her, and without realising why, she yearned to experience these quiet places, the solitary landscapes and the mystical atmosphere that had made such an impression on her mother. When they had their weekly telephone calls, Brontë told Nell how much she had come to love West Cork already and that she now understood her mother's deep affinity with this place.

At first, Bridget had worried that Brontë might be bored, but as the weeks went by, she became more concerned that her granddaughter did not seek out company; she seemed to like being on her own and enjoyed the peacefulness of her surroundings. School had so far presented no problems; she had adapted to the new routine and quiet discipline at St Teresa's; so reassuringly different from Lamberham and was already well ahead in most subjects.

Sometimes Brontë would take herself off for a walk after coming home from school. "Don't worry Granny, I need the exercise, and I want to lose a bit more weight before the wedding". Brontë tried to explain to her grandmother that she liked to explore the area further down the boreen where the track met the road, she loved the fact that she was unlikely to meet anyone else on her walk and this gave her a sense of freedom just to be herself, something she felt able to do here where no one would judge her or expect too much. Bridget felt sure that Brontë would be perfectly safe, but was sure to put some boundaries in place so that she did not get lost or stay out too long, it was nearly October and nights were drawing in.

Brontë had made some firm friends at St Teresa's; Cora Lynch and Kitty Devlin who had shown her round on the first day. The girls here are nicer, thought Brontë. They're not so competitive or streetwise as back home; it may be because it's a Catholic school or perhaps the quiet time in the morning calms everyone down. She no longer dreaded getting up for school as she had done back in Drover's Cross, where she knew she would face taunts and unkind comments on the bus. Instead, she was greeted by a wave and a smile from her new chums and a warm welcome from the Sisters as she walked into the school grounds.

As she settled into her new life in West Cork, she felt that although she missed her family, especially her mother, she could at last put the past behind her and start to become the person she wanted to be.

Chapter Forty-Five

"It's a very worthwhile thing to do, but not everyone is cut out for it". Nell and Patrick had asked for her parents' opinion on the prospect of fostering, and the four of them were sitting in the drawing room after the youngest children were in bed, and Arthur and Henry were watching television in the breakfast room. It was now early October; Arlo had begun to sleep through the night and at that point Nell had started to establish a bedtime routine for him, whereby he would settle to sleep in their bedroom in his Moses basket, away from the general hum of activity downstairs.

Neville continued. "But it's something that the whole family would need to agree on, feel part of. Taking on someone else's child is a huge responsibility. In a way it's more daunting than having a child of your own, because usually you have an active choice whether to foster. But I do understand that this situation was thrust upon you, you didn't choose it. That has made it far more complicated. You never had the chance to discuss it first, to see if it was the right thing for you all. You're having to make all these decisions after the event. By which time Arlo has become part of your family, which has begun to cloud your judgement already, I can see that". He looked at his daughter affectionately, with a knowing smile. "My eyes do not deceive me".

Lois was sitting by the window, looking out at the half-light. Summer is over, she thought, it's growing dark earlier. I want to stay in England longer, I have so much to make up for, so much I need to say to my daughter, but could I cope with a winter here? She had been listening carefully to her husband's words, then turned to face the others.

"I suppose one thing to consider is the reason you might want to foster Arlo? Ask yourself – yourselves – why. Nell, could it be to compensate for Brontë leaving? That was such a hard decision for you to make, and I know how you agonised about letting her go, because you felt it was the right way of helping her. But there's no doubt, she has left a big gap in the family".

Patrick nodded his agreement. "I think you may have a point there, Lois". He could see the difference in his mother-in-law; it was not so long ago that she would have been uncomfortable taking part in any such conversation and would have felt awkward and self-conscious. But here she was, making a very valid contribution to an important matter. The transformation was undeniable.

Nell had so far said very little but thought that everyone had failed to recognise one important aspect. "Daddy, you're right about Arlo now being one of us – that seemed to happen very quickly. The children have accepted him. And yes, if I'm honest, I have come to love him. But all I can think about is that he had no part in this situation. He did not choose to be abandoned by someone who should have loved him yet didn't care what happened to him. He is the one who will be affected for the rest of his life because of decisions other people make now, however well meaning. I just feel that he deserves better than that. Mum, I know what you're thinking about Brontë, but truly that is not the reason I'm thinking of us fostering Arlo, I would have felt that way even if she were still here".

"I can see how strongly Nell is feeling about this," said Patrick. "I don't feel quite the same, to be truthful, but I do understand why she cares what happens to him and I know she loves him, after all she's looked after him more than anyone. If you are all happy to go ahead with fostering, I will do my part to make it work. But there are a few hoops to jump through before it's official, and...." He looked at Nell lovingly. "I just don't want you to be hurt, Nelly. If by some miracle that fellow comes back and claims Arlo, you would have to hand him over. Or if for some reason we were not approved for fostering. It's not a done deal yet".

Neville stood up and walked around the room. The light was fading fast; they had all been so intent on the conversation that they had not noticed.

"From what you told me, the social worker seemed keen on the idea" he remarked. "I seem to recall that she said you have every advantage here. Which of course you do. Any child being fostered into such a loving family with a comfortable home in beautiful surroundings and the prospect of a good education would be very fortunate indeed. There can be no harm in finding out more. But before you do, I would suggest talking to the children and of course involve Brontë. They must all be on board with the idea and you would need to listen to any objections they might have".

Patrick and Nell looked at each other. "You're right Neville, it's not going to work if any of them are against it." said Patrick. "Let's talk to them tomorrow".

"From what I've seen of her, Emer will have plenty to say". Neville was smiling. "But I think she will probably agree in the end".

"Knowing Emer she will use it as a bargaining chip for something else she wants" said Patrick wryly. They all laughed, as Nell went to switch on the lamps and put a match to the fire. "While we're on the subject, we'd better warn your parents about Jacob".

Neville and Lois looked up in alarm. "Not another child? Please!" said Lois in disbelief.

"It's ok, Mum, Jacob is a donkey. We're rehoming him; it's through a charity. He's arriving in a couple of weeks. He's for Emer. I had the idea when we were looking at your photos. She's been asking for a pony; well, that's out of the question but we thought that a having responsibility for an animal might calm her down a little and encourage her to think a bit less about herself. We've yet to see if it will work, of course".

"And guess who will be doing the looking after if she loses interest?" Patrick looked resigned, and the others all laughed again. "Don't be giving the game away now". He went on to tell Neville and Lois of the plan. "It's going to be a surprise;

she's going to a birthday party that weekend and hopefully Jacob will be here before she comes home".

"Brontë said Emer will love to boss him about, but Patrick thinks he may turn out to be as stubborn as she is", said Nell. "Let's see who wins".

* * *

The following evening straight after dinner Nell rounded up the children and they sat in the breakfast room. Neville and Lois were in the drawing room; Patrick had suggested that they joined in the discussion, but Neville said no, this was a matter for the immediate family and that he and Lois had already given their opinions; it was now for the children to give theirs.

Nell explained to Ronnie and Emer what was meant by fostering, and that if they decided to go ahead it would be something that affected them all. The four children were all only too aware that Arlo had been left in their care; Ronnie, mature beyond his years seemed to understand the dilemma that faced the family, but Emer posed many questions, all prefaced with 'why', about how the situation had come about, which of course Patrick and Nell were unable to answer.

"Fostering means that Arlo would become one of our family, for a time, anyway. We don't know for how long, it could be weeks, months or even years. The main difference is that it would be official, the council would give permission and would check in with us regularly to see how Arlo is getting on". Nell thought it unnecessary to explain about the fostering allowance.

"It will be like us becoming temporary parents to Arlo," said Patrick. "It will be as if you have a new baby brother, the only difference is that at any time we might have to hand him back, supposing his real parents are traced".

Henry spoke next. "Isn't that what you and Mum are doing already? We can just carry on as we are, can't we, even if it is under the council. We should foster him. It won't be any different to how you are looking after him now".

"That's right," said Patrick. "The only change will be that the council, Children's Services will be in charge of the arrangement and will want to be sure that Arlo is well and happy and that he has everything he needs. Which of course, he will have, we will see to that".

"What about Brontë?" said Arthur. "Surely we need to know what she thinks?".

"I shall be explaining it to her when we next talk on the phone. Nothing will be decided unless all of you agree. And even then, it's up to the council whether to approve us as a foster family". Nell wanted to make sure that they understood every aspect of the plan.

"I feel sorry for Arlo" said Arthur thoughtfully. "He has no one to speak up for him except us. I think we should go ahead with the fostering".

Nell felt a surge of emotion at her son's words. He feels the same as I do, she thought. How grown up he is, how mature. Her eyes misted over for a moment.

"I like Arlo" said Ronnie simply. "And I think he likes us. He is happy here, isn't he Mum? Let's be his foster family".

Emer had been unusually quiet after her first outburst of questions. "Yes, we can be his brothers and sisters". Then, as always preoccupied with names, asked: "Mummy, will he be Arlo Walsh?".

"That's a very good question, Emer, and another one which I can't answer".

Chapter Forty-Six

Kathleen had decided to remain in Ballymere until her final divorce papers were received, this being the address she had given when applying. But having stayed for a fortnight Adam reluctantly decided to go back to Spain ahead of Kathleen, feeling unable to leave the restaurant any longer. Also, to everyone's surprise, Neville and Lois had announced that they would be extending their stay in England, so Adam had agreed to keep an eye on the apartment for them.

"Rafael is more than capable, and I'm not worried about leaving him in charge" he said to Kathleen on the evening before his departure. "But he really needs a holiday as well, and Hayley can't be expected to manage on her own". Hayley was an English girl who had come to Spain on holiday two years previously but had decided to stay and had accepted the offer of a job at Martina's.

"I shall miss you" said Kathleen sadly. "I don't suppose I shall be back in Spain for a few weeks yet".

"It's a good opportunity for you to spend some time with your Mam". Adam could see how much Bridget loved having her daughter to stay. "The time will soon pass. And you can get well ahead with the wedding planning while you're here. But I'll be coming back before the wedding, next time I'll stay for longer. And there are some places I want to look up".

Adam had done some research into his family tree and discovered that his paternal great grandfather came from Ireland and emigrated to Australia in the nineteenth century. He had pieced together information from a passenger list, official records and his parents' knowledge; some of the latter he was unable to validate but he was told that his great grandfather, who came from County Galway met a girl during the sea voyage and that they married soon after their arrival at Sydney. Kathleen was fascinated by the story, and the fact that the man she had fallen in love with and become engaged to had Irish ancestors seemed to cement their relationship. She was as excited as Adam at the prospect of finding out more. "Let's take a trip up the west coast next time and look for Lankerris" she said, knowing that it was something so important to Adam. "Yes, and while we're there I shall look up the parish records" he said. "Who knows what else we might find? I may have distant relatives living in the area".

Connor drove Adam and Kathleen to Cork airport on a Friday morning. It was a drizzly early autumn day, the leaves were just beginning to turn, but without any sunshine everywhere looked drab and dull. After a sad farewell, Adam waved goodbye as he made his way through the departure gate, and Connor and Kathleen returned to the car park.

"He's a grand chap you've got there," said Connor. "And you both look so happy together. I'm glad things worked out for you, Sis, look how everything has changed for you since you left Ballymere".

"Yes, I'm very lucky Connor. Sometimes I wonder where I would be now, if I hadn't made that move when I did".

* * *

The following morning, being Saturday, Bridget went off into Ballymere to do some grocery shopping, leaving Kathleen and Brontë to linger over their breakfast.

"How is school going?" asked Kathleen cautiously. "I know St Teresa's is a good school, Orla went there, she got on well. I went to the comprehensive school; I wasn't so clever". She laughed and poured them both another cup of tea.

"Actually, I like it very much. I'm getting on ok in most subjects and I've made some friends. I'm glad Mum and Dad decided to send me there".

"So a big improvement on your last one then?" Kathleen knew all about the unhappy time Brontë had been through, and Nell had hinted that Brontë might need to talk about it in confidence at some point, just to get it out of her system.

"It's so different, Auntie Kathleen. The girls and the Sisters are really kind. When I think about Lamberham...." She paused and looked tearful for a moment. "You know all about the bullying, don't you, and that horrible rumour that people spread about me".

Kathleen's heart went out to Brontë. "I do know, and it was a wicked thing that happened altogether. I'm not surprised that your Mam and Dad took you away".

There was silence for a few moments; Kathleen wanted Brontë to speak up if she needed to, but did not want to dig too deeply for fear of stirring up feelings that were perhaps beginning to fade.

"Arthur was teased at school because of his red hair. And Henry was called HP Sauce, because of his name I suppose, HP Walsh. They didn't seem to care, and I wouldn't really have minded that, but I was always bullied about being fat. That hurt so much, it was every day with no let-up. Ronnie, well he's an angel, everyone loves him. And Mum and Dad have always said that Emer would never be bullied in a million years, she's too bossy".

"I was bullied at school too," said Kathleen. "In my case it was because they all thought I was stupid, everyone mocked me. I came bottom in everything, never did well in any subject".

Brontë looked at her aunt in surprise. "I can't believe it! You're... you've done so well, you've had some nice jobs, you are happy with Adam".

"It wasn't always like that Brontë. Before I came to England, I was a mess. Michael bullied me as well, he tried to control me, but he never loved me, I know that now. He would taunt me about how I looked, he'd say I was useless, that I'd never come to anything. He kept me short of money, he undermined everything I tried to do, so much so that I was close to giving up. I drank more than I should, I was a horrible person. Even my own parents didn't know what to do with me".

Kathleen let her words sink in.

"But do you know how it all changed? Your Mam, that's how. Your Mam had faith in me when nobody else did. She helped me out and found me that first job in England when I was at the lowest point in my life. I still don't know why she did what she did, it must have been just because she's a good person who wanted to do something to make a difference. I'll never be able to repay her for her kindness. But let me tell you, I wasn't very nice to her when we first met, in fact I was a.... well, I said some wicked things to her. I was jealous, I suppose, she seemed to have so much. I'll never forgive myself for that".

Brontë listened, wide-eyed at Kathleen's revelations. "I had no idea you were unhappy too" she said, realising that her aunt had spoken with honesty and a great deal of regret about her past. "I didn't realise that Mum sorted out a job for you".

"She did so much more than that. And Barbara and Jonathan too. They gave me self-respect, confidence that I was worth something. But then as if that wasn't enough, your Nanny Lois asked me to go to Spain with them, to help them out and do a little bit of housekeeping. I'd never travelled you see, except to England, never been to a holiday destination, somewhere hot. It was like a dream come true, and then I met Adam. He's the love of my life".

"It all sounds like a fairy tale" said Brontë, still taking in everything Kathleen had told her.

"In a way, it is. So when your Mam and Dad asked me to be your godmother, I thought, here's my chance to repay their kindness. You know, I do understand what you've been coping with because I went through a lot myself in the early days. Your Mam was very wise; she knew that, and it was why she asked me".

"I guess there's hope for me yet" said Brontë with a half-smile.

"Brontë you're not even fifteen. You have so much ahead of you. You're clever, you're kind like your Mam, you have a family who love you to bits. And..." Kathleen paused. "When

I saw you in that bridesmaid dress the other week, you looked beautiful. I'm not just saying that because you're my niece and I love you. It's true, you looked stunning. You have your Mam's lovely hair and skin, and you know, you've slimmed down even since you've been here. I know you've been careful about what you eat, and you've been taking exercise, but it's more than that. I think you feel at home here, you've relaxed, and a lot of the worry has gone out of you. It's made all the difference; I can see it and so can your Granny".

As she went off for her morning walk along the boreen, Brontë gave a great deal of thought to what Kathleen had told her. She said I looked beautiful, she thought. No one has ever said that to me except Mum, and she's biased. Perhaps things are beginning to change for me. As she crossed over at the bridge and took the coast road, she felt that despite the rough terrain, each step had become a little lighter.

Chapter Forty-Seven

October 1997

There had been something puzzling Helen Kimber ever since she had visited the Walshes. In many ways they were one of the closest, most stable and loving families she had come across during all her twenty-five years in social work. Added to that there was a happy and secure home environment, enough money for a pleasant and fulfilling lifestyle, excellent role-models and support and encouragement from intelligent parents. She had worked with many families where all those ingredients were absent; where every negative force, failure and disadvantage meant poor parenting and dismal life chances for the children. So it was because of this one remaining nagging doubt that she dialled the number for Lamberham School and asked to be put through to the head of Year Ten.

"Mr Franklin, I'm Helen Kimber, Kirchington Children's Services. I believe you know the Walsh family; I'm working with them in the matter of a baby that was left with them, it's a bit of a mystery and on the face of it it's quite an unlikely story, but they have expressed an interest in fostering, which is why I'm looking into the family background. In particular I'm concerned about the eldest daughter, Brontë. I think she was in your year?".

Terry Franklin paused for a moment and was cautious in his reply. "Yes, I knew Brontë. She left us recently. As a matter of fact, I taught both of her elder brothers. They're a lovely family".

"Did you have any worries about Brontë as to why she left? Have her parents been in touch about her education?"

"Her mother wrote to me last week, asking me to remove Brontë from the school roll. She said she was making other arrangements for her schooling. There had been problems for

Brontë while she was here, especially during the last year. She was experiencing some bullying from the girls in her class, but we weren't aware of the extent of it in time to tackle the situation, and unfortunately by the time Mrs Walsh came to see me, things had deteriorated and Brontë never returned to school from that day".

"What form did the bullying take? What was the cause? Can you be more specific, Mr Franklin? Because you see, I may be jumping to conclusions here but I'm wondering if there is a connection between this baby and the reason Brontë was taken out of school".

"Mrs Kimber, I did have a most difficult discussion with Brontë's mother on this very subject. There was an extremely worrying rumour going around the school that Brontë had given birth to a baby during the summer holidays. I had to confront Mrs Walsh about it as you will understand, for reasons of safeguarding. She explained to me the circumstances about this baby arriving in their household, and although at the time it seemed far-fetched, I did believe her, and that it was nothing to do with Brontë. She is an overweight child, and sadly overweight children are often bullied. But I think things had gone a good deal further than routine teasing; Mrs Walsh told me how much damage the unkind treatment had done to Brontë and that she would need a fresh start to get over it. In the light of this, we have reviewed our school policy on bullying, and we have been quick to dispel any further untruths or gossip on this matter".

"Mmm. So you think there was no foundation whatsoever for this rumour, that it was a rather unpleasant piece of spite from some of her classmates?"

"I do think that, and between you and I, I'm deeply ashamed about the way she was treated by some of the girls. Unfortunately, Brontë was an easy target. It's a great pity because she showed great promise in several subjects; she was a good student, worked hard and was well above average".

"So you weren't aware that Brontë is now going to school in the Republic of Ireland?"

"Her father is Irish; they probably have family out there. But all I knew was that her parents had decided to send her to a different school, or possibly to home-school her. Mrs Walsh did not strike me as someone who would neglect her daughter's education".

"Thank you, Mr Franklin. I agree with you there, and it's good that Brontë is still in school, that's one thing I'm less concerned about. But it's the reason why they took such a drastic step that seems unusual. Next time I meet the family I may press them a little more on this".

* * *

To everyone's surprise, Neville announced that he and Lois would not be returning to Spain just yet. Adam had reassured them that he would make regular visits to the apartment to check that everything was in order, and that in the unlikely event of any work needing to be carried out, he would arrange for it to be done and would keep them informed.

Nell was concerned. "It's lovely that you're going to stay a bit longer, Mummy. But we're nearly halfway through October, winter is round the corner. Will you be able to cope with the cold?"

"I feel so much better, Nell. I really think I can. At least I should like to see how things go; we can always return to Spain at short notice if it turns out that I can't manage. But we're going to move back to the Swan's Rest. They have our usual ground floor rooms available, and I think they're glad of a long-term booking; they're very quiet during the winter months".

"Well it will be nice to all be together at Christmas. I'm pleased you feel so much better Mummy". Nell could well understand that her parents might be looking forward to some peace and quiet away from Moongarth; in particular her mother had made huge strides over the past few years, both in terms of her illness and in re-connecting with the family, but Lois was now 70 – not by any means old, but at a time in her life when she needed to slow down and to be mindful of her health.

"We won't be far away; we can visit every week. And you and Patrick can come and have a meal with us at the hotel – let the boys try their hand at cooking for the others sometimes".

Nell laughed as she thought of what culinary disasters might lie ahead if that ever came to pass, but she liked the idea of dining with her parents at the hotel – she rarely had a break from cooking, and they seldom ate out. This was not because of any lack of money, more to do with time always being in short supply. Never enough hours in the day, she said to herself, but her mind turned to Bridget who had brought up seven children, had run an overcrowded home with very few modern conveniences and still had time to help her husband on the farm in her younger days. The thought of Ireland reminded her of Brontë. How she missed her. She knew her daughter was happy – their weekly phone calls confirmed that, and she seemed to have settled well at St Teresa's. Sometimes you must make sacrifices for the greater good, she realised. It had been a sacrifice to part with Brontë, to make the decision to allow her to go to Ireland where she could have a complete break from all the unhappiness. But it had been the right one, she was sure of that. And Brontë would be coming home at Christmas, the time would soon pass.

* * *

The renovations at Hackett's Guest House near Ballymere were nearly finished and Angela turned her thoughts to hiring some temporary staff to cover the Christmas bookings. After a slow start, the diary was looking promising, and there were still several weeks to go before the grand opening. Not all the accommodation was complete, but the builders were putting the finishing touches to the main dining room and the modern spacious kitchen, and six en-suite rooms were now ready for occupation.

The idea of a guest house was something Angela had been thinking about for some time, and she had also felt a compulsion to return to Ballymere which was her childhood home. It had taken almost a lifetime for Angela to contemplate that move; Ballymere was after all the place where in her youth she had undergone a heartbreak from which she thought she would never recover. Living in Limerick for over forty years had at least placed her at a distance from the anguish and the cruel ordeal that she had experienced, but she knew that in some ways her wounds could never heal; no matter what she did or where she went, the torment would follow her until the end of her days. So with that in mind, knowing that in Ballymere she would be near family and that starting a new business would give her the distraction and challenge she needed in her later years, she and her husband Fergus moved down to West Cork. Fergus had recently retired and had a sum of money to invest, and together with their savings and the proceeds of their house in Limerick they were able to purchase the freehold of Castleway House in Ballymere and finance the extensive work needed. Despite being a year older than her sister Bridget, Angela was still in good physical health, strong and active, with a vigorous energy that was the envy of women half her age.

During the third week in October, Angela and Fergus took up residence in the guest house which had adjoining accommodation for the owners. Her first task was to place an advertisement in the local paper for two hotel cleaners, a chef, a receptionist, a bartender and some waiting staff; preferably two but she could manage with one at a pinch. She and Fergus would fill in any other roles; he would cover as relief bartender and act as handyman.

Visiting Bridget on the first weekend after their arrival, she was introduced to Brontë.

She had known of her great-niece of course; Bridget had kept her sister fully up to date regarding family matters during the intervening years although Angela's visits to Ballymere were very rare. But Bridget had kept her counsel and had not told anyone else the details of the trauma Brontë had gone through; and she was certainly not about to risk causing Angela any upset which the story might provoke.

Brontë thought that Aunt Angela's was the saddest face she had ever seen, and she resolved to ask her grandmother about it when there was an opportunity. But there was a certain intensity about her that spoke of someone who was determined to hide that sadness and find things to be grateful for. She smiled at Brontë, asked after her family and how she was liking West Cork.

"I love it here, Aunt Angela. I feel as if I've lived here for months. Everyone is so kind, I'm doing ok at St Teresa's, and I've made some new friends".

At the mention of St Teresa's, a shadow fell across Angela's face, then disappeared and the smile returned.

"That's good to know. It's not everyone who settles in so quickly here, there's nothing much for young people to do. But I'm hoping that when the guest house opens, it will provide some jobs for people and bring in a few tourists. If you'd like to earn some pocket money at weekends, there'll be plenty to do, making beds, cleaning and putting up decorations in December. What do you say to that?".

Brontë had never given money a thought. Her father sent Bridget a cheque every month; this was partly to cover her keep and for some spending money for his daughter. But she had saved it up, mainly because in Ballymere there was little to spend money on. Nevertheless, the thought of earning some of her own was a welcome one; it made her feel more grown-up, and it would be something to do at weekends. She couldn't spend all her time on homework and reading.

"Will that be all right Granny?" she asked Bridget.

"It will be grand, as long as you don't get behind with your studies. But don't forget to tell your Mam when she rings you next week".

"Well, it looks like I have my first member of staff," laughed Angela. "And maybe Aisling too, when she's a bit older. It's a family business already".

Chapter Forty-Eight

October 1997

The next fortnight was a busy time for the Walshes. Firstly, Patrick had to work out how to build a stable in the meadow for Jacob in advance of his arrival. That was not so easy; he had purchased a large second hand shed which they could adapt for a shelter but how to assemble it without arousing Emer's attention was going to be difficult. In addition, darkness came early at the end of October; Arthur, who would normally have helped his father was having driving lessons most evenings. In the end Nell sought help from the mother of Emer's friend Kirsty, who agreed to have Emer to play with her daughter on the following Saturday while the stable was being built.

"Thanks so much, Joanne" said Nell gratefully. "We'll make a date for Kirsty to come to us to see the donkey as soon as things have settled down. And don't put up with any nonsense from Emer!"

In the end, Patrick and Arthur built the stable just out of sight of the house. The field was slightly L-shaped, and the stable was tucked away, but near to the end of the track beside the house. It was impossible for Emer to see it from her bedroom window.

Just as they breathed a sigh of relief that all had been accomplished in the end without too many problems, The Willows Donkey Sanctuary telephoned with a suggestion. Jacob had been used to being with other donkeys during his time at the rescue centre and as with most herd animals, he liked company. Would Mr and Mrs Walsh consider re-homing two?

The Sanctuary needed a quick decision. Patrick thought two would not be much more work than one, and maybe the donkeys would be happier as a pair. Nell agreed as long as they were both boys. "We can't be doing with baby donkeys" she said. "We have enough to cope with".

* * *

On the next Wednesday evening WPC Tina Drummond telephoned. Nell answered, her heart in her mouth. She realised that whereas as few weeks ago she would hope every day for news of Arlo's parents, she now found herself praying that there were no developments; she had come to love this baby as her own and would find it so hard to part with him now.

"Have you found out anything?" Nell asked, nervously.

"Well, Forensics did manage to extract a DNA sample from some hairs on the rucksack, probably from Denny Reid, but unfortunately, they were not able to find a match. And the same with the swab from Arlo, there was no match on the database. We're keeping our enquiries open, but we have so little to go on. How is the baby doing?"

"He's fine, growing fast. We're still looking after him of course".

"We will keep in touch, Mrs Walsh. You never know, sometimes there's a breakthrough. But the likelihood is that Denny Reid has left the country".

"What about CCTV at the airport? Isn't that worth checking?"

"It might be if we knew which airport, destination, flight number, date and so on. But it would be a stab in the dark without any of those details. The same applies if he took a cross-channel ferry. Denny Reid may be a false name. Come to that, we don't even know if Arlo was born in this country".

"I see. So you're not thinking of doing a press conference?"

"Unlikely. Now if Arlo had been reported missing that would be one of the first actions we'd take. But this way round, well it's difficult, it could result in all sorts of false claims to the baby, or at the very least it would mean lots of time wasters would come forward, some well-meaning but with nothing of any substance. It's been decided to keep the case open to see if we receive any reports of a missing child, and then we can start to piece the jigsaw together".

"Ok, I understand. What happens now?"

"Well, as I said, we'll keep our enquiries going and let you know if anything comes up. Have you seen Children's Services again?"

"Yes, Mrs Kimber has taken over now. She's asked us to consider fostering. We're still thinking about it, but I think we'll probably go ahead if we're approved. Our children think we should as well".

"That's good of you. Not every family would agree to take that on. I hope it all goes well. Goodbye Mrs Walsh".

Nell put down the phone. That's it, then, she thought. We're more or less on our own now. If Patrick agrees, I think we should tell Mrs Kimber that we would like to foster Arlo and make it official. I'll talk to him later. But first I need to telephone Brontë.

Nell usually phoned her daughter on Friday evenings, so it was a surprise when Bridget's phone rang at 8 o'clock on the Wednesday, just as Brontë was finishing her homework.

"Is everything ok Mummy?"

Did Nell imagine it or had Brontë picked up just the slightest Irish accent?

"We're all fine," said Nell. "Or grand, as they say out there. I'm just ringing to talk to you about Arlo. The police haven't come up with anything and they're no nearer to tracing his parents. So, the social worker has suggested we could foster Arlo. We haven't finally made up our mind but I'm ringing to ask what you think about it". She went on to explain what fostering would involve, that it was a long-term commitment that would affect the whole family and that once they had been approved, there was no going back because Arlo needed love and stability from people who cared about him.

"What do the others think, Mummy?"

"I have spoken to them, they're all in agreement. They've come to love Arlo; well we all do. But I need to know your thoughts on the matter. You see, we all need to be in favour of the idea. It won't work otherwise".

Brontë was quiet for a moment.

"I think it's a good idea, Mummy. It would be wonderful for Arlo to have a family like ours. He needs us, doesn't he? I've only got one question". She lowered her voice. "I'd just want to be sure that Arlo living with the family wouldn't stir up those rumours about me again. I don't think I could bear that. You see, I've just got settled here and I'm really happy. I hardly ever think about the bullying now; I've left those days behind me. Please don't let that start up again". The tremor in Brontë's voice was unmistakable.

"Brontë, you have my word. I would never, ever subject you to that again. I'm glad you're happy and you're gradually getting over it. But if you agree in principle, we'll go through the application process with Mrs Kimber and see if they give us the go-ahead. There's still a chance it may come to nothing".

Brontë went on to talk about school, her friends and that Aunt Angela had offered her a weekend job at the guest house. For a moment Nell felt a pang; it seemed that Brontë had settled in so completely that she was not really missing her family or her home as much as she had expected her to. In a way, the idea of giving Brontë a fresh start in Ireland was working too well, if anything. But she understood how her daughter had fallen in love with the area, the way of life and something else – that she felt somehow protected, by seventy miles or so of the Irish Sea, from everything that had hurt and humiliated her back in England.

Chapter Forty-Nine

Neville and Lois came to Moongarth on the afternoon of the donkeys' arrival. Lois had enjoyed her visit to the sanctuary in Spain and after recovering from the shock of hearing that Nell and Patrick had agreed to not one but two further additions to the family, they were excited to see Emer's reaction.

Nell was reassured to see her mother in good spirits and looking well, despite the weather having turned colder towards the end of October. The suite of rooms at the Swan's Rest were comfortable and she knew her parents were happy there, within easy reach of the family but enjoying the quiet atmosphere which the hotel offered during low season.

Patrick and Arthur had been busy all morning fetching supplies of haylage, straw and vitamin pellets, enough for the winter months. They had even thought of grooming brushes and a currycomb. Together they fitted an extended hosepipe to the stable for a water supply and filled a trough, then set up an electric fence across a third of the field. "This is to prevent them from over-grazing" Patrick explained to Nell. "Some animals don't know when they've had enough, they'll just keep eating and end up overweight. We can move the fence around so that each part of the field has a chance for the grass to re-grow".

The donkeys arrived at three o'clock in a horse box towed by the manager of the sanctuary. They trotted happily down the ramp and into the field as if they knew they were coming to a good home. All the family stood behind the fence at the edge of the field to watch the spectacle; all except for Emer who was still at her friend's house. Jacob was deep brown with a white muzzle, and Jay was a paler colour with a white underside. They inspected the stable then apparently disliking an audience, or perhaps having discovered their food supply, did not come out again for a while.

"I'm Martin Warren, good to meet you". He shook hands with Patrick and looked around him at the meadow, the hastily built stable and the impressive house and garden in the background. "It's a nice set-up you have here, ideal for them. I normally come out to check things over before bringing the animals, but I'm rushed off my feet at the centre at the moment and I could tell from your phone call that everything sounded about right. I'm sure they will settle in quickly. There are just a couple of forms for you to sign. You said the donkeys are for your daughter?"

"Yes, well I expect all the family will be involved. But mainly for our daughter. We thought she needed to learn how to look after animals and we'd decided against a pony for her. She doesn't know yet, it's to be a surprise. She'll be back later".

"You do realise they've never been ridden? Well not since they've been in our care, anyway, and they're probably a bit old to start, but if you think that's something your daughter wants to do, contact us first. You will need to have them shod if they're to be taken out on a hard road surface, even if you're just leading them. They've both been seen by the vet and given the all clear, they've had some vitamin shots recently. But they're old boys now, they need a quiet retirement".

"Don't we all" said Patrick, and they both laughed.

At four thirty Joanne brought Emer home from the birthday party and Nell went out to the car to thank her. "Do bring Kirsty in if you'd like to" she said, still trying not to spoil the surprise.

"There's a present for you in the field" said Patrick as Emer and Kirsty walked through the door. "Two presents, in fact". The rest of the family all followed the girls outside. Nell held her breath. What if it all went horribly wrong, and Emer was disappointed that the surprise was not a pony but two donkeys?

Dusk was beginning to fall but there was still enough light to watch the girls disappearing for a moment round the far side of the field towards the stable. Then there were shouts and squeals of excitement. Nell and Patrick exchanged glances. "So far, so good", said Patrick. Soon afterwards, Emer came running back, tears streaming down her face, closely followed by Kirsty. Oh no, thought Nell. Please don't let this have been a mistake.

"Daddy, thank you. And Mummy, thank you, are these really my donkeys?"

"Yes, Jacob and Jay. They are for you; this is their home now. You are to take care of them, feed them, brush their coats, fill up the water trough. You will also need to clean out the stables regularly and put fresh straw down. Do you think you can manage that?"

"Yes Daddy. I'm so excited! You see, Chloe and Olivia both have ponies, Ava's father keeps horses but no one else has donkeys! I shall be the only one who has! All my friends will be so jealous. I promise to look after them really well". Always highly strung, Emer became even more emotional, her voice shrill and high-pitched with enthusiasm, and after kissing both her parents raced off again across the field to the stable with Kirsty in pursuit.

"Well! I feel quite exhausted after that" said Lois, laughing.

"I'm sure we all do. And relieved," said Patrick. "Trust Emer to turn this into an opportunity for a bit of one-upmanship. I think we all need a cup of tea now".

* * *

While all this was happening in Drover's Cross, four hundred and fifty miles away in Ballymere Kathleen was feeling elated after receiving some long-awaited news.

She arrived in Bridget's kitchen carrying two bottles of champagne. Her mother looked up in alarm. "Would you believe it; I had to go to O'Malley's for this. First time I've set foot in there since I don't know how long, I don't think anyone recognised me. And I bet it's the first champagne they've sold for a while; they had to dust off the bottles". She noticed her mother's expression then laughed. "Don't worry Mam, I'm not about to disappear down the slippery slope. You know I hardly ever drink these days. But tonight, we're celebrating. My divorce papers came through this morning. I'm now a free woman".

Bridget could not help but be pleased for her daughter. Kathleen had waited a long time for this moment, and she deserved every bit of happiness that marrying Adam would bring her. In an ideal world it would have been different, she thought, Kathleen and Michael would have made a success of their marriage, had children and stayed together through thick and thin. But the world was changing; Ireland was changing. Women had more choices now; they did not have to tolerate husbands who ill-treated them or even stay in relationships where love had long since departed. But it's taken generations to get where we are now, she reflected. Hopefully it will all be for the best.

"Let's ask Aunt Angela if we can have a little party tonight at the guest house Mam, Connor and Gráinne can come over with Aisling, Aidan and maybe Orla and Finn can make it if Orla's off duty. It's just a shame Adam's not here to join in. But I did phone him to tell him the good news". At that moment Brontë appeared, looking in surprise at the bottles on the table. "You can have a little taste of champagne tonight as well" said Kathleen, smiling at her. "And we'll be drinking a toast to your Mam for sure. I wouldn't be where I am now without her, and that's a fact".

* * *

It was Tuesday evening and half term week. The clocks were due to go back one hour at the weekend but even now the light was fading by four thirty in the afternoon; Patrick and Arthur went to work in the dark and returned home in the dark. A meeting had been arranged with Helen Kimber after dinner, and she was bringing a colleague with her whom she referred to as a fostering lead. This time she wanted to meet the children as well.

"This is Charlie Weston, he's in charge of fostering at Kirchington Council" said Helen, introducing a tall young man with a closely trimmed beard and short fair hair. He shook hands with everyone, and they all said their names.

"I have two donkeys" said Emer, to no one in particular. "Sshh" said Nell. "We're here to talk about Arlo".

"How is Arlo?" asked Charlie. "I've heard all about him, of course, it's extraordinary that he was left with you like that".

"Yes, well, we've got over the shock of it now, but it's taken a while," said Patrick. "The little fellow's grand, he's growing fast. And recognises us, he smiled at me this morning".

"The policewoman telephoned the other day" said Nell, wondering if Children's Services had been contacted. "They did manage to extract some DNA but weren't able to find a match".

"Mummy what's DNA?" Emer looked at her enquiringly.

"It's very complicated. Now don't interrupt".

"Mrs Walsh, let us have a chat with the children then perhaps they can leave us while we go through the application forms". Helen Kimber asked each of the children to talk about themselves for a few minutes, and how they felt about becoming Arlo's foster family. The boys all said they were in favour, each of them telling Helen how he had already become like a little brother. Emer, seizing the opportunity to take centre stage for a moment, said she would love to be Arlo's big sister because up to now she had always been the youngest and she found that sooo difficult.

Nell looked at Patrick who rolled his eyes.

"Does anyone have any worries about Mum and Dad fostering him? Are there any questions?"

"Only what would happen if his real parents showed up. Would we have to give him back?" Arthur had been wondering about this for some time.

"That would depend on the circumstances," said Charlie. "It's a very serious thing to abandon your child, that would take some explaining. We would have to make absolutely sure his parents were capable of looking after him. Everything we do, every decision we make is based on what is best for the child, it's not necessarily what the parents want. And supposing Arlo had been happy and settled with you for some years, it would be unfair, some might say cruel just to uproot him. In many cases the Family Court would make a ruling".

After the children had left the room, everyone's attention turned to the completion of forms. This took nearly an hour, and halfway through, Nell went out to fetch a tray of tea for them all.

"We've dealt with as much as we can today, I think," said Charlie. "There will have to be a full home inspection in due course, and you will need to be interviewed by a panel before you can be finally approved, but it's all looking hopeful. I can see no reason why you would not be accepted as foster carers".

"So Arlo stays here with us in the meantime?" Nell asked tentatively.

"Yes, he is settled here and as you say, doing well. We won't disturb him tonight, it's late, but next time I should like to see him if we visit during the day. Anything else you'd like to ask?"

"I need to register Arlo with our GP," said Nell. "I don't know what vaccinations he's had; he may not have had any so I will need advice on that. But the receptionist at the medical centre asked for his birth certificate before they can take him on as a patient. Obviously, we don't have one".

"It's a good point. Normally with fostering there is a birth certificate which would be provided at the beginning, but as we've said before, the circumstances are all back to front. We can give you an official letter confirming that for now, you are his legal guardians. That should suffice for the GP. We are jumping the gun in a way because you are not formally signed off as foster parents yet, but Arlo's health comes first in this situation. Looking further ahead, we will need to apply to the Registrar General for Arlo's birth to be registered retrospectively. My department will deal with that for you. It's quite rare to have to do this but as the police have been unable to trace the birth parents it's the only course open to us. Arlo will need this as he grows older, for a passport and so on".

Patrick nodded. There were so many complications, things that he hadn't thought of.

All this time, Helen Kimber had been making notes, then after a while she put down her pen.

"Mrs Walsh…"

"Call me Nell".

"Nell, I telephoned Mr Franklin at Lamberham School the other day because I still have a few concerns about your daughter Brontë. You didn't quite tell me the full story before regarding the bullying, did you? I understand that there was an unpleasant rumour doing the rounds at school that Brontë had given birth to a baby during the summer holidays".

Nell was infuriated. "He had no right to discuss that with you. It was the most despicable piece of gossip, and it all came about because she was bullied about her weight. You must know how spiteful some children can be, especially girls. I went to see Mr Franklin about the bullying, and I was horrified when he told me what was being said about Brontë, so I put him in the picture about Arlo and that there was no truth in the rumour whatsoever. I also insisted that he put a stop to the gossip, and I decided there and then to take Brontë out of that school. You know the rest".

"We – Mr Franklin and I – do have every right to discuss such matters where there is a question of safeguarding. You really should have been more open with me about it. Look at it from our point of view – we have to follow up on every suspicion of this kind, otherwise the school staff would not be doing their job and neither would I".

Patrick looked furious. "We were trying, for our daughter's sake to put it behind us. To keep going over it with different people would have been to add fuel to the rumour, we all just wanted to forget it. The last thing Brontë needed was someone else asking her questions. She was in a very fragile state, we were so worried about her, that episode had done her immense damage".

"So you decided to send her away?"

"You make it sound like a punishment! It was no such thing. We made arrangements for her to live with my mother in southwest Ireland for a while so that she could get over all the upset and have a fresh start. We were not trying to hide anything, there was nothing to hide. She is going to school at the local convent there which has low numbers and small classes, she has settled well. We have notified Lamberham. You were just saying about everything you do being in the best interest of the child, well that's exactly why we made that decision. It would certainly not have been in her best interest to leave her where she was".

"Ok Mr Walsh, I accept what you say. I just wish you'd given us all the facts. As prospective foster carers you will be in a position of trust. Please don't hold anything back from us in future, we need to work together in full co-operation".

Patrick and Nell nodded, both feeling that they had been ticked off like naughty children and were relieved when the meeting was over.

"Whew! I wouldn't like to get on the wrong side of her too many times" said Patrick, closing the front door. He was still visibly angry.

"I suppose it's how things will be from now on if the fostering goes ahead" said Nell thoughtfully. "Our lives will always be open to inspection; nothing will be private. It's something we will have to get used to".

Chapter Fifty

Kathleen had thought the day would never come when she could finally call herself a single woman again, even though it would only be for a short time as her wedding was at last arranged for the following summer. The celebration of her daughter's divorce was the first party Bridget had attended for many long years. The wake following the death of Dermot could not have been described as a party even though as with many wakes in Ireland, that had descended into revelry after the first few hours. But this was a happy occasion, with many of her family eager to join in, and when the champagne ran out there was Guinness and wine enough to keep the conversation and the craic flowing.

So it was not surprising that Bridget looked forward to a quiet few days during the week that followed. One weekday evening, Brontë went to sit with her in the living room for a while.

"Granny, do you mind if I ask you something?"

"Of course dear, ask away".

"Has Aunt Angela had a very sad life?"

Bridget paused and looked at her granddaughter. This day was bound to come, she thought; the subject can't be avoided for ever.

"She has, and there's a reason for it. You're surely old enough to understand, but I'm afraid you won't find the story very easy to listen to". She looked fondly at Brontë.

"Angela was not much older than you – fifteen. She went to St Teresa's like you do, she was doing well at her lessons. Anyway, she started walking out with this boy, Shay his name was. He was eighteen, he came from Skibbereen. Don't ask me how she met him".

"What's walking out?"

"Well, what do you call it now, dating, I suppose. Anyway, to cut a long story short, after a couple of months Angela was pregnant. Now you may not think that's so terrible these days but remember this was Ireland in 1947. Being pregnant before marriage back then, and underage was considered a mortal sin by the Church, some still think that way. For the family it was a terrible scandal and when the school got to hear about it, which was sure to happen, they took matters into their own hands and tried to hush it up. St Teresa's was far stricter in those days than it is now, let me tell you. And something else you may not realise, the Church had a great deal more control over peoples' lives at that time, much more so than today".

"Mummy told me once that she was expecting Arthur before she and Daddy got married".

"That's right, and to be honest I wasn't happy about it when I first heard the news but England in the 1970s and 80s was very different to Ireland, in many ways it still is. They were able to get married and bring up their child. It all turned out well. But for Angela it was nothing short of a disaster. Shay disappeared, and the next thing was, Angela was sent to a mother and baby home run by the Church in County Galway, St Teresa's arranged it all in a hurry. That's a long way up north. The family had no say in the matter. She had a terrible time there, the girls had to do very hard domestic work and laundry for long hours in the home to pay for their keep. The family weren't allowed to visit, and the girls were more or less kept prisoner. There was no escape. But there was worse to come. She had a dreadful time with the birth, no pain relief and no sympathy from the nuns. They told her that she was wicked and that it was punishment for her sins. They were so cruel to her".

Bridget was finding it hard to hold back tears; Brontë listened intently.

"Anyway, it was a boy. A little boy, Kieran. He survived, but the nuns took him away. Angela was never allowed even to hold him or feed him. Each day she peeped into the nursery, but the nuns were always watching, they sent her away every time.

A few days later they told her it was time to leave. Apparently, the little boy had been taken for adoption. Angela was heartbroken. She could not give permission as she was only fifteen, the nuns arranged it all and they would give her no information about who had adopted him.

After that she came home in disgrace. She never went back to school, so she didn't finish her education. She took jobs in Ballymere, cleaning peoples' houses and did some work on the land. Our parents felt the shame until the day they died, but it was worse for Angela, because for years she tried to trace her son but never did, she was blocked at every turn".

Brontë's eyes were wide with horror.

"How could people do that to her, Granny? The Church is supposed to care for people. When I go to Mass the priest talks about forgiveness, Jesus taught us to love our neighbour. Where was the kindness, what happened to love? And the baby boy was taken away from his mother. That was wicked, not anything Aunt Angela did".

"My dear, you've so much to learn about the world, especially over here. It's full of contradictions. It should be so simple, as you say, but it's not. The Catholic Church in Ireland has always been very judgmental about sex. It's very hard for some of us to come to terms with these things. Anyway, life did improve for Angela in the end, she met Fergus after a few years, and they've had a long and happy marriage. He stood by her; he didn't care about her past. But they never had children. I don't know for sure why, but I have my suspicions that too much damage had been done, in more ways than one".

By now Brontë was in tears. She felt every emotion at that moment, sorrow, anger, sympathy for Aunt Angela and a sense of injustice, just as years before, her mother had done when Patrick had tried to explain about the harshness and inconsistencies of life in rural Catholic Ireland.

"It's done now dear; nothing can change it. But I'm telling you so that you can understand just a little bit about what Angela has been through. There were many like her. It's all right to cry, my dear, it's a sad tale altogether. The Lord knows Angela and I have shed enough tears since it happened". Bridget crossed herself. "But you're not to go on worrying about it. This was all a long time ago and she has a better life these days. She's a good woman, despite her unhappy past; for years she's been a volunteer in a hospice in Limerick, giving end-of-life care. She knows what suffering is. And isn't she about to go into business and open the guest house now? She's a marvel altogether, taking that on at her age. And you'll be part of it Brontë, having a little weekend job there now. Your Daddy isn't the only one to have started a family business you know". She laughed and Brontë smiled.

Despite Bridget's words, Brontë could not help but dwell on the story. In some ways she felt trusted as a grown-up with such an important family matter. But she couldn't help thinking how she would have felt, being at almost the same age as her great-aunt was then; pregnant when little more than a child, then shunned and disgraced, with no support from her family or the baby's father, and the Church acting without a shred of humanity, yet Aunt Angela had later found the compassion within herself to comfort dying people. Her mind returned to her own situation at the beginning of term – only a few weeks previously – yet so much had happened since then. She began to think that the bullying and unkind treatment she had received from her classmates, even the evil rumour that had been spread around seemed insignificant compared to what Aunt Angela had experienced. As she reflected more and more about what she had been told, it seemed that her own troubles receded a little and she was able to look at them in perspective. Without Brontë realising it, the healing had begun.

Chapter Fifty-One

Brontë was trying to explain to her cousin Aisling about Bonfire Night.

Last Friday when her mother telephoned, Nell had explained that they would not be holding their usual November the Fifth firework party in the field behind the house as the noise might frighten the donkeys. Instead, Arthur, Henry and Ronnie had made a guy and hauled it down to the village green where a communal display was to be held. The bonfire had been under construction for over a fortnight and was now over eight feet high, so they had difficulty placing the guy on the top.

"What's a guy?" Aisling wanted to know. It was something she had never heard of.

"Well, we take men's old cast-off trousers and jackets, stuff them with straw and newspaper and put on a mask and a hat for his head. It's like a great big puppet. Then we set fire to it on the bonfire".

"But why?"

Just then, Brontë was reminded of her little sister Emer who prefaced most of her questions with 'why', or more often 'can I have', and for a fleeting moment felt a little homesick. Then she went on to tell Aisling about the Gunpowder Plot, when Guy Fawkes and his associates attempted to burn down the Houses of Parliament in London in order to assassinate King James the First in 1605.

"He was stopped in time; the plot was discovered, and Guy Fawkes was sentenced to death. It's commemorated every year on November the Fifth. People have bonfires and light fireworks". Brontë saw that Aisling was still looking puzzled, then realised that this event did not really feature in Irish history, so was probably not taught here in schools, at least not in the Republic.

The following Saturday Brontë was to start her weekend job at Hackett's Guest House. Aunt Angela was only allowing her to do four hours on Saturdays as she was still only fourteen, and she had promised Bridget that she would not neglect her homework, but to Brontë, earning a little pocket money was a huge step towards independence. Aisling, being not yet twelve was too young but could work a couple of hours each week after her next birthday.

The Guest House was an odd mixture of old and new; the original building dated back to 1900, but a new ground floor extension comprising a double suite of rooms, and two singles with shower rooms had been added. Together with six double en-suite rooms on the first floor and two further twin rooms with bathrooms on the second floor, there was ample accommodation for families, couples or single visitors. There was a large communal lounge, bar and dining room, and a separate one-bedroom flat adjoining the main building which Angela and Fergus occupied. Every room had been re-plastered and freshly decorated, modern furniture put in place, and it was Brontë's task to help with making up the beds with brand new linen, put out towels, clean the bathrooms and dust and vacuum. On the first morning she worked with Niamh who was one of the regular hotel cleaners. Niamh was curious about the reason Brontë had come to stay in West Cork.

"Sure and isn't it most people I know can't wait to get out of Ireland" she said, shaking down a pillow into its case. "I can't understand why people would want to come to live here, except for holidays I suppose. There's nothing here, really. I was lucky to get this job".

"That's why I like it" said Brontë, tucking the sheet neatly under at the corner of the mattress as Niamh had shown her. "It's peaceful, no one's rushing around trying to out-do everyone else. Everyone's kind. I'd like to live here forever". Niamh looked at her in amazement. Brontë stopped, suddenly realising what she'd just said. Did she really mean that, forever? To not go home and live with her family again?

It seemed disloyal; she loved all her family very much and she missed them. But somehow, in a strange, unexpected way, she felt she fitted in here, amongst the quiet fields, the rocky coastline and the bleak landscape. Her mother loved it here too, she would understand. But it was only ever meant to be temporary; in a few months' time she would have to return to England. But not yet; please not yet.

* * *

Armed with a letter confirming her status as guardian for Arlo, Nell had successfully registered him at the Medical Centre in Drover's Cross and booked an appointment for vaccinations. The practice nurse had never before come across a situation where a baby's parents were unknown and no immunisation history could be established, so Nell had to wait while she consulted the duty doctor. He had in turn conferred with colleagues and decided that administering a possible double dose of all vaccinations needed for a three-month-old baby would be less harmful than the risk of leaving him unvaccinated. Arlo's development was pronounced normal for his age; Nell could only give his approximate date of birth as late July or early August. The nurse shook her head as though she found the whole story impossible to believe, and Nell realised that if she and Patrick were to be accepted officially as foster parents, this was the first of many difficult explanations that she would have to give over the coming months and years.

During the next few weeks there were several visits from Charlie Weston. Sometimes Helen Kimber accompanied him, on another occasion he brought a trainee social worker along. Each time he asked to see Arlo who was now alert, reaching out and showed signs of early teething. He was making above average progress now; this had been confirmed by the Health Visitor when Nell took him to the baby clinic at the village hall. Charlie was shown over every inch of the property and grounds and interviewed Nell at length, asking searching questions about her childhood, her family, her education and her marriage. During evening visits, Patrick was subjected to the same questioning. At times it became tiresome, and they began to wonder why they had allowed themselves to be placed into a position where every detail of their life was being held open to scrutiny. Jenny, Neville and Lois were interviewed as well, but Neville understood why everyone's background had to be checked so thoroughly; during his teaching years he had once been consulted when a boy at his school was to be adopted after losing his parents in the Second World War. Arthur now had a girlfriend Abby who had become a frequent visitor; even she did not escape the enquiries of the social workers.

Nell and Patrick were asked to give names of referees who had known them for several years but were unrelated. Without hesitation, they named Joe, Caroline, Jonathan and Barbara, all of whom had been friends for some time. The next step would be for them to attend a panel, where a decision-maker would look at all the evidence, reports and references and give a determination as to their suitability. That might not happen until the new year; there was a great deal of information to be examined, but until then the weekly visits would continue, and Arlo's development monitored.

As the weeks moved on to December, Nell turned her thoughts to Christmas, and she realised with pleasure that her family, including her parents would all be together for the first time. During her Friday night telephone call to Brontë she asked if her daughter would be coming home by ferry or whether she would prefer to take a flight from Cork to Gatwick?

There was a pause. "Mum I shan't be coming home for Christmas. Aunt Angela has asked me to work at the Guest House, they have a lot of bookings".

"But of course you're coming home! That was always the plan, that you'd come home at Christmas".

"I'm sorry Mum".

"No Brontë it's all been decided, you're to come home. We haven't seen you for three months".

"Couldn't you come out here for a few days, Mum?"

"It's impossible, I can't leave Arlo. We're going through the fostering process as you know, I can't be absent just now. You must come home".

Brontë gave a sob.

"Let me speak to Granny".

Brontë handed the receiver to Bridget and rushed out of the room in tears.

During the conversation that followed, Bridget did her best to explain to her daughter-in-law how quickly Brontë had settled in and was doing well, both at school, socially and in her little part time job. In so many ways the visit had been a success. But she could well understand why Nell wanted Brontë to come home for the festive season.

"She's happy enough here Nell. She seems to have put all that upset behind her. Well, she never speaks of it at all, obviously I don't know if it's still on her mind. So as far as that's concerned, I think the visit has been a success. But what we don't know is, how will she be back home in England?"

"I never thought that she'd like staying with you so much that she didn't want to come home, not even for Christmas".

"Nell, in a way this was an experiment altogether. None of us knew how things would turn out. We've both been doing our best for her. And she's still a child, sometimes she doesn't understand her own feelings".

"I know Bridget, and I'm truly grateful for everything you're doing for her. It can't have been easy; we threw you in at the deep end with very little notice".

"That's all ok, I've loved having her. But let's leave things to settle down for a week or so, I shan't put any pressure on Brontë one way or another. She may come round to the idea. And as for her working for my sister over Christmas, yes that has been discussed but it's only a few hours here and there, nothing that can't be overcome".

Later that evening Patrick found Nell in tears in the bedroom. She told him of the telephone call.

"Patrick, she doesn't want to come home for Christmas. It's all gone wrong. Almost as if she's turned against her home, she prefers her life out there. Well, she didn't say that in so many words but that's what it amounts to. Patrick, we're losing her". Nell's voice cracked with sobs. "We're losing our daughter".

"Nelly that's not happening. It's good that she's doing well, finding her feet, getting over all that business. She will always be our daughter, but perhaps it's too soon, maybe we're expecting too much. It's only been three months".

"But I was so looking forward to seeing her at Christmas. Our first one as a complete family".

"I know. But there will be other Christmases, birthdays, holidays, there's the wedding coming up in the summer. Lots of chances for us all to be together".

"If it wasn't for Arlo, I would take the next flight out to Cork and see for myself how things are". For the first time Nell realised the restrictions looking after Arlo had placed on her; more so than on any other family member. "I don't think Charlie would agree to me taking him along".

"No, probably not, he would be out of the council's jurisdiction in Ireland. But that might change once we are fully approved. We'd be allowed to take him on holiday with us surely?"

"I hope so, otherwise it would mean I'd be a prisoner in the UK for ever. Or at least until he's eighteen".

"Nell, aren't you getting a bit ahead of yourself? All this time they've been finding out about our backgrounds, our family history. They know I have relatives in Ireland and that we will want to visit them now and then. It's obvious that if Arlo is being looked after as one of the family, he will come with us. We just have to wait until we have the all-clear. Then perhaps we can go out there for a week or so in the spring. And as far as Christmas goes, well you never know, we may be able to work out a compromise with Brontë. Let's do as Mam says, give it a few days for her to think it over".

Chapter Fifty-Two

It was the second week in December and although the weather was turning noticeably colder, Lois seemed to be surviving the winter so far and no mention had been made about returning to Spain. She and Neville were comfortable at the Swan's Rest; their suite of rooms was well heated and looked out onto the hotel garden where someone had thoughtfully placed several bird-feeders, and one of their greatest pleasures in the morning was to identify the birds flocking in to feast on the nuts and fat-balls, and watch a squirrel hastily gathering up any morsels that had fallen to the ground.

Knowing that Kathleen would only be able to live with them in Spain for a few more months at the most before her wedding, Neville had been considering how Lois would manage back at the apartment without any help, and whether they really wanted to think about engaging a new companion, who would inevitably be a stranger. He was reluctant to entertain this idea; although many years had elapsed since the fiasco with Evelyn, he could never completely forget how close they had come to disaster in those days. Lois has really improved, he thought, not just in health but in contentment. She has overcome so much, he reflected; even her consultant was surprised at how the illness had stabilised and could only put it down to the climate in Spain and that the periods of remission were more frequent. In the meantime, Neville deliberated whether they might after all stay in England indefinitely. The possibility of selling the apartment occurred to him.

For Nell, the welcome prospect of having both of her parents at home for Christmas was marred only by the thought that her eldest daughter might be absent. Taking the advice of both Bridget and Patrick she was careful not to pressurise Brontë but remained hopeful that she would come round to the idea of returning home, at least for a while.

It was Kathleen who came to the rescue. She was still in Ballymere but had planned to travel to Spain to spend Christmas with Adam. The café bar would be quiet during the winter months, and they were looking forward to some time together. However, a bridesmaid dress needed to be chosen for Emer; when she was last at Moongarth she had promised to take her shopping, and time was ticking by. There might not be many more opportunities to see Emer before the wedding.

"Nell is upset that Brontë doesn't want to go home for Christmas". Bridget had confided in Kathleen one morning after Brontë had left for school. "I don't want to take sides over this, it's a difficult one. In a way Brontë is so much better than when she first arrived here, but it's not my place to tell her what to do. It's a bit of a problem altogether".

"Let me have a think about it, Mam. I might have an idea".

Later that evening Kathleen took Brontë to one side. "I need to talk to you about something. You know I'm going back to Spain to spend Christmas with Adam? Well, I'm staying at Moongarth for a couple of nights on my way. While I'm there I want to buy Emer's bridesmaid dress. I'm planning to fly from Cork on the twentieth of December. The thing is, I hate flying". She looked a bit embarrassed. "Before I went to work for Nanny Lois I'd never been on a plane and I was so looking forward to it, but between you and me, I hated every minute of it. It wasn't so bad last time when Adam was with me, but I'm really dreading going on my own".

"Couldn't you go across by ferry?"

"I could, but I'd still need to fly from Gatwick to Malaga".

Brontë seemed to understand. "I've never been on a plane yet", she said. "We always came here by ferry. But I would like to fly one day. I don't think I'd be nervous".

"The other problem is, about the dress. Your Mam is busy with Arlo and has lots of meetings at the moment. She can't come with me. But I don't know if I can cope with Emer on my own".

Brontë looked at Kathleen sympathetically. "I know. She can be very tricky, my sister. She argues a lot, it really gets Mum down. I can usually handle her though. Sometimes she listens to me".

"I wouldn't know what to do if she threw a tantrum in the shop now, it's been worrying me. But I really need to sort out her dress before Christmas in case it needs any alterations. July will be here before we know it. What I want to ask you is, would you travel back with me to Gatwick? I'd feel better if someone was with me on the plane. I know I'd have to do the journey to Spain on my own, but if your Dad took me to check in and Adam met me at the other end I could just about cope. And I'm sure that between the two of us we could manage Emer".

There was a pause. "I wasn't planning to go home at Christmas" said Brontë slowly. "I explained all this to Mum the other day. "I'd be letting Aunt Angela down for one thing, the guest house is going to be busy. And, well, I just don't know if I'm ready to go back yet".

Kathleen knew that the worst thing she could do at that moment was to push too hard. "I suppose if I were in your shoes I'd be a bit unsure. But with some things, the longer you wait, the harder it gets. Maybe if you just went home for a few days, knowing you could come back here straight after Christmas it would break the ice. And you'd be doing me a big favour. I'd like you to take your bridesmaid dress with you and put it on to show Emer the colour we've chosen. You wait until your Mam and Dad see you in that, won't they be impressed!"

Brontë thought of the dress hanging upstairs in her wardrobe underneath its filmy protective cover. She had tried it on again several times and looked herself in a full-length mirror. She felt that it transformed her whenever she put it on, each time it gave her confidence and that instead of letting her aunt down she would be a credit to her; there would be no need to try and hide when the photographs were taken. She would love to show her mother.

"Well, I suppose I could go home for a few days, just until after Christmas" she said at last. "I would really love to go on a plane and keep you company. I could help you with Emer. But what about Aunt Angela?"

"Leave Aunt Angela to me, I'll explain. There are bound to be staff who are happy to do a few more hours and shifts to earn some extra money before Christmas. Then you could work your normal hours again when you come back".

Brontë was still thinking about the arrangements as she undressed for bed that evening. She did have a few doubts about going home, but the thought of travelling by air for the first time was exciting and irresistible. Another thought occurred to her. Up until now, she had been seen as a problem, by the school, her classmates and although they would have denied it, even her parents at times. But now she was helping Auntie Kathleen with her problems – her fear of flying and her worries about not being able to deal with Emer. The realisation made Brontë feel useful, helpful and more grown up. Things are changing for me, she said to herself. My life has changed since living here, I shall be happy to go home for a while. Everything will be all right.

The next day Kathleen booked the flights and checked that Connor could drive them to Cork Airport on the twentieth. Brontë telephoned her mother to say that after all, she would be coming home for Christmas and that she hoped that Emer hadn't taken over her old bedroom because Auntie Kathleen would be needing it for a few days. Nell was overjoyed and at last felt that she could really look forward to the holiday season and make it extra special. The only cloud – if it was a cloud – on Nell's horizon was the forthcoming foster panel; the date for the final interview was the ninth of January. We can't do any more to prepare for it, Nell thought. It's not like an exam where we need to give the right answers. We just need to be ourselves so that the panel can see that we are responsible people who will always love and care for Arlo, give him a happy and secure home and do our best for him.

Chapter Fifty-Three

December 1997

Neville treasured every moment spent with Lois and their lives were so much happier as a couple now. His only regret was that this blissful state of affairs had not been possible sooner; so many years of their marriage had been sacrificed to misfortune, Lois's fragile health and the destructive intentions of a third party. But most of the time he was able to put those disappointments behind him and be thankful that at last they had found a place of contentment; reconciliation with their family, no financial worries and reassurance that Lois's condition was manageable.

It had not been possible for him to pursue his interest in astronomy in Solibrio. He had set up his telescope in the apartment in the early days but in such a residential area there was too much light for any meaningful study of the Mediterranean skies, and it would have been necessary for him to travel some distance to find the right conditions. Kathleen would have taken excellent care of Lois in his absence, but he had decided to postpone his hobby until some future date. Nell had once told him with excitement about the dark skies in West Cork and at that time his interest had been piqued. With the prospect of visiting the area for Kathleen's wedding, his enthusiasm resurfaced. He mentioned this when they next visited Moongarth, a few days before Brontë's return. To his surprise, Henry had a suggestion.

"Grandpa, I would really like to learn more about astronomy. I saw a poster in Kirchington about the Planetarium, and one of the teachers at school goes to their meetings. There are some interesting talks and exhibitions, but they need volunteers and speakers. Could you and I go there one evening?"

Neville was delighted to think that his grandson was showing an interest in a subject that was so important to him. His hobby would be more fulfilling if there was someone likeminded to share it with, and he readily agreed, then realised that as the meetings took place in the evenings, this would inevitably mean leaving Lois alone for a few hours. But surprisingly, she did not mind; she would be perfectly safe on her own, she said; she would watch television, listen to the radio or sit in the hotel lounge and talk to the other residents for a while.

He smiled and looked at her lovingly. What a transformation from the woman who a few years ago was frightened of her own shadow, would never venture into a social situation without a companion, and would be reluctant to strike up conversation even with people she knew.

The next talk was entitled "The Moon – Earth's nearest neighbour" and was to take place on the Friday before Christmas, just after Henry's birthday. Neville was tremendously excited – not just because astronomy was his passion, but also because his grandson had suggested it and was to accompany him. The possibility of reviving his hobby and meeting new people who shared his interest was an exciting one, and even more so because Lois was in favour of it.

* * *

"I was rather hoping I could wear blue".

It was to be expected. If Kathleen had decided on blue, Emer would have preferred pink or yellow, any colour but the one the bride had chosen. Kathleen looked desperately at Nell.

They were discussing bridesmaid dresses the evening before the shopping trip. Brontë had put on the dress they had bought in Ireland, and Nell had gasped with delight as her daughter stepped shyly into the room. The dress had fitted perfectly in the shop, but it was now looking slightly loose.

"Brontë, you look amazing! Patrick come and see!" Nell was ecstatic and Patrick whistled as he put his head round the door. "Who is this gorgeous young lady?" he joked. Then, "you look beautiful" he said fondly, and there was a slight catch in his voice as he spoke.

"The bridesmaids are wearing dark green with white trimmings" Nell said firmly to Emer. "There is no argument, it's not about what you want. Anyway, the colour will suit your hair perfectly".

"But..."

Kathleen still looked anxious. "You can choose the style, Emer. It's the colour I have decided on. Your Mam's right, it will look lovely against your auburn hair. You are so like my sister Orla".

The thought did not mollify Emer but to everyone's relief she did not pursue the point any further. She seemed excited at the prospect of shopping the next day with Kathleen and Brontë, and for a moment Nell felt upset that she could not accompany them. But she and Patrick had an appointment with Charlie the following morning, the last meeting before Christmas. Instead of sending them on a series of courses in readiness for fostering it had been agreed that Charlie would make additional visits to them, covering the main content of the course material and to prepare them for the interview panel. The circumstances were exceptional, he explained. This suited Nell and Patrick better in fact, as they could not leave Arlo for whole days; Jenny could only assist for a few hours at a time.

Returning to Moongarth had been less traumatic than Brontë had feared. She had felt a little nervous at the thought, and the reasons for the move to Ireland came back to her in a rush as Connor drove them to the airport. But the worries were fleeting; she tried to hide the excitement of taking her first trip by plane out of respect for Kathleen who was feeling slightly sick at the moment of take-off. As she walked through the front door of the house where she had lived all her life until a few months ago, she realised how much she had missed her family, yet already she thought of Ballymere as her home, which was unsettling, and she felt unable to explain this to anyone.

The shopping trip proved more difficult than expected. Hoping to see some more individual designs, Kathleen suggested they avoid the High Street; they looked briefly in a few smaller shops and boutiques, but none had anything suitable for Emer in the right colour. In the end they decided to go on to Darcey's, which was the main department store in Kirchington. As they made their way through the revolving doors, Kathleen's heart sank as she looked at the crowds of Christmas shoppers. Perhaps this was a mistake, she said to herself, I should have waited until the new year. But as they travelled up the escalator to the first floor, she was relieved to see that the bridal section was quiet; perhaps very few brides decided to shop for their gowns during the week before Christmas. The shop assistant looked hopefully at them as they approached; she was probably the only member of staff not feeling exhausted by the Christmas rush.

After spending a great deal of time examining fabrics, trying on different styles and comparing shades of dark green, there remained three dresses suitable for Emer in her size. As Kathleen had promised, she allowed her niece to make the final choice, and to Brontë's surprise, she chose the simplest empire line style in soft velvet with three quarter length sleeves and a narrow white lace trim at the sleeve edge and hem.

The shop assistant had noticed Kathleen's accent. "That shade is called Emerald, madam" she said, wrapping the dress in tissue paper before placing it into a large carrier bag.

"You see, I knew that should be my name" said Emer, as if proving a point. "It's a sign". Kathleen gave her a puzzled look, not understanding. "I'll explain later" said Brontë as they walked towards the escalator.

As it started to descend, they looked down at the ground floor counters. From their vantage point they could see the cosmetics and perfumery section below, busy with people shopping for last minute gifts. Then to her horror, Brontë noticed two girls trying on lipstick: Zoe Jordan and Kelly Banks, her chief tormentors from Lamberham School. One of the girls glanced in Brontë's direction, sneered and nudged her companion who looked up and laughed unpleasantly.

Brontë felt panic grip her; too late she reached out to clutch the moving handrail. Down and down she spiralled into inky blackness with pinpricks of silver piercing the edge of her vision.

*** * ***

"It's very hot and crowded in here, I think that must have caused her to pass out for a moment". Kathleen said worriedly to a member of staff who had run to their assistance. Emer looked frightened.

They were sitting in the staff rest room with a manager and a first aider who had taken Brontë's pulse and was covering her with a blanket.

Brontë was wide awake now and seemed confused momentarily, not knowing where she was. "What happened to me?" She sat up, suddenly feeling rather foolish, but was immediately aware of pain on her right thigh and upper arm.

"You fainted on the escalator and tumbled to the bottom. Fortunately, we weren't far from the ground floor, or it could have been much worse". Kathleen was holding her hand, wondering if they should call an ambulance.

"I don't think there are any fractures" said the first aider, carefully checking for swelling or signs of limbs at an unusual angle. "Try to stand up gently. If you can't then I think we should ask for medical advice".

Brontë got to her feet slowly. "I think I can walk ok" she said, taking a few cautious steps. "But everywhere hurts".

"You will probably have lots of bruises tomorrow. That was quite a nasty fall you had". The first aider was packing up her kit; there was a graze on Brontë's hand which she had dressed. "If you feel sick or your vision becomes blurred you should see a doctor. Just as a precaution" she added. "Make sure you have rest and quiet for a day or two".

"How are you getting home?" asked the manager.

"Bus, I'm afraid" said Kathleen, resignedly.

"I don't think you should stand around waiting for a bus. I'll call you a taxi, it's the least we can do".

"But we live out at Drover's Cross".

"No matter. We have a duty of care to our customers".

Nell was astonished to see her family return home by taxi and her first thought was to telephone Dr Ferris when she heard what had happened.

"Mum I just want to go to bed. Please don't fuss. I'll be ok in the morning". Brontë was already starting to mount the stairs, trying not to show how painful she was finding every step.

While Nell was filling a hot water bottle for Brontë, Kathleen knocked on her niece's door.

"Can I come in for a moment?"

"Of course,"

Kathleen sat on the bed. "Brontë, don't tell me anything if you don't want to, but can you remember what made you fall? Because I saw the look on your face, just before it happened".

Brontë looked at her aunt with terrified eyes. "I saw them" she whispered. "They were there, by the makeup counter".

"Who was there?"

"Two girls from Lamberham school. I hate them, they were horrible to me for months. They saw me on the escalator, I thought here we go again, I can't escape. I don't remember any more after that".

Kathleen took Brontë's hand and spoke gently. "They can't do anything to you, Brontë. That's all in the past. Your life is different now".

"I should never have come back to England. I can never be free of them. I need to go back to Granny's, I was just beginning to feel ok there. I can't live here".

Kathleen thought she had never heard anything so sad as her young niece not wanting to be in her own home with people who loved her.

"Brontë, do I have your permission to talk to your Mam and Dad about this? Because they really need to know". Kathleen felt torn, sensing the importance of keeping Brontë's trust but at the same time feeling out of her depth and realising that Nell and Patrick had a right to know that their daughter needed expert help to overcome her fears.

"Ok but it won't do any good. They don't understand. I think Mum will expect me to stay here now I'm back. She always said I'd only go to Granny's for a few months".

"Perhaps it was too soon to come back. Let me talk to them. All we want is for you to feel better and to be happy".

With a heavy heart Kathleen walked slowly down the stairs, wondering how this situation was ever to be resolved.

Chapter Fifty-Four

That same evening, Neville and Henry took the planned trip to the Kirchington Planetarium. The foyer was crowded; it was the last event before Christmas and Neville was surprised to see people of all ages gathered round the various exhibitions and posters, waiting to be ushered in to hear the speaker. He paid for their tickets and then studied a list of forthcoming talks: The Giants of the Solar System, The Moon Landing of 1969, Winter Skies, The Northern Lights. He would love to attend every one of them, and saw that Henry was looking at the same poster with excitement. "Grandpa wouldn't it be great if we could go to all of these? Some of them would be useful for my science project. When we go home, I'll show you how far I've got".

At that moment a middle-aged man approached them. "Hello Henry. Glad you could come".

"This is my grandfather, Neville Garth. Grandpa this is Mr Davenport, my science teacher. He's tonight's speaker".

The two men shook hands and Neville explained that this was his first visit to the Planetarium for many years but that he had a lifelong interest in astronomy and was looking forward to attending regularly. As he said the words, he acknowledged that already he was taking it for granted that he and Lois would not return to Spain, but somehow the thought did not concern him; without realising it, they had both settled into their lives in Sussex. Lois was coping with the colder weather so far and had made no complaints.

"It's good to see a new face. Many people here tonight are members, they come regularly. We always welcome volunteers you know, if you'd like to get involved. There's more to putting on a display or a talk than people realise. And educating children is one of our main aims. Anything to do with space travel always fires their imagination, we try to build on that to include all aspects of astronomy. And of course it comes into the science syllabus at school".

"I agree with you about education. If you can spark children's interest in a subject by making it exciting and relevant, you're halfway there. I used to teach at Kirchington Grammar, in fact I was head there for several years until I retired. Maths and Science were my subjects too".

Chris Davenport was immediately interested. "I had no idea. We should get together for a chat sometime; we must have a lot in common! Perhaps you would have some ideas for our future programme. Here's my card".

At that moment an announcement was made for the talk to begin, and as Neville and Henry took their seats, Neville felt elated. He was nearly seventy-eight but here was a younger man suggesting that he still had knowledge to share on a subject close to his heart. Life could be full of surprises, even at his age. He settled down with anticipation to listen to the speaker, suddenly feeling that maybe, just maybe he yet had something to offer to the world.

* * *

The first aider had been right; the following day Brontë was covered in bruises down the right side of her body. Every muscle ached as though she had run a marathon or swum the English Channel. But her physical symptoms were insignificant compared to the feelings of fear and nervousness that at times threatened to overwhelm her.

Nell had instructed Brontë to stay in bed for the day, and Jenny brought her breakfast on a tray.

"Don't you go thinking this is a regular thing now. You're not going to be spoiled just because you're home for a few days" she teased. But privately Jenny was as worried as the rest of the family; she could see that Brontë was far from well. The bruises would fade in time but the trauma that a few seconds panic had unleashed would need expert help to heal.

It was Saturday. All the adults assembled in the drawing room after lunch, including Neville and Lois. Arthur was out on a driving lesson; Henry was catching up on homework in advance of Christmas, and Ronnie and Emer were cleaning out the stable. Patrick had insisted that the job must be finished that day or there would be consequences. He did not elaborate on what these might be, although Emer who was always keen to prevaricate, asked him several times.

Arlo was sitting in a bouncy chair, smiling and reaching out for the soft toys hanging from the frame.

"While we're all here together, we need to talk about Brontë". There was a note of desperation in Nell's tone. "We thought she was so much better when she arrived on Wednesday, but there's been one little upset and we're back where we started".

"She may not see it as a little upset" said her father slowly. "It was a huge setback for her".

"She has been fine at Mam's," said Kathleen. "At least, she's settled in well at St Teresa's, she's not spoken about the bullying at all. We all thought she was getting over it. I really thought we'd have known by now if she had been bottling it up".

"Perhaps it was a mistake, expecting her to come home so soon". Patrick avoided looking at Nell, knowing that she disagreed with him over this.

Lois had been following the conversation. "Sometimes you just need to be listened to. Brontë may be only fourteen, but she has a great deal of self-awareness. Perhaps she knows what's best for her better than anyone else does".

"So have I been handling the situation the wrong way? Wanting my daughter home with her family?" Nell was defensive, which was unlike her.

Neville sighed. "Of course it's not wrong. But it's not straightforward either. She has been suffering from the effects of trauma for some time, then seeing those girls yesterday triggered a panic and brought it all back. Perhaps it will take her longer to get over it, really get over it than any of us expected".

"In that case what do we do? She's too young to make such important decisions".

"I don't like telling parents what to do where their children are concerned. It is not my business. But since you ask, I think there are a couple of courses open to you".

Nell and Patrick looked at him expectantly.

"One option is to seek professional advice. Ask for a referral to a psychiatric service for young people. That's quite a long-term solution; it may take many sessions for Brontë to build a relationship of trust with the counsellor and much longer to get to the root of the problem. Even then, there are no guarantees".

Neville stood up and wandered over to the window. There had been a frost that morning and the shaded part of the lawn still showed a sheen of white.

"I agree with Lois. The other possibility is simple. Just ask Brontë what she would like to do, let her decide". He saw that Nell was about to protest and pre-empted her objection. "No, don't look on it as giving in to her. Treat her as an adult and she will respond like one. I know you are anxious to have all your family back together my darling, but you may have to wait a little while for that. She's wiser than you think, but for reasons we don't fully understand, she is a very troubled girl. Now I think she may well ask to go back to Ireland straight after Christmas, and if she does, let her go with your blessing, explain to Bridget and the school and see how she is when we all go over for the wedding. Review the situation then. She won't be missing out on her education; by all accounts she's doing well at St Teresa's, and Kathleen says that she was happy at her Granny's."

"But the wedding's seven months away!"

"I know. But the time will pass quickly. If she had a serious physical illness, you wouldn't think twice about her undergoing months of treatment. I do think she will get over this in time but Patrick's right, it may have been too soon for her to come home after three months and hope that everything was going to be fine. But if she takes this at her own pace, then the recovery will follow, I'm sure of it".

Arlo, deciding that he had been ignored for long enough, started to wail. "He needs changing. I'll see to him". Nell picked him up, trying to hide her tears. On one hand she knew that her father, with all his years of experience and wisdom was right, but it didn't make it any easier to accept.

She attended to Arlo and settled him down for his afternoon nap. Then wearily she climbed the stairs to the second floor; Brontë was using the spare attic room while Kathleen was staying in Brontë's old bedroom.

"How are you feeling, sweetheart?"

"Still sore, and really tired. But I'll be ok, Mum. Can I get up for dinner?"

"Of course, if you're up to it. But let's have a chat now, while Arlo is sleeping. I've come to ask you what your plans are, for after Christmas, I mean".

Brontë looked at her mother in surprise. "Well Mummy, I would really like to go back to Granny's and to St Teresa's for the start of term. But I wasn't sure what you wanted me to do. I've been so worried. I know you'd like me to stay".

"We want whatever will help you the most, Brontë. And if that means returning to West Cork for a while longer, then that's all right. I know Granny is happy for you to go back. We will all miss you, that goes without saying, but we can see how you are at the end of the summer term, when we all come over for Kathleen's wedding and the baptisms".

Saying those words to Brontë was one of the most difficult things Nell had ever had to do. All her instincts were telling her to hold on to her daughter, to keep her close, to protect her. Yet perhaps to let her go was, in a way, to do what was best. The relief and gratitude on her daughter's face left her in no doubt that it was.

Chapter Fifty-Five

Christmas was everything Nell could have hoped for. All the family were present, except for Kathleen who had left for Spain the day before Christmas Eve. Some of the preparations had been left until the last minute because Nell had been preoccupied with Brontë, and Arlo who was showing signs of teething, needed a great deal of her attention. By the day before Christmas Eve, she was feeling more stressed than usual and wondered how everything would be ready on time. But somehow, with all the family helping, and Jenny staying on an extra hour here and there, it was.

They had all taken a hand in decorating the house with greenery, fairy lights and coloured baubles, and a magnificent tree stood in the hallway. Patrick had found one that just fitted, its top branch almost touching the ceiling. Arlo, watching them hang strings of stars and shiny decorations on its branches reached out from his baby chair and gurgled happily. Arthur and Henry fixed up some outdoor lights along the front of the house and these could be seen from the road below, twinkling through the trees and hedgerows at dusk.

Brontë tried to take part but at times was very quiet. She was sad to say goodbye to Kathleen whom she now thought of as an ally; someone whom she could trust and who really understood her – more so than her own parents. If only she had known that those feelings towards her parents were typical for a fourteen-year-old; as it was, the guilt was another burden to add to the layers of panic and terror she experienced every time she thought of the incident in Darcey's. But her mother had reassured her in one way; she could return to Ireland soon and Brontë was certain that everything would be better there. She imagined herself standing on the cliff top near the bay, only the sound of the wind and the gulls breaking the silence. She would find peace there again, no one would be unkind or spiteful, or put pressure on her.

Christmas Day passed in a haze of gift-opening, noise, games, music and treats. At three o'clock the family of nine sat down to a sumptuous turkey dinner. Despite all the distractions of the last few days, Nell had surpassed herself, but she was quick to deflect praise and reminded everyone how much help she had received from Jenny who also had Christmas in her own house to organise and cook for. Arlo was still too young for a highchair, but Patrick propped him up in his stroller beside the table so that he could see everything that was going on. Lois could not remember a Christmas she had enjoyed more; in Spain their celebrations were invariably low-key and quiet, but a boisterous family Christmas at Moongarth was anything but peaceful. Neville was pensive for a moment, remembering a time long ago – could it really be more than sixty-five years? – when he and his brother Henry spent a magical Christmas in this very house with Aunt Phoebe and Uncle Frederick. Dear Aunt Phoebe, who had spared no effort in making everything so special for them during that Christmas in 1931, which was to be Henry's last. This house has seen its fair share of sorrow in the past, he thought; but he watched his grandchildren laughing and shouting as they pulled crackers and read out jokes and riddles, the volume of happy noise rising and filling the room and felt that the balance was being restored.

They all shared in the clearing up after dinner, then Neville suggested a walk. Zacky, who was by now getting old, pricked up his ears to show his approval as they all wrapped up in coats and scarves and made for the front door. Lois decided to rest for half an hour, and Brontë said she would stay home too. "My leg still hurts, Mum. I'll keep Nanny Lois company".

As they walked down Hasker's Hill towards the village, Nell fell into step beside her husband. "Do you think Brontë is still in pain, Patrick, or is it an excuse not to go out?".

"I don't know. It's only been a few days since that fall. She had some bad bruising; it takes some getting over".

"She surely can't feel threatened on Christmas Day in her own village with all of her family around her?"

"I'm just as baffled as you are, Nelly. Who knows what's going on in her head?".

* * *

Lois, meanwhile, was glad of a few moments alone with her granddaughter.

"Things will get better, you know. Perhaps you just can't see it at the moment. There were times when nothing seemed to go right for your Grandpa and I, but now we've never been happier."

"I'm so pleased, Nanny. It's been lovely, all of us together for Christmas".

"For what it's worth, I think your mother and father have made the right decision to let you go back to stay with Granny, if that's where you feel you need to be. You're old enough to make up your own mind about this. Of course we'll miss you, your mother especially, but perhaps you did come home too soon. It's easy to be wise afterwards. But you will get over this upset; it's been a misfortune; one you could have done without but in a few months, you will look back and realise it's just something that happened in your life that you overcame. Something that made you brave and strong. Now tell me all about the guest house where you have this little job. I'm so looking forward to staying there when we come over to visit in the summer".

On Boxing Day, visitors came; Barbara and Jonathan, Joe and Ruth and Jenny and her husband Phil. Patrick insisted that Nell should have a day off from cooking, so a cold buffet lunch was laid out in the breakfast room. While Arlo was having a nap and the children were playing board games, Patrick opened a bottle of Irish whiskey for the adults while Nell and Barbara put on their coats and took a stroll through the garden and orchard, down to the edge of the field. Jacob trotted over to the fence immediately knowing that Nell might have some carrots in her pocket and as soon as this was confirmed, Jay followed in the hope of having his share.

"Something's bothering you" said Barbara knowingly. "Is it the interview? That's coming up soon, isn't it?"

"Well yes, it is, but I'm more worried about Brontë. You see, I thought three months in Ireland would be enough for her to get over all that business at school. I was looking forward to her coming home for good. She was reluctant to come home for Christmas, but Kathleen persuaded her, then on Friday...." Nell went on to tell her friend about the incident at Darcey's. "Barbara how did I get this so wrong? Patrick and I have had to agree to her going back, at least until next summer because that was the only thing that calmed her down. She's convinced that everything is fine over there, that's how it seems to her, but how can I explain to her that it's inside her head, it doesn't matter where she's living. Or perhaps I'm way off the mark, I just don't know what's best anymore".

"Mmm. It's difficult, but perhaps she really does feel better for being far away. Just for now. Even if that upset in Darcey's hadn't happened there might have been another trigger at some stage. I know you'll find it hard to part with her again but think of it this way – it's for a few more months now but maybe it will benefit the rest of her life. If you rush things, the recovery might take longer in the end".

"I suppose you're right. But is it being selfish, wanting your children with you?"

"Of course it's not. You're her mother, it's only natural that you want to protect her. But perhaps the best thing you can do for now is to let her go and not to let her see you're upset, that may make her feel worse. Tell her that if she's happy, you're happy. Even if it's a bit of a white lie. Go and ask her if she'd like to go back by ferry or does she feel up to flying to Cork on her own?"

Nell forced a smile. "You always make me feel better. Even when I'm close to giving up".

"Giving up? Not you. That's not the Nell I know. Let's go back in, it's getting chilly, and that mulled wine won't drink itself".

* * *

Brontë fastened her seat belt and looked forward to take-off. That's the part Auntie Kathleen didn't like, she said to herself, but I think it's exciting. As the engine roared and she felt the immense power lifting the aircraft off the ground, her next thought was, I'm going home. It was an extraordinary admission, since only three hours ago she had left the place where she had lived most of her life and had been brought up. But she could not deny it; those three months spent in West Cork had forged such an impression on her that she felt she belonged in the quiet lanes and desolate landscape, by the rugged coastline and in the cool sacred corridors of St Teresa's where she felt accepted and at ease with herself. She knew for certain that deep down, her mother understood but felt torn; Brontë's one regret about going back to Ireland was that she had created a dilemma for both her parents, and she felt a pang of guilt whenever she let those thoughts encroach on her mind.

Patrick and Nell had driven Brontë to the airport, having left Arlo with Jenny for the morning, then walked with her through the airport lounge as far as security. She felt grown-up, taking her first flight unaccompanied, but as she looked back and waved, she saw her father's comforting arm held tightly around her mother's shoulders and realised how hard it was for them to say goodbye to her. But I know it's the right thing for me, she thought, as the queue pressed forward. I know I'm right.

Chapter Fifty-Six

In no time at all it was twelfth night, and the interview panel was only a week away. Nell could not remember feeling more nervous when she was taking her 'A' levels or her driving test. She confided her fears to Patrick, who, being more pragmatic, reminded her that the Fostering Panel would put them at their ease and would be friendly, after all, they needed good responsible foster parents and would want them to succeed, they were not trying to catch them out.

Recalling the stern words from Helen Kimber about being open with her on all family matters, Nell telephoned her a few days before the interview to explain the upset Brontë had experienced just before Christmas, and that they had decided to let her go back to Ireland for a few more months. Mrs Kimber still sounded puzzled about this and asked Nell how she felt about splitting up the family again. Nell replied that she did not see it that way; it was a solution to a very difficult problem, and they needed to tread carefully. They all hoped to be reunited in the summer.

In Solibrio, Kathleen and Adam decided to close the bar for a few weeks' break during the winter; Adam needed to catch up on the business accounts and carry out a stock-take. Neville and Lois had made up their minds to stay in England permanently and Neville had signalled his intention to put the apartment in Spain up for sale; Adam was offered first refusal. The price Neville was asking him was a competitive one, several thousand below the market value, but he was hopeful of a quick sale, wishing to avoid the worry of long-drawn-out negotiations. There were other considerations too; he felt indebted to Adam for looking after the apartment while it was empty and for the small repairs and maintenance he had done for them. Lois had a more sentimental reason for them offering it to the couple; she was very fond of them both, especially Kathleen and somehow, she liked the thought of them being the next owners and living there, rather than strangers.

* * *

Sister Francis had only half-expected Brontë to return to St Teresa's for the new term. Nell had indicated in her letter in September that she was requesting a temporary placement for her daughter, but there had been no further details as to what 'temporary' might mean. Brontë's appearance in class on the fifth of January was therefore very welcome but had not been taken for granted.

Nell had written another letter to the school, explaining that Brontë had experienced a further emotional setback during the Christmas holidays and that as a result, her daughter had returned to live with her grandmother in Ballymere, at least until the following summer. In view of this, she would like to continue the arrangement with St Teresa's. Again, Nell had decided against divulging the precise nature of the bullying or the setback, but unlike Helen Kimber, Sister Francis was not given to speculation and accepted that unless Brontë herself ever wished to disclose more information, the subject would not be raised. The fact that Patrick had enclosed a generous cheque towards school funds did not influence her; St Teresa's was funded by the Catholic Church in Ireland and by donations from some of the parents and other patrons, but whatever their background, the girls were all treated alike. Nevertheless, Sister Francis could see that Brontë might need some specific help; she had watched with interest her progress during the previous term and noted that on the surface, she had settled well and seemed content. But experience told her that a slow and gentle approach, perhaps with some less conventional therapy, might help Brontë to overcome whatever was troubling her so deeply.

On the second day of term, Sister Francis asked to see her.

"I'm very pleased you have returned to us for a while longer, Brontë. You made a good start last term, your test results in most subjects were well above average. The change in schools doesn't seem to have impacted you at all. Well done!"

"Thank you, Sister. I was very happy to come back. I feel better already...." Her voice trailed away, hoping that she would not be asked to explain.

"Good. Now I have a suggestion for you, well, as a matter of fact, I need some help with something, and you may be the right person". She paused for a moment and looked out of the window.

"Do you like gardens, Brontë?"

"Yes...well I suppose so. We have a big garden at home, with an orchard and lots of flowers. In the summer we have meals out there and picnics". Brontë wondered where this was leading.

"We have extensive gardens here; you will have seen them. Sister Bernice is our gardener, she doesn't have a teaching role, but she is in her eighties now and has arthritis in her hands and hips. How would you feel about helping Sister Bernice in the garden? Perhaps for an hour or so after school some days when the evenings get lighter in the spring, and occasionally during the lunch hour or free study time?"

"Yes Sister, I'd like to do that. I don't know much about gardening though, but I could help".

"I should explain, Sister Bernice came to us from a silent order. Do you know what that means?"

Brontë shook her head.

"At her previous order, the nuns didn't speak, only out of necessity. It's a spiritual devotion, a form of holy discipline. It's believed that this helps the Sisters feel closer to God. But it's not for everyone. Here, we are mainly a teaching order, that is our calling".

Brontë listened, intrigued. "I think I can understand that a little. There are many times when I just wish everything could be quiet, so that I could sort out my thoughts".

"Exactly so. Silence is very under-rated in this modern world, in my opinion. That's why I introduced the quiet half hour at the beginning of the school day. So, do you think you could work with Sister Bernice? She does communicate now, but mainly to give instructions or to answer questions. There will be no gossiping, no trivial chit-chat. But you will learn a great deal, and there is much to be said for watching things grow, tending to plants, and listening to nature".

"When should I start?"

"Not this week – settle back into class and go and see Sister Bernice next Monday. Remember your schoolwork is still important and you have made some nice friends. You will want to spend some time with them. Thank you Brontë, I am sure this will work out well".

Brontë left the Sister's office feeling bemused. To be asked to work in the school garden with an elderly Sister who rarely spoke was the last thing she expected. But the more she thought about it, the more the idea of spending time gardening in companionable silence appealed to her. She felt that she could learn from the experience, and suddenly she understood why some people found that working closely with nature could be curative. I can't wait, she thought.

At the weekend Brontë returned to her little job at Hackett's. There was a new young man working behind the bar. He introduced himself as Ruari and it turned out that he was the elder brother of Kitty, her friend from school. He asked her how she had enjoyed her Christmas holiday.

"It was ok but I'm glad to be back at Granny's" she said shyly. She had so little experience of talking to boys, except for her brothers. At Lamberham she rarely had anything to do with the boys in her class in case it became the cause of taunts and unpleasant comments. But Ruari seemed nice, he was friendly without being pushy or over-confident.

Like Niamh, he was surprised that Brontë had wanted to return to the area when so many young people couldn't wait to leave. But he was wise enough not to ask questions; there was something about her, he realised, something troubled. Maybe one day he would find out, but sensed that whatever it was, it must have been serious enough for her to leave England and her family. A mystery, he thought, but not my business. If I'm meant to find out, then it will happen.

Chapter Fifty-Seven

January 1998

It was the ninth of January, and the interview day had come. Numerous visits, meetings and training sessions had taken place over several months, and all family members and friends had been questioned at length. Pages of notes had been made by the social workers, and innumerable questions asked. Arlo's health and development had been closely monitored, and the family home had been inspected. Even the couple's finances had been scrutinised. But at the end of this journey – or was it the beginning of another – Nell and Patrick sat waiting to be called in for the final important meeting with the Fostering Panel, who would decide whether they could be confirmed officially as foster parents.

They had brought Arlo with them – they could not leave him with Jenny for what might be an unknown length of time, but also because Nell and Patrick felt that as this meeting was to decide his future, he should be present. They were to be interviewed separately and together. Charlie Weston, who was to support them through the interview process joined them in the waiting room. Nell was called in first with Charlie, while Patrick waited outside with Arlo.

The panel consisted of Helen Kimber as Chair, Mary Curtis who was deputising for the head of Children's Services and Colin Wheeler from the Council Education Authority. Three other people introduced themselves, two of whom were already foster carers and a senior paediatric nurse.

The circumstances around Arlo being left with the Walshes was explained to the panel by Helen Kimber and Charlie added some background information. Nell had the impression that none of them apart from Helen and Charlie had any prior knowledge of how he had come to live with the family, so she felt that they had no preconceived ideas about the situation. That's good, she thought, they've not had time to become biased one way or the other. The panel members were welcoming and amiable; Patrick had been right when he said that they would all be keen to have a good outcome and to be certain that Arlo would be cared for in a loving and secure home.

Nell was questioned about her parenting skills and the upbringing of their five children, how did she ensure some individual time with each of them, how did they get on with each other, how did she manage such a large family? She was asked how her children had received the news that their parents were planning to foster Arlo. Was there any jealousy, any resentment? How did she deal with conflict? The panel seemed less interested in the children's educational achievements and were more concerned as to how they interacted with others and the level of support and encouragement they received from their parents. She then had to describe a situation where a difficult decision was made regarding one of her children. She explained how they had re-homed two donkeys to help their youngest daughter overcome a tendency to self-importance and to learn a sense of responsibility; this was already proving a success. Then, deciding it was better to volunteer the information rather than have to react to difficult questions, and taking a deep breath, she told the panel of her eldest daughter's experience with school bullying and how she and Patrick had arranged for her to stay with her grandmother in Ireland for a time in order to recover, and to continue her schooling there.

This was received with some surprise by most of the panel members; one commented that it must have been very serious bullying to have necessitated a move to another country. Nell replied that it was, mentally crossing her fingers that she would not be asked to go into detail. No one did ask; but Nell added that the bullying was such that it was a cause of great concern, and due to her daughter being extremely sensitive she had struggled in mainstream education for some time. The regime and low numbers at the convent school were more suited to her, and she was doing well. To her relief, the panel seemed to accept this and moved onto the subject of Nell's support network and family background.

Patrick was asked similar questions and how he felt about fostering a child when his own children were growing up. He replied honestly that becoming a foster parent had not been his first thought when Arlo was left with them and it had taken him a while to come round to the idea, but he fully supported his wife's wish to go ahead with fostering, and he spoke of the close bond which had developed between Nell and the baby; as time went on he had become fond of Arlo himself. When asked about his own background he explained that he was one of seven siblings, so he had grown up in a large family. Two of his brothers had also moved to England and lived locally so the extended family were very much a part of their lives; one of his sisters was a frequent visitor and was godmother to his eldest daughter. At the end of the interview, he was questioned about his future expectations of fostering. Patrick found this difficult to answer. He replied that he had no real expectations other than to provide a safe and happy home for Arlo and that as a family they could give him a good start in life, despite such tragic beginnings. This seemed to go down well with the panel; they nodded in agreement but clearly were not going to give anything away as to their decision at that stage.

Finally, Nell was called back in, and the panel were introduced to Arlo, who was at that moment wide awake and alert. "He's teething" said Nell, explaining his red cheeks. Some more general conversation followed, mainly about the procedures for decision-making and timescales. Helen thanked them for attending and for coming forward as foster parents, and for the excellent care they were providing for Arlo. The decision would be notified to them within the next two weeks.

"Well! That wasn't too bad, was it?" said Patrick as they made their way out of the council offices to the car park.

"No, you're right, so why did I feel as though we were being interrogated, or having to prove something? I almost felt as though I was in the wrong somehow, even though we are offering to do what not many people would do, take on an unknown child as our own for an unlimited length of time, without really knowing how or why he came into our lives. It's all a bit strange, isn't it?"

"It is, and that's a fact. You realise, don't you, that we may never have answers to those questions. And when Arlo is older and starts to ask about his birth parents, we won't be able to tell him much. I was thinking the other day, we're not even sure if Denny Reid is his real father. We don't know if anything he said was true".

Nell stopped in her tracks. "Patrick! You've just given me a thought. The police took a DNA swab from Arlo, and they extracted some of Denny's from the rucksack. Surely that would prove whether he was the father or not? Do you think the police only looked for a match on the database? The database as it was then, before Denny's or Arlo's samples were entered?"

"I don't see what you're getting at...."

"Well, they said there wasn't a match on the database, but did they compare the two samples to test for parentage? If they did, they certainly didn't tell us the result".

Patrick looked thoughtful. "You could have a point. It's so obvious now you've mentioned it. But we don't know how these things work, we're not experts. Those forensic people, they're so highly qualified. Surely they couldn't have missed something like that in plain sight? And as you say, why didn't they tell us? This situation has more twists and turns than a crime novel".

"Should we go back to the police and ask them? I know it won't change anything where the fostering is concerned, but as you say, when Arlo asks questions in years to come, at least we can say with some certainty that either Denny was his father, or that both of his parents are unknown. He has a right to know that much".

Patrick looked at her, and then at Arlo, now sleeping contentedly in his stroller. "Poor little fellow. It's a very basic right to know who your parents are. Even adopted children are allowed to find that out these days. But if no one knows, how can he ever find out...? I feel so sad for him. We must do whatever we can".

"Foundlings" said Nell, pensively. "That's what they used to be called. Abandoned babies, I mean. I read it somewhere, I've just remembered. It's an old-fashioned word, isn't it? I suppose it happened more often in times gone by. Even less chance of tracing the parents in those days. I think the babies were often named after the place where they were found".

"Let's make Arlo a sort of scrap book, Nell. The children can help. You know, anything we can piece together to give him what information we can. We'll start with some photos of him and our family from last September. You could write a sort of journal for him, telling him what happened and all the efforts that were made to find out about his parents, and why we fostered him. Then we could give it to him when he's old enough to understand".

"Good idea. We'll start straightaway. I forgot to ask the panel what surname Arlo should be given. At the doctors I gave his name as Arlo Walsh, I hope that was ok. Let's just hope we're approved as his foster family, after all this!"

Chapter Fifty-Eight
January 1998

Kathleen purchased her wedding outfit in a small exclusive vintage shop 'Bella Antigua' in Malaga during the few weeks while Martina's was closed.

When she thought of the cheap, ugly dress she had been forced to wear at her first wedding twenty years ago, she cringed with embarrassment and occasionally with anger. She had never felt less like a bride that day; in fact, she was glad that there were very few photos of her wedding as it was not something she wished to remember. But this time it would be different; the outfit would be her choice, on her terms; this dress would be special.

Acknowledging that she was now approaching forty, Kathleen was careful to choose a dress that was suitable for a more mature bride but at the same time she wanted it to be glamorous and eye-catching. It was not too much to ask, she thought, for a bride, whatever her age, to be the centre of attention on her wedding day but it had to be the right sort of attention. She dismissed the thought of meringue-style gowns with full skirts and corset tops; what she had in mind was something more unusual. She had retained her slim figure; middle-age spread had not yet become a problem and only a very few traces of grey could be seen in her hair, but the dress she had set her heart on was one which very few younger women would have chosen.

The dress was not new, but she suspected it had only ever been worn once, probably decades before, possibly for a wedding or a special occasion. It was still immaculate, and the shop assistant assured her that it had been dry cleaned with the utmost care. It was a nineteen twenties flapper dress in ivory silk, sleeveless but calf length, with a neckline low enough to be in keeping with the style and high enough to be modest. But what made it perfect as a wedding dress was the sheer overlay in filmy, cream coloured organza, which was fastened to the main garment with two strands of beautiful pearl beading at the neck and shoulder. Two further bands of the same beading had been added just above the hemline of the underneath layer. The overall effect was stunning; it was like no other wedding gown Kathleen had ever seen but it was exactly right for an older bride for whom a traditional dress in virginal white would not have been appropriate.

To complete the outfit, Kathleen chose cream low-heeled shoes and a cloche hat in a matching colour with a narrow brim, trimmed with satin ribbon and a cluster of pearl beads and sparkly crystals on one side. She had originally wanted to wear elbow length white gloves but decided that it would be too fiddly to have to remove them during the exchanging of rings.

When she looked at the ensemble in the full-length mirror in the shop, she felt elated and thrilled at her reflection, and something else – empowered. Adam would be proud of her she felt sure, and her mother would be unable to deny the transformation of her once dowdy daughter. This time she looked forward to having lots of photos taken and maybe her wedding would be featured in the Ballymere Post. So what if Michael saw it, so much the better. She wondered if he would even recognise her.

* * *

Late one afternoon during the first week of term, Henry went to see his grandfather at the Swan's Rest. Something was troubling him, but his parents had been preoccupied that week with the Fostering Panel, and he did not want to bother them; also he thought he knew what his mother would say about his dilemma, even if his father was more likely to be open-minded.

"Grandpa, can I talk to you about something?"

The request took Neville back to his teaching days, when pupils might ask his advice but in a more formal way.

He met Henry in the hotel lobby. Lois was not having a good day and was in a great deal of pain, more than she would admit to. It was the worst time of year for her as the cold weather often made a flare-up of her condition more likely, so rather than join her husband and grandson in the coffee lounge, she said she was happy to stay in their own suite of rooms and listen to some music on the radio. This was a very different Lois from times gone by – she was more self-sufficient now and able to manage her symptoms in a way that was less dependent, less needy. It had taken decades, but Lois had matured; the emotional development in her early life was stunted by the domination of her mother, and her youth and best years had been marred by ill health and trauma. But now it seemed that the butterfly had at last emerged from the chrysalis and was making up for lost time, despite the occasional setback.

Neville ordered tea and cakes for them both and asked him what was on his mind.

"I don't know what to do for the best, Grandpa. Uncle Sean has arranged for some work experience for me at Lovells, they're a civil engineering firm here in Kirchington. If it all works out, they could offer me an apprenticeship later on when I've taken my 'A' levels. It would lead to a degree. But I know Mum is set on me going to university. She will be so disappointed if I don't".

"What does your father think?"

"To be honest, Dad still thinks in terms of me learning a trade. That was so important when he was growing up. A proper apprenticeship would be much more than that, of course. But I know he doesn't like to oppose Mum's wishes over this sort of thing, so he hasn't said much so far".

Neville looked thoughtful.

"The one thing I've learned over many years, Henry, is not to tell people what they should do. Occasionally you have to, of course, but in my experience, it's better to set out the options for people and then let them decide for themselves. So that's what I propose to do". He refilled their cups.

"Your father has a point. A trade, with practical skills is always a good plan. You would be able to earn decent money after a while, like your Uncle Niall. He's done well in your father's firm, hasn't he? There is always work in the construction industry. And you might be able to train others, in time.

On the other hand, as you say, a formal apprenticeship in civil engineering would be a wonderful qualification. We will always need highly trained engineers and there are lots of different branches of engineering to explore. It's what keeps the infrastructure, the modernisation and the safety of our country going. Engineers build a better world, find solutions for the future. That's hugely important.

A university degree, well that's different. It doesn't really matter what subject you read, it's partly an indication that you've been educated to a high level and been disciplined enough to persevere and get through your finals. But it's so much more than that – and I think I know why your Mum is so keen on it. It's the whole experience of university life, the gaining of independence, self-reliance, mixing with a whole range of people from very different backgrounds. It helps you to navigate your way through life and to sort out your ideas, your priorities, your strengths. Often it is an opening to a great career, or sometimes it's just something people want to do, so they can say they've done that and have letters after their name. Your mother would most likely have gone to university, if things had been different. She certainly had the brains, and the motivation. She worked very hard at school, always had good grades".

Henry looked uncomfortable. "Grandpa, are you saying that Mum sacrificed all that for us?"

For the briefest of moments, Neville was tempted to say 'yes, she did'. He had not completely forgotten how his hopes and dreams for his only daughter had been dashed, many years ago. But instead, he smiled at his grandson and shook his head.

"Your mother never had a moment's regret. Family life means everything to her, and Nanny and I are proud of you all. You see, she had a very lonely childhood, no brothers or sisters, no cousins, very few friends. It's understandable that she wanted to be the centre of a big family – that has meant just as much to her over the years as a university education. I'm not surprised to hear that she would like to see you go to university, it's something she never managed to do herself. But the only advice I shall give you on that score is, don't take the university option just to please your Mum, or to do it because she wasn't able to. Make up your own mind based on what you want, whatever you feel is right for you. You have quite a few months before you need to decide, take that time to think it over and you will make the right choice in the end, I'm sure of it".

As Henry waited for the bus to take him home to Drover's Cross, he reflected on his grandfather's words and felt that a huge weight had been lifted from his shoulders. He alone would decide where his future lay, and he would make that choice for the right reasons.

* * *

A fortnight later, the all-important letter arrived for Nell and Patrick, preceded by a congratulatory phone call from Charlie Weston. They had been officially accepted as foster parents.

Chapter Fifty-Nine

The letter contained further papers to be signed, information leaflets, contacts for help and support and a statement reminding Nell and Patrick of their responsibilities towards Arlo and any children they might foster in the future. Patrick looked at Nell with a wry smile when he read the last paragraph.

"That's a bit ambitious. I'm not used to being a foster parent to Arlo yet, let alone any further children".

"This may be a one-off, Patrick" said Nell seriously. "In a way, it's a solution that was made to fit the circumstances. Very unusual circumstances. But thank goodness we have been approved, at least Arlo can have some stability with us, and we know where we stand officially".

There was a further document explaining the fostering allowance to which they were entitled, and a separate fund for expenses, which was to ensure that Arlo would receive the same material benefits as Patrick and Nell's own children. Considering that this was backdated to when they first started looking after Arlo, it came to a substantial sum. Patrick looked thoughtful.

"We may need to buy a bigger car, Nell. One that can seat all the family in comfort. We will need that when we go home for the wedding". Patrick still referred to Ireland as 'home', even though nearly half his life had been spent in England. "I'll start looking next week".

Nell went back into the kitchen where Jenny was feeding Arlo some baby porridge. She had started to wean him after Christmas; the health visitor had agreed that assuming Arlo was now six or seven months old, Nell could introduce him to some solid food, but his face was showing some puzzlement at the feel of the spoon in his mouth. She sat at the table and looked at him, feeling a well of emotion as he recognised her and smiled. "You're now one of us, Arlo, it's official. This is your family; we all love you. No one can take you away now". She said those words hoping that over the years to come, they would be proved true – and that with every passing week, the possibility of anyone claiming him might become less likely. Occasionally she woke in the night in a panic, the thought of Arlo being handed over to a stranger was a distressing one. At those times Patrick tried to calm her, reminding her that even in the unlikely event of both of his birth parents turning up on their doorstep, the authorities would first and foremost consider the fact that Arlo was settled, happy and much loved in his foster family and that abandonment of a child, for whatever reason would probably disqualify his own family, whoever they were, from claiming him when it suited them. Knowing Patrick to be right, and that his words echoed those of the social workers did reassure Nell to a certain extent, but the fear continued to lurk in a far corner of her mind, although she did her best to disregard it most of the time.

* * *

Torrential rain prevented Brontë from making any meaningful progress in the school garden for the first few weeks of January. She did make several visits to the garden between the showers and was always surprised to find Sister Bernice there whatever the weather, sometimes cleaning garden tools, reading seed catalogues or raking up dead leaves and cuttings. She must be so tough, despite being in her eighties, thought Brontë, and for a moment felt slightly ashamed that she, at the age of fourteen, could be put off outdoor work so easily. But in February there was an improvement in the weather and Brontë started to help in earnest, having been given permission to work in the garden during free study periods three times a week. She was unused to physical work and after the first week of preparing vegetable seed beds, weeding, laying mulch and pruning, her limbs ached, and her hands felt rough and blistered. But this feeling of tiredness was different from the mental fatigue caused by sitting at her studies for too long; working in the fresh air had given her a healthy glow and she felt a sense of well-being. Already she was learning from Sister Bernice, and Brontë soon discovered that despite having been told that her mentor spoke little, instructions and information necessitated more conversation between them than she had been led to expect. Sister Bernice explained how to prune shrubs and roses correctly to encourage the maximum re-growth and flowering later in the year; how to cut back hardy plants that had over-wintered in the greenhouse, and Brontë was permitted to choose a variety of sweet peas to sow indoors from seed. "These are my mother's favourite flowers" she said without thinking, then almost regretted speaking, wondering if that comment would have been thought trivial and therefore unnecessary. But Sister Bernice nodded and smiled, looking pleased.

That first evening Brontë started a gardening journal. She decided to write it in two sections each day: 'What I did today' and 'Things I have learned'. It was quite basic and sometimes the information overlapped, but that didn't matter. Time spent trimming and pruning led on to the rules and techniques she had observed, what type of secateurs were best for different tasks, what time of year was best to prepare the ground for seedlings, and why some plants thrived better in light sandy soil, and some needed more shade or moist ground. On a day in late February when Sister Bernice pointed out some tiny green curls emerging from what Brontë had rejected as a bundle of dead dry sticks but was in fact a clump of ferns, she was excited and couldn't wait to make it a feature of that day's journal entry.

One afternoon, Sister Bernice showed her the kitchen garden which would soon need digging over and weeding. Brontë's face must have betrayed a trace of dismay, but she tried to hide it, remembering that in previous years Sister Bernice would have dug the whole patch and weeded it single-handedly. When she was shown the planting plan which the Sister had drawn and mapped in some detail,

Brontë could see in her mind's eye the rows of salad, beetroot, carrots and cabbage which would be harvested in the summer, and the thought made her dismiss the prospect of heavy work, knowing that there would be rewards later. As well as the vegetables there was to be a herbery; herbs for cooking and for healing, explained the Sister, nodding wisely; and strawberry beds, raspberry canes and some blackcurrant bushes, with several apple and plum trees promising autumn fruit in abundance.

Often Brontë was given instructions then left to work alone. She did not mind this; it gave her some precious thinking time and being at one with her thoughts with birdsong all around her and occasionally a drift of choral or hymn singing coming from the chapel was both calming and uplifting. Having spotted a robin perched precariously on the handle of a spade, she watched as he flew off round a corner. On an impulse, she followed him quietly. He's like the robin that showed the way in The Secret Garden, one of her favourite stories, she thought. Hearing a gentle murmuring, she saw Sister Bernice standing beside a beehive, clutching her rosary beads. Fearing that she had interrupted the Sister at prayer, Brontë turned to leave, but Sister Bernice called softly to her. "Come, child. Wasn't I just telling the bees that you have come to help me in the garden. And thanking God that He has sent you. It's always right to tell the bees about any changes, or anything that is on your mind. They have a wisdom all their own, and they like to hear good news, just as we do". She smiled enigmatically. Brontë nodded but didn't know what to say. It was the longest speech that she had ever heard the nun make. She returned to weeding the herbaceous border, all the time thinking what an extraordinary piece of knowledge the Sister had just imparted. Was it hocus pocus or superstition? She didn't think so. Bees were creatures of great skill and importance in nature, vital for pollination of crops and flowers, she knew that, and of course they produced honey which she sometimes spread on her breakfast toast, and she had heard that it lasted for decades without spoiling.

So they must be very special and extremely clever. Somehow, talking to such amazing insects didn't seem ridiculous at all. They would be worthy of a whole page of her journal, not forgetting the robin who had led her to them.

* * *

Kathleen and Adam were to return to Ireland for a few weeks at the beginning of March. The visit was primarily for them to finalise their wedding arrangements, and they were also to take the planned trip to County Galway so that Adam could find out more about his Irish ancestors. But they were to stop over for a few nights to see Nell and Patrick and the children on the way.

The packing and transporting of her wedding outfit for their flight from Malaga to England gave Kathleen some nervous moments. She had a recurring nightmare that her suitcase or the contents were seriously damaged or never appeared on the luggage carousel, to be lost forever. She checked the terms of their travel insurance several times, then decided that even if the worst came to the worst, no amount of financial compensation would enable her to replace the unique outfit that she had chosen so carefully. The second part of their journey from Drover's Cross to Ireland was to be by hire car and ferry, which somehow Kathleen felt gave her a greater amount of control over the precious items.

The family at Moongarth were overjoyed to see them, although it had only been a few weeks since their visit just before Christmas. The news about Nell and Patrick's acceptance as foster parents for Arlo was the first topic of conversation, and Kathleen picked him up and cuddled him, as excited as everyone else that he was now officially one of the family.

Soon after their arrival, Patrick, Arthur and Henry took Adam down to The Herders in the village for a beer while Nell finished preparing dinner for them all. Kathleen took the opportunity to ask Nell about Brontë.

"She's back with your Mam, of course" said Nell, basting a joint of beef and returning it to the oven. "I wasn't keen on the idea of her going back again but she's happy, that's the main thing. To be honest Kathleen, I'm grateful to your Mam but I feel a bit of a failure that my own daughter can't be just as happy at home here with us". Her eyes were full of tears.

Kathleen felt a huge wave of sympathy for her sister-in-law who had done so much to help her over the years and to change her life, yet who was completely unable to resolve her own dilemmas. "You're not a failure Nell, never think that. You're the perfect mother. Look at your lovely family, they all adore you, especially Brontë. She hasn't rejected you, or any of you, she just needs space and time away from everything that's happened. It's the circumstances that have caused this, not anything you've done or not done. Think of Ireland as a solution, not a problem".

The two women hugged, then Nell, drying her eyes said, "I think that as the men are all in the pub, we deserve a glass of something". She knew that Kathleen did enjoy a drink occasionally and that she had long ago taken control of a habit which, had her life not taken a very different turn, could have been her downfall. But at that moment Emer rushed in, demanding that Auntie Kathleen must come and see the donkeys before it grew dark. As she walked with Emer to the back door, Kathleen watched Ronnie playing with Arlo, who threw down a soft toy and laughed when Ronnie picked it up for him to repeat the game time after time. For just a fleeting moment, she experienced a pang of envy. She had met Adam too late in life, she realised, to have a family of her own. It was not impossible, but unlikely. Then she gave herself a mental shake. She was to marry the man of her dreams whom she loved more than she could say and who loved her unconditionally. What was that line from an old movie? Don't ask for the moon; we have the stars. A happy future with Adam was all she would ever need.

Chapter Sixty

March 1998

Lois, Neville, Sean and Niall joined the family for the evening meal, so it was a large gathering that sat down to dine, a little later than planned. There was a great deal of discussion about wedding plans, and inevitably the subject turned to dresses, flowers and music. Kathleen, as with all brides, refused to reveal any details of her outfit, saying that they would all just have to wait for the big day, and Lois, who was especially fond of Kathleen, said she was absolutely right to keep it a secret, but Emer was having none of it. "I really must know what your dress is like, it's important as I may have to carry the train."

Kathleen smiled. "Here's a clue. There's no train, so no need to worry. That's all I'm telling you".

Emer looked disappointed for a moment, but not to be outdone, turned to the subject of her own wardrobe. "I have two new dresses, one as a bridesmaid and one for my Holy Baptism. One is dark green, the baptism dress is white, and I shall wear the same white shoes with both dresses. I may carry different flowers...."

Ronnie spoke up. "It's not a fashion parade Emer, you aren't going on the catwalk".

"What's a catwalk?"

Nell and Patrick rolled their eyes, and the others laughed. "Does she ever give up?" said Patrick despairingly. "Well, it's nothing to do with cats, for a start. And Ronnie's right, the wedding is not all about you and what you are wearing, it will be Auntie Kathleen's day. And as you're going to be baptised, it's time you learned what it means, and it's not about dressing up. I'm going to arrange for you and Ronnie to go to classes with Father Egan to prepare you, and Granny will be checking up to make sure you've been listening".

After the younger ones left the table and Nell took Arlo to be bathed before bedtime, Patrick mentioned the DNA samples and that they were wondering if the police had tested them for a match. "You see, they said that neither of the samples matched with the database" he explained. "But what we don't know is whether they've been compared to see if Denny is in fact Arlo's father. Surely the police would have picked this up".

Adam agreed that it was very unlikely that the forensic department would have missed something so obvious. "But there's no harm in ringing them to check. If there was no match, they probably didn't think it was worth telling you. But if there was.... well.... it's a start. You need every bit of information"

"I'll ring them tomorrow," said Patrick. "Now how about a glass of Irish? We're going to be brothers-in-law; I need to know your poison. How about you, Sis?"

"Going back to the subject of the wedding, Patrick" said Kathleen, refusing the whiskey but opting for a tonic water instead; "as Dad is no longer with us, will you give me away?"

Patrick looked at his sister fondly. The transformation in her never failed to astound him. He thought of how she was twenty years ago before he came to England; angry, depressed, down-at-heel, losing hope with her life and with no motivation to change. Yet before him now was this smart, confident, stylish woman who had completely reinvented herself and exuded happiness. "I'd be honoured to give you away, Kathleen" he said, and meant it.

* * *

It took a long time for WPC Drummond to come to the phone when Patrick telephoned the police station the following day.

He had decided to take a few hours off work that morning; apart from the phone call he had some paperwork to

419

complete, and he wanted to take the opportunity to spend some time with Kathleen and Adam before they travelled on to Ireland. It would be the last time they all met up before the wedding. "No point in being the boss if you can't please yourself occasionally" he said, jokingly.

Patrick asked the WPC if there was any further information she could give him regarding the DNA testing. There was a pause.

"We did report back to you on that, Mr Walsh. There was no match".

"What I am getting at is, did you compare the two samples?"

"We did. A small amount of DNA was recovered from the rucksack, but it was not of sufficient quality to prove without doubt that there was a match between Arlo and Denny Reid. So nothing conclusive I'm afraid. I know you must be anxious to find out, but there's no more we can tell you at this stage. I'm sorry".

"Ok. It was only a long shot, I suppose, but we thought it was worth asking".

"How is Arlo?"

"He's grand, we are officially his foster parents now, so that's a load off our mind. We expect him to be with us for the longer term, so he's really one of the family already".

"It's a good thing you're doing. As he's so young, he won't remember what happened to him when he was left with you. It's a strange story, isn't it? We would have expected to have more leads by now, but there simply haven't been any".

"We try not to think about it too much now," said Patrick. "Speculation doesn't get us anywhere and it just makes Nell upset. In a way we would rather things stay as they are; Arlo is settled and happy and we love having him".

"Well, if there's a breakthrough we'll be in touch". She rang off.

Patrick made light of this conversation to Nell. There was, as he had remarked to Tina Drummond, no point in wondering. They both thought of Arlo as their sixth child now, and his health and happiness were all that mattered.

* * *

Bridget and Brontë couldn't wait to welcome the travellers home in early March. This time Kathleen was to remain in Ballymere until her wedding, although they would be taking a few days out to travel on to Galway for Adam to research his family tree, after which he would need to return to Spain for a while, although no date had been decided. The plan was for them to stay with Connor and Gráinne at the farm where there was a spare bedroom, but as always there would be many visits between the houses for meals and cups of tea, and Kathleen was anxious to see Aunt Angela to check the number of rooms at the guest house to be set aside for wedding guests.

Knowing that Nell was keen to have firsthand news of her daughter, Kathleen took Brontë to one side as soon as she had an opportunity to see Brontë alone.

"You look well, Brontë. Your skin looks beautiful and you're so slim, what have you been doing?"

Brontë hugged her aunt, and they walked down the laneway together for a little way. Kathleen needed to stretch her legs after the long drive.

"I work in the garden at St Teresa's now, a few times a week when I have free study time. I really like it; I think the exercise has helped me lose a bit more weight. I've learned a lot. I help Sister Bernice; she doesn't speak much but she's very kind".

This was not what Kathleen had expected to hear, and if she was surprised at the revelation, she did her best not to show it. "Well, it's certainly doing you good" she said approvingly. "But don't lose any more weight or we'll have to have your bridesmaid dress altered!"

"Will you be back for St Patrick's Day, Auntie? There's going to be a big party at Hackett's, we've been planning the decorations, Aunt Angela has booked a band and there'll be dancing". Her eyes shone. How different from the girl she had said goodbye to before Christmas, thought Kathleen. But at the same time her heart went out to her sister-in-law whose dearest wish was for her daughter to be with her family in England, and who might have felt sad to see how Brontë sparkled with fun in a way she seldom did back home.

Later, after Brontë had gone to bed, Kathleen and Adam sat for a while with Bridget who was full of excitement about the forthcoming wedding, and as he could tell that the two women were clearly set on discussion of every detail, Adam decided to walk up to the farm to see Connor.

He too, felt at home here in West Cork. He had been brought up in New South Wales and had lived for many years in Spain but there was something about this place, something magical that he could not define. He could understand in a way how many people, even after years of exile or separation could still feel the pull of their Irish homeland, despite its sad history, constantly changing weather and the financial hardship experienced by so many. Kathleen is different here too, he reflected. She has slotted back into her native country as if she'd never been away, yet she loves our life in Spain. He was excited about the trip to Galway – how strange that he had discovered he had Irish ancestry soon after he had met Kathleen. Would there still be any Keenans living in Lankerris; if so, should he make an approach? He knew only a very few facts: that his great grandfather William Keenan was born in eighteen thirty in Lankerris and that his name was on the passenger list of a convict ship which sailed from Limerick in eighteen forty-eight. He thought it possible that William Keenan might have been a convict, although some emigrants did travel independently on such ships if they could pay for their fare; their main aim being to search for a better life than Ireland could offer. Adam knew that the Great Hunger in Ireland which he had learned about from his history lessons happened in the mid nineteenth century, although poor harvests and famine continued for decades after that. If William was not a convict it was likely that he was trying, like many others, to escape poverty and starvation. The story about William meeting his future wife during that sea voyage was hearsay; he had no way of verifying it, but he did know that William married Roisin Murray soon after arriving in Sydney; that was on record, although her name was not on the list of passengers. It sounded like an Irish name, so it could not be ruled out.

* * *

If Adam and Kathleen had hoped for a wealth of local knowledge about the Keenan family at the church of St Mary the Immaculate Heart at Lankerris, they were to be disappointed.

They had travelled up to County Galway on Saturday and stayed that evening at a bed-and-breakfast guest house overlooking Dingle Bay. The journey along the Wild Atlantic Way was stunning, the coastline certainly living up to its name on that blustery March day. Kathleen realised how little she knew about her own country, not having ventured any further than Cork City in her early life; in fact, the trip to Rosslare when she first crossed the Irish Sea to England had been an adventure to her. Strangely, she realised she was more familiar with the Mediterranean coastline than the shores of the Atlantic on the west coast of Ireland where she had been brought up. Perhaps you take more notice of places where you are happy, she reflected; if so, her feelings for Ireland might be about to change for the better. With Adam at her side and her dream wedding only a few months away she could not fail but to be elated and optimistic.

After an early start on the Sunday, they drove into Lankerris village by mid-morning in the expectation of finding the parish church and that they would be able to speak to the priest at the end of Mass. He was sure to be familiar with the names of local people in such a small community, and with any luck he might have known more than one generation.

But on arrival, they found the church to be in ruins. The roof had long since fallen in and only two of the stained-glass windows were still intact. Evidently the entire site was dangerous, with steel railings preventing any attempts to gain closer access, and several 'Keep Out' notices explaining the risk of falling masonry.

It was a major setback, but the graveyard was still accessible, although the grass was knee-high in places. Wordlessly, they wandered among ancient crumbling gravestones, many of which leaned over at precarious angles. Clearly no one had tended these graves for decades; most of the lettering had been eroded by age, weather and the overgrowth of moss and lichen. Occasionally a letter or number could be deciphered but all in all, it was a huge disappointment. The atmosphere was one of neglect and decay, but now and then birdsong broke the silence, and the distant bleating of lambs could be heard.

"There's nothing here to help us" said Adam, regretfully. "I wonder what happened to the church. I suppose there just wasn't enough money for upkeep, it's only a small village".

They were about to return to the car when an elderly man appeared, walking through what remained of the pathway from a gate at the far side. He looked at them curiously.

"Sure and there's not many visitors to this church now, it's nearly forgotten altogether" he said in a friendly way. Obviously, any stranger looking round an abandoned churchyard would attract a certain amount of speculation. He had bright piercing eyes and a shock of white hair. "Is it a family grave you're looking for now?".

Adam explained that he was an Australian and was researching his family tree, and that his great-grandfather came from Lankerris. He was hoping to find some clues from the church records, or the priest about any other relatives who might still be living in the area.

"I've lived here all my life, and there's not much I don't know about it. Lucky it is that I saw you, I was just on my way back from checking my sheep. There's a new church building now, the other side of the village" said the old man helpfully. "Don't they have a new young priest too, Father Healy. But you won't be finding anything here. It's the newer graveyard you'll be needing". He pointed with his stick to another gate in a gap in the hedge and led Adam and Kathleen through into a sunlit, open space.

This part of the churchyard had been recently tended, the grass mowed between the graves and the hedge neatly trimmed. Fresh flowers had been placed on some of the graves and here the lettering on the stones was more clearly legible.

"This looks more like it" said Adam, hopefully.

"What names would you be after looking for?" asked the old man. "I'm Colm Brady, by the way, senior of this parish". He gave a laugh which turned into a wheezy cough.

Adam introduced himself and Kathleen. "The name's Keenan. I'm Adam Keenan and my great- grandfather William Keenan lived here, then emigrated to Australia in eighteen forty-eight. I know that much. But I'm wondering if he left any brothers or sisters here, or cousins even".

Colm gave him a long, penetrating look. "Keenan, now that's a name you might find in the North of Ireland" he said carefully. "But there was a Keenan family in Lankerris. Harry Keenan still lives here in Forest Road; he's in his eighties now. He had two sons and a daughter, I think they're all still alive, but they moved away. He keeps himself to himself now, I haven't seen him for months. There were several cousins. But Harry is the only Keenan here now".

Kathleen had wandered off and was looking at some of the recent graves. "Here's a grave for a Michael Keenan" she called excitedly. "He died in nineteen thirty-two. And look, he was married to a Mary Walsh, she survived him by twenty years. It's not a coincidence though" she continued. "Walsh is a common surname in Ireland. And here's another – Francis

Keenan. He died in nineteen twenty-five. They could have been brothers".

Colm nodded. "They were. And there were two more brothers, James and Declan. They all died young. One died in the Battle of the Somme, fighting for the British. Ireland was all one country then, if you know your history. The other died in the Easter Uprising in nineteen sixteen. Harry Keenan is their cousin".

Adam felt excited at this breakthrough. "Thank you, Colm. You've been really helpful. I think we'll try and call on Harry Keenan while we're here".

"Ask anyone in Forest Road," said the old man. "Turn left just after Reilly's bar. They'll tell you what number, I forget. But don't expect too much from Harry, that's all I'll be saying about that. Good day to ye".

Kathleen had been taking down all the details in a notebook; names and dates from the gravestones and the information Colm had given them.

"I think we should go and find some lunch and decide what to do next," said Adam. "It would be a shame to come all this way and not look up this Harry Keenan while we're here".

Chapter Sixty-One

The front garden of the little cottage in Forest Road was overgrown with weeds, nettles and brambles. The house itself looked dilapidated and neglected, and at first it was hard to imagine anyone living there.

Adam knocked a couple of times, but no one came to the door, although they both thought they could hear someone shuffling about inside.

"What shall we do? Should I go on knocking?" Adam was reluctant to abandon the idea of making contact when he had come so close to finding a potential relative, but at the same time did not wish to annoy or upset the man. Colm Brady had cautioned them to not put their hopes up.

"Do we have to go back home tonight?" asked Kathleen. "There are rooms at Reilly's, we could stay there overnight and try again tomorrow. Don't let's give up just yet".

The following morning yielded more success. After the second knock, they heard the scrape of bolts being drawn back and the door opened with much creaking and grating. It seemed that Harry Keenan rarely welcomed visitors, and this fact was confirmed by his angry glare.

"Hello Mr Keenan. I'm sorry to bother you but I'm visiting from Australia, and I think we may be related. I'm Adam Keenan. This is my fiancé Kathleen".

Harry Keenan looked unimpressed and surly. He was unkempt, unshaven and his clothes had seen better days. He leaned heavily on a walking stick. When he spoke, it was with a rasping, croaky voice. "I don't have time for family. What have they done for me now? Left me here in my old age, no one to help me. What is it you want?"

"Just to chat really" said Adam, wondering if after all this had been a bad idea. "We spoke to Colm Brady at the churchyard, he gave us your address".

"Did he now? He had no right; he should mind his own business".

Kathleen spoke up. "We saw some graves, Mr Keenan, with the family name. Colm said they were your cousins. Adam may be related to you as well but we're not sure how the family tree all fits together".

"Hmm. Well, you'd better come in. You'll have to take me as you find me, no one ever comes here".

They followed him along a dimly lit hallway to a living room at the rear of the cottage. The furnishings were stained and none too clean, the curtains frayed and torn in places, and the kitchen which was visible through a second door looked grimy and unsanitary. I hope he doesn't offer us a cup of tea, thought Kathleen, looking round her carefully as their host invited them both to sit down.

"Well?" Harry was obviously not going to volunteer any information yet. This left Adam no choice but to explain.

"My great-grandfather was William Keenan. He emigrated to Australia in 1848..."

"He did no such thing. He was a convict, a felon, a horse thief. He was transported".

Adam looked uncomfortable for a moment. He had suspected this, but in Australia there was no longer any stigma in having a convict as one of your ancestors; these days it was thought of more as a badge of honour.

"You know something of your family history, Mr Keenan, I can tell that much. So how are we related?"

"I know a thing or two. My great grandfather was Eamonn Keenan, he was the brother of Thomas Keenan, William's father".

"We are definitely related then". Adam was trying to work out the exact relationship.

"Whatever. So what d'ye want from me now?"

"Well, you may be my only living relative outside of Australia. I was hoping we could get to know each other".

Harry looked impatient, puzzled, then sad. His eyes filled with tears.

"Don't I have two sons and a daughter now? The boys are in the North. I'll never forgive them for that. And Rose, she's in England, nursing. She hasn't been back to see me since Nora died. Why couldn't she stay here? They've all gone. I have nothing left now".

Despite his sullen, unwelcoming behaviour, Kathleen felt sorry for the old man. Clearly, he was vulnerable and there was a sad story behind his words; a family feud perhaps, or maybe Harry could not accept that his children needed to move away to find work, to improve their prospects.

"So, my father, Edward Keenan must be your third or fourth cousin once removed as you are a different generation".

"If you say so".

No one spoke for a while and for a moment Adam and Kathleen wondered if there was any point in continuing the conversation. Then, in a flash of inspiration Kathleen said:

"Mr Keenan, you said all your family have left you, but here you are now with a distant cousin turning up on your doorstep. And you have more in Australia. Isn't that some good news altogether? Even though William Keenan did something years ago that you're not proud of?"

Harry looked at her with a fixed gaze. "I never said I wasn't proud of him. I said he was convicted of horse theft and transported. That's the truth. But he was one of many, facing starvation. I would have done the same in his shoes. So that's an end to it". He crossed himself and hobbled to the window, turning his back on them. Adam and Kathleen looked at each other, unsure what more to say.

"Mr Keenan, we're staying in West Cork, near Ballymere. We'll be driving back there later, but I'd like it if we could meet up again. Do you have a telephone?"

"I do".

"Here's my number. Let me have yours and I'll call you soon. Next time we visit we'll go out for a beer at Reilly's and talk some more".

Harry Keenan looked at Adam as if he had suggested a trip to the moon. "It's a long time since I drank at Reilly's.

But maybe I'll surprise them yet". As he wrote down his number the surly expression changed to something resembling a smile.

* * *

"Adam, that poor old man" said Kathleen as they drove away. "That house is in a terrible state, and he looks none too steady on his feet. Can't we do anything?"

"I know" said Adam, looking worried. "It's strange, we only met him an hour ago and yet I feel responsible for him".

"There must be some way we can help him. It doesn't look as though anyone else does".

"Mmm. I'd like to. But we would need to tread carefully. We can't just arrive out of the blue and start interfering in his life, however much he needs looking after. Old people can be very private and mistake any help for charity. That could make things worse. Let's go back in a week or two and see how things go when we take him for a drink. I'll ring him in the meantime".

Chapter Sixty-Two
March 1998

At Hackett's the St Patrick's Day party was in full swing, and the family had turned up in numbers to support the first big event since Christmas.

Angela had given Niamh, Ruari and Brontë free rein with the decorations and they had fixed balloons, banners and friezes all around the bar and the dining room. The tables were covered with white runners trimmed with shamrocks and some of the staff were wearing fancy dress with top hats and green outfits. By eight o'clock several guests had drunk more Guinness than was good for them but Fergus, knowing that this was the one night of the year when people really let their hair down, was not minded to be too hard on them unless they became violent or upset other partygoers.

The folk music band 'The Luna Scutters', having tuned up, launched into a medley of traditional Irish dance numbers and several dancers took up positions. Brontë was secretly hoping that Ruari might ask her to dance although she could see that this type of dancing was performed in lines but without a partner; the hands were held straight at the sides while the feet and legs did all the work. She watched, fascinated. Ruari came and stood beside her.

"It looks so difficult – how do they find the energy and stay in time with each other?" Brontë wondered if they were professional dancers.

"A lot of kids learn the dance before they even start school" said Ruari. "They take it very seriously and practice several times a week".

After a while, the band performed some well-known songs and encouraged the audience to join in. Brontë didn't know the words but soon picked up the choruses. Everyone was in high spirits, the atmosphere raucous and noisy. The Irish really know how to enjoy themselves, thought Brontë. At that moment Angela appeared, smiling. "I need you both to carry in trays of snacks and refreshments now. It's a good crowd that have turned up, I hope we've made enough to go round".

A year ago, Brontë would have been horrified if anyone had asked her to mingle with complete strangers, many of whom were well on the way to being drunk, and to wait at table making friendly conversation. Yet here she was, waitressing, laughing, chatting with the assembled company without a care in the world. Angela had asked Ruari to keep an eye on Brontë in case she called for help, but there was no need.

After a while they were allowed to have a break and Ruari brought her a glass of lemonade. Together they watched the dancers for a few more moments. The rhythm slowed to a waltz and several couples took to the floor: Orla and Finn among their number. Soon after, Connor and Gráinne followed. Ruari took her hand. "Let's join in, come on".

Despite wanting very much to dance, Brontë protested. "I don't know how to waltz" she said, uncertainly.

"It doesn't matter. Nor do I, come to that. Most people are too drunk to put one foot in front of another anyway".

My first proper grown-up dance with a boy, thought Brontë, as she stepped into the crowd. Angela and Bridget watched them, pleased to see Brontë enjoying herself so much but at the same time both feeling protective of her. Kathleen, sitting this one out with Adam, was delighted to see her niece on the dance floor, but another thought struck her as she watched the couple circling round the room. If Brontë has a boyfriend here now, she's even less likely to want to go home in the summer. Something else to complicate matters, she said to herself. But on the other hand, it was another huge step forward for Brontë, a rite of passage and perhaps a breakthrough, progress that would help heal her sadness and give her confidence to go back to England in time without fear of past unhappiness returning.

* * *

Adam telephoned his parents in Sydney to tell them all about Harry. He spoke to his father at length, explaining the difficult situation.

"Harry is my third cousin, then," said Ted. "Well done on tracking him down. But it sounds as though he might be struggling a bit. You say he's, well, not living in comfortable circumstances?"

"That's an understatement, Dad. To be honest, he lives in squalor. Kathleen and I are wondering how best to help him. But it's not going to be easy, he's quite a difficult man from what we've seen and he's very bitter that his children seem to have abandoned him. We don't know the full story, of course. Anyway, you'll see for yourself when you come over for the wedding; we'll take you to meet him".

There was a pause. "Sorry mate. We aren't going to be able to make it over for your wedding".

"Dad! You're joking?" Adam's dismay could be detected across ten thousand miles.

"It's your Mum. She's had a little heart scare. It was a warning, let's say. She's ok, taking it easy and on some new medication. But the doc's advised against flying. She's very disappointed, it's two years since we've seen you, and we were both longing to meet Kathleen".

Adam was shocked. Recently his mother had seemed in good health, active, energetic, always busy. "When did this happen, Dad?"

"About three weeks ago. We didn't want to bother you, at first, we thought it was nothing to worry about. But we must follow the doc's instructions. She'll be ok if she doesn't overdo it".

"Oh Dad, I'm sorry. Poor Mum. She'll be sad to miss the wedding. The doc's probably right, she wouldn't be up to a long-haul flight. But perhaps Kathleen and I can get over to Aus soon. I'll have to work out when I can have a few more weeks off from the restaurant. I don't seem to have been there much lately. And I've got a honeymoon to fit in as well". He laughed.

433

Another pause.

"Just a suggestion. Why don't you come here for your honeymoon? You could spend a few days with us in Sydney, then go up north or take some road trips. I know it will be winter here in August but if you don't mind that, it means you could kill two birds with one stone, kind of thing".

"Thanks Dad, that's certainly an idea. I will talk to Kath later. What about Jack, is he ok?"

Jack was Adam's younger brother and had agreed several months ago to take some long overdue holiday in Europe and combine this with the wedding celebrations.

"He's fine, looking forward to seeing you. You'll have your best man, don't worry about that".

"Can I speak to Mum now?"

She's resting, mate. Next time you phone let me know in advance and I'll make sure she's with me".

His father rang off, and Adam had to be content with that. Feeling deflated, he wandered out into the laneway. He was full of conflicting emotions; sad and worried about his mother's health, and disappointed that neither of his parents would be with him to see him marrying Kathleen. That would have meant so much to him. He would have Jack for support; he was fond of his brother but there would be only one relative on his side whereas Kathleen's extended family were numbered by the dozens.

After a few moments he shook off his doubts. It wasn't a competition. Weddings created all sorts of unusual circumstances and dynamics where families were concerned. The main thing was, he was to marry Kathleen, whom he loved with all his heart. He had never expected to fall in love again after Martina, much less re-marry. Later he would suggest to Kathleen the prospect of a honeymoon in his home country. He had come to love Ireland, even more so since discovering that it was the home of his ancestors. Perhaps Kathleen would feel the same way about Australia in time, although they could only take in a small part, even during an extended visit.

* * *

"Do you fancy a honeymoon Down Under?" Adam and Kathleen had decided to take a walk down to see Bridget after dinner. It was now late March, and the evenings were growing lighter.

Kathleen gasped. "Australia? Are you serious?"

"I certainly am". Adam went on to tell her about the conversation with his father, and as predicted, Kathleen's first reaction was concern for his mother's health. "I'm so sorry, Adam. Your poor Mum. But it sounds as though your Dad is taking good care of her. She will be upset to miss the wedding though".

"She is. But getting back to the honeymoon...."

"That would be wonderful" said Kathleen, her eyes shining with excitement. "Of course I'd love to. You see, years ago I never thought I'd travel anywhere. Just getting on the ferry to Britain was a massive thing for me. Since then, I've lived in Spain and travelled by air several times, I'm beginning to overcome my fear of flying. But going to Australia with you would be such an adventure, and I could meet your parents".

"That's settled then" said Adam, opening the farm gate. "We can start to make plans".

Kathleen had an idea of her own. "What about Harry? Shall we invite him to our wedding? He's your family, after all".

Adam looked thoughtful. "We won't rule it out. But we need to take it step at a time, we've only met him once. But let's see how things go when we visit him next".

Chapter Sixty-Three

Although the wedding was still four months away, there was discord in the Walsh family about the travelling arrangements. And the divisions did not end there.

Arthur had not yet passed his driving test despite two attempts. It was a source of annoyance and embarrassment to him that his girlfriend Abby had passed her test first time two months previously and had a little car. Nevertheless, he hoped that he might be successful on his next test which was booked for the end of May, and Patrick had promised to buy him a car as soon as he passed.

Abby, and Henry's new girlfriend Lucy Dixon had been invited as plus-ones to the wedding, and Henry thought it would be a great idea if the four of them could travel together in Abby's car. However, Diane, Abby's mother was not at all happy at the thought of her seventeen-year-old daughter driving onto a car ferry and in a foreign country with only a couple of months experience behind the wheel, and certainly not with three other teenagers in the car. She telephoned Nell as soon as she heard about the plan that had been hatched.

"I agree with you totally," said Nell. "They're all too young and inexperienced to travel together like that. But it is a problem; we have bought a bigger car now, it's a seven-seater but it won't be enough for everyone plus our luggage. I think I'll have to ask our friends if they have spare seats. Leave it with me".

Neville and Lois had decided to fly to Cork Airport and pick up a hire car there, but Jonathan and Barbara did have room in their car for two extra and so did Joe and Ruth. This seemed to Nell to be a solution but when she told Arthur and Henry one Saturday afternoon it sparked a family row.

"The four of us want to go together Mum" said Arthur crossly. "We don't want to travel with the others. Couldn't Dad buy me my car now, then whatever happens I could drive it, and Abby could sit beside me as she's a qualified driver".

"Arthur, I don't know if that's legal at Abby's age" said Nell, despairingly. "And even if it was legal here, it might not be in Ireland. That's just not going to happen".

Patrick was equally adamant. "I've promised you a car when you pass, Arthur, and I won't go back on that. But even if you do get through before the holiday, I wouldn't be letting you drive over there until you've had a lot more experience. Your mother's right, and there's the insurance to think about. You'll be travelling with our friends and that's an end to it".

Arthur went out, swearing and slamming the door behind him. Patrick looked furious but Nell tried to smooth things over. "Patrick he's eighteen now, he's nearly grown up. He wants to do things his way, he's frustrated about not passing his test, it's holding him back and he's angry. You know I agree with you, but don't be too hard on him".

It was the first serious sign that Arthur was trying to find his feet as an adult. He was doing a man's job now; two years working with his father and other skilled men had taught him a great deal in the building trade, and he was earning well. He was as tall as Patrick now and equally broad-shouldered, with a similar muscular build. Whenever she looked at him Nell was reminded of the man she fell in love with all those years ago. But Patrick had matured, there were more grey hairs visible now and just a little more flesh around the jawline. The responsibilities of a large family and an ever-growing business had left their mark. Occasionally he was short-tempered with the children and quickly ran out of patience, even over minor disputes. It was a relief to Nell that Ronnie gave them no trouble at all, and she often wondered how he had come to have a wisdom older than his years, always diplomatic, good-natured and warm-hearted. In many ways he reminded her of Patrick's brother Aidan, who was calm, placid and always considerate. It was also fortunate that Emer seemed to have settled down a great deal in recent weeks; she was less demanding, less truculent. This was just as well because Arthur and Henry, both leaving childhood behind were starting to rebel against the limitations of home life and family rules. Normal behaviour perhaps, thought Nell. Her two eldest sons, moving through adolescence into adulthood were sure to test the boundaries of their upbringing from time to time.

It was not just the driving. Arthur had let slip that he and Abby wanted to live together and have their own space. Nell knew that she had to tread carefully with this. She and Patrick had never made any secret of the fact that she was pregnant with Arthur when they married and that she had been only just eighteen at the time. It was to be expected that Arthur would remind her of this fact as soon as she voiced any objections, but Patrick would not remember so easily; he would be more likely to lay down the law or refuse to discuss the matter. Two male redheads under the same roof, locking horns – it was bound to happen, she thought ruefully. It seemed that just as her worries about Brontë were beginning to ease, concerns about Arthur and Henry had taken over. The latest letter from her daughter told Nell just how happy she was at school; how she had enjoyed the St Patrick's Day party and the progress of her nature journal as she learned more about gardening under the expert eye of Sister Bernice. Once again, the thought of her daughter, content and settled in Ireland was bitter-sweet; would Brontë ever feel the same way in her own home? For a moment she felt tearful.

Just at that moment Arlo gave a squawk, signalling that he had woken from his afternoon nap. He was starting to shuffle along on his bottom, sit up unaided and say a few words. It was a blessing that he was a happy baby, seldom grizzly and this only when teething was troubling him. Nell knew that she had Ronnie to thank for this; he spent a great deal of time with Arlo, down on the floor, playing with him, talking to him. Ronnie had endless patience for a ten-year-old and could be trusted to watch Arlo when the other children might be less reliable and more easily distracted.

It was after one such altercation between Arthur and Patrick that Neville arrived one weekend.

Nell as usual had been trying to keep the peace between father and son but feeling torn both ways. Neville took one look at his daughter and followed her as she went into the kitchen to fill the kettle.

"Emer?" he asked, raising his eyebrows quizzically.

Nell laughed, despite feeling at her wits' end that day.

"No, for a change Emer is behaving much better recently. Perhaps she's just growing out of that difficult stage, she's not so argumentative these days. We really seem to have turned a corner with her. No, it's the boys". Nell went on to explain about the travel to Ireland. "In a way it's nothing serious but it seems to have blown up out of all proportion, and now there's a rift in the family. No one will give way. Arthur is becoming as stubborn as Patrick can be, and Henry follows his lead".

Neville put a comforting arm around his daughter. "I'm sure it can't be that bad. Go and get Arlo, we'll have a cup of tea, and you can tell me all about it".

He listened as Nell poured the tea and told him of Arthur's plans to leave home; how should they deal with it? "Dad, it feels as if my family is falling apart. Brontë, Arthur, Henry.... Ronnie is the only one I don't worry about, then I feel guilty that I don't pay him much attention because he never gives me any bother".

"Of course it's not falling apart. You're overthinking this and mixing up a lot of issues here". He gave an amused smile. "I seem to remember not that long ago, a young lady who couldn't wait to be with her boyfriend".

"I knew you'd say that, Dad. But this is different. There's no talk of them getting married and Abby's not pregnant – at least I hope not. They just want to live together".

"Well, that's what young people do nowadays. He's eighteen, he's an adult in law, he can move out if he wants to. Why not let him try? See how he gets on, finding a place, budgeting, being independent. But if Abby is younger, her parents may not be so keen so they may have to wait, and that will mean you can't be accused of interfering".

Nell looked surprised. "Do you really think that could work, Dad?"

"I think it's worth a try. Put the ball in Arthur's court. Now where the trip to Ireland is concerned, perhaps look for another solution. I agree that the four of them travelling in one car is not a good idea. But they want to go together as a group?"

Nell nodded.

"Here's a suggestion. They can all travel together by air. I'll pay their return fares, all of them. Call it a gift from me. Then they can take a train from Cork or perhaps Connor will meet them. And it can be on a separate flight from your mother and I, in case they think we're trying to keep an eye on them. I don't know about the girls, but Arthur and Henry have never flown before, so the idea may appeal to them. You can even see about booking the seats together".

"That's very generous of you Dad. I think you may have hit on something there. They would be together but not in a car. I'm sure Patrick will think it's a clever idea as well, I'll tell them all later. Thank you so much".

"That wasn't so bad, was it? Two problems solved". He looked affectionately down at Arlo. "Now let's see how this little chap's doing".

Later Nell reflected on the conversation. Her father always helped her to see things in a different light, gave her a new perspective. Neville was right, Arthur was not wanting to do anything unreasonable, he just wanted to spread his wings, as she had done at his age. Agreeing to his plans was not necessarily giving in to him. Sometimes letting go was the right thing to do and perhaps, in so doing, she would keep him close. Would that be the same with Brontë? Only time would tell.

Chapter Sixty-Four

It was early April, and the school garden was bursting into life. The weather from the Atlantic was milder; winter storms had passed and were replaced by warm breezes. The daffodils were nearly over but fruit blossom was abundant, and delicate primroses, brightly coloured tulips and purple aubretia lined the pathways. Brontë watched the birds flying back and forth with twigs and wisps of straw in their beaks; several weeks ago, Ruari had, with permission from Sister Francis fixed up some nesting boxes on the side of the shed one weekend; all now had tenants. She wondered why she had never really noticed these things before, but now every new discovery of buds and green shoots brought her delight and excitement. Tomato and vegetable plants were putting on growth in the greenhouse and the garden was changing before her eyes every day. With so much happening in the garden it was tempting for her to spend more time there than she should, and Sister Faith, her geography teacher had noticed that she was frequently late for lessons and asked to see her at the end of the school day.

"It would be a shame altogether if you neglected your studies" she said, not angrily but with a firm note in her voice. "It's a grand thing you are doing there, helping Sister Bernice but you will have the Leaving Certificate exams in the summer. You're a clever girl Brontë, don't be letting me down now. Just try to be on time for your lessons in future".

Brontë apologised and promised to improve her timekeeping. She knew that being allowed to work in the garden during school hours was a great privilege and it wouldn't do to risk losing this concession. As well as schoolwork, she spent time on her nature journal each day and she began to understand why her mother took such pleasure in writing, and how that had led to Drovers' Diary being a regular feature of the local newspaper. Perhaps one day I can have something published like Mummy, she thought, and resolved to mention this in her next letter home.

Ruari had become a regular visitor to Bridget's cottage since the party. Brontë would have denied that he was her boyfriend if anyone had asked, but she had grown very fond of him and liked the fact that he made no demands on her, just seemed to enjoy her company. Bridget could not fail but to notice this, and after one such occasion she walked down the laneway with Ruari as he left.

"I need to tell you a little about Brontë. She's been through a great deal; she had a troubled time at school back in England". On no account would Bridget divulge any further details. "That's why she's staying here. You're to keep it to yourself, I'm only saying this because you are her friend. Now if I find out that you've hurt her or upset her, you'll have me and Mrs Hackett to reckon with. She's just beginning to get over all her problems. You look after her now, and no funny business. She's only fourteen remember".

"Thank you for telling me, Mrs Walsh. I had a feeling that there was a reason she came here. I promise to look after her, you can trust me to do that".

Bridget and Angela had previously shared their concerns about the growing attachment. Angela might have been forgiven for seeing certain similarities to her own situation many years ago and was fiercely protective of her great-niece. But they needn't have worried. As time went on, and Bridget could see that Brontë and Ruari were perfectly content to sit and chat in the living room or just to walk down the laneway in sight of the cottage, their fears receded, and they began to see the friendship in a positive light.

* * *

Meanwhile, Adam had started to make plans to return to Spain later in April. With a shock he realised that it was several weeks since he had left. He knew that Rafael was experienced in running the café bar and that Hayley was a reliable and capable assistant, so he had no doubt that they would manage perfectly well without him. Still, it didn't seem fair to leave them with all the responsibility indefinitely. He would arrange to return within the next fortnight. But first, he had an obligation to fulfil, a commitment, if not exactly a duty. It had been troubling him since his visit to Lankerris and the meeting with Harry. He must, somehow, help the old man. Giving him money, whilst in one way would be the easiest thing to do, was not an option; Harry was clearly a proud man and would most likely be offended. No, he had guessed from their brief conversation that Harry was lonely and felt abandoned. Could he, or perhaps Kathleen, persuade him to move south? To leave that ramshackle cottage and relocate to Ballymere? Surely they could arrange that somehow. Initially the idea seemed preposterous. He had only met Harry once and that exchange had not been a resounding success. Who were they to suggest such a thing, to interfere in his life in that way?

He and Kathleen were sitting at the bar in Hackett's with Angela later that evening, and as Fergus poured their drinks, Adam explained to about Harry and their dilemma.

"He really shouldn't be living alone. He can't look after himself, and his place is, well, to put it mildly, in need of attention. In fact, I don't really think he's safe".

"It didn't actually feel right leaving him," said Kathleen. "I almost wish we'd never been there and met him, because now that we have, we can't just forget about him. Especially as he's Adam's relative".

Angela listened attentively. "It's quite a puzzle you have there" she said thoughtfully. "It sounds as if he owns his house, no landlord would allow it to get into that state. Did you say you might invite him to the wedding?"

"Yes, we're definitely going to do that". Adam went on to tell Angela about his mother's illness and that only his brother would be coming over from Australia. "Jack will be my only relative at the wedding unless I can persuade Harry to come, even though he's a stranger really".

"Mmm. Well shall I be booking a room for him, just in case?"

"Yes, can you do that Angela, please? If he refuses to come, I'm sure you'll be able to let the room to someone else".

Angela went to the reception desk and made a note in the big diary. She had an idea, but it would keep. Perhaps it would come to nothing; she would talk to Fergus and Bridget about it later. One step at a time, she thought. Let's see how their next visit goes.

* * *

The second journey up to Lankerris was, if anything, more purposeful than the first. This time Adam was determined to persuade Harry to come to Reilly's with them for a drink or two, then they would gradually introduce the subject of his wedding. He had come armed with a bottle of best Irish Peat Whiskey as an icebreaker; he had yet to meet an Irishman who would refuse such a gift.

Adam had rung ahead to arrange a time when they would collect Harry to take him to the bar, and for a bite to eat. At first, he had received a few grunts in reply, but Harry seemed to remember him and agreed to be ready for six o'clock that evening. But nothing could be taken for granted; it was quite possible that when they arrived in Forest Road the old man would either refuse to answer the door or say he had changed his mind.

It was therefore a surprise when Harry opened the door to them and appeared to be ready for his first night out in a very long time. He had shaved after a fashion and put on a collar and tie. Kathleen realised that his clothing spoke of a generation past, when any outing other than work would call for more formal attire. He accepted the whiskey graciously and as he climbed into the front seat of the car beside Adam, she felt a huge wave of relief that the first hurdle had been overcome.

Heads turned as they walked into the bar. The bartender seemed to recognise them from their previous stay, and although he was surprised to see Harry, he made no comment as he took their order of pie and mash, pints of Guinness for Adam and Harry and a tonic water for Kathleen.

There were a few other customers although it was early evening. One or two men recognised Harry and nodded to him; a third turned his back and ignored him. Harry did not seem too worried by this and after he had downed his first pint he relaxed visibly. "They didn't expect to see me in here" he said, with a glimmer of a smile, looking almost triumphant.

"Do you remember I said that Kathleen and I are to be married in July?" Adam wanted to broach the subject as early as possible.

Harry nodded and accepted a second pint.

"I also mentioned that I don't have any other relatives in Ireland apart from you. My brother is coming over from Australia to be my best man, but that's all. Kathleen has a big family. We've both been married before, so the ceremony will be held in a Registry Office".

At that moment the food arrived so the conversation paused while they began their meal. Adam was worried that the opportunity was lost and looked meaningfully at Kathleen.

She came to the rescue. "Harry, what Adam is trying to say is, will you be a guest at our wedding in Ballymere?"

Harry looked astonished and for a moment was speechless. Kathleen thought she saw the faintest hint of a tear in his eye then quick as a flash he blinked it away.

"I never go anywhere. You're the first visitors I've had for a long time. I've not been out of this village for fifteen years. I wouldn't even know how to find Ballymere. Why would ye want me at your wedding? I'm a miserable feckin' bastard".

An elderly man at the next table overheard the last comment and muttered "Amen to that".

Adam tried again. "We're inviting you because you're one of our family. Now that I've tracked you down, I don't want us to lose touch".

445

"My family would like to meet you as well," said Kathleen. "And don't be worrying about how to get there, we'll come and fetch you in the car. My aunt runs a guest house nearby where you can stay, she has some nice ground floor rooms, there'll be no stairs. What do you say? Will you at least think about it?"

Harry said nothing but left the table and shuffled off in the direction of the toilets. Adam and Kathleen looked at each other. "Well? Do you think he'll agree?" asked Adam. She shrugged. "It's hard to tell. But he hasn't refused, so let's see how things go when he comes back".

A few moments later Harry returned. They looked at him expectantly, but he said nothing for a few moments, gazing into his glass. His eyes had misted over.

"Me and my daughter Rose had a falling out, years ago. Right ructions, you might say. All over her going off to England with that Sasenach and leaving me here, and her mother not long passed. The boys had already gone, they're in Belfast, they set up some building firm together. Why could they not have stayed here? I don't hear from any of them now. None of them care about me. It breaks my heart not to see Rose, she surely thinks I'm still angry with her. But I don't know where she is or how to find her. So now ye know why I'm a grumpy old sod, not much to be happy about these days. But the answer is, I'll come to your wedding and thank ye. Bad luck to the rest of them".

"That's great, Harry! How about another pint to celebrate, then we'll take you home".

* * *

As they drew up outside Harry's cottage, Kathleen's heart sank. What a bleak, cheerless place to come home to. They waited while he unlocked the door and stepped into the gloomy hallway. "We'll come in with you for a moment, Harry. Shall I be making you a cup of tea now?"

"No, I'll away to my bed, thanking ye".

Adam looked at the steep stairs leading up to the first floor, and aware that Harry had consumed three pints, wondered for a moment if he should escort him up to his bedroom. As if he had read his thoughts, Harry laughed. "Don't I sleep in the parlour for the last ten years? I never set foot up these stairs now".

Relieved, Adam shook his hand, and on an impulse, Kathleen kissed the old man's whiskery cheek. Harry's eyes softened as he looked at her and clasped her hands tightly. "Won't you be making a beautiful bride, now? You're a lucky man, Adam, and that's a fact".

They took their leave, Adam promising to telephone soon to give details of the wedding arrangements.

"Thank ye. Slan go foill". Harry closed the door behind them.

Chapter Sixty-Five

In January Neville had mentioned to Adam that he had decided to sell the apartment in Solibrio and was offering it to him at a very favourable price, partly because as a private sale they could both avoid paying some professional fees, and also because Lois had set her heart on the soon-to-be newlyweds becoming the next owners. At the time, Adam jumped at the chance; the proximity to Martina's made it a very convenient bolt hole – near enough to be within easy walking distance of the café bar, but far enough away to create some distance between their home and place of work.

However, with his mind occupied with his forthcoming wedding and the search for the Keenan family in County Galway, no progress with the purchase had been made, so Adam was full of apologies when Neville telephoned at the end of April to ask if he was ready to proceed.

"I should have been in touch sooner, I'm sorry Neville. We do want to go ahead; Kathleen is very excited about the apartment and I'm due to fly back to Spain on Thursday so I can get things moving with my solicitor. Wouldn't it be great if we could complete the sale before the wedding? We have three months yet".

"I don't see why not, Adam, let's aim for that shall we? I also wanted to ask you about the contents. Lois and I bought the apartment fully furnished; it was easier than trying to move everything out and buy new, also we liked the furniture, it suited us to do that. But you may wish to make other arrangements, if so, I can set the wheels in motion to sell it all...."

Adam said he wouldn't hear of Neville going to so much trouble and, in any case, he agreed that the apartment had been furnished to their own taste as well. Kathleen might, sometime in the future wish to make changes but he was all for keeping things simple for now which would speed up the process. He promised to keep Neville informed and that he would see him next in Ireland just before the big day.

* * *

"When you come back to Ballymere our wedding will be only a few days away". Kathleen was seeing Adam off; Connor had driven them to the airport and was now keeping at a discreet distance in the departure lounge while they said their goodbyes.

"We've always spent so much time together; it'll be strange to be apart. But three months will soon pass, in fact it will be less than that, I'll be back mid-July. We both have plenty to do in the meantime. I need to take up the reins of the bar again, look at the accounts, and get things moving on the apartment. And if I have any spare time, I'll book our flights to Australia". He laughed, hugging her close.

"You'd better remember that" replied Kathleen with mock severity. "And if I have time to catch my breath in between wedding plans, I'll keep in touch with Harry. We don't want him to be forgetting about us". So, with a last embrace, Kathleen waved him off and went to find Connor.

* * *

It was the beginning of May and with the promise of summer and warmer days, Lois had made an important decision.

Her wheelchair, which since her first diagnosis had remained an unavoidable presence in her life, would not be coming with her to Ireland.

It had accompanied her from Moongarth to Spain and back again to Sussex on each journey; an essential if unwelcome encumbrance. In the early days, as her illness advanced, she had been glad of it at times when pain, and the exhaustion of coping with pain became too much, and fatigue and weariness made even the shortest walk impossible. Now it stood folded in their luggage cupboard at the Swan's Rest, seldom needed, always resisted. Recently Lois had made supreme efforts to manage without it, especially when milder weather or periods of remission had rendered it unnecessary. But the wheelchair seemed to have taken on a personality of its own, taunting her, creating doubts in her mind and pouring scorn on her attempts to walk unaided, becoming an obstacle to her independence. As if to shut out those intrusive thoughts, Lois closed the cupboard door firmly and concentrated on the prospect of attending Kathleen's wedding holding on to nothing but her husband's arm.

Neville was delighted with Lois's determination. "You are always so much better during the summer months, my darling" he said, not for the first time offering up private thanks for this transformation in his wife and her resolve to not give in to her illness, even now at the age of seventy-two when she could have been forgiven for taking the easier option. "And what's the worst that can happen? If anything unexpected crops up, we shall drive into Cork and hire one for you. But I'm so proud of you my dear. This is one more thing to look forward to this summer".

Patrick was not so sure, and voiced his concerns to Nell one evening after her parents had visited.

"Ireland isn't like Spain in summer, especially not in the southwest. Sure, July is one of the warmer months, but there can be a dozen changes of weather in a day, and your Mam may find it hard to adjust. She may not benefit from the time of year as much as she's expecting to".

"Don't say anything, Patrick. Mum has made up her mind to try to do without the wheelchair and I think we should encourage her. Dad is all for it, as you can see, but knowing Dad, he will have a plan if anything should go wrong".

She was right, but ensuring Lois's well-being was not the only idea in Neville's mind. Long ago Nell had spoken excitedly to her father about stargazing in West Cork, and from time to time the idea returned to him. The visit to Ireland would provide a real opportunity to study those dark skies. By chance, whilst carrying out some errands in

Kirchington one Saturday morning he bumped into Chris Davenport from the Planetarium and invited him back to the Swan's Rest for a cup of coffee.

"It's strange, I was going to call you, Neville" said Chris, accepting a slice of carrot cake. "Do you realise it was before Christmas when we talked about meeting up, that was over four months ago".

"Yes, you're right, before you know it weeks have passed" agreed Neville. "I always seem to be trying to catch up. Not enough time to do everything. That's what happens when you retire". They both laughed.

"I was hoping to pick your brains about the summer programme," said Chris. "I'm trying to think of fresh ideas. It's strange, astronomy is such a vast subject but we're in danger of repeating the same talks time after time. They always go down well, of course, and attendance is good, it's usually a full house. I'd like to introduce different themes, a new angle. But it has to be something that will appeal to a wide age range, detailed enough but not too technical or you risk losing your audience. That's where I get stuck and tend to go for the safe options".

"Mmm. I see your point, Chris. Have you thought about giving your visitors a questionnaire? You know, ask if there are any subjects they'd like to know more about. You'd need to allow that some ideas might be unworkable, but if you had five good suggestions out of say, thirty or forty questionnaires, that would be a start. I used to do that occasionally in school, partly because it made the boys feel more involved".

"Yes. I think I might try that. Nothing to lose, and as you say, it would be worth it for one good idea".

"What about a field trip? Depends on the weather of course, but if you have a dozen members with their own telescopes you could arrange to meet out of town where there's no street lighting, perhaps up in the hills. You could point out constellations, whatever planets are visible at a particular time of year, help them learn to navigate the night sky. Just a thought, it would be a change from a formal talk".

"I think you've got something there Neville. Yes, I'm sure quite a few would be interested. Glad I asked you now. You've given me quite a lot to think about. I don't suppose you would like to give a talk sometime? One evening this summer? You could decide on your own subject".

Neville was hoping to be asked this but had been reluctant to push himself forward. "I'd be delighted" he said. "But I shall be away for a couple of weeks in July". He went on to tell Chris about the forthcoming family wedding. "We'll be staying in West Cork. I'm planning to take my telescope and a good camera with me. My daughter wants to take me stargazing, as she calls it. It's very rural where we're going, close to the Atlantic coastline, and I'm hoping for some good views".

"Neville, you're jolly lucky to be going there. Do you realise that southwest Ireland has some of the darkest skies in Europe? That will be a wonderful experience. You could include it in your talk. And while you're over there, see if you can find out if they have a planetarium or an observatory in the area. Just out of interest".

The two men shook hands, promising to keep in touch sooner this time and Chris took his leave. As Neville walked back along the corridor to find Lois, he felt elated that he had been asked to give a talk. This time it was a specific request, not just a general invitation. And without Neville even realising it, Chris had planted another seed in his mind.

Chapter Sixty-Six

May 1998

There were ten weeks before the wedding, but Kathleen's head was already in a whirl. Her dress was carefully wrapped in a delicate cover and hung in her mother's wardrobe at the cottage along with her shoes and accessories. The Registry Office had been booked several months previously as soon as the divorce was finalised but there were still a few things to organise in the way of flowers, order of service, photographer, and transport. The reception was to be held at Hackett's so Kathleen, Bridget and Angela had spent many hours discussing décor, seating arrangements and buffet menus. Kathleen and her mother had agreed on most things, but Bridget was overruled on the matter of a jaunting-car; Kathleen had decided on something more discreet to take her to and from the Registry Office. Everything else was going to plan and Angela, who was methodical and thorough, had no intention of allowing anything to be a disappointment or to go wrong for her niece on her wedding day. The only misgiving, which no one could do anything about was the weather which in West Cork was notoriously unreliable. This was Kathleen's one tiny regret. When Adam had first popped the question and she had accepted, for a moment she had visions of a beach wedding on the Mediterranean coast where warm sunshine would be guaranteed. She thought dreamily of the two of them exchanging vows in front of a calm aquamarine sea under clear blue skies and a white canopy decked with flowers. But she soon realised that the prospect of her entire extended family travelling to Spain was unlikely and she would not contemplate a ceremony without all her relatives and friends present. She had, on one occasion made a passing reference to a beach venue when she and Adam were first making wedding plans but had quickly dismissed the idea.

By the middle of May, Kathleen was beginning to suffer from wedding nerves and anxiety, so much so that both her mother and her aunt started to notice that she was becoming cross and irritable over the slightest thing when really there was nothing to worry about; by then all the preparations were well in hand. One afternoon, noticing that Kathleen had become upset that the printers had made some minor mistakes on the order of service, Bridget decided to take matters into her own hands.

"Hear me now, on Sunday we are going to have a day off from all this, or your Aunt Angela and I will be frazzled wrecks before your wedding, and you'll be even worse and will not be fit to be seen as a bride, your face is full of wrinkles and frowns altogether as if you had the world on your shoulders instead of a beautiful day to look forward to".

Kathleen burst into tears, just as Brontë walked in the door after school. Brontë looked at Bridget in dismay and ran to sit beside her aunt.

"Granny what's happened?"

"Nothing to worry about dear, your auntie's just been overdoing things a bit lately. I've told her that we need a rest from wedding plans this weekend. We'll take a trip out somewhere".

Kathleen, screwing a sodden tissue into a ball nodded. "Yes, let's do that. We all need a break. Sorry Mam. I just want everything to be perfect".

"And it will be, have no fear on that score. I'll make the tea. Now where would you like to go?"

Kathleen was silent for a moment and while Bridget went into the kitchen to fill the kettle, Brontë went upstairs to change out of her uniform. When she returned, the tea had been poured and there was some discussion about whether to drive to Cork or Glengarriff for the Sunday outing. As nothing was decided, Brontë spoke up.

"Do you think we could go to meet Harry? Auntie you said you would keep in touch with him while Adam is in Spain. I'd love to see a bit more of the west coast as well".

Kathleen looked uncertain. "Yes, I did promise to do that. We could take a trip there.... but it's a long drive up to Galway, do you think you can manage it, Mam?" Not for the first time, Kathleen regretted not learning to drive at the same time as her older brothers. Momentarily her thoughts went back to the inequalities in her earlier life which she had resented for so many years. Then she reminded herself that she had left those regrets behind, along with the person she used to be. There was time enough to do all those things; her life was different now, with endless possibilities still ahead.

"I can do that" said Bridget, pouring a second cup. "I'm not in my dotage yet. It'll be grand".

At seven thirty on the following Sunday morning the three women climbed into the ancient Land Rover and set off. Bridget rarely missed Mass on Sunday mornings but said she felt sure she would be forgiven for one absence. The guest house was fully booked that weekend, and Bridget realised that Galway held nothing but sad memories for her sister but nevertheless extended the invitation. Angela laughed. "Won't the poor man already be outnumbered with the three of you turning up mob-handed? Don't you be frightening him off now, Adam wants him at the wedding for sure".

Kathleen had telephoned Harry the previous evening to check if it was all right to visit. She had no doubt that he would be at home but there was a pause when she asked if she could bring her mother and young niece.

After a couple of seconds there was a grunt. "Haven't I lived here alone for years and seen no one, and then there are three visits from ye within a few weeks? And now more of ye? Well, bring your family but don't be expecting much. You know I don't entertain company".

Kathleen hastily reassured Harry that they were not expecting hospitality; Bridget had thought of bringing a food hamper and flasks of tea and taking Harry out somewhere for a picnic. This would relieve the old man of any worry.

"When you see the hovel he lives in you'll understand, Mam" said Kathleen as they left Glengarriff behind and motored north towards Killarney.

"What's a hovel?" asked Brontë from the back seat, wondering if it was a style of architecture or a house design not seen in West Cork.

Kathleen was momentarily at a loss for words.

"It's well…it's a house that's not very well cared for" she said at last. "A place that needs a lot of work to bring it up to standard. And before you say anything Mam, yes, I remember when my own place in Ballymere wasn't much better. You had a thing or two to say about it in those days".

"I did" agreed Bridget. "And that's all in the past, thank goodness. Now Brontë you're not to repeat what we just said. Harry may live in a poor way but it's his home and we must respect it".

The journey took more than four hours but just before lunch time they drew up outside Harry's cottage in Forest Road and sat for a moment with the engine turned off.

"Well, here we are" said Bridget, taking in the tangle of briars and brambles covering the front garden, and the clumps of nettles encroaching over the path to the front door. But Brontë's sharp eyes had noticed a deep pink rose climbing defiantly above the banks of weeds and stretching its tendrils across a grimy window, and here and there a few foxgloves pushed their pink spears through a mass of bindweed and ground elder.

After a few moments, Harry greeted them at the door and Kathleen went to make brief introductions, but instead Bridget, mindful that he might be feeling a little overwhelmed, took the plunge. "Lovely it is to meet you, Mr Keenan. I'm Bridget, Kathleen's Mammy. And this is my granddaughter Brontë. Thank you for inviting us".

"You invited yourselves. But no matter. Call me Harry. I've nothing to offer ye, but you're welcome to come in".

They followed Harry through into the dingy back room, Bridget and Kathleen determined not to show any expression of surprise or concern at the squalid surroundings, the sticky stained carpet and layers of dirt in the sink and on the cupboard doors. Brontë looked around in wonderment; it was the most run-down dwelling she had seen in her life, but remembering her grandmother's words, asked politely:

"Harry, is that a rambling rose or a climber on your front wall? There's one just like it in the school garden. It's an old-fashioned rose, isn't it? It has a beautiful scent".

Harry looked at her intently. "You're the first person to notice that in many years. Nora planted it after our daughter Rose was born. It needs pruning, I don't know how to do it. She always looked after the garden; the sadness would be on her if she saw it now". He looked away and crossed himself, overcome for a moment. "Do ye like flowers, then?"

"Yes, I help in the school garden with one of the sisters. I've not been doing it for long, but I've learned a lot. Sister Bernice showed me how to prune roses, and which secateurs to use".

* * *

Harry needed some help to manage the steps up into the Land Rover but once settled in his seat, seemed to enjoy the trip through Lankerris, pointing out some landmarks and commenting on a shop that had changed hands and that another had closed since his last visit. The picnic was a success. They drove out of the village for half a mile to common land where a few horses grazed untethered and occasionally a dog walker came into view on a footpath at the far side of the field. Kathleen unfolded some canvas chairs while Bridget set out the food on a picnic table. To their surprise, Harry ate ravenously everything he was offered, as

457

though it was his first meal in a long time and drank two large mugs of tea.

Bridget was keen to encourage the old man to talk. He spoke emotionally about his late wife who had died ten years previously, and his daughter, now somewhere in England whom he would like to trace, but he had no idea how to go about it. When it came to the matter of his two sons leaving for work in Belfast, his face darkened. "There are some in this village who won't speak to me because of that" he said angrily. "I had no part in it, and yet I am blamed. My sons were never unionists". Clearly a sectarian undercurrent ran close to the surface here, and seeing that Brontë was looking puzzled, Bridget decided to steer the conversation in a different direction.

"Did you go to Mass this morning, Harry?"

"I did not. Nor to Confession these last ten years"

Clearly that was also a controversial subject. Bridget tried a different tack.

"Let me tell you about the arrangements for Kathleen's wedding. Adam will collect you in the car on the twenty second of July. That's a Wednesday. He'll be in touch about what time. The wedding is on Saturday the twenty fifth, but we thought you might like a few days to settle in beforehand and meet the rest of the family. My sister Angela owns the guest house, she has a nice ground floor room set aside for you, with its own bathroom. There's a bar and a lounge if you want to sit and chat with other guests, or a private garden if you'd prefer some peace and quiet. Breakfast and dinner are included but I hope you'll come and share a meal at my table with us sometimes".

"Hmm. What's all this going to cost me then?"

Kathleen interrupted hastily. "Don't worry about that for now, Adam has it all covered. You'll be our guest".

"I'll not be beholden".

Once again, Brontë, who had taken no part in the discussion looked mystified. There's still so much about grown-up talk that I don't understand, she thought. To her, it had seemed so simple, but a kind and well-meaning invitation was becoming complicated.

They took Harry back to his cottage, and as they walked with him up the overgrown path, Brontë had an idea. "Harry, when Uncle Adam comes to collect you for the wedding, I'll ask if I can come as well. I was wondering if you could show me your back garden and if you like I'll bring some secateurs and prune that rose for you. Only if it's finished flowering, of course. And I'll ask Sister Bernice if I can have some rose feed. I'm sure she won't mind. Then you will have lots of lovely blooms to look forward to in August and September and next year".

Harry looked at Brontë, his eyes misting over. He nodded, unable to speak for a moment. He held her hand as they all took their leave. "Thank ye cailin. You remind me of her" was all he said.

* * *

"Well! He certainly does need looking after" said Bridget as they returned to the main road and headed south. "I think that poor man was starving. Did you see him eat? I can't wait to welcome him to Ballymere and I shall be feeding him up for sure. And Angela will have an idea or two of her own".

"Go carefully though, Mam. We hardly know him, and I don't want to risk upsetting him. Or Adam, for that matter. You could see how he didn't like the thought of being under any obligation to us over the guest house. Let's see how he settles in. He's going to be in an unknown place with a lot of strangers. That's a great deal for an old man to take in after years of his own company".

"You're so right, Kathleen. Best to see how things go".

Brontë sat quietly in the back seat, half-hearing the conversation as she watched the views of the coastline flash past along the Wild Atlantic Way, but her thoughts were back in the overgrown garden in Forest Road with its few bold flowers and shrubs determinedly pushing their way through the neglected borders, and how she would love to find out what undiscovered treasures still lay dormant under their cloak of weeds. Would it be thought trivial to tell Sister Bernice about the garden? Somehow, she didn't think it would.

Chapter Sixty-Seven

There were celebrations in the Walsh household at Drover's Cross on the twentieth of May; Arthur had passed his driving test.

On the previous weekend, Patrick had been as good as his word and had bought Arthur his first car; a second-hand black hatchback with low mileage and a service history. Arthur had eyed some of the racier, sleeker models in the showroom with interest, but his father brought him back down to earth by reminding him of the huge insurance costs of such a vehicle for an eighteen-year-old, and that a smaller, more economical car would be far more suitable. After tearing up his L-plates, Arthur climbed eagerly into his car but instead of roaring up Hasker's Hill as Nell had feared, she was relieved to see that he edged cautiously out of the driveway and set off at a sedate pace with no crunching of gears or fast acceleration.

Henry watched, feeling envious. "Your turn next" said Patrick, punching him playfully. "It won't be long, you'll see. And maybe you'll pass first time and show Arthur how it's done".

As they returned indoors, Henry followed his mother into the kitchen as she prepared Arlo's evening bottle. He decided, noticing that as she had relaxed somewhat after Arthur's departure, that this was as good a time as any to broach an important subject.

"Mum, I've come to a decision, about after I leave college, I mean".

"Oh?". Nell looked at him expectantly.

"Assuming my grades are good enough, I'm going to apply for an engineering apprenticeship at Lovells. That way I can earn a salary while I'm studying for my degree. They've already offered me work experience starting in September. Uncle Sean arranged it for me".

"Henry! What about university?" Shock was etched on Nell's face. "Have you thought about this? Really thought about it, I mean. It was always the plan, that you would go to university. You could still read engineering, but university would offer you so much more than a degree. Why have you changed your mind?"

"Mum it was you that had made up your mind, I'd not decided until now. I've done nothing but think about it for ages. I went to see Grandpa and had a chat with him a while ago".

Nell was somewhat reassured by this. "Well, I'm sure Grandpa would have been in favour of a degree."

"He agreed that I should train for something or continue my education, but he suggested various options and we talked about the pros and cons. He said I should make up my own mind, but it should be an informed choice".

For a moment Nell smiled to herself despite her disappointment. How like her father not to tell Henry what to do, but to set out all the possibilities so he could decide for himself. She remembered that not so long ago, Neville had used the same tactic, if it was a tactic, when she was trying to work out what was best for Brontë. In hindsight, it had led her to the right decision. How wise he was. It occurred to her that her ambitions for her children were often clouded by what she wanted for them, when that might not be the best thing at all. She suddenly realised that even at the age of thirty-six she still had a great deal to learn.

The dispute about the journey to Ireland had been resolved; Neville's offer of air tickets to Cork had been accepted with a great deal of excitement. The parents of Abby and Lucy both wrote thank you letters to Neville, and Arthur, Henry and the girls called at the Swan's Rest with some flowers for Lois and a bottle of whiskey for Neville, all chorusing their thanks and that they were looking forward to seeing them at the wedding. Neville and Lois were thrilled to have a visit from 'the young people' as Lois called them, and tea and cakes were ordered while they chatted, much to the boys' delight.

* * *

Brontë's letters home were always something to look forward to. With the increasing use of text messages and emails, the art of handwriting personal letters was beginning to disappear, but Brontë was still making the effort to write a letter to her mother every couple of weeks. Nell had always believed feelings and events could be expressed more deeply and descriptively on paper, and recently she had noticed that Brontë was beginning to hone and perfect her writing style in much the same way as she herself had done years before.

On the day when the latest letter arrived, Nell tucked the letter into the pocket of her jeans, made a cup of coffee and went to read it after she had settled Arlo for his morning nap. The first couple of pages were full of family news, her progress at school and the latest details of the wedding plans. It was all beautifully written, the punctuation and grammar correct, and there was something more – each paragraph was carefully crafted, the sentences flowed. But the next page drew Nell's interest.

'Mummy did I tell you that I was asked to work in the school garden to help Sister Bernice? Well, that's been going on since I came back after Christmas. I wasn't sure about it at first, but now I simply love it, and of course since the weather has improved and the evenings are lighter, I can spend more time there. The thing is, I've learned such a lot from Sister Bernice even though she doesn't say much because she is a silent nun. Do you know, I might even think about landscape gardening or horticulture as a career. And guess what! I have started to keep a gardening journal. I started off by writing down what I did in the garden each time, things I observed and what I'd learned. I've called it "The Restorative Garden" because Sister Bernice has explained how plants and flowers have powers of healing, and the garden has helped me to feel better about everything that's happened. I can't explain it any more than that, but I shall ask Sister Francis if when you come in July, I can show you around. Writing the journal reminded me of the diary you write for the local paper every week. If I can ever write half as well as you do, Mummy I shall be very happy.

PS don't worry, I always hand my homework in on time!"

Before continuing to read the rest of the letter, Nell put down her cup and gave a little sob, feeling full of mixed emotions. The very fact that Brontë was showing such an interest in writing and was inspired by Nell's own small successes was a huge consolation to her; but the separation, with which Nell had come to terms as best she could, still had the ability to reduce her to tears and she could rarely view it in an objective light, however much she tried to convince herself that allowing Brontë to return to Ireland had been the right decision.

She read on.

'My birthday is next month, and Aunt Angela is organising a little party for me at the guest house, just family, a few friends from school and some people I work with on Saturdays. I wish you could all be there, Mummy but by then the wedding will only be about a month away. So, what I was wondering was, you'll be staying for a while after the wedding, won't you? Can you and I go out for the day somewhere, just the two of us? There's so much I want to tell you and talk to you about. Last weekend I went to meet Harry, he's Adam's cousin, with Granny and Auntie Kathleen. It was the strangest house I have ever been in Mummy, Harry's a really sweet old man but so sad. He doesn't look after himself very well and has a garden that is so overgrown and neglected that I wanted to work on it there and then for him! You'll meet him at the wedding too".

Nell folded up the letter, lost in thought for a moment. It was a happy, positive letter, written as though Brontë was saying those words sitting at the table beside her. There was no doubt, she was growing up and showing maturity, losing that crippling shyness and self-consciousness. She couldn't wait to see her, and the prospect of a day out for the two of them was something Nell would look forward to even more than the wedding.

Chapter Sixty-Eight

Neville had given a great deal of thought to the telescope and photographic equipment he might take to Ireland. He guessed he would need a wide-angle lens to take in the panoramic views and capture the broad horizons in West Cork so the following week he purchased one in Kirchington after a long discussion with the sales assistant who seemed determined to sell him more accessories than were necessary. But Neville resisted the sales talk, conscious of the fact that Jenny and Phil had agreed to take these items to Ireland in their car, thus avoiding the risk of them being damaged by careless baggage handlers.

On the way back he called in at Moongarth. Nell was down on the floor of the drawing room with Arlo who, having learned to pull himself up on the furniture, was attempting a few wobbly steps but was still not sure about letting go.

"This little chap's doing well, isn't he" said Neville, laughing as Arlo gave him a beaming smile.

"Yes, he's mobile now, I shall have to start thinking about stair gates and moving everything out of reach. No peace from now on". She gave a wry smile. "How are you, Dad?"

"Well, I've been out buying some camera equipment for the holiday. I know it's going to be a busy couple of weeks out there, even after the wedding but I wanted to ask if you and I could spend an evening travelling off-road, where I'm likely to get the best views and widest skies, you know the area. I really want to make the most of our time, because this may be the only opportunity I get. But of course, it will depend on the weather so it may have to be at short notice. What do you say?"

"Of course, Dad, I'd love to. I've been hoping we'd have a chance to do this. And there will be plenty of people to help with Arlo, and lots of company for Mum while we're out".

"Thank you my dear. And while I'm at it, I want to take plenty of shots of the family, not just wedding photos but over the whole holiday".

Emer came into the room and overheard this. "Grandpa, I was going to ask if you'd take some photos of me at my baptism. But at my baptism class Father Egan said it's a sin to be vain and to think about yourself all the time. He said we should be thinking about other people more, and how we can help them. Do you think it's a sin for me to want to have my photo taken?"

Neville looked at her gravely, while Nell tried to hide a smile. "It can be, I suppose. It depends on your reasons. It's not wrong to have photos taken if it's to remind you of happy occasions or important events. It becomes vain if it's because you think you're more important than anyone else".

"Oh…I see. I don't think I am more important. I am trying to be a better person, Grandpa. Daddy said I'm not so bossy as I used to be, but I have to be firm with Jacob, or he would never do anything he's told. The donkeys are very stubborn, so I must show them who's boss".

Neville, who thought privately that no one could be in any doubt who was boss when Emer was around, tried to keep a straight face. "Well, perhaps it's different when you're dealing with donkeys" he said at last. This seemed to satisfy Emer, and she kissed Neville goodbye as he went to put on his jacket.

"Do you see what we're up against, Dad?" said Nell as she walked down the driveway with her father. "Patrick wanted the children to go to the classes, particularly because Emer was so full of herself. But it seems to have backfired, now she's talking about herself in terms of how much she's trying to improve, how she's putting all the teaching into practice. It's still all about her. I don't know where we're going wrong".

Her father smiled. "You're not going wrong, my dear. Some of this she may grow out of in time. And there's an honesty about Emer, even if she is a little…. what shall we say…over-confident? I'm sure that she will settle down. The main thing is, she has a loving family and some excellent role-models, her mother for one". He kissed the top of Nell's head. "I must be going".

At that moment Ronnie came running breathlessly out of the house. "Grandpa, I was going to ask you something before you go. Please will you come up and see my Airfix models? I'm building World War Two aircraft".

Neville laughed and took off his jacket again. "Go on then, let's see what you've made". He followed Ronnie up the stairs to his room and admired the various models; a few finished ones hung on wires from the ceiling, others were in various stages of completion.

"This one's a Messerschmitt, ME 109 and this is a Spitfire, of course. Spitfires helped win the Battle of Britain, didn't they Grandpa? Next, I'm going to make a Flying Fortress and a Hurricane. And I'm saving up for a Lancaster and a Stuka".

"You've done an excellent job on these. I can see you've got the markings right on the fuselage. Did you use the correct paint?" Neville was impressed as much by Ronnie's enthusiasm as the models themselves.

"Yes, it comes in tiny little tins. I have to use a very fine brush".

"When I was a young man during the war, there was a dogfight not far from here – a Messerschmitt and Hurricane crashed up in the downs, on the next hill along from Low Barrow. I expect there are still a few remnants of the aircraft up there if you knew where to look".

Ronnie looked at Neville, his eyes wide with excitement. "Will you take me up there, Grandpa? Just to see?"

"Sorry Ron, I'm a bit too old to make it up there now. But perhaps your Dad or your brothers will take you. I'll want to hear all about it if you find anything, of course".

As Neville turned to leave, his mind returned to his time at Fenborough Academy during the early years of the war. How frightened they all were then; how close the war had seemed. Yet he had had an easy war compared to some. There was still a twinge of guilt in his mind about that, even after sixty years. He remembered times even further back when he thought of Uncle Frederick who had returned from the First World War an empty shell of a man and resolutely refused to discuss his experiences. Now both of those wars were consigned to the history books; within a few decades they would be beyond living memory. Even now, they were something distant, remote, as they were to his grandson who was learning about them in the same way as he learned about the Battle of Hastings or the English Civil War.

"Grandpa, I was thinking. I'm ten now, look at my muscles! When we go to Ireland I can push Nanny's wheelchair for you. Sometimes I push Arlo in the stroller for Mummy so it can't be very different".

Neville was touched by this and smiled. "Well Ron, that's a very kind thought but the good news is that Nanny has decided that she won't be taking her wheelchair to Ireland. She says she can manage without it now if someone is with her".

"That's great, isn't it Grandpa? She must be feeling much better. Well, she can take my arm sometimes, then. Except at my baptism, I expect I'll be at the front of the church with Emer that day. We've been going to classes".

On the way home, Neville reflected on his two youngest grandchildren. Fenborough Academy and Kirchington Grammar had both been founded on Church of England principles, so he was largely unfamiliar with the teachings of the Catholic Church, but he was aware that it involved a certain amount of ritual. He respected Patrick's views and would never interfere, but Neville wondered to himself about the need for these classes. Did an innocent nine-year-old girl really need to be worrying about sin? When he thought of the many boys he had taught and come to know over the years, he was convinced that the important things were a close, supportive family, unconditional love, a stable home and positive examples, which Emer, Ronnie and all his grandchildren had in abundance. The main thing was, they were being brought up in the Christian faith, and surely that was what mattered.

Chapter Sixty-Nine

June 1998

It was just past midsummer. Brontë's birthday was on the twenty fourth of June which was a Wednesday, but it was agreed that her birthday party would be held on the following Saturday.

Bridget had made the day as special as possible for Brontë, realising that she would be missing her family very much, this being the first birthday spent away from them. She gave Brontë a book called The Discerning Gardener, which gave insight into the properties of various plants and herbs, and how to plan and tend a garden with healing in mind as well as colour and scent. Brontë wanted to start reading it straightaway and pronounced it her favourite present, but at that moment Nell telephoned to wish her daughter happy birthday.

Brontë went to work as usual on the Saturday morning but at one o'clock Angela hurried her out of the guest house and back to the cottage where there were still cards and presents to be opened. The family had been generous; gifts of toiletries, accessories, pretty pyjamas and several more books that she had been wanting to read were all unwrapped and exclaimed over. Adam had sent her a beautiful traditional red and black lace scarf from an exclusive boutique in Malaga.

The card read: "To my adopted goddaughter, with love on your birthday".

As she changed out of her work clothes and deliberated what to wear to her party, Brontë thought back to her last birthday when she was shy, awkward and saw herself as ugly and unattractive, but ever since she had first tried on that bridesmaid dress, she had begun to feel more confident and self-assured. What a lot had happened in that year, she reflected. This time, things were different. She had bought her first pair of jeans with some of the money her parents had sent, these were slim fitting without being tight and teamed with a colourful top the effect was stunning. She really did look slimmer, she decided as she looked at her reflection in the full-length mirror. Despite not needing makeup, she put on a little blusher and lipstick anyway. It's my birthday after all, she thought.

Angela and the staff at Hackett's had put up bunting, streamers and had hired a disco with a light show, although as darkness did not come until after ten o'clock in June, the full effect would not be seen until later in the evening. The chef had made a special effort with the buffet, designed with teenagers' tastes in mind, not too childish, not too grownup.

Her friends Kitty, Cora and Maeve from school had been invited and Jimmy, who was introduced as Maeve's boyfriend. The girls presented Brontë with a huge birthday card signed by the Sisters and her year group. There was a gift from them all: a framed print of 'The Peace of Wild Things' by Wendell Berry, a poem which they knew that Brontë loved. Most of the Hackett's staff joined the party except for those working at the bar or in the kitchen, but these were soon relieved by Fergus who wanted them all to have some time off, and by seven thirty all the guests had arrived. The atmosphere was already lively and relaxed, the music of the year's hit tunes booming out across the lounge which was once again doubling as a dance floor. Ruari, who had begged Angela to let him have the evening off, didn't leave Brontë's side and was intent on making sure that she enjoyed every moment.

Soon after eight o'clock, a taxi drew up outside, unnoticed by most of the guests. Then the front door opened, and someone stepped into the room.

"Mummy!" squealed Brontë and flew across the dance floor.

The only person who looked slightly disappointed at that moment was Ruari, such had been his determination to give Brontë the best birthday party and to spend every available moment with her. But he was generous natured and could see how thrilled she was to have an unexpected visit from her mother, realising that there was nothing else for it but to take a back seat for a while. He was sure there would be an opportunity to get some time alone with Brontë later.

"How come you're here, Mummy?" said Brontë, linking arms with Nell as she took her mother across the floor to where Bridget and Angela were waiting to greet her. "What a lovely surprise!".

There were hugs, exclamations and shouts as the family gathered round to welcome Nell. Only Bridget knew of her daughter-in-law's plan to fly to Cork for Brontë's party and had been sworn to secrecy.

"Well, it was your father's idea", explained Nell. "He and Ronnie said they could look after Arlo for a day or so; Ronnie's really good with him as you know. Jenny is coming in for extra hours over the weekend. It won't hurt for them to manage without me for a while. And of course, Emer is there to keep them in order". They all laughed.

It had been nearly six months since Nell had waved goodbye to her daughter after Christmas; a time Brontë preferred to forget because of the unbearable memory of that day in Darcey's when the sight of the two girls mocking her and taunting her in public had caused her to pass out on the escalator. At the time that setback had seemed so overwhelming, so insurmountable that she did not think she could ever regain the small amount of progress she had made until then. But Nell's eyes did not deceive her; here was Brontë, smiling, vivacious, sparkling, everything a young girl should be at her fifteenth birthday party yet there was something more; a contentment. Brontë was at peace with herself; seemingly she had wrestled with her demons and banished them.

"Mummy I want you to meet Ruari. He's my good friend" said Brontë, not wishing to give her mother the idea that he was officially her boyfriend but wanting her to know that he was now someone special in her life.

"I'm very pleased to meet you, Mrs Walsh" said Ruari, shaking Nell's hand nervously. "It's a great party, isn't it? Mrs Hackett knows how to put on a good hooley".

Nell liked Ruari on sight, noticing his friendly natural manner, his courtesy and his obvious affection for Brontë.

"He's nice" said Nell, as they made their way to the buffet table. "You have some lovely friends here Brontë. And while we're on our own, let me tell you, you look fabulous! All grown up, so slim, your skin is beautiful, your hair, and you look so, well, happy! This last six months has really done you a great deal of good. What's your secret?"

"I am happy, Mum, but it's not any one thing. It's school, my friends, the garden, Ruari, living here with Granny in the peace and quiet, nobody expecting too much, just accepting me for how I am. It's what I needed, Mum, thank you for letting me come back".

At that moment, Connor, emboldened by several pints of Guinness came and asked Nell to dance. "Sure and if my brother can't be here to walk his wife on to the dance floor it's myself that should have that honour" he said, seizing her hand and steering her into the throng of dancers. Ruari saw his chance and quickly propelled Brontë into the laughing, shifting crowd. No one really knew one dance from another by then, everyone was just swaying in time to the music, not worrying about steps or formalities.

After that there was a queue of partners for both Brontë and Nell. Neither of them was used to dancing and by nine thirty it was a relief when Angela called a halt, and Brendan, the chef carried in a spectacular birthday cake, adorned with flowers and birds in sugar icing. The lettering said 'To Brontë, Flower of Ballymere'. Fergus followed with a tray of sparkling wine for a toast, and Nell took out her camera and snapped a whole reel of film, wanting to capture the atmosphere of the party while it was in full swing and before she was too tired or caught up in the moment to remember.

Angela did indeed have the knack of hosting the perfect party. She knew exactly how to find the right balance, encouraging plenty of revelry and good-natured banter, reinforced by just enough alcohol where the adults were concerned to ensure a pleasant, relaxed and jovial atmosphere, but stopping short of anything getting out of hand or uncomfortable for her guests. And together with the music, dancing, light show and an excellent buffet it was an evening to remember. As the deejay called everyone onto the floor for the last slow dance of the evening, Ruari lost no time in claiming Brontë so that they could spend the final special moments of the party together, and as the song ended, he took her in his arms and kissed her; her first real grown-up kiss.

* * *

"Thank you for a wonderful time, Aunt Angela" said Brontë, hugging her great-aunt after saying goodbye to her friends.

"Away with you" said Angela fondly. "Sure, isn't it some practice I'm needing before the next big event? The wedding will be on us before we know it".

Nell was to share Brontë's room at the cottage; she was to sleep in her daughter's bed while Brontë used the sofa bed in the same room. As they settled down for the night, mother and daughter exchanged confidences. Brontë confessed to liking Ruari very much and that she hoped that Nell would approve. Nell had noticed the glow in her eyes, had seen the metamorphosis of her traumatised, self-conscious daughter into a confident, happy young woman who was at ease with herself, and she could not but feel that although she, as her mother had been unable to bring about this change, this was not a failure on her part. Allowing Brontë to return to Ballymere was the catalyst; she could see that now. There were other benign forces at work here; perhaps the timeless aura of this beautiful place was weaving its magic in a way that so few outsiders could comprehend. But Nell had felt it, had witnessed it herself many years ago, and understood.

Chapter Seventy

July 1998

Where will they all sleep?

This was the question Angela was asking herself as she considered the details of accommodating all the family and friends of the bride and groom at Hackett's. Many months ago, she had booked out the entire guest house for the whole week from the Wednesday preceding the wedding, thinking that planning well ahead was the answer. But the guest list had grown; not excessively but in proportion to the number of rooms available it was a challenge, to say the least. A small marquee was to be set up in the garden as they could not rely on good weather; this would provide additional space for the reception but would not solve the problem of bedrooms. In addition, some guests, although travelling together were not couples, so could not be expected to share. She thought of Arthur and Henry who were both bringing their plus ones; should she allocate them double rooms with their partners? She thought not, despite the fact that the boys would no doubt be in favour. Angela scratched her head and asked Donal to bring her a fresh pot of tea while she mulled over the numbers and tried to make sense of them.

Neville and Lois would have the double ground floor en-suite room and Harry would have one of the singles. This was easy and could not be changed. But the remainder of the accommodation was just insufficient whichever way she looked at it. She felt annoyed with herself; she was normally so well organised, nothing fazed her. There must be a solution, she thought, but right now she just couldn't see one. With a sigh she reached for her address book and picked up the telephone.

A couple of hours later she was on her way to solving the problem. She booked out the remaining single room on the ground floor to Jack. Moving up to the first floor, the doubles were allocated to couples. Nell and Patrick would have the largest as they would have Arlo with them. Four further doubles were set aside for Barbara and Jonathan, Joe and Ruth, Sean and Amy (his fiancé) and Jenny and Phil. The sixth room was reserved for Adam and Kathleen, although they would be departing on the day after their wedding. Adam and Jack were to stay in a hotel in Clonakilty on the Friday before the wedding; traditionally the bride and groom would spend that night apart.

The top floor presented more of a dilemma. There were two twin en-suite rooms. She knew that Arthur and Abby regarded themselves as a couple now, but did that mean they would share a room? And if they did, would that mean that Henry and Lucy would share also? Their relationship was much less serious. Angela felt uncomfortable about that and in the end decided that she would err on the safe side and book the two girls in together in one twin room and the boys in the other. If there were objections, she would leave those to Nell and Patrick to sort out. That took care of most of the guests. But that left three single people: Niall, Hayley and Rafael. Angela was on the point of hiring some converted shepherds' huts, but that would come at a cost at such short notice. Mmm.

After a further half hour, the answer came to her, and following a discussion with Bridget and Gráinne, it was decided that Aisling and Emer would share Brontë's room at the cottage. This left two rooms free at the farm for Hayley and Rafael. Ronnie would sleep on an air bed in their dining room. A quick call to Aidan confirmed that he would be able to offer Niall his spare room. Job done. If there were no further additions to the guest list, this would do very well. She gave another sigh of relief, put down her pen and ordered a gin and tonic from the bar.

* * *

In Kirchington, Lois was full of excitement about the forthcoming wedding. She realised with a shock that she had only attended only two weddings in her life: her own and her daughter's. Most women in their seventies had been to dozens during their lifetime, she reflected. Never mind, even more cause for celebration. She was extremely fond of Kathleen whom she regarded as family; she would always remember her kindness when she and Neville first returned to Spain, both still nervous and full of trepidation after the debacle with Evelyn. Yet somehow, she had trusted Kathleen implicitly from the start, despite her being a most unlikely choice of companion. There was an honesty about Kathleen and a readiness to admit to her past mistakes. But as she began to know her better, Lois did not regard them as failings. Kathleen had been unlucky and during those early years had not had the opportunities that a good education might have afforded. But from that first invitation to come to England, Kathleen had shown she had spirit and a determination to better herself. She had just needed someone to show faith in her. Nell and Barbara had done that, but the rest was down to Kathleen's own hard work and resolve. Now, at the age of thirty-nine and in love, real love for the first time she had blossomed; but some of her happiness was due to people trusting her, offering her those important chances and Kathleen having the courage to accept them.

Lois turned to the beautiful aquamarine silk suit hanging in its delicate cover. She and Nell had chosen it together in Darcey's a few weeks ago. It was expensive; a designer outfit, complemented by a frivolous hat – an ensemble that was intended for a special occasion; the London season, a society garden party, or an afternoon outdoor concert in palatial surroundings. Lois had so rarely ventured into company that she had never given a great deal of thought to such an addition to her wardrobe. But this wedding, the most exciting event that she had ever been invited to deserved the very best; it would be a day to remember. Not just because it was for

Kathleen, it was more than that; it was a holiday, a visit to a new country and she would be with friends and family, people whom she knew and loved. Most of all, she wanted Neville to be proud of her. She never forgot that fate had given them a second chance.

Meanwhile, Neville had packed up his telescope and camera equipment with as much care as Kathleen had packed her wedding outfit. He was excited about the holiday for the same reasons as Lois but he was also looking forward to spending time with Nell and taking those excursions to the desolate, dark corners of West Cork she had spoken of, and searching those jet-black night skies with the promise of brighter stars and myriad constellations in all their brilliance which he had never been able to study in England or Spain. He wanted to make the most of this chance; it might be the only opportunity he would ever have to indulge his hobby for a few nights in such surroundings, knowing that Lois would be in pleasant company and well taken care of.

* * *

Jack Keenan had arranged his trip around Europe so that it ended in Solibrio, prior to the onward journey to Ireland. The plan was for him to stay at the apartment with Adam for a few days and take the opportunity to explore the Costa del Sol, relax, swim and make up for lost time with his brother whom he had not seen for more than two years.

There was a strong family resemblance but whereas Adam was tall and lean, Jack was more sturdy, muscular and shorter than his brother. Both men were deeply tanned and had the same luminous light blue eyes, but Jack's hair and eyebrows were blonde, bleached by the Australian sun, while Adam's colouring was slightly darker, although his temples were showing streaks of grey.

They had decided to fly from Malaga to Cork on the fifteenth of July, leaving plenty of time before the wedding for

Adam to take care of any last-minute tasks and to travel up to Lankerris on the twenty second to collect Harry as arranged. Adam had told Jack of the first awkward, strained meeting with their Irish cousin, but how on the second visit Harry had mellowed slightly and had shown an unexpected willingness to come to the wedding. He related how he and Kathleen had seen a deep sadness in the old man, no doubt hiding some long-buried resentment and anger; but that now and then a spark of humour and defiance had broken through the surface. Since then, he had heard from Kathleen that she had visited him again along with Bridget and Brontë, and how Harry had taken a liking to her young niece who had forged a sort of connection with him despite being three or four generations younger.

✳ ✳ ✳

Patrick was long overdue for a break from work and despite the pressures of work he was eagerly anticipating the extended holiday in Ireland, for the wedding and later for the children's baptisms. He couldn't wait to see his family back home, as he still called Ballymere; it was a long time since his last visit which, he realised with guilt had been for his father's funeral ten years ago. Where had that time gone? His business seemed to take up more and more of his attention; this was due to its success, but Nell complained that the only time she and the family saw him was when he was rushed or tired.

Something was worrying Patrick, and one evening as they were snatching a few minutes peace and quiet after Arlo had been settled to bed and the rest of the family were occupied, he confided in Nell.

"I'm a bit nervous of leaving the business for so long while we're away" he said at last. "It's the first time Joe and I will both be absent. I can't rely on anyone else in the same way".

"You must have a holiday, Patrick. You're on site six days a week as it is, and on Sundays you're still thinking about work. You do need to delegate more. What's the point of the business doing so well if none of us see any benefit from it? You'll be ill if you go on like this, and then where will we be?"

"I know, I really do need a rest".

"Patrick, it's a couple of weeks before we leave. Take that time to plan the work while we're away, get everything as organised as you can in advance and who can best take over the reins for a short time. There must be someone, you said you have several teams of good men on the contracts now".

"Well yes, there may be a couple who could step up for a while".

"There you are then. Get onto that tomorrow, Patrick. And don't forget, Joe won't be staying in Ireland as long as we will. He's not a godparent this time, remember. He'll be back to work before you are".

Patrick brightened a little when Nell reminded him of this fact. "You're right. I think it will just about work out. Thanks Nelly". He kissed her lovingly.

But privately, Nell realised that although she might have won this particular battle, there would be more ahead. She was determined to make Patrick slow down during this holiday and to take the opportunity to have a re-think about his work-life balance. She was aware that his father had died of an undiagnosed heart condition, and although she didn't want to frighten Patrick, she must find a way of making him see that by continuing to overwork in this way he was in danger of putting his health at risk.

Chapter Seventy-One

Excitement was building at Ballymere as one by one the guests started to arrive well in advance of the wedding. Adam and Jack were the first, Adam having left Rafael and Hayley in charge of Martina's for a few more days until the relief staff took over.

Nell, Patrick and the younger children would be travelling by ferry but had to wait until the end of the school term on the seventeenth of July. Arthur, Henry and their girlfriends were flying to Cork on Sunday the nineteenth, to be met at the airport by Connor. Neville and Lois, having agreed not to travel on the same flight had decided to travel a day later. The remainder of the guests would be arriving at various dates during the week before the wedding. Angela was happy with this arrangement; staggered arrivals meant that she could welcome each set of travellers and settle them in separately, giving the personal touch which made every guest feel special.

* * *

Summer Term at St Teresa's ended on the fifteenth of July. Sister Francis asked to see Brontë on the last day. "Brontë, you have done exceptionally well during the last two terms, and your progress towards your Leaving Certificate has been impressive. As you know, your results will be issued later in August, but I am certain that that you and your family will be very pleased with them".

"Thank you, Sister,".

"Have you given any thought as to what you will do now?"

Brontë was silent for a moment. "I do have an idea for a future career, but first I shall need to find out about training".

"And what career is that?"

"Sister, ever since you asked me to help Sister Bernice in the garden, I have realised that I would like to study horticulture, botany, something to do with plants and flowers. Perhaps landscape gardening. Sister Bernice has taught me so much, thank you for letting me work with her. I've kept a garden journal, you know. And...there's something else". She paused. "Sister Bernice...the garden... has helped me get over....my problems" she said lamely, not wishing to explain but feeling sure that somehow, Sister Francis understood.

"Sister Bernice has unusual powers", Sister Francis said at last. "She has a healing ministry, there is no doubt about that. Not everyone is comfortable with it, of course; I shall say no more on that score. But I am not a bit surprised that she has helped you. She does indeed have great gifts, and I am very glad that you have benefited from her knowledge and wisdom". She turned to look at the papers on her desk. "We will miss you, Brontë. I have some forms here for your father to sign, as you will be leaving us. I gather that your parents are visiting for a family wedding?"

"Yes, my aunt's. I am to be a bridesmaid".

Sister Francis smiled. "So you will be going back to England with your family afterwards?"

"I...I don't know. Yes, sometime soon, I expect". Brontë was still unsure about returning but knew that this reality would have to be faced before long.

* * *

Brontë liked Uncle Jack, as she called him, on sight. He was a lot of fun, she decided, and she loved hearing his Australian accent which was so much more pronounced than Adam's. On the way up to Harry's at Lankerris he told her of Sydney Harbour with its famous Bridge and Opera House, swimming and surfing in the warm, clear waters off Bondi Beach with its white-gold sands and unforgettable sunsets. She laughed at his description of kangaroos running wild even on busy roads, and how drivers had to give way to them. When he went on to describe diving off the Great Barrier Reef, she was fascinated at the thought of swimming amongst the coral gardens and the most exotic and colourful fish, yet concerned to hear that because of its popularity, the reef was now beginning to become endangered and threatened. It's a world away from the garden at St Teresa's, she thought, yet lately she had come to realise that there were so many forms of beauty in nature, and that she had only just started on her voyage of discovery. With that thought in mind, she had come armed with pruning secateurs, rose feed and some lightweight shears, which she hoped Harry would allow her to use in her quest for uncovering some long-abandoned plants and shrubs in his garden and that with a little help, sunlight and a good watering, they might be encouraged to flourish once again.

Adam had explained to his brother that Harry's place was.... he tried to put it politely.... unkempt, in fact he shared his concerns with Jack that it was an unhealthy and possibly hazardous environment for an old man with failing eyesight and poor mobility. He confided to Jack that maybe after the wedding, or on their return from the holiday in Australia he and Kathleen would try and persuade the old man to move to somewhere more suitable, but so far, they had not thought how that might be achieved, knowing that Harry was inclined to be stubborn and would probably regard it as interference.

After the first introductions had been completed, Brontë went off to start work in the back garden, Harry having given her free rein to do whatever she wanted as long as she didn't hurt herself, as the back garden was full of unwanted clutter; old household items, broken tools and unidentifiable metal and wooden objects. Adam had warned her that she would not be able to spend very long; they had another four-hour drive back to Ballymere ahead of them. About an hour or so, he said. During that time, Adam and Jack had decided to risk a cup of tea in Harry's kitchen before helping him to gather his few possessions into an old shabby suitcase. Angela had provided them with a packed lunch for four people, knowing that they would not wish to add time on to their journey for eating out, but Brontë took hers into the garden, now and then taking a mouthful of a sandwich, but really wanting to make the most of her time outside. She began by raking up a mountain of dead leaves and vegetation, only to find another layer of weeds underneath, completely stifling any plants brave enough to survive without light or space. But here and there were red stalks of peonies, defiantly pushing their stems up alongside some ground elder, and some Asiatic lilies. These should have flowered in June, she thought, then realised that everything was delayed because they were smothered by last year's foliage. She set about making a space around the plants, pulling the weeds well away to give them room to thrive. Maybe they will catch up now, she thought, finding a rusty watering can and filling it from an outdoor tap. Moving the can which had almost taken root revealed a cluster of pinky-mauve cranesbill, and as she continued to clear away weeds with her bare hands she found some stalks of what she thought were golden rudbeckia, a clump of Lady's Mantle, its leaves still clinging on to some sparkling pearls of moisture, and a trio of hostas which even the slugs seemed to have deserted. Nora must have loved this garden once, she said to herself, wondering what had happened in Harry's life to make him give up on it. If only I had enough time here, I could really make it come alive again, she thought, wishing Sister Bernice could see the task before her and knowing that the nun would have nodded encouragement and in a very few words given the best advice and direction. Lastly, not forgetting her promise to Harry, Brontë moved round to the front garden and tackled the rose by the window. It had not been pruned for many years, she concluded; some of the stems were thick and woody but there was visible new growth, which would yield blooms later in the season. Remembering Sister Bernice's instructions, she made diagonal cuts with her bypass pruners, firstly removing all the dead wood, then concentrated on trimming the younger stems just above the bud-eye as she had been taught and finally gave it some of the rose feed she had brought with her. When she was satisfied that she had shaped the rose as best she could, she stood back to survey her handiwork, hoping that it would meet with Harry's approval.

Harry had tried to make an effort with his appearance, sporting a passably clean collar and tie, but he had made an unsuccessful attempt to cut his own hair, which now looked jagged and uneven. "I've made a mess of it altogether" he said regretfully to Adam, with a tinge of embarrassment.

"No matter" said Adam, trying to spare the old man's feelings. "There's a visiting hairdresser at the guest house, I'm sure she will tidy it up for you before Saturday".

When Harry saw the difference Brontë had made to his garden in one short hour, and that many forgotten plants were now visible and lending some colour to the previously neglected wilderness, he clasped one of her small hands in both of his and whispered in a husky voice: "Thank ye, cuilan, you have worked wonders. She would love to see this. She would have loved you too".

Brontë guessed that he was talking about his late wife, and feeling suddenly shy, took Harry to the front garden to show him the rose. "It's a climber I think, so it should flower again well into the autumn" she explained. She saw with discomfort that Harry had tears in his eyes. "You must come back and see it when it is in bloom again" he said hoarsely.

"You can drive back" said Adam, tossing the car keys to Jack. "Don't worry, you know we drive on the left here, same as Aus". They both laughed as they climbed into the car. Harry was helped into the front seat and Adam sat with Brontë in the back. "You've done well today" he said, looking at her with admiration. "It's not many people who would tackle that garden. You've really made an impression on it".

"It's what I love doing" said Brontë modestly. "I just wish I'd had longer; I could do so much more".

* * *

Angela and Kathleen were waiting at the door of Hackett's to welcome Harry. After a brief tour of the guest house, he was shown to his en-suite room, which he looked at in wonder, as if he had been offered a room in a palace.

"Dinner is at six-thirty" said Angela, placing Harry's suitcase on the luggage stand. "But feel free to have a rest until then, you've had a long journey. Bridget will be over to see you later. Call me if there's anything you need, anything at all". She pointed to the telephone on the bedside table. "We're so pleased you decided to come. Doesn't it mean a lot to Adam and Kathleen now? You're one of the family already, you know". She smiled at him and left the room.

Harry didn't know what to think. He was nearly eighty-one and had resigned himself to spending the rest of his life in his ramshackle home without family, friends or company. Some of that he had brought on himself, he acknowledged. But in the blink of an eye this had changed; suddenly he had two young cousins and more on the other side of the world. He had been welcomed into this kindly, caring group of people who had accepted him without question, did not judge him and had offered him hospitality and friendship despite barely knowing him. Perhaps life still has some surprises in store for me, he reflected, taking off his shoes and laying down on the soft, comfortable bed. Within seconds he had drifted off into a deep sleep.

Chapter Seventy-Two

1998

It was the sixteenth of July. At the same time as the family were beginning to assemble in Ballymere for Kathleen's wedding, Nina Mason, wearing over-large sunglasses and her hair tucked unbecomingly under a baseball cap was seated at a corner table of Dimitri's Coffee Lounge which was conveniently situated down a quiet side street in Trentingham, a small town about forty miles from Drover's Cross. She was early; she had finished her coffee already. Should she order another? From time to time, she glanced down at her phone and then occasionally at the entrance which was in her line of sight. She had insisted on discretion for this meeting, but now she was wondering if she should have arranged it at all; it had been at her suggestion that they had cut off all contact since last year. But recently something had been nagging at her; was it conscience, curiosity or some other unfamiliar instinct that had been waking her in the night and threatening to rob her of whatever peace of mind she had been able to scrape together? It must be because it was coming up for a year since it happened, she thought. Jessie was the only person she could talk to; she had not heard from Denny since that day.

She did not recognise Jessie at first when she walked through the door. Gone was her long chestnut hair, replaced by a sharp blonde bob. She had lost weight and looked too thin. Her skin was clear but there were lines on her face that hadn't been there before. There was no doubt, Jessie had aged in the last year. I expect she thinks the same about me, thought Nina ruefully. All this has taken its toll on both of us. Well, we're not here for girl talk. I'll say what I came to say and gauge her reaction. Then we can both go our separate ways.

"You were the last person I expected to hear from" said Jessie, sitting down opposite Nina. Clearly, she was not going to waste time with pleasantries. "I thought we'd agreed to draw a line under everything. Have you heard from Denny?"

"No, nothing. I expect he's somewhere in Europe. Jessie, I wanted to ask you a couple of things. It's a year next Friday since....do you want a coffee?"

Jessie ignored this. "I hope you're not having second thoughts, Nina. You know there's no going back now on any of it".

Nina stirred the spoon around her empty coffee cup.

"I know. I don't regret my decision. The only thing I do regret was ever meeting Denny. It was a one-night stand you know, I was lonely. Doug had been working abroad for months, and he was supposed to come home on leave, then at the last minute he telephoned to say all leave was cancelled, the project was behind schedule. I was angry. Denny wasn't even my type, I didn't know he was a potential criminal until it was too late. He had debts, I knew that, and people were chasing him for money. Even then, if he'd done what I expected him to do and cleared off, I could have coped. I'd booked myself into a clinic and no one would have been any the wiser. But he had to interfere, and you couldn't keep your mouth shut, could you?"

"You know what happened, he kept on and on at me until he completely wore me down. As a matter of fact, I was frightened of him at one point. I had no choice too, just remember that. You've told me all this before, why are you bringing it up now?".

"I just needed to talk to someone about it, there's no one else. It was a terrible thing we did, Jessie, unbelievable. But even now when I look back, I don't see that I had any other way out. He wanted money, Jessie, a lot of money, that's why he made me have the baby, he wanted to have a hold over me. Making sure I had his baby was his way of tying himself to me, or to my money, more to the point. He wanted me to go away with him, but I refused. In the end he settled for taking the baby and the money, but really it was just the money he wanted. He needed to get away, he'd been a witness to a murder, for God's sake! Exactly how involved he was I don't know but telling me that was his big mistake because it gave me some leverage, and I was almost out of options. I could have gone to the police straight away. But I didn't because I couldn't tell what he was capable of. I had to find a solution before Doug came home, thank goodness he didn't come back until months later. I really don't know how I managed to hide the pregnancy all that time".

"I still don't understand why you've asked me here, Nina.". Jessie was becoming impatient and glanced down at her wristwatch. "We shouldn't be seen together".

"I can't get it out of my mind, Jessie, I've been having sleepless nights lately. Maybe it's because he would be one year old next week. What it amounts to is, I paid Denny ten thousand pounds to take my baby away for good. I still can't believe that I did that. The baby was no more than a bargaining chip to both of us. Ok I've never had maternal feelings, I never wanted children but what kind of a person does that? Some sort of monster? Is that what I am?" She paused. "And in the end, what was it all for? Doug and I never really got back together, he's met someone else now, we're getting a divorce".

"Like you said, you had no choice. You were under a huge amount of pressure at the time". Jessie checked her watch again.

"What I wanted to ask you was, well, I've been thinking whether I should try to trace him. My baby, I mean. I can't help wondering how he is, where he is.... I never gave him a name...I don't even know if he's still alive. I know that would mean giving Denny away and I promised not to do that, it was part of the deal...".

Jessie's face went white with shock. "Nina you can't mean that! No way, absolutely no way. I can't believe you're even considering it. You couldn't even make anonymous enquiries without arousing suspicion. Denny may be well out of the picture by now but what about us? What about me? Have you any idea of the consequences?" She lowered her voice. "Concealing a birth is a serious crime. I would be struck off the register of midwives for gross misconduct, I'd never work again, I'd kiss goodbye to my pension and we'd both go to prison. Even failing to register a birth is against the law. I would never have had any part in it except I had such money troubles back then. We're in this together for the long haul, you and I. You must accept that. I've never breathed a word to a soul, and you agreed to do the same. If we both hold our nerve it may get easier in time".

"Hmm...I guessed you'd say something like that. But what about if he tries to trace me, later on, when he's older?"

"Unlikely. He could be anywhere in the world by then, where would he start looking? There would be nothing to link him to you. Your DNA isn't on any database, you have no criminal record".

Nina stared into space for a few minutes. "What do you think I should do, then?"

"You do nothing and say nothing. Not ever. We are both going to put this behind us, as if it never happened. Are you listening to me Nina? We both move on".

Nina got up from the table and slung her bag over her shoulder. "That's it, then. No more to be said. I'll have to start afresh, make a new life somehow. I'll go abroad, find a job. Try to forget".

Jessie looked at her friend and for a moment the harsh edge disappeared from her voice. "I'm sorry for all you've been through Nina. I know it's worse for you, I can't imagine how you must be feeling. But you must see, what I've said makes sense. The alternative is...well...impossible".

"Yes...well, ok Jessie. We'll leave it at that. Don't worry, we won't be meeting up again. Goodbye, and...have a nice life".

One by one the two women left the coffee shop and walked away in different directions.

Chapter Seventy-Three

Emer did not know quite what to make of Granny Bridget. This was her first visit to Ireland; she had not been born when the family came over for Dermot's funeral; her brother Ronnie had been only two months old then. So Emer was uncharacteristically cautious. She decided that her grandmother was very kind but was also a no-nonsense person who could not easily be argued with and who would be very quick to correct any misdemeanours. This was unfamiliar territory for Emer who, although her behaviour had improved significantly over the last six months still had plenty to say for herself and was always inclined to want the last word. Her parents watched this unusual reticence with a mixture of relief and amusement. "I knew she would meet her match with Mam" said Patrick, witnessing a conversation between them and noticing that Emer was nodding obediently instead of contradicting. "I can see you've been paying attention in your baptism classes, Emer" Bridget was saying. "Haven't I been telling Father Sweeney all about you when he visits? And your brothers and sister too".

Bridget had been surprisingly tearful when Nell carried Arlo through the front door of the cottage on that first afternoon. "Dear little soul. His parents may have abandoned him, but the Lord will never give up on him, poor lamb" was all she said, crossing herself.

A few tense words had been exchanged between Patrick and Henry over the matter of the sleeping arrangements. Arthur and Abby were to share a room at the guest house; this had been agreed as they were going to live together in a flat in Kirchington soon after they returned from holiday, so there seemed no point in separating them. But Nell was insistent that Henry and Lucy could not share; they had known each other only a short time, and she and Patrick were answerable to Lucy's parents and responsible for her during this holiday. So much to Henry's disappointment, it was decided that he was to have the other second floor room and Lucy was to share the twin room with Hayley at the farm. Another crisis averted, thought Nell as she pushed Arlo in his stroller from her mother's cottage up to Hackett's to meet some of the other guests who had already arrived: her parents, Jack, Harry, Jonathan and Barbara. After the evening meal she planned to take a walk with Brontë and later she and her father would be taking a trip out with his telescope; the weather was fair and so far, there was not a cloud in the sky.

✻ ✻ ✻

Patrick was behind the wheel of the Land Rover. The Mizen was too lonely a place for Nell to drive her father to at night, he had insisted, aware that she had only visited the area a few times in her life and then most of their excursions had been during daylight hours.

At first, Neville was slightly disappointed by this. Secretly he had hoped for a trip out just with Nell so that together they could discover those vast, uninterrupted dark skies she had promised; where there was no light pollution, where there were no buildings or forests to obscure his vision and no traffic disturbance or aircraft noise to shatter the peace. But as they set out just before dusk on that July evening, he had to admit that Patrick was right; this was a forlorn, desolate landscape where the only sounds were waves crashing onto the shore a mile or so below them and the cries of a few birds flying home to roost in the bushes. No danger lurked there; he was sure of it; this was a friendly, welcoming country but its very isolation meant that it would be easy for an unwary traveller to lose their way.

"What's that mountain?" asked Neville, pointing to a peak a few miles distant.

"That's Mount Gabriel" replied Patrick. "I've climbed it a few times when I was a lad. The views are breathtaking – you can see Roaringwater Bay, lots of islands and the Beara

Peninsula. They say that it's where the last wolves in Ireland roamed, back in the eighteenth century. That may be just a legend though" he grinned.

Nell shivered. Even though they were travelling in countryside that she knew and loved, the thought of wolves wandering around freely in the dark was unnerving.

"This is the only light pollution you need worry about" said Patrick, stopping the Land Rover and indicating the Fastnet Lighthouse on its rocky promontory several miles out to sea, just as he had pointed it out to Nell so many years ago. He and Neville stepped out onto the road for a better view.

Neville watched, fascinated for several minutes. It was true, it was the only light visible, and he could understand the solace that its reassuring beam, flashing every few seconds would be to sailors and to those ashore. Nell, cheered by the comfort of the light sweeping across the bay, forgot about wolves and climbed out of the Land Rover to join the others.

It was a perfect night for sky-watching. For a change, a high-pressure weather system had settled over West Cork, and this ensured an absence of cloud, hardly any wind further from the shoreline and clear, pure air. The moon had not yet risen, and the skies were a deep, ebony black, like a curtain of velvet draped across the heavens, dotted with thousands of pinpricks of silver light. Neville thought he had never seen so many stars with the naked eye.

"We'll need to turn inland a little way for the best conditions" Patrick said, starting up the engine again. "If we make for that slope further up – there's a rough track we can follow – then the shoulder of the next hill will obscure the light from the Fastnet".

"What's that?" As they climbed higher into the hills, Neville pointed to a derelict building a few yards from the laneway. Patrick parked up and switched on his torch, so they could have a closer look. It was run-down and obviously abandoned; a rough dwelling constructed from stone blocks, a few of which were crumbling. Thorns, brambles and weeds had for countless years taken over and covered the walls and part of the roof. But the structure looked sound, even in its neglected and dilapidated state.

"It's one of the old Poor Houses" explained Patrick quietly. "A kind of workhouse. During the Great Hunger, if people were turned out of their cottages by the landowners because they couldn't pay the rent, they could take shelter here and would receive just about enough food to survive. Some, if they were starving but owned land would have to give it up in exchange for sanctuary here. They were grim places, very grim. Disease was rife. Whole families were split up, and they had to do pointless, back-breaking work on the land in return for the smallest ration of food. It was only just slightly better than total starvation".

For a few moments they stood in silent contemplation. This had been a scene of immense suffering; haunted by misfortune, cruelty and despair, separated from the present day by only a few generations. How many families had sought refuge here on this very spot, Nell wondered, left with no other option but to throw themselves on the mercy of a brutal, inhuman regime that offered them only the most meagre existence, devoid of all hope. For the second time that evening, she felt a tremor of fear and unease. It was not a happy place.

Neville was the first to break the silence. His mind had travelled in a different direction. The brow of the hill on which they stood had a commanding view of the night sky, with broad horizons in each direction. His eyes had gradually become accustomed to the starlight and as Patrick had predicted, the light from the Fastnet could not be seen from this position. Apart from Mount Gabriel it was one of the highest points in the area. As far as location was concerned, he could not have imagined a more perfect place to site an observatory. In a way he felt excited, enthusiastic, impatient, as if at last he had found what he had been searching for. Chris Davenport would have agreed with him, he felt sure. But Neville was also a sensitive man; he could well understand that recent history was never far from the surface in these parts; this ruined building had been left as it was for nearly a hundred and fifty years as a solemn reminder of past injustices and in memory of those who had entered its walls out of desperation, clinging on to the barest threads of life. He knew something about the political tensions between Britain and Ireland that had existed for centuries. How could he, an Englishman on holiday here, ever think of making such a suggestion and upsetting such deep-rooted feelings?

"Who does it belong to?" he asked Patrick.

"The council, probably. Or maybe a charity. Why?"

"No matter. Just a thought, that's all. But while I'm here, I'll set up my telescope, if that's ok".

Patrick wondered what was on Neville's mind and could only guess. But he also knew that his father-in-law was a man of integrity, known for his fair mindedness and deep thinking. If he was about to devise a plan, it would be well thought out and researched, taking into account peoples' feelings and sensitivities. Time would tell. He felt sure that Neville would keep any scheme to himself until he was ready to share it and had considered every aspect of how it might affect others. He felt a huge respect for this man, and looked at Nell, who was standing motionless, lost in thought. How like her father she was. He moved to her side and put a comforting arm around her shoulders. "It's a sad place altogether" he said, understanding how troubled she was by what he had told them. "But sometimes things can change for the better. Good can come out of bad". She looked up at him and wondered what he meant. But his face was inscrutable.

Chapter Seventy-Four

During the days leading up to the wedding, the family spent more time at Hackett's, which was within walking distance of the farm. It seemed the natural thing to do; guests were arriving every day and everyone wanted to get together as much as possible, so the daily gatherings were like a continuous pre-wedding party. Nell didn't worry too much about the children's bedtimes; they were on holiday after all, and apart from one or two last-minute SOS pleas from Kathleen about place cards and buttonholes, there was nothing to do except relax and look forward to Saturday. There was to be a hen night of sorts at the guest house on the Thursday evening; it would be a toned-down affair as the younger children would be present. But the men, including Arthur and Henry were going to Clonakilty for the stag night which looked likely to be uproarious. Harry declined regretfully, saying that his pub-crawl days were over and that he liked to be in bed soon after ten o'clock, but if it were all the same to Adam, he would drink his health here in the bar. Neville, unable to remember any such occasion even in his youth, was flattered to be invited and accepted, thinking there was a first time for everything, and there was a part of him that wanted to experience every bit of life in West Cork even if it did involve Guinness, for which he had never really acquired a taste.

Adam and Patrick were amused to see how well Harry was settling in and enjoying the company. They looked across at the table where he was seated along with Angela, Bridget and Lois, all of them talking animatedly. Every now and then laughter could be heard and the clink of glasses signalled that the mood was jovial and carefree.

"Look how he's lapping it up with the ladies" said Patrick in amazement. "From what you told me I thought he would be a grumpy old so-and-so. But I think he's having the time of his life. He's probably not had so much attention for years!"

Adam nodded. "You're right, he does seem to be fitting in with the family no problem. It's as though once he'd made up his mind to come, he decided he'd make the most of it. Fair play to him, I say. And your Aunt Angela will never let anyone sit on their own or feel left out".

Nell was touched when after having been introduced to Harry, he told her how fond he was of Brontë. He had only met her twice before, he said, but what a lovely daughter you have, so thoughtful and she worked wonders in my garden in less than an hour.

They were sitting in the lounge together while Angela and Bridget prepared the dining room tables for the evening meal.

"She does love gardening; she wants to make a career of it. But she's been through a great deal" said Nell, not wishing to go into detail but feeling the need to make conversation.

"She'll be grand" he said. Nell noticed the affection in his eyes and could tell that he saw something special in Brontë, something he had in a way connected with. Who'd have thought it, she said to herself. Our daughter is still full of surprises.

"We're hoping that Brontë will come back to England with us". Nell wasn't sure how much Harry knew about the circumstances which had brought Brontë to Ireland; probably very little, she decided. Bridget had been discreet and could be relied on to keep her counsel. "We've missed her of course. She's done well at school here; she's made a lot of friends and she's been happy. But she can't stay here indefinitely".

Clearly, Harry was not going to ask questions. "Family is everything" he said, with a sad note in his voice. "Being together, well ye don't realise what that means until you're left alone".

Nell wondered for a moment what to say. "Have you lost touch with your family, Harry? Do you ever hear from them?"

"Not these ten years". He paused for a while and then continued. "It's my daughter Rose that I would like to find. We didn't part friends, if ye understand me. Most of that was my fault. But I'm getting on now, I'd like to put things to rights before I die. But all I know is she's a nurse; she lives somewhere in England".

There was a part of Nell that though it might be wrong to interfere. She hardly knew this old man. But somehow, she couldn't just ignore what he had told her without offering to help.

"Harry, you can tell me to mind my own business if you like. But there are ways of tracing people, in England anyway. Would you like me to try? The Salvation Army helps track down missing people, I could check the electoral roll if you have any idea where in England she might be living. We could use a private enquiry agent. And I think there's a register of nurses and midwives. I have a good friend who's a nurse in London. What's your daughter's married name?"

"It's Anderson. Rose Anderson. Her husband is Keith".

"Do you give me permission to try to find her, Harry? When I go back to England?"

"If ye can do that, I shall die a happy man". He reached for her hand, and she gave his a squeeze.

"I can't guarantee that I will find her, Harry. But I promise you that I will do my best".

* * *

Later that same afternoon, Harry took himself off for a walk around the garden and noticed Brontë knelt by a flower border.

"Whenever I see ye, you're digging or pruning, or you have your hands in the earth" he said in amusement.

"Well sometimes Aunt Angela asks me to keep the flower beds tidy and do a bit of weeding instead of working indoors. This week she wants the garden to look its best for the wedding. The marquee is going up tomorrow, so I'd be in the way then". She brushed the soil off her hands and went to sit beside Harry on a bench.

"I've been talking with your mother. Ye have the look of her". He gazed at Brontë fondly. "Ye have a grand family, Brontë. Especially your Mam".

"I know. She's the best".

"She's going to try to find my daughter Rose when she goes back to England. That is something that would make me happy, Brontë, to see Rose".

"Mum will do everything she can, Harry. Once she starts something she won't give up".

"There's nothing so important as family, Brontë. And being together. Ye don't realise this until things have gone wrong. And then, if you're like me, ye do nothing about it until it's nearly too late".

"I'm sure it won't be too late, not if Mum has anything to do with it. And you never know, if she manages to find Rose, well Rose might be in touch with your sons? You could all get back together".

"Maybe. But if I weren't such an old fool, I'd never have let pride get in my way. I'd have made the first move years ago". He looked at her intently. "I don't know why ye came to live with your Granny. It's not my business to know. But whatever it was, don't ye be letting anything come between you and your family. That's all I'm saying. My life would have been different, even after Nora passed, if I'd remembered that". He turned away and crossed himself. "Don't make the mistakes I made".

"I wasn't sure if I was ready to go home. I love all my family, really I do. I want to be with them. It's been difficult.... but perhaps it is the right time. Thank you, Harry. You've helped me decide". She stood up, put her arms around his neck and kissed his cheek, then walked across the garden to the shed, leaving Harry alone with his thoughts.

Chapter Seventy-Five

There were audible gasps as Kathleen entered the room on Patrick's arm.

Many years ago, there had been a time when Kathleen turned heads for all the wrong reasons. No one who had criticised her all those years ago would have thought this transformation possible, but as she made her way down the aisle of the Registry Office toward her future husband the reaction was overwhelmingly complimentary, positive, full of admiration. Kathleen looked stunning in the outfit carefully chosen for being unconventional yet undeniably stylish, with perfect makeup and a hairstyle so fitting for the overall look she had created. It certainly had the impact she had been hoping for.

As he saw Kathleen walking towards him, Adam's expression was one of amazed delight and adoration. Kathleen looked back at him with undisguised devotion; it was one of those moments suspended in time which everyone would remember, and which would be described many times when the highlights of the day were recalled and recounted in detail.

The three bridesmaids Brontë, Aisling and Emer in their deep green dresses gave a perfect contrast to the bride's cream ensemble. Opting for simplicity, Kathleen had decided against fussy head-dresses for the girls, and the hairdresser had instead woven tiny white flowers into their hair. They carried posies of pale coloured gerberas, echoing those in the bride's bouquet. It was a picture of understated elegance, and spoke of everything a happy occasion should be, but for Kathleen it said more than that; it was a triumph of present over past, of hope over despair.

Bridget was overcome with pride, and although she was rarely given to displays of emotion in public, her eyes were full of tears as she watched her daughter taking her vows, knowing with certainty that this time they were said with real love, not just for the sake of outward propriety or expediency.

This was an occasion the family had looked forward to for so long. Everyone looked their best. Only the groom and best man wore morning suits, but all the men looked smart and handsome; Harry had accepted the services of the visiting hairdresser and Angela had arranged for his suit to be brushed and pressed. The weather that week had been kind, meaning that the ladies could dispense with coats and umbrellas in favour of light, floaty dresses and suits in pastel shades or floral prints, and dainty, impractical hats or fascinators.

This time there was no hiding away from the camera for Kathleen or Brontë; they stood confidently, enjoying their moment in the limelight and smiling at the photographer, ready to follow his instructions to form into various groups and poses. But when they returned to the guest house the best shots were the less formal ones of Kathleen and Adam embracing in the garden by the trunk of an old silver birch tree, and groups of family and friends against a colourful backdrop of flowers and shrubs.

Angela and her team of helpers had surpassed themselves; every aspect of the décor, seating, menu and music had been arranged with care; no detail had been forgotten. Everyone was relaxed, and after the speeches and toasts, many couples took to the dance floor as the evening wore on. Ruari, who was thrilled to be Brontë's plus-one, took every opportunity to be by her side and to claim her for every dance. Patrick and Nell looked on in amusement. "That's three of our children paired up already," said Patrick. Then his eyes widened in amazement as he saw Harry leading his mother onto the floor for a slow waltz. "Well! Who'd have thought it!" he exclaimed. It wasn't clear who was more surprised – Bridget or Harry.

Lois and Neville were dancing too; it wasn't that long ago that Lois thought her dancing days were over – if indeed they had ever really started. But although she knew the steps of the waltz she clung to Neville, secure in his embrace and swayed in time to the music. No longer just an onlooker, she felt part of things – not excluded by her illness or having to watch from the sidelines. Secretly, Neville had made a music request to the band; he and Lois moved slowly around the floor to the strains of 'By the Sleepy Lagoon' – a favourite from their courting days, and they looked into each other's eyes like young lovers once again.

The younger children: Ronnie, Emer, Aisling and Orla's two boys Liam and Declan were excited at being allowed to run free in the garden or in and out of the marquee, make up their own games, come in whenever they liked to have drinks, help themselves to the buffet and dance if they wanted to. Even Arlo laughed as he tottered along for a few cautious steps here and there holding Nell's hand. There could not have been a more relaxed or joyful family gathering.

* * *

Just before ten o'clock, Patrick's phone buzzed in his pocket. Who could be phoning him at this time, he wondered? He didn't recognise the number and was about to ignore it, but something told him it could be important. Stepping outside to hear more clearly, he confirmed "yes, Patrick Walsh here".

The caller was WPC Drummond.

"I'm sorry to ring you so late, but there's been a development. Can we call round to see you?"

"Well, I'm afraid we're on holiday in Ireland for a couple of weeks. I'm at my sister's wedding. Can it wait until we come home?"

There was a pause at the other end of the line.

"In that case, Mr Walsh, is it convenient to talk now?"

"Yes, that's ok". Patrick could detect the urgency in Tina Drummond's voice.

"Two days ago, a man's body was discovered in Trentingham Forest. It had probably been there for several months, impossible to identify I'm afraid. But a postmortem has been carried out, and DNA recovered. The DNA is a match with Arlo, there is no doubt. This man was Arlo's father".

Her words hit Patrick like a hammer blow.

"So.... the man was Denny Reid?"

"We don't know that. We never knew if that was a false name, an alias. All we can be sure of is that this man's DNA matches Arlo's. The cause of death is so far undetermined, so more investigations will be needed. It may have been an accident or natural causes. At present we are treating it as an unexplained death".

"I see". Patrick was at a loss to know what else to say.

"There's nothing for you to do, I'm just telling you because I promised to let you know if there was any news. It may help to give you the closure you've been looking for, but obviously we are no nearer to tracing the mother. We will let you have this in writing as soon as possible, and of course we will be notifying Children's Services".

"Thank you....". Feeling a mixture of emotions, Patrick ended the call just as Nell came out to look for him.

"Who was that on the phone, Patrick?"

He had never once, in all their years of marriage, lied to Nell. But just for one brief moment, hearing the buzz of conversation, the lilt of music and the strains of laughter coming from the dance floor on his sister's special night and wishing to protect his wife, he was tempted to.

"Patrick what is it?". She could see he was worried and holding something back.

"Where's Arlo?"

"Barbara's looking after him.... Patrick what's going on? Tell me!" Nell was looking frightened.

"If I tell you, you mustn't say anything to anyone, not tonight".

Gently, Patrick took her hand and led her to a bench at the far side of the lawn, away from the marquee. Fairy lights and artificial candles had been strung across the trees, music and happy chatter floated through the open windows of the lounge. The air was mild and still, the atmosphere magical.

"Nelly, it's been such a lovely evening, the best. But what I'm about to tell you will come as a shock. I'm only telling you because we don't have any secrets".

Without going into any of the more unpleasant details, Patrick told her of the phone call.

"Oh Patrick! To hear that news tonight of all nights!"

"I know. What can I say? She was only doing her job, and she had promised to tell us if there were any developments. But don't let's tell anyone else tonight. Nothing must spoil this night for Kathleen. She doesn't need to know until she gets back from her honeymoon. We'll just tell your parents and maybe one or two others in a few days' time. There's nothing anyone can do".

"Yes, you're right, Patrick. There's nothing we can do, come to that. It just means that one piece of the jigsaw has fallen into place. Another tiny fragment of knowledge for Arlo to be told one day".

Patrick put his arm around her and held her tightly as a waning moon rose beyond the silver birch tree and shone through the tracery of the branches.

Chapter Seventy-Six

Kathleen and Adam had come to say their goodbyes to the family and friends who had assembled in the bar the following morning.

"Mam and Angela, thank you for everything you've done. You've made our day so special. I never thought I could be this happy. It's been wonderful". Kathleen clung to her mother as Adam hugged Angela and then walked round the room to take his leave of the rest of the company with a great deal of hand shaking and kissing. He then presented each of the bridesmaids with a narrow box trimmed with satin ribbon. Inside were silver bracelets decorated with tiny pearls, nestling on a blue velvet lining. Brontë gasped with delight and hugged him, then the two younger girls did the same.

The newlyweds were to take an early afternoon flight from Cork to Heathrow, then onward to Sydney with a forty-eight-hour stopover in Singapore. Kathleen could hardly contain her excitement. Even with the prospect of a long-haul flight ahead of her she had managed to conquer her nerves, knowing that her husband would be by her side.

This time Sean drove them to the airport. Everyone came out of the guest house to wave them off, then as the car disappeared up the laneway, they trooped back inside, all feeling a slight sense of anti-climax. But Angela had anticipated this and had prepared a sumptuous buffet lunch with some relaxing background music, and Donal appeared with glasses of sparkling wine on a tray. Ruari had devised a treasure hunt in the garden for the younger children and some outdoor games which he and Brontë supervised.

"Just a few days for me to catch my breath then it will be the baptism next Sunday" said Angela to Bridget as they carried out the last of trays of canapés.

"No time to relax just yet" agreed Bridget.

Later, Ruari saw Patrick sitting on his own in the garden watching the children and made his way over to sit beside him.

"Mr Walsh? Can I ask you something?"

"It's Patrick. What's on your mind?"

"I'm thinking of leaving Ireland to work in England, I wondered if you could help me?"

Patrick smiled. "How many times have I heard that? I know there's not much going on here for young men, that's why I went to England twenty years ago". He gave Ruari an amused look. "It wouldn't have anything to do with my daughter would it, by any chance?"

Ruari blushed. "I'm very fond of Brontë. We get on well. Apart from anything else.... well, she's my best friend. But she's not the only reason. I want to get on in life, make something of myself. It's a grand job I have here and Mrs Hackett's a great boss, but I don't want to be a barman for ever".

Patrick was reminded of his decision to look for work in England when he had been about Ruari's age, and how in hindsight it had been the best move he had ever made. He would never have met Nell, never had this wonderful family, would never have become a successful businessman employing dozens of men if he had stayed here in West Cork. The least he could do would be to offer a helping hand to someone else looking for the same prospects.

"Does Brontë know you want to come to England?" he asked.

"No, we've not really discussed it. She knows I want to get a better job though".

"Ok. I'll help you all I can. But this is the deal. Don't tell her about this conversation, not just yet anyway. Nell and I are hoping that she will come home soon. But we want that to be for the right reasons, that she's moved on from...well...all she's been through. Not because you're coming to England, that would influence her, and we want her to come home because she is ready to.... sorry, it's difficult to explain and

506

I can't go into details with you. Just accept what I say and keep your plans to yourself. Just for now".

Ruari nodded. "Thanks, Patrick. I really appreciate that. I shan't say anything to Brontë, I can see why you need her to make the decision just for herself".

"Leave it with me for now. We'll talk again soon; I may have a couple of ideas".

* * *

Neville had told Lois about the trip they made up into the hills on the Mizen, the wide skies and the intense darkness. When he described the building they had found, and that its position would be perfect for an observatory, she found the idea unsettling.

"It has a very tragic history, Neville. Do you think people will want to come, knowing what happened there?"

"I've been wondering that. But with a change of use it could have a new lease of life, a new purpose. It could be an amenity for the area, there would be no cost to the council because it would be at my expense. This is not a wealthy area, Lois but the unique situation, the darkness, the isolation – those are things that money can't buy. If I made an investment in converting the building and setting up the equipment the local people would benefit, it could be a free hobby, a new interest, right here on their doorstep. This could make something good out of a sad past".

"I see...." Lois could tell that Neville was very taken with the idea, and in so many ways she wanted to support him. But she was concerned that he might have underestimated the opposition to such a scheme.

"Neville, I think you need someone else in your corner if you're going to go ahead with this. Someone who knows about these things. Why not ask Chris Davenport to come over, you could show him the site and maybe approach the council together?"

"Yes, good idea. When I spoke to Chris about us coming here for a holiday, he was really interested. But first I'll check with Angela to see if she has any rooms available for a few nights".

* * *

Since the phone call on the night of the wedding, Patrick had been giving a great deal of thought as to whether to tell the others about it. After much deliberation, he and Nell agreed that for now, they would just tell Neville. He found a moment to speak to his father-in-law when no one else was in earshot.

Neville was, as expected, thoughtful. "Hmm. It's strange. We've waited so long for answers then when one comes along it just opens up more questions. What happened to him? What went on in between him leaving Arlo with you and his death? Was he out for a walk in the forest on his own and had an accident? Was he ill? Was it suicide? Or was someone pursuing him? We don't know if it was foul play, of course. And as the police officer said, it still gives us no clue about the mother".

"No. It doesn't really change anything where we're concerned. The only difference now is that we know that the man we call Denny Reid was Arlo's biological father".

"Yes...." Neville smiled. "But the important thing is that you are Arlo's father now in all the ways that matter. You will always be the father figure in his life. He will not remember Denny".

* * *

Having consulted with Angela about accommodating an extra guest, Neville lost no time in telephoning Chris. It came as no surprise that his friend was eager to visit West Cork and see for himself the possibilities of setting up an observatory. But Neville warned him that there were several obstacles to be overcome and that nothing could be guaranteed. They decided to take another trip to the area first and then get their heads together about how they would make an application to the council.

He realised that he would need to involve Patrick in these journeys, at least until he became more familiar with the area. He could hire a car but that would not help much; he had no hope of finding the place on his own, even in daylight. Patrick had mentioned that even the local people did not always know their way around this remote territory; if their ideas were to come to fruition then signage and maybe map references would be necessary.

Lois surprised him later that evening as they sat together on a bench in the garden, enjoying the remaining warmth of the sun after what had been by West Cork standards, a scorchingly hot day.

"I feel as well here as I did back in Spain" she said happily, tucking her hand into Neville's arm. "I've been thinking, could we spend the rest of the summer here? I mean, not go back straight after the baptisms?"

Neville studied her for a moment. "Do you mean, stay here at Angela's long term?"

"Yes Neville I do mean that. I know the winters here in West Cork will be too hard for me, but we could go back to the Swan's Rest as soon as the weather turns colder. Then return in the spring. I love it here". She gazed across the garden to where the sun was just slipping behind the distant hills. Another beautiful sunset; red, pink, gold, even pale green shades against the fading blue of the sky. "Angela takes such good care of us here; we are so comfortable. We've made friends among Patrick's family. But there's another reason". Lois paused for a second. "If your idea about the observatory goes ahead, you will want to spend time here, setting it up, overseeing it, especially in the first year. You've sacrificed a great deal of your life to my care Neville, I shall never forget that. The least I can do is support you with this project, I know how much it means to you".

Neville was overcome for a moment. He had not dared suggest staying longer, thinking it would be too difficult for Lois. But as she had brought up the subject, he realised that there was no reason not to extend their stay. If things didn't go to plan, they could return to England at a moment's notice. But Lois seemed determined.

"Thank you, my darling" he said at last, putting his arm around her and kissing her cheek. "It would be wonderful if we could stay for another couple of months. I'm hoping that my plan will be accepted, but even if it isn't, we can still enjoy some more time here. This is what I always wanted, you and I together. We've nothing to lose, have we?"

Chapter Seventy-Seven

Angela was relieved to see that Harry was quite content to stay on at Hackett's after the wedding, in fact he had not mentioned anything about leaving, although Jack had agreed with Adam that he would take Harry back to Lankerris when he was ready.

However, when Harry found out that before he left on honeymoon Adam had settled his bill for a fortnight's stay, he was angry.

"Was he thinking that I cannot pay my own way now?" he said crossly to Angela.

"Sure and it was nothing of the sort" she replied. "He hired a lot of the rooms himself; it was all part of the arrangement. Is your room not to your liking, Harry?"

"The room's grand, I could not wish for better. I'm sorry, Mrs". He looked apologetic.

Bridget arrived at that moment. "Will you come for a meal with us at the cottage later, Harry? It will just be the three of us, you, me and Brontë". Emer had moved into the farm to share with Aisling a few days previously.

At the mention of Brontë the old man smiled. "Thank ye, I'll come. Not wishing any disrespect for your cooking, Mrs Hackett". He winked at her, his anxiety about the bill forgotten.

"No offence taken" said Angela laughing. "And call me Angela".

Bridget had two aims in mind: to feed Harry well and to raise her concerns about him returning to his cottage. As expected, he enjoyed the plate of lamb stew that Bridget served up and accepted a second helping, followed by apple tart and cream.

"I could get used to this, all these grand meals I'm having. And the room your sister has given me, it's so comfortable. I can't remember enjoying myself so much, it's the first holiday

I've had since...." he didn't finish the sentence, but Brontë guessed he was speaking about Nora.

"We'll why don't you stay longer, Harry?" asked Bridget "My sister will offer you a special rate, as you're family. You've no need to go home yet surely?"

"Yes Harry, please stay. We love having you, don't we Granny?" Brontë kissed his cheek then asked if she could be excused, she wanted to take Arlo for a walk with Nell.

"Indeed we do, we do," said Bridget. Then, as the door closed behind Brontë, she cleared away the plates and sat down opposite him.

"Harry, I'm one for plain speaking, in case you haven't noticed. I'm worried about you living alone". She thought that was more tactful than referring to the neglected state of his house.

"Oh away with ye, haven't I been used to my own company for years now?"

That wasn't quite what Bridget meant.

"Harry, your house is unsuitable for you. If you tripped and fell, no one would know. Your house needs some work to make it safe for you now. Look how much better you've been staying here, a decent bed and bathroom, your meals cooked, your washing done. All help on hand. You said yourself you're enjoying it here".

"I did. But I can't go on accepting hospitality...."

"It wouldn't be hospitality, you'd be paying".

"Well, I'm not looking forward to going home, truth to tell. I suppose there's no reason why I have to go back yet. I can pay the going rate, if that's what you're wondering, I have a bit put by". He tapped the side of his nose with his finger. Old men are so proud, thought Bridget. But if he could afford to stay on, why not? She was determined to persuade him.

"That's settled then" she said briskly. "You can arrange it all with Angela when you go back later. And we can tell Jack you won't be needing a lift after all".

"You women. Ye have it all worked out, don't ye?" He laughed and could see that he had been outmanoeuvred, but Bridget thought she could see relief in his eyes.

"We do, that's what we're good at. Now how about a cup of tea?"

* * *

Nell had not forgotten about the plan to have a day out with Brontë. On the Tuesday after the wedding they set off, Nell behind the wheel of the family car. She had a vague idea that they would follow the route she and Patrick had taken on her first visit to Ireland all those years ago, and was certain she could find the way to Crookhaven. But when Patrick heard about the trip, he was concerned.

"I'll drive you; Mam will look after Arlo. You can't be driving all that way on your own".

"Please, Patrick. I promised Brontë it would be just the two of us. Nothing personal" she added, jokily. "It's a girl's day out. We'll be fine. You know where we're going, if we're not back by six then you have permission to come looking for us".

Patrick sighed as if he knew that it was useless to argue.

But first, they were to visit St Teresa's. Brontë wanted her mother to meet Sister Francis and if possible, Sister Bernice. Although term was over, the sisters were still in residence; St Teresa's was their home after all. But Nell was determined that their day would not be spoilt by any discussion about Brontë's future plans. That subject was off limits today, and Nell had thought how she might deflect any such questions.

Sister Francis welcomed them both into her office and shook hands with Nell. "We've so enjoyed having Brontë here at St Teresa's, Mrs Walsh. She has been a credit to the school, and we shall miss her".

"I'm so grateful to you, Sister. It has worked out really well. Brontë has loved her time here".

"What will you do now?" The question seemed intended for Brontë, but Sister Francis was looking straight at Nell.

"We...we're going to be staying in Ballymere for the rest of the summer. My parents are staying on as well. My father is hoping to set up a...well, if it all works out you will hear about it".

"Harry is staying too" said Brontë.

"Ah yes, Harry". Sister Francis smiled. "You did some gardening for him, I remember you telling us. You've learned a lot with Sister Bernice, and I think your choice of career will prove to be the right one. You have a gift, and you must nurture it; you need to have a feel for nature as well as head knowledge. You have the beginnings of both, Brontë".

Nell took two envelopes from her bag. "Sister, I know you don't accept personal gifts. So this is a cheque for the school funds. I've enclosed a second cheque to be spent on garden tools or equipment to help Sister Bernice and to make her work easier".

Sister Francis accepted both graciously. "That will be very welcome, thank you. I hope you will keep in touch with the school, Brontë. You have made an impression here, and we will follow your future with interest. Now go and see Sister Bernice and show your mother the garden".

* * *

"I can see why you loved spending time in the school garden, Brontë" said Nell as they took the road west and headed for Roaringwater Bay which was to be their first stop. "But it must have been strange, working with someone who hardly spoke to you. How did you ever get used to it?"

"I liked it, Mum. It was one less pressure, the silence helped me to think. Do you know, after a while the need to speak just seemed to disappear. There was a kind of communication without words, I can't explain it. It wouldn't work for everyone, I suppose".

As they motored further west, the countryside looked less brooding in the summer sunshine; golden and russet rather than green, with colour provided by clumps of flame-coloured crocosmia. Although Brontë had experienced the very worst of the weather here through the storms of winter she felt an affinity with the windswept moorland, the rocky crags and the relentless wind, and tried to describe her feelings to her mother. But there was no need. Nell told her daughter that years ago she had felt the same rapport with this mystifying, enigmatic place and that it was in these bleak surroundings that she had first been compelled to write down her impressions of what she saw and the feelings that the landscape evoked.

As they drove along, Brontë told her mother about how well she had fitted in, how she had adapted, not just to school but into the way of life. "Do you believe in reincarnation Mummy? Because sometimes I really feel I belong here, I was meant to be here. Does that make any sense? I felt I was coming home; it was as if I have lived here before in a previous life. Sorry, I'm not rejecting my home back in England. I just wanted to try to...."

"It's ok. I don't know anything about reincarnation, but I do understand that you feel this is where you were meant to be. But it doesn't mean for always, Brontë. It may be just for a particular time in your life. You're only just fifteen, you have so much ahead of you".

They chatted easily, happily, Brontë telling her mother about her school friends and that she was going to write to them. This is a good sign, thought Nell, carefully navigating the subject. It meant that already, her daughter was thinking in terms of leaving. "I shall miss Ruari most of all" she said regretfully. "He's been a good friend to me. I'm very fond of him, you know". She gave her mother a sideways glance as if to test her reaction, but Nell only smiled. "He's Kitty's brother. They're the best friends I've ever had".

The landscape was now more rocky and barren. The roads were narrower, with only occasional passing places for other vehicles, but so far, they hadn't met any. "Is this near where Grandpa wants to set up the observatory?" asked Brontë. "Shall we go and have a look?"

"I don't think I'd be able to find it," said Nell. "And in any case, we don't want to be going there today. It gave me the shivers, to be honest".

"I know what happened here, Mum. Granny took me to the museum at Skibbereen. She said I needed to know the history. It was awful Mum, all those poor people starved to death here in West Cork or died of disease. I cried, but Granny said that sometimes it's right to cry, people should cry over something so terrible".

"It's true, it's the least we can do, to pay tribute to them, to acknowledge what they went through".

"Mum, maybe if Grandpa gets permission, it will change the way people think about that building. It could be a new beginning".

"Let's hope so, Brontë. Now here we are at Roaringwater Bay. I stopped here at this very spot with your Dad, and he showed me the Fastnet Lighthouse". She pointed to the rocky outcrop about five miles out to sea, with its pencil-slim, white structure pointing upwards from one side. Today in the bright sunlight its beams could not be seen, but somehow it was a comfort to think that as darkness fell, come what may, the light would shine out across the bay in all weathers to warn shipping of the treacherous rocks, and to give reassurance to those on land.

"I love going to places where you first went with Dad" said Brontë. "Once Auntie Kathleen took me to Markham's, I told her that's where you and Dad went on your first date".

Nell smiled at the memory. In some ways it seemed like yesterday. How much has happened since then, she thought.

At Crookhaven, Nell parked the car close to the beach at Barleycove and Brontë rolled up her jeans and kicked off her sandals. "I'm going to paddle" she shouted, running down to the water's edge. "Are you coming, Mum? Oh, it's freezing!" she squealed, as the water splashed round her knees. "Well, it is the Atlantic, after all" laughed Nell, taking a photograph.

O'Sullivan's bar was busy with tourists that day, but they found a table outdoors, in view of the harbour and ate crab sandwiches with a shared bowl of chips. Brontë is just eating normally, thought Nell. No hang-ups, no obsessions, just a healthy appetite for a teenage girl. She realised how much there was to be thankful for. They wandered round the village after lunch, sat on the shore eating ice creams, watched the boats sailing in and out of the harbour, and browsed in the gift shop. As they made their way back later that afternoon, both women felt a new closeness and a strengthening of that invisible bond between mother and daughter. Without any words being spoken, it seemed that the worries that had not long ago overwhelmed them had lifted and could finally be relegated to the past.

Chapter Seventy-Eight

Chris Davenport and his wife Jane arrived the following day. Having been shown around the accommodation and introduced to all the remaining family, he was keen to take a trip out to the Mizen after dark with Neville and Patrick. Jane stayed behind to talk to Lois and Angela in the lounge; most of the staff had been given the night off after working extra shifts over the wedding weekend, so Fergus was manning the bar. It was a relaxed, comfortable evening; the pressure of the wedding was over, said Angela, and the baptism party would be a quieter affair.

The area was new to Chris although he had heard of its potential for astronomy many times. A deep blue twilight had settled over the landscape so although he could just make out the contours of the terrain, it was hard for him to gain a more detailed impression of the countryside; that would have to wait until daylight. But tonight, he was looking forward to seeing for himself the open spaces, the elevated position and above all the wide, dark skies that Neville had described.

He was not disappointed, if anything he was more excited than Neville. The situation could not be more perfect, he agreed, and he could visualise straightaway the building's suitability, assuming it was basically sound, and how it could be re-purposed. The most complicated and expensive part would be the dome, which would require expert design and construction as it was the key element of the observatory itself.

Neville had only been able to give Chris a brief description of the origins of the building, and he asked Patrick to explain more fully. As expected, Chris understood straightaway the possible drawbacks of the plan, and that to make changes to a building with such painful associations would inevitably arouse resentment and opposition amongst some of the local population.

Patrick was careful not to give a view one way or another. As a local man, he felt torn; he had known from boyhood, through accounts passed down through generations of his own family how badly people had suffered here. That would never be forgotten. But he could also see how Neville's plan could give something back to the community; a facility for education, a family activity, a meeting place and a chance to observe the night sky from arguably one of the best locations in the whole of Europe. And if he understood his father-in-law correctly, all this would be achieved without any call on the public purse; it would be Neville's investment.

"For what it's worth, my advice would be to approach the Council," said Patrick. "Prepare your pitch, tell them what you have in mind, do your costings, explain how the venture would be funded. I know you'll be diplomatic; they'll see you've done your homework and you're not about to ride roughshod over people's feelings. But you might be surprised, maybe your plan has come at the ideal time. People might be ready to accept change if it's done in the right way".

* * *

James Dolan, Senior Planning Officer had sat on the planning committee of Ballymere Council for seven years. It was not the most demanding of roles, he concluded after the first two; very few applications came across his desk, mainly because there was an acute shortage of money in the area, so new developments or even proposals for change of use were increasingly rare. So it was with some surprise that he welcomed the two Englishmen into his office and wondered what was behind their request for an urgent meeting.

After making brief introductions, Neville explained his connection with the area; that some years ago his daughter had married a local man who had come to England for work. This was his first visit to West Cork, but his daughter's family came here more often, and his granddaughter had attended St Teresa's until recently. James Dolan knew of the Walsh's farm, he said; he had made a site visit there a few years ago to advise on the construction of a barn. Neville then went on to outline his proposal for an observatory on the Mizen. James Dolan listened in amazement.

"If anyone had told me this morning that someone would be coming here with such a proposal, I would have laughed them out of the door altogether" he said, barely able to conceal his astonishment.

"I wish to make it clear from the beginning that I am not looking on this as a commercial proposition," said Neville. He wanted to set out his vision early in the discussion before any assumptions were made. "It will not be a money-making venture, nor am I expecting any funding from the council; I shall invest in the project, I shall pay for the renovation of the building and provide the equipment. My idea is for this to be a community facility from which the local people will benefit. All I am seeking from you is permission......and.... I suppose, approval".

There was a long pause. James Dolan stood up and walked to the window, his back to them. He seemed deep in thought for several minutes. When he sat back down again, he still did not speak, and Chris felt compelled to break the silence.

"We do appreciate there may be strong local feelings about the plan, Mr Dolan, which is why we thought it best to have an informal conversation with you first. The last thing we would want to do is cause an upset. If you think this is a non-starter, the discussion need go no further. We don't want to waste your time, or the council's".

"I can see how this might appear," said Neville. "Strangers – British – wanting to come in and make changes, stirring up old memories, throwing their money around. I can understand how people might feel about us. Just let me say this. All my life I have been a keen amateur astronomer, but for reasons I won't go into, I haven't been able to follow it in the way I would have liked. But when I came here and saw the scenery, the landscape, the extreme darkness, I knew that

I could search for years and never find another such perfect place for an observatory. Then, when I fully understood the history of that building on the Mizen, the Poor House, I also felt that here was an opportunity to use it for a good purpose, something positive, educational, and maybe, through introducing people to the wonders of the night sky, over time it could bring about a kind of healing......" He stopped short, wondering if he had said too much, or if his well-intentioned words might in themselves be thought insensitive.

James Dolan spoke at last. "It's a grand idea you have there, Mr Garth, and thank you for thinking of investing in the area. I can see how this might work; you've explained it very well. But yes, you're right, there may be dissenters. Personally, I think it would be a wonderful opportunity for Ballymere. And if it went ahead, there might be a possibility of a grant; I would need to investigate that. Have you thought of applying for charitable status? But as you have mentioned, there are hurdles to overcome and I think the normal procedures for planning applications and objections might not quite cover this situation. I should like to give this a great deal more thought, discuss it with some colleagues before you go to the trouble and expense of having plans drawn up; we might be able to consider it under change of use. Leave it with me for now, perhaps we can have another meeting – say – early next week?"

He opened the door to show them out. "I will do all I can to help you with this" he said, as he shook their hands. "As a matter of fact, my wife used to love sky-watching, as she used to call it, and I know she would have been in favour of this idea. She died three years ago. But I mustn't let that influence me. I'll see you both soon".

Chapter Seventy-Nine

The interior of St. Brigid's Church in Ballymere was cool and dark after the bright sunlight and unrelenting heat outside. For the last fortnight, the area had sweltered under an unaccustomed heatwave although any prolonged period of warm weather was described thus in West Cork, where continuous lashing rain and high winds were more likely even during the height of summer.

Ronnie and Emer were to be baptised by Father Sweeney, successor to Father Donovan whom Nell remembered from her first visit to the church when Arthur was a small baby. Permission had been given by Father Egan in Lamberham for the actual service to take place in Ballymere, although the children had completed their induction classes back in Sussex.

Despite her parents' fears, Emer seemed to be taking seriously the whole concept of baptism and was no longer thinking of it as a photo-opportunity. She was wearing the white dress and carrying white flowers as promised by her mother but talk of posing for photographs and expecting attention had been replaced by a solemn, thoughtful mood and an understanding of the prayers and sacrament as she made her baptismal promises. Ronnie, only a little older in age but with an insight beyond his years showed a similar disposition. Both children had been subjected to some gentle questioning by Bridget who, whilst being overjoyed that her two grandchildren were being baptised here in her parish was nevertheless anxious for them to understand their commitments and that the baptism was not an end in itself but the beginning of a lifetime of faith, as she put it. Emer had acquiesced, still feeling too much in awe of her grandmother to argue or ask questions.

The church was full, all the family and friends who had remained after the wedding had taken their place on the front pews, and even Harry, Jack, Chris and Jane who barely knew the children were seated at the back. Sean and Jenny, as godparents made their promises to guide and care for the children and at the end of the service Emer and Ronnie were presented with their Certificate of Baptism and a candle which would be lit again at their first Holy Communion.

"That went well" said Patrick as they drove back to Hackett's for the party.

"Yes, it was a lovely service, Patrick" agreed Nell. "And I think they both took it to heart, don't you? Emer really surprised us".

"I am here, you know" piped up a voice from the back seat. "I think I did well and I'm sure Granny Bridget was pleased with me. I expect she will have some words of encouragement for me".

Her parents exchanged glances. "I'm sure she will" said Patrick drily.

After the quietness and intensity of the church service, the younger children were all ready to let off steam as soon as they arrived at the guest house and the garden was suddenly alive with noise and shouting while Angela and Fergus carried in trays of tea and glasses of wine for the adults.

"You're so good at this, Angela" said Nell as she looked at the mouthwatering buffet laid out in the dining room.

"Well, I've had a lot of practice lately," laughed Angela. "Christmas, St Patrick's, birthdays, wedding! And now a baptism. But things should quieten down a bit now, there are no more big events booked for a while. I'm just going to concentrate on the day to day running and try to catch up on paperwork and a few things I've been putting off".

"I'm so pleased Mum and Dad will be staying on for a while. And Harry too! That was a surprise".

"It's good to have some longer-term residents," said Angela. "It gives a feeling of stability altogether. I'm still building up a reputation, too many empty rooms are not good for business".

* * *

Harry had spotted Bridget sitting alone at a table, and he sat down to join her just as Fergus appeared with fresh cups of tea for them both.

"I'm just about ready for this, I don't know about you" said Bridget thankfully.

"So would this be a bad time for me to ask a favour, Mrs?" Harry looked slightly embarrassed.

"Ask away," said Bridget. "As long as you're not going to ask me to get up and dance" she joked. "My legs are aching today; I think it's the heat". They both laughed.

"Would ye do me the kindness of giving me a lift into Cork? Whenever is convenient, mind. No rush".

Bridget looked at him in surprise. "I can certainly do that. How about Tuesday?" She didn't feel able to ask him what errand he could possibly have in Cork, but after a few moments Harry gave the beginnings of an explanation.

"I have a bit of business to attend to" he said at last. "With a solicitor". There was a pause, as he seemed uncertain whether to continue, then added: "It's about my Will. I need some advice".

After a lifetime of organising a farm and a large family, Bridget was tempted to ask for more details or at least offer help. It was in her nature to be at the helm and take command. But she stopped herself, realising that if Harry wanted her to know any more, he would tell her when he was ready.

"I'll leave it to you to choose a solicitor and make an appointment then, Harry" she said. "Then we can leave in good time and go for a cup of tea afterwards".

"Thank you, Mrs" he said gratefully, draining his teacup.

* * *

Henry, noticing that both his parents were in a relaxed mood after the baptisms and had each drunk at least two glasses of wine, decided that this was as good a time as any to raise the subject that had been on his mind.

Leaving Lucy to help Brontë carry round some trays of food, he joined them in the bar.

"Mum, Dad, can I have a word?"

"Have as many as you like" said Patrick, pulling up another chair.

"I just wanted to tell you; I've made up my mind. Provided I get the grades I need next summer, I'm going to apply for an engineering apprenticeship at Lovells. I shan't be going to uni."

Ever since their conversation a few weeks previously when Henry had first hinted that he was having second thoughts about university Nell had known that the subject would come up again before long. She had hoped that he would change his mind. It was not so much the degree; she knew that apprenticeships offered a good degree pathway, and he could earn a salary at the same time. But it was the whole university experience that she had wanted for him, even though she acknowledged that this was her ambition talking rather than his. When she saw Patrick nodding in approval, she knew that she was beaten.

"It's a good decision," said Patrick. He looked at Nell and saw her disappointment, yet he couldn't deny that Henry had made the right choice and had no doubt thought about it over many months. He knew that Sean would not have suggested it to Henry unless it had been a suitable option with good prospects.

"Grandpa thinks it's a good idea" said Henry, torn between feeling relief at having told his parents but not wanting to upset his mother.

"I know, Henry" said Nell, trying to adopt a brave face. "I'm sure it will turn out to be the right thing for you. Take no notice of me, I'm a bit emotional today after the baptisms. Now who's going to get me another glass of wine?"

Chapter Eighty

"Would you be willing to speak at a public meeting?" James Dolan telephoned Neville early on Monday morning. "I think that will give us more idea of the general feeling about your plan. If we rely on formal written objections, it won't give us quite the same cross-section of opinions; often it's only the very determined who bother to do that".

"Yes.... I'd be happy to, but can we make it soon? I'm not sure how much longer Chris will be staying, and to be honest I will need another ally". Neville didn't want to be overly pessimistic but if he was to face a lot of opposition he would need the support of his friend.

James suggested the following Friday evening which would give him time to advertise the meeting in the local newspaper which had a wide circulation, and have some posters displayed around the town.

That gives Chris and I a few days to prepare, thought Neville. Time to have some copies made of similar observatory structures so that people would have an idea of what was planned. And we can anticipate some of the questions and draft out replies. He was excited, even if slightly nervous; it was a new challenge and, in a way, it took him back to his time in the classroom when he would be tasked with explaining a difficult concept to a class of boys and feeling that sense of satisfaction when they understood.

* * *

Bridget drove Harry into Cork late on Tuesday morning and parked the Land Rover as close as she could to the solicitor's office, knowing that he could not walk far, and that the city was unfamiliar to him.

Harry's appointment lasted nearly an hour, but when he came out of the office, Bridget thought she could detect a look of relief on his face. She wondered if he would tell her the nature of his business that day, but once again tried to contain her curiosity. Instead, she suggested driving west out of the city on their homeward route and stopping off at a coffee shop on the outskirts.

"Don't you want to know what I've been doing at the solicitor's?" asked Harry with a slight twinkle in his eye. They found a table near the window and ordered a pot of tea and some sandwiches.

"Only if you want to tell me, Harry" replied Bridget. Had he read her thoughts?

"Well, I've had a new will drawn up. I've saved a bit of money over the years, not a fortune but it's a decent sum. And I have my two good pensions, isn't that enough to keep me going at your sister's for as long as I want?". He took a bite of his sandwich.

"I told ye I don't have any contact with my children anymore. Your daughter-in-law, Nell, what a lovely girl she is now, she's going to try to track down my daughter in England and if she manages to, well, there'll be a sum of money in my will for Rose. But the main thing is, my cottage. I know it's a disgrace, you and your family, well you're all too polite to say what you're thinking. I know, I know. It's my own fault; I never wanted the fuss and bother of builders and all that work going on around me. But it's sound as a bell underneath all that mess, and with a bit of work it would make a grand home. But I may never go back there, I'm getting used to a bit of luxury at your sister's place! So, what I've done, Mrs" Harry paused. "Is this. I've left the cottage to Brontë. For when she's twenty-one".

Bridget was open-mouthed. "Harry! Are you sure about this? It's very generous of you. But what about your children, and you may have grandchildren for all you know".

"Maybe I do. But they haven't come near me these ten years, so if they have families, they've not bothered to tell me. No, Brontë, that little cailín, well she was the only one to show my garden some love, she didn't judge or ask awkward questions, she just got on with it. Nora would have loved her. She's a very special young lady, that one. Ye must be proud of her".

Bridget felt quite overcome, and for a moment she was tempted to tell Harry the whole sorry tale of how Brontë came to be living in Ireland and the trauma she had been through. But she knew she mustn't. That wasn't her secret to tell; only a very few members of the family knew about it.

"I am proud of her Harry, and I love her dearly. You are a very kind man to think of leaving her your cottage. It's not many that would do that, you haven't known her that long".

"I know all I need to know," said Harry. "But you're not to tell her about this. Nor her family. She will find out when the time is right. Now, Mrs, shall we have another pot of tea?"

* * *

The Ballymere school hall was crowded and buzzing with conversation. Public meetings were rare here, mainly because very little happened. Although it was, some said, a shabby little town, on the whole it was respectable, and crime rates were low; in fact, the residents often joked that the Garda would ride into town sounding their sirens if someone dropped a piece of litter or uttered a curse on a Sunday morning. Change came slowly if at all, so a public meeting, open to all the townspeople and arranged at short notice had generated a great deal of excitement and curiosity.

Most of the family had turned up, including the Walsh children; Henry had a particular interest in the plan ever since he had started attending the planetarium in Kirchington with his grandfather. Even Jack and Harry had agreed to come along with Bridget to support Neville. Angela said that as it was a Friday evening she couldn't leave the guest house but was happy to put her views in writing if they were needed. Brontë noticed Sister Francis, Sister Mary Luke and Father Sweeney seated halfway down the room; there was

Mrs Byrne from the grocery store, some of the staff from O'Malley's and Gard O'Hagan; the rest of the company was a mixture of young and old, families and couples, and what seemed to be at least half of the remaining population.

James Dolan called the meeting to order and introduced Neville and Chris. Neville stood up and thanked everyone for attending but feeling he should first explain a little more about his link with the town, mentioned that he was father-in-law to Patrick Walsh. There was a murmur of approval; many of the farming community present remembered Dermot Walsh and knew the family. Neville went on to give the reason for calling the meeting and outlined his plans for an observatory in the area. He was met with a sea of blank faces at that point; few people understood what this was, so he found himself having to explain in some detail while Chris distributed photographs of a similar building in England. Neville described the ideal location of the site he had earmarked and stressed the importance of the absence of light pollution from streetlights, traffic and houses. He confirmed that he would be investing in the project himself, providing the telescopes, employing local labour wherever possible, and that it would not involve public money; this would be a not-for-profit venture. It was to be a community facility for the benefit of the townspeople, it was an enjoyable hobby, had educational merits and would be free of charge. But he would not take this any further if public feeling was against it and knowing he could not avoid the subject for much longer, he took a deep breath and explained that the building he had in mind for conversion was the Poor House on the Mizen in the hills above Ballymere.

As expected, the room went quiet for a moment while everyone took this in. Then people started to talk amongst themselves and at this point James stood up, saying that Mr Garth and Mr Davenport would be pleased to answer questions or hear the views from the floor but one at a time.

"Do you know the story of the famine, Mr Garth, and what happened in that building? It would be a terrible thing now to desecrate the memory of such a tragedy". Once again there was a rising volume of voices as an elderly man stood up and posed the question.

"I do know, and I appreciate the strength of feeling," said Neville. "It was never my wish to upset anyone. I understand, as much as is possible, how past generations suffered here. My only thought was to give the building a new purpose, and that creating an amenity for the town might bring about some more positive associations. I could apply for permission to construct a brand-new building in the area, but to my mind that would be a wasted opportunity, why not use an existing building and give it a new lease of life?"

Chris came to his rescue. "Any changes would be carried out with the utmost respect for the history of the building. It's not as if we are proposing to open a noisy bar or a night club. And we want to consult you all at each stage; that's why we've called this meeting before we go any further. It will be your facility; all Neville and I will do is provide the funding and the expertise".

Sister Francis stood up. "You mentioned education. Would the facility offer talks and visits for schoolchildren?"

"Indeed it would, Sister" confirmed Chris. "This is a subject close to our hearts. Neville is a retired head teacher, and I am still in teaching. We shall always encourage the educational aspects for children, but of course education and learning can apply to any age group".

"Shouldn't we leave the past as it is and not disturb it?" asked a stern looking woman from the front row.

"It's not a grave now, Maureen" said another woman from the row behind.

Mrs Byrne from the shop raised her hand. "I suppose it would bring in people, tourists into the town, if it's the only obs...ob... Observatory in the area? Visitors would be spending their money here in Ballymere"

"Typical of you, Oonagh, always remember the bottom line" chimed in another voice from the back.

Seamus Doherty, manager of the betting shop got to his feet. "I don't see the point at all. What do we have in Ballymere but rain most of the time? And that means cloud. What are the chances of seeing anything else in the skies around here?"

"Trust Seamus to be thinking about the odds" muttered someone, and several others laughed.

"Actually, the gentleman has a very good point," said Neville. "Stargazing, astronomy, call it whatever you like, is dependent on the weather so sometimes events would have to be arranged at short notice when a clear sky is forecast. But at other times when the weather is unsuitable, we can arrange talks, exhibitions, films. I would set those up and organise publicity, perhaps a calendar of events. If anyone is interested in becoming a volunteer to help with that even in a small way, that would be most welcome".

A boy of about Ronnie's age stood up to speak. "I'd like it if we could have an observatory. We're learning about the solar system next term at school". Ronnie caught his eye and gave him the thumbs-up.

The room went quiet again as Harry shuffled to his feet. "Forgive me for speaking up. I'm not from these parts, as you can see. I'm a Galway man. But my grandparents knew hunger. We have long memories of the famine too. The past will never be forgotten. But there comes a time to make changes. Changes that will make a difference, improve lives, give people a better future. We need that in this country. If it were my town, I'd say go ahead and do it. Thank ye for hearing me out". He sat down again in silence, then suddenly a ripple of applause from the back of the room became a roar, and a few people stamped their feet on the floor. Neville and Chris looked at each other in surprise, and James stood up to ask for quiet as several people still wished to ask questions.

Another old man leaning heavily on a walking frame asked to speak. "I agree with that gentleman. We need change here. We can't be stuck in the past for ever. Us old people, we've had our day. Do something for the young ones".

A young woman who seemed anxious to speak and was obviously being encouraged by her husband, stood up next. "Like many people here, I had ancestors who died in the famine. Making changes when it involves something so tragic is always going to be difficult and may divide opinion. I think we should thank Mr Garth and Mr Davenport for taking an interest in our little town and for wanting to set up this facility for us. But make no mistake, we shall call you to account if you go back on your promises and fail to show respect or consideration for our community over this." She sat down again to another round of applause.

"That's Mary O'Shea, she's a teacher from the primary school" whispered James.

Neville was then asked what the next steps would be. He explained that if permission were to be given for change of use, he would firstly engage a surveyor to check the integrity of the building, then an architect to design the dome and any other structural changes needed. After that he would invite tenders from local building firms to carry out the work on the conversion. He was due to return to England eventually, but he and Chris planned to return frequently to hold observation evenings and in time, any local people who were interested might perhaps come forward to be trained in the operation of the retractable roof, and with the aid of star charts the residents of Ballymere could have use of the facility to study the night sky throughout the year. He would supply monthly updates to the town in the form of newsletters and would leave his contact details in case anyone had further queries.

There were no more questions, so James asked for a show of hands and the majority were in favour of the project. They all thanked the audience once again and the meeting drew to a close.

"You did well" said James, as they filed out of the building.

"Yes, I thought we got away lightly. I expected a great deal more opposition". Neville looked tired but relieved. He glanced at Chris, who nodded in agreement. James gave them a meaningful look. "They mean what they say though. Keep to your word over this and the town will be behind you".

Chapter Eighty-One

The fine weather continued, enabling Neville and Chris to make several more forays into the Mizen to look again at the site, make notes and some rough sketches of how the building should be converted. Although these trips took place in daytime, they were still dependent on Patrick for transport, but Neville took more notice of the route now, realising he would soon have to make his own way when Patrick returned to England. Being able to find the site was a priority; even local people might need help, but James had indicated that assuming the project went ahead, provision of signage would fall within the council's remit.

Nell was in no hurry to return home; the only reason for going back, in her mind, was for the children to start the new term in early September. Right now, that seemed a blissfully long time away. During the fortnight that they had already spent in West Cork, Patrick had visibly relaxed and the frown lines on his face had faded. He had not mentioned work for over a week and then only to give some parting instructions to Joe as he left after the wedding. She was relieved to see him joining in with his brothers, lending a hand around the farm and doing small jobs for his mother and Angela; she saw this as a break from the pressures of business which recently had been in danger of taking over family life and more importantly, compromising his health. It's the West Cork effect, she decided, smiling to herself. It touches all of us in some way; makes us slow down, puts life into perspective, reminds us of what really matters.

Brontë came to help as Nell was pegging out some washing for Bridget in the garden of the cottage. "Mum, I've decided something".

This was so like the words Henry had spoken a few days previously that instinctively, Nell's senses, always fine-tuned where her children were concerned, went onto high alert.

"What is it, darling?" She tried her best to appear calm.

"I'm coming home with you at the end of the holidays. I want to be back with my family again".

Nothing Brontë could have said would have given Nell greater happiness at that moment. She whirled round and clutched at her daughter. "Brontë that's wonderful news. I'm so delighted, everyone will be. Have you made any plans?"

"Well, I'm predicted good grades in my Leaving Certificate. I won't know for sure for a few weeks of course. But I thought, could I study at home for my 'A' levels? Perhaps with a tutor. Obviously, I won't be going back to Lamberham. Then, if I do ok in the exams, I'd like to apply for a course in landscape gardening, take some sort of qualification, even if it's not degree level. I really want to have an outdoor career, Mum. That's one thing I have learned over this last six months". She looked Nell straight in the eye. "It's over, Mum. They can't hurt me. I don't hate them anymore; I hate what they did but I don't hate them. That's something else I've learned. I'm a different person now, well in some ways I am. I've lived a new life here and it's changed me, it's made me stronger. Things will never go back to how they were".

Nell was open mouthed. Brontë had this all worked out, and there was no sign of apprehension or nervousness at the thought of returning to Sussex. It was like a miracle. Another one wrought by this place and its people, she thought. There was going to be no need for persuasion, for negotiation or for any further dialogue; Brontë had thought it all through. Nell was ready to agree to any terms if it meant that her family would be reunited.

"I'm sure you've made the right decision, Brontë" said Nell, hugging her daughter. "Go and tell your Dad and Granny Bridget now. They'll be pleased, I know". She realised Bridget would miss Brontë but that would be for the best of reasons.

* * *

"Did I tell you that Ruari is coming back to England with us?" Patrick said to Brontë later that day, knowing full well that he had not told her, and nor had anyone else; it had been a well-kept secret. As soon as his daughter told him of her plans to return with them, he mentioned to Ruari that there was no longer any need for secrecy as Brontë had come to the decision herself.

"Oh Dad, that's even better!" Brontë was beside herself with excitement, and if any tiny doubt about going home had remained, this latest piece of news successfully put it out of her mind. "Thank you, Daddy. He's my best friend you know". She lifted her face up to kiss him. "Will he be working for you?"

"Maybe. Or Lovells. There are several possibilities. And while he's looking around, I'm sure the Swan's Rest would take him on, they always want staff, and he has experience as a barman".

Brontë and Patrick were walking up the laneway from the cottage up to Hackett's, taking turns to push Arlo in the stroller.

Patrick continued. "Ruari will be staying with us for a while, so it'll be all change when we go home. Arthur will be moving out, so Emer can have his room, and that will free up the attic en-suite for Ruari. You will want your old room back. Henry will stay where he is, Ronnie likes it on the top floor so that's everyone catered for, I think, until Arlo needs a room of his own". A murmur from the stroller reminded them that Arlo was very much a presence in their lives and they all now thought of him as the youngest member of the family; Emer often referring to him as 'my baby brother' which, in every sense that mattered, he was.

* * *

Before he left on honeymoon, Adam had left a sum of money with Jack and instructions to make an approach to Harry about having some work done on his cottage to make it safer and more pleasant for him to return to.

Jack had agreed but was not comfortable with the thought of raising such a delicate matter. He barely knew Harry and although it was clear from his only visit to the property that it needed a great deal of work but he anticipated that the old man would give a dozen reasons why he did not want anyone to interfere and was likely to say that his cottage was grand as it was. So it was with trepidation that one evening that week after a couple of pints, Jack opened the subject, but to his relief, Harry interrupted him.

"It's all right. There's no need to worry about it. I won't be going back to live there. I have made some plans, and it's all official. I'm not about telling ye what they are, mind – but yes, a deal of work will need to be done, and I've set aside the money".

Jack felt that he had been let off the hook and there was no point in arguing. "Ok mate. Sounds like you have it all in hand, I'll tell Adam. So what will you do now?"

"I'm staying here. Angela, well now, she's made me very comfortable, and I want for nothing. And to be honest with ye, I like the company. Oh, I know some of ye will be leaving soon, but people come and go all the time, it's never dull. I will do very nicely here and have no worries. I've put my house in order, as they say. And if Nell can trace my daughter, well then, we shall be having another hooley here and the drinks will be on me".

Chapter Eighty-Two
August 1998

Lois had been giving a great deal of thought to Neville's project. She knew it was gaining momentum and there was every likelihood that the change of use would be approved. Then it would be a short step to the plans being drawn up and construction work starting. Neville would not be ready to go back to Sussex in September; he would want to be here, overseeing the work through to completion and during the first few months after the grand opening. The previous evening, she had astonished him by suggesting that they spend the winter at Hackett's.

"Lois surely you're not serious? The winters here in West Cork can be terrible. I don't think you'll cope with it, darling. We've been lucky with the weather over the last few weeks, it's been perfect for the wedding and the holidays, but Bridget says it's quite exceptional. It won't last much longer, unfortunately". He looked out of the window at the deepening dusk; the twilight had taken on a shade of dark lavender. The sky was still cloudless. He had been hoping that this clear spell would continue; a meteor shower would be visible later that month if conditions were right.

"At least let me try, Neville. I may as well be here indoors in the warm as at the Swan's Rest. Angela will make sure that I'm comfortable. And if the worst comes to the worst, I give you permission to put me on a flight to Gatwick, Patrick will meet me at the other end. Please. I want to do this for you".

He gathered Lois into his arms and kissed the top of her head. "All right. If you are sure, we will stay a while longer and see how things go. Thank you, my love, you're right, I do need to be here at this stage of the work. Chris can only stay for another week. But I shall be keeping my eye on you. Any sign of a flare-up and we shall be on the next plane back to Sussex".

* * *

Nell and Aidan had promised to find the time, amidst all the comings and goings and general excitement of the last few weeks to chat together about their latest book recommendations. Aidan was now a teacher of English and History at St Brendan's College for boys. This was a small, church-funded school between Ballymere and Skibbereen, similar to St Teresa's in numbers but not exclusively staffed by clergy or Catholic Brothers. Aidan rented a small cottage nearby but some of his duties involved being present on site so despite not being far away from the farm he did not make it home quite as often as he would have liked.

They spoke of their first conversation nearly twenty years ago when they had discovered their shared love of literature and discussed the importance of education. Aidan said he had often remembered Nell telling him about her father's teaching career and how this had helped him decide to go into teaching himself. He had said as much to Neville during one of their opportunities to talk since the wedding; it was something he had never regretted. Nell felt gratified on her father's behalf; she was proud that even in his late seventies he could inspire people in this way, just by being the person he was.

With a slight touch of embarrassment, she told Aidan of her own literary efforts; Drover's Diary was to continue in a monthly format instead of weekly, and her first children's story had been accepted for publication several years previously, with another two currently at various stages of completion. But it was with pride that she described Brontë's journal and how well her daughter's writing style was maturing – this gave Nell as much pleasure as any of her own successes. Aidan was equally excited. Writing, second only to reading was, he thought, the gateway to so much more in learning, in education – and in life.

"We will talk again soon" said Aidan, as they exchanged reading lists. "Aunt Angela's guest house has changed everything. We can all meet up more often".

* * *

Gradually, regretfully, the company was breaking up. Jack, Niall, Sean and Amy were due to leave on Saturday morning, and Chris and Jane a few days later, so everyone met in the bar at Hackett's for a farewell get-together on Friday lunchtime. All the guests but especially the family had become used to what had turned into an extended party, and although they knew this could not last forever, they were determined to make the most of these last few hours. It was a noisy gathering; laughter, music and good-natured banter could be heard in every corner of the guest house and garden. They all reminded each other that England was just a short hop from Cork airport and only a few hours away by ferry; now that accommodation at Hackett's could be arranged there was no reason why they could not all meet up again soon, maybe at Christmas? Many drank to that idea; in fact, within a short time, they were toasting everything they could think of; the absent bride and groom, Neville's project, Brontë's exam results, the fostering of Arlo, and when they ran out of ideas for toasts, they toasted Angela herself, who had made this family gathering possible.

As the day wore on, some of the ladies sought shade in a corner of the garden and relaxed in the golden warmth of the late afternoon sunshine and the haze of champagne, reminiscing about the success of the last few weeks, the wedding, the baptisms, new friends made and plans in progress.

Five women across three generations at a point in time, joined together by family ties, circumstances and personal challenges, all those challenges brought about in some way by babies and children, what had happened to them and what might have been.

Angela had been haunted for a lifetime by one action – who was to say if it was a mistake? – leading to years of heartbreak and searching, never to find the child cruelly taken from her, never knowing if he was still alive and if he ever wondered about her or tried to find her. Yet she had found some peace in a long and happy marriage, a selfless vocation and now a thriving business that at a time in her life when most women were slowing down, would give her fulfilment and channel her vision and energy in the years to come.

Lois. A woman whose early life had been blighted by a domineering and dictatorial mother, wishing only for a family of her own and yet who for a time, unfathomably had alienated her only daughter whom she loved with all her heart. Her best years had been marred by illness, miscarriages and a still birth, with which for so long she had been unable to come to terms, leading to bitterness and self-recrimination that had so clouded her judgement that it had threatened her marriage and future. Yet she had pulled back from the brink and had dug deep to repair the damage and restore lost relationships with her family, and in so doing, most importantly of all, had opened a new chapter in her life with Neville.

Bridget, like so many Irish mothers had waved goodbye to three of her five sons as they left their homeland to improve their fortunes. She had been proud of them in a way for doing so but never took for granted that she would ever see them again, and she had hidden her personal grief for the sake of their futures. And now, despite the loss of her husband she refused to give into sadness but drew strength from her faith, feeling blessed to have all her family together for a while, however fleetingly.

Nell had experienced a lonely and secluded childhood. But becoming pregnant at the age of seventeen changed everything for her, leading to a happy if unconventional marriage, and she had created and nurtured the large family she had promised herself and Patrick in the early days. Five children all so different, each with their individual strengths and mysteries yet with nothing but love and determination to draw on she had raised them and had learned so much about them and about herself. As if this was not enough, had with no warning taken on an abandoned child as her own, and in becoming a foster mother had developed as strong a bond of love with Arlo as with her own children.

They thought of another woman – Kathleen, now on honeymoon on the other side of the world. At the age of nineteen she had all but given up on herself and her life as it was. Yet a few people saw her potential and gave her those vital opportunities to change and accept that her life could be different. She had found the courage to embrace those chances and grasp happiness and fulfilment. Now a bride for the second time, she radiated contentment and gratitude for the new life ahead with the man she loved more than anything. She too had been granted a second chance and would never forget that she had others to thank for it, rarely acknowledging that her own efforts had played a part. And as if to restore the balance of good fortune, she had come to a place of acceptance that happiness found a little later in life sometimes came with compromises; she knew that having children of her own was becoming a vanishing hope – not impossible but doubtful. For a time, she had struggled with disappointment but took comfort in her role as aunt to her many nieces and nephews, and as godmother to Brontë, to whom she was as close as it was possible to be.

Brontë, when scarcely more than a child herself had been the subject of a cruel rumour that she had given birth to a baby; a malicious lie from the distorted imagination of a few spiteful people who had no idea of the trauma and pain that their thoughtless remarks had unleashed. Consequences that had changed the course of Brontë's future, affecting her family, her education and her outlook on life. Yet those consequences had in time brought about strength, self-discovery and love of nature with all its powers of healing. And had granted her, at the age of fifteen an understanding beyond her years, resilience.....and the capacity to forgive.

These women, unaware of the invisible bonds that had brought them together and held them there in strength, solidarity and love sat there in companionship, talking, laughing, yet conscious of an unspoken affinity that would remain long after the magic of that summer had scattered and drifted into memory.

And somewhere in the world, another woman not known to the rest, lived daily with the knowledge that she had taken a momentous and secret decision to give away her newborn child into an uncertain future – an action illegal and impossibly cruel in the eyes of most human beings. A baby whom she had never held, never nursed, never named, and whose birth had never been formally registered, denying him even the right of his existence being recognised in law – surely the most basic right of all. A never child. A little boy whom she would never see through the milestones of infancy and childhood; his first smiles, steps and words had been witnessed by others as would be his first day at school, sporting triumphs, prize giving, graduation. In time there would be a career, perhaps a wedding, and grandchildren whom she would never know. Did she think of it as a sacrifice worth making; was it a solution, a relief, or a regret too overwhelming to put into words? Would those five women sitting in the garden on that summer afternoon ever have understood her torment or shown her compassion? It was a question never to be answered, never to be put to the test. Their lives would continue in ignorance of her situation, only the consequences of an unknown set of circumstances would ever touch them.

* * *

Neville carried his drink over to the open door and looked out at the group, relaxed, smiling, content with each other. They had all been through a great deal in different ways, that much he knew. How like stars they are, he mused, or was it the third glass of wine talking? But then he allowed his mind to continue along that train of thought. Stars are only visible in the darkness, he reminded himself. They need an absence of light for their own brightness to be seen. In the same way, these women have all come through dark times to find their strengths and discover their potential to shine. They were stars. Stars that had travelled on a long journey to be where they are.

Chapter Eighty-Three

January 1999

It seemed no time at all before the plan, vaguely and tentatively discussed on that last, glorious summer afternoon, came into being and the whole family returned to Ballymere for Christmas. All that is except for Adam and Kathleen who were enjoying their first Christmas as a married couple at the apartment in Solibrio previously owned by Neville and Lois. Kathleen's brief, passing mention of a beach wedding had not been forgotten by Adam; as the weather turned warmer towards the end of their stay in Sydney, he secretly arranged a blessing of their marriage under a flower-strewn marquee on Bondi Beach instead of the Mediterranean, with her new Australian family looking on; Kathleen wearing a white beach dress instead of her wedding outfit.

Also missing from the reunion was Jack, who had returned to Australia soon after the wedding; but the holiday and the area had made a lasting impression on him, and within a few weeks he was experiencing the emotional pull of West Cork in the same way as it had cast its spell over so many who were fortunate enough to have spent time there.

Lois had managed well; the autumn temperatures had not been overly cold, but she had been prepared for days when she was 'confined to barracks' as she put it. On the most difficult days she resorted to the help of a walking stick or even a walking frame but she had been resolute in declining the use of a wheelchair, not venturing out in the wind and rain but contenting herself with staying indoors talking to the other guests, in particular with Harry who had proved to be surprisingly good company and of course Bridget who visited often, and Angela and Fergus whenever they were not busy. This was a lean time for the Hackett's after a full house during the summer months, so Angela was relieved to have three long term residents as well as a few frequent visitors and occasional travellers.

The autumn months had been busy ones for Neville as his plans for the observatory gradually came into fruition. There had been an anxious wait for the change of use to be approved, followed by a prolonged search for an architect who was willing to take on such an unusual commission. The reasons for these refusals puzzled Neville, who could not decide if their reluctance was due to lack of expertise, pressure of work or an uneasiness with the plan itself. Another hurdle then presented itself; Neville had been insistent on inviting tenders from local builders who would have been glad of the work during the winter months. But finding a local firm who had the skills and experience to construct the retractable roof-dome – an essential part of the design – was problematic. In the end a compromise was reached by engaging a team of specialist builders for that part of the work, with the remainder of the conversion undertaken by Coyne Construction of Ballymere. All obstacles having been overcome, work started in earnest in mid-October.

Before leaving Ballymere at the beginning of September, Patrick had confided to Bridget, Angela and his brothers about the discovery of Denny Reid's body, and back in Drover's Cross they explained the situation to the older children as delicately as they could, without causing alarm or concern. Soon after their return home, WPC Drummond told Nell and Patrick that that the coroner had determined that death was due to natural causes in the absence of any evidence to the contrary. She said that an element of doubt might always remain in peoples' minds but that their enquiries were now closed as far as Denny Reid was concerned, although if any information ever became known as to the identity of Arlo's mother, then obviously, they would be in touch. However, as over a year had elapsed since Arlo was abandoned with them, the likelihood of that happening was becoming increasingly remote.

This knowledge went some way to reassuring Nell that Arlo was not about to be taken away from them suddenly, but Patrick was acutely aware of her fears and that she could not fully relax, even knowing that as time went on, Arlo's position in his foster family became more and more secure. One evening after Nell had settled Arlo to bed, read him a story and sung him to sleep, Patrick sat down with her, poured them both a glass of wine and suggested that they apply to adopt Arlo. They talked about it for hours, knowing somehow that it was the right thing to do, and in the end agreed that the finality of Denny's death and the realisation that no one was about to claim parentage of Arlo gave them the impetus they needed. The next day they explained to the family that they would be starting the process of having Arlo legally declared as their own child. The children, as expected were all in favour but they had already thought of Arlo as one of the family for many months now and this would never change. On one occasion Nell confided to Patrick that she wondered if it would be kinder, when Arlo was old enough, to tell him that Denny always intended to return for him. Patrick disagreed. "We can't be certain of that, Nelly" he said gently. "It may only have been something he said to persuade you to look after Arlo that afternoon. The truth is that we just don't know, and we will never know. We always promised to be honest with him." As time went on, Nell had to concede that Patrick was right, and that one day, Arlo would understand as much as they were able to tell him.

While this was going on, Nell had, as promised, contacted the Salvation Army to see if they could help in tracing Harry's daughter Rose. They had agreed to help, but there were formalities to be gone through, and of course they could not guarantee success. Nevertheless, Nell kept Harry informed at each stage; he was not to give up hope as there was every chance that eventually they would find her.

Arthur and Abby had moved into a small, rented flat in Kirchington which they could just afford. When Nell saw it, she was immediately reminded of the tiny flat she and Patrick had lived in soon after their wedding when she was expecting their first child. But she also remembered how, at that age, the most important thing was to be together. They would manage; Abby had started to train as a dental receptionist and Arthur worked hard in Patrick's business, occasionally reminding his father that the company name was Walsh and Sons, so when could he expect to be made a partner? Patrick had laughed at this, but Nell gently pointed out that it was a family business and wasn't that what they had planned for all those years ago? What was the point of it being a family company if only one member shouldered all the risks and mental load? She was concerned constantly about Patrick's tendency to overwork and his reluctance to delegate which had returned with a vengeance after their holiday. Her next mission had been to insist on a reduction in his workload and if that meant Arthur and Niall stepping up, then so be it. Patrick was not yet ready to hand over any part of the reins to them, but after some tense family discussions during which Nell threatened to hide his van keys and his phone if he did not make some changes, Sean offered to leave his job at Lovells and join Walsh and Sons as co-director which would be a hands-on role and take a great deal of the responsibility from his younger brother. And thus, the family element of the company was strengthened, and Patrick started to take a few important steps back.

After making a few enquiries, by late September a tutor was engaged for Brontë three afternoons each week. She had done well in her Leaving Certificate with Higher Level grades in all subjects. Mr Gifford, the tutor was impressed; he had taken the trouble to research the structure of the Irish Examination system and concluded that Brontë was significantly ahead of her age in taking it at fourteen so he had no doubt that she would prove to be a dedicated and conscientious pupil. Although Brontë admitted to science subjects being her weakest, she had decided that Biology 'A' level would be an essential requirement as a landscape gardener, Geography and Social History making up the other two subjects needed to be eligible for the Landscape and Design diploma she had set her heart on. Nell was so happy to have her daughter back at home, contented, relaxed and full of enthusiasm for her future that she willingly offered to give up her writing room as a study for Brontë. The room has been used for several purposes, thought Nell, as she tidied up her papers ready for Brontë to take up residence. Firstly, it was a maid's bedroom in the time of Great-Grandfather Geoffrey. It was used as a storeroom when Frederick and Phoebe lived here. After that it was Daddy's observatory room, then my writing room and now Brontë's study. This house has served the family so well.

Neville was excited to hear that Henry, who was a year ahead of Brontë, was to move to Kirchington Grammar to take his 'A' levels. This was of course the school where Neville had held the post of Head Teacher until his retirement. It gives a sense of continuity, he reflected, and was pleased to hear that Henry was keeping in touch with Chris Davenport about the progress of the observatory on the Mizen. Chris was planning to make a flying weekend visit for the inauguration and Nell and Henry were to accompany him.

Ruari was now recognised, by anyone who mattered, as Brontë's boyfriend. He had settled in well on the top floor at Moongarth and after a spell of work as part time bartender at the Bridge Tavern he had been taken on as a trainee scaffolder by a firm called Corrigan's, which Patrick had recommended. This was well-paid work, even for an apprentice and enabled him to pay his way and start saving up to learn to drive. Everything was at last falling into place and Nell and Patrick began to look forward to calmer waters ahead. Ronnie, as always uncomplicated, good-natured and diplomatic showed no sign of losing any of those characteristics and remained the stalwart of tact and tolerance within the family; Nell hoped that the forthcoming move to Lamberham Comprehensive school would not change him. Emer.... well, she was still Emer, occasionally argumentative, always questioning. But her behaviour had been a little more restrained of late; tantrums were rare – perhaps Bridget's firm words to her, as they left Ireland after Christmas had been understood. "Be sure to be a good example to Arlo now, he's your little brother, he will look up to you".

* * *

There was to be a dedication of the observatory on the evening of the ninth of January, followed by the official opening. The event was open to all comers – Neville was determined that this would be a facility available to everyone and it was his sincere hope that many of the townspeople and visitors alike would find a new interest and in a small way share in what had been to him a lifetime's pursuit.

Surprisingly, Ballymere Council had been generous. It had come forward with a small grant for some of the work and as promised had funded signage and publicity, but James Dolan had been working away behind the scenes and had managed to procure a Millennium award. There was also an anonymous donation from an unidentified well-wisher. Neville was puzzled initially, wondering who the mysterious donor might be, but had his suspicions. One afternoon, knowing that James's late wife had had an interest in astronomy he asked if he thought she would have approved of the venture. "Wholeheartedly" was his reply. "How she would have loved this".

For some reason, Neville asked him her name.

"Stella. Her name was Stella".

As had happened before at significant times of his life, Neville felt with certainty at that moment that he had been given a sign. Stella was the Latin word for star. He went away with another idea in his head.

It seemed that most of the town had made the journey across wild country on that freezing January evening to witness the opening. For many it was out of genuine interest, others out of curiosity, and for some, a pilgrimage. Regretfully

Lois was unable to accompany her husband on this important occasion; her health would not permit her to venture out on a cold dark winter's night but Bridget and many of her family were there with Nell and Henry, all of them in awe of the changes Neville and Chris had made and amazed at the number of people queuing at the entrance. The weather was not completely clear, but the clouds were patchy, offering some visibility and the chance of a good view of the night sky. As they filed into the building, a few people noticed a discreet sign above the main door which read:

The Stella Society

In the observatory room, all eyes were drawn to a plaque on the far wall, and as everyone read the wording, all fell silent and a few blinked back tears.

**This facility is given to the people of Ballymere
in honour of all those who suffered and died
here during The Great Hunger.
Their stars will for ever shine more brightly
than those we look on now.**

**"You will shine among them like stars in the sky".
Philippians 2 v 15**

**"He telleth the number of the stars; He calleth
them all by their names"
Psalm 147 v 4**

Neville had never considered himself to be a religious man and had consulted Father Sweeney about the wording. At first he had been unsure about the plaque in principle, but the priest agreed that it would be a fitting tribute and would dispel any remaining doubts in the minds of local people as to Neville's sincerity and that the changes would be for the better. Light, he said, can transform the darkest of places.

Neville gave a brief introduction, welcoming everyone and thanking the Council for their support. He and Chris demonstrated the workings of the retractable roof and then small groups at a time were able to look through the telescope as he pointed out the planets and constellations visible that evening. There were gasps of excitement and wonder; for many this was their first ever opportunity to look through a professional-grade telescope and see objects in the night sky magnified and explained.

As well as the telescope being the main attraction, there were several stands containing information leaflets, posters notifying forthcoming events and talks, and a small area set aside for refreshments. Neville did not want any aspect of the facility to be run for profit, but it would need to cover costs, so prices were to be kept extremely low. There was a buzz of conversation; not one word of dissent could be heard, and several people came up to thank Neville and Chris for their hard work and generosity in making the facility available. As the evening drew to an end Neville made a closing speech, thanking the people of Ballymere for taking a risk with them, as he put it; for supporting their endeavour and for all those who had come forward as volunteers to run the tea bar, print posters and even to put out chairs. But no one seemed in a hurry to leave.

Neville continued to look around the room, wondering at the number of Ballymere residents who had turned out on this January night for no other reason than to be part of this gathering, and to witness something which, for most of them was outside their experience. Apart from Chris, James Dolan and family members eager to witness his achievements, he knew no one. Yet this small rural community had trusted them, not only to deliver on their promises but to honour and respect the tragic associations of this place.

He glanced at Nell and Henry, both in earnest discussion with visitors. How proud he was of them – of the whole family – what they had accomplished, how they had grown in wisdom, overcome obstacles in their lives and how they had shown him unfailing support and faith in his enterprise. His mind took him back to his reverie at the end of the summer and his musings on the metamorphosis of five women in his life, how they had struggled through hard times to shine like stars.....but in fact this applied to every single one of his family, even the youngest, he acknowledged; each had in their way achieved something priceless in their lifetimes. Neville was a modest man by nature and took no credit for making these things happen, but somehow, he had been part of this remarkable journey.

Suddenly he realised, with a feeling somewhere between excitement and relief that if tonight's success was the high point of his seventy-nine years, so be it. If I never do anything else in my life worthy of note, I have done this, he reflected; in pursuing a lifelong passion I have helped bring about positive change and given something worthwhile to Ballymere, a place which means so much to my family.

Unexpectedly, the conversation around him became a murmur then slowly ceased. It was as though the volume had been turned down by some unseen force, and the lights had dimmed slightly. Neville looked across the room and standing beside the plaque on the opposite wall he saw his brother Henry; no longer a young boy but a man of his own age, yet they recognised each other. He walked across the room to Neville, embraced him and patted him on the back. They stood there together for a few seconds suspended in time; two brothers joined by an unbreakable bond in silent companionship. Then gradually the vision faded, and Neville was alone once more, conversation around him resumed and his surroundings shifted back to the present. It was unmistakable. Once again, at an important milestone in his life, his brother Henry had been with him. He could not explain it, yet it was as real and comforting as Nell slipping her arm through his as she came to congratulate him at the end of the evening.

As people gradually drifted out of the building, some chatting animatedly, some lost in thought, all felt somehow that the atmosphere of the building had lightened. Although the past sadness would never be forgotten, there was now a new energy, a new purpose and a new hope within its walls.

Neville returned to Lois later that evening, his mind still racing with elation. They sat together in the bar, and he ordered two glasses of whiskey.

"Well?" enquired Lois, unable to hide her eagerness to hear of his success.

Neville smiled at her, his tone self-deprecating. "I think it went very well" he said.

* * *

Epilogue
September 2006

A pick-up truck, loaded with luggage and household items drew up late one afternoon outside number forty-three Forest Road in Lankerris. On the side of the truck was printed "**Devlin Garden Design**" followed by the wording "**Your vision – our commission**" with pictures of a shamrock and a rose. The shamrock, said Brontë was in memory of Harry, and the rose was a homage to his daughter with whom he had been reunited six months before his death.

Ruari climbed down first, then Brontë stepped down from the passenger side and turned to lift a small girl from her car seat.

They stood for a while looking up at the freshly painted window frames and front door, the neatly clipped hedge and newly paved path.

The child held tightly to her mother and in the other hand clutched a limp, fluffy toy rabbit. Together, the three of them walked through the gateway.

"Look Saoirse. This is our new home". Ruari smiled down at his daughter then took a bunch of keys from his pocket and passed them to Brontë.

The rose, which Brontë had pruned all those years ago was clinging vigorously to the front wall, displaying a profusion of deep pink blooms in their second flush of the season. As the breeze ruffled the leaves, the flowers seemed to nod in approval as if to welcome the new occupants.

For the second time in her young life, Brontë had come home.

* * *

About the Author

After a long career as a civil servant, Mae Wellcome started writing in retirement.

It is her observations of the human condition and her own life experiences that fire her imagination, and curiosity about everyday scenes and sights which compel her to write.

Mae cherishes family life in West Sussex with her partner, children and grandsons. A keen singer and pianist, she has led a local choir, has volunteered for a national charity and enjoys nurturing her cottage garden.

"Stars from there to here" is her debut novel.

www.ingramcontent.com/pod-product-compliance
Lightning Source LLC
Chambersburg PA
CBHW030742030726
47497CB00001B/94